THE HISTORY OF
MARGARET CATCHPOLE
A SUFFOLK GIRL

BY

RICHARD COBBOLD

WITH AN INTRODUCTION BY
CLEMENT SHORTER

The World's
Classics

OXFORD UNIVERSITY PRESS
LONDON : HUMPHREY MILFORD

RICHARD COBBOLD

Born; Ipswich 1797
Died . . . . . January 5, 1877

'Margaret Catchpole' was first published in 1845. In 'The World's Classics' it was first published in 1907 and reprinted in 1912, 1923, 1929, and 1931.

PRINTED IN GREAT BRITAIN

477. 32

INTRODUCTION

THREE personalities interest us in reading the novel of *Margaret Catchpole*—the author, the heroine, and the author's mother, in whose service the real Margaret Catchpole was employed. Neither the author nor his mother has been the subject of much biographical effort, although Richard Cobbold was an industrious novelist, poet, and essayist for a long period of years, and wrote this one book that will always, I think, be read. His mother, Elizabeth Cobbold, made some reputation as a writer of verse, and is immortalized for us in Charles Dickens's Mrs. Leo Hunter. Fortunately we have a sketch of her by one Laetitia Jermyn, dated 1825, and attached to a volume of *Poems*, published at Ipswich in that year.[1] Laetitia Jermyn tells us that Elizabeth's maiden name was Knipe, and that she was born in Watling Street, London, about 1764, her father being Robert Knipe of Liverpool. In 1787 she published a little volume of verse entitled *Six Narrative Poems*, which she dedicated to Sir Joshua Reynolds, evidently by permission. It is clear that in girlhood she had made the acquaintance of the great painter. Her biographer says nothing about her being an actress, but it is a tradition in Ipswich that this was for a time her profession. In 1790 she was

[1] *Poems by Mrs. Elizabeth Cobbold, with a Memoir of the Author.* Ipswich: Printed and sold by J. Raw in the Butter Market. 1825.

married at Liverpool to William Clarke, a Portman of the borough and Comptroller of the Customs of Ipswich, who was apparently about sixty years of age and in very delicate health. The sprightly young wife wrote the following lines to her husband on St. Valentine's Day, soon after their marriage :—

Eliza to William this Valentine sends,
While ev'ry good wish on the present attends ;
And freely she writes, undisturb'd by a fear,
Tho' prudes may look scornful, and libertines sneer.
Tho' tatlers and tale-bearers smiling may say,
" Your Geniuses always are out of the way,"
Sure none but herself would such levities mix,
With the seriousness suited to grave twenty-six.
A Wife send a Valentine ! Lord, what a whim !
And then of all people to send it to him !
Make love to her husband ! my stars, how romantic !
The Girl must be certainly foolish or frantic ;
But I always have thought so, else what could engage
Her to marry a man who is twice her own age ?
While the tabbies are thus on my motives enlarging,
My sentiments William may read in the margin.

On the wings of old Time have three months past away
Since I promis'd " to honour, to love, and obey,"
And surely my William's own heart will allow
That my conduct has ne'er disagreed with my vow.
Would health spread her wings round my husband and
        lord,
To his cheeks could the smiles of delight be restor'd ;
The blessing with gratitude I should receive,
As the greatest that Mercy benignant could give ;
And heedless of all that conjecture may say,
With praise would remember St. Valentine's day.

I quote this valentine at length because it is a fair sample of the quality of our poet's efforts. At the end of the eighteenth century, and far into the nineteenth, a rhyming faculty of this kind was quite sufficient to make a literary reputation in an English provincial town, and in the case of Mrs. Clarke it was followed up by the writing of a novel, *The Sword*, published at Liverpool in 1791. It is interesting to find the name of Roscoe the historian among the subscribers for this book. In the same year—within six months of her marriage—the writer lost her husband.

The interest of Elizabeth Knipe's life, however, begins for us when very shortly after this she became the wife of John Cobbold, of the Cliff Brewery, Ipswich. Cobbold was a widower. He had already had sixteen children, of whom fourteen were then living. When it is remembered that by his second wife he had six more children it will be seen that there was a large family, and it is not surprising therefore that the Cobbold name is still very much in evidence in Norfolk and Suffolk, and particularly in Ipswich. "Placed in the bosom of this numerous family", writes her biographer, "and indulged in the means of gratifying her benevolent and liberal spirit, 'The Cliff' became the home of her dearest affections, the residence of taste, and the scene of hospitality." One need not complain of the lady that she was not very much of a poet, for she had otherwise a versatile character. In addition to being, as we are assured, a good housekeeper, she was, if her self-portraiture be accepted, a worker in many fields :—

A botanist one day, or grave antiquarian,
Next morning a sempstress, or abecedarian ;
Now making a frock, and now marring a picture,
Next conning a deep, philosophical lecture ;
At night at the play, or assisting to kill
The time of the idlers with whist or quadrille ;
In cares or amusements still taking a part,
Though science and friendship are nearest my heart.

Laetitia Jermyn tells us much about her charity and kindness of heart, her zeal in behalf of many movements to help the poor, and she dwells with enthusiasm upon her friend's literary achievements.[1] But the scope of this Introduction to her son's book does not justify devoting more attention to the mother, although her frequent appearance in Margaret Catchpole's partially true story demands that something be said about her "mistress". Elizabeth Cobbold died in 1824. Her husband outlived her for eleven years. John Cobbold (1746–1835) traced back his family in the direct line as landowners in Suffolk to a Robert Cobbold, who died in 1603. He was a banker as well as a brewer, and lived first at "The Cliff" and afterwards at "Holywells", which has ever since been the seat of the head of the family. It was the fourteenth child of his first marriage—Henry Gallant Cobbold—who was saved from drowning by Margaret Catchpole.

It was Richard Cobbold, one of the six sons of the second marriage of John Cobbold, who was the author of this story. When he was born he had ten nephews and nieces awaiting him, the children of his brothers and sisters of the first family, and he was at school with his own nephew, who was just a fortnight younger than himself. The nephew was John Chevallier Cobbold, who for twenty-one years represented Ipswich in

---

[1] The three most talked of books by Elizabeth Cobbold were:—*The Mince Pye*, an Heroic Epistle, humbly addressed to the Sovereign Dainty of a British Feast, by Caroline Petty Pasty, 1800. *Cliff Valentines*, 1813. *An Ode to the Victory of Waterloo*, 1815. The suggestion is made in the *Dictionary of National Biography* that she was descended on the mother's side from Edmund Waller the poet, but this is exceedingly improbable.

Parliament. For this information I am indebted to a grandson[1], who also sends me the following anecdotes:—

When John Cobbold—the father of twenty-two children —was High Sheriff, he once persuaded the Judge to come to dine with him on condition that there should be no one to meet him except his (J. C.'s) own family. When the Judge was shown into a drawing-room full of people, he was very angry, and said loudly before the company, "Mr. Cobbold, you have deceived me." Explanations followed, and the Judge was introduced to the various members of the family.

Elizabeth Cobbold was in the habit of saying that when she married her husband she found no books in the house except Bibles and account-books.

Brewing was such good business in those days that John Cobbold was able to give to each of his two youngest sons (twenty-first and twenty-second children) a University education, and to buy for each of them a church living worth £1,000 a year.

Richard Cobbold was educated at Bury St. Edmunds and at Caius College, Cambridge, was destined for the Church, and when he married he was a curate in Ipswich[2], but his father obtained for him the living of Wortham, near Diss, where he was Rector from 1825 until his death in 1877. He was also rural dean of Hartismere. Several years after celebrating his golden wedding—Dr. Spencer Cobbold informs me—he and his wife died within a day or two of each other; the

---

[1] Dr. Spencer Cobbold, of Batheston, Somerset, a grandson of Richard Cobbold, and the son of T. Spencer Cobbold, M.D. (1828–1886), the distinguished helminthologist, who was the youngest F.R.S. of his day. He had made some original investigations concerning Entozoa, and was the author of many books on "Parasites" and kindred subjects.

[2] At the Tower Church. He lived at St. Margaret's Green.

survivor did not know the other was gone; both were buried at the same time. Of the three sons who survived, one became Rector of Hollesley, another was the father of the well-known amateur footballer, W. N. Cobbold, and the third was the Fellow of the Royal Society, to whom I have already referred, and to whose son I am indebted for so many interesting facts.

That Richard Cobbold was not particularly honoured in his own country may be gathered from many quarters. One writer speaks of his " little vanities, his amusing egotisms, and his good natured pomposity ". It was clearly not Suffolk that helped to make his fame, if we may accept one of the few printed references to him that I have been able to find : —

I confess I never knew a Suffolk man at home or abroad who would take any pride in being the fellow countryman of this clerical novel-writer ; but in different parts of England I have seen reason to believe that our division of the eastern counties has a place in the minds of many thousands of people only by reason of the Rev. Richard Cobbold and his works, that the ancient town of Ipswich, which we hail from as if it were a niche in the temple of fame, has never been heard of except as the scene of some of the chief adventures of Margaret Catchpole.[1]

Other books are assigned to our author in the catalogues, but I doubt if one of them survives other than *Margaret Catchpole*, which not only survives, but is really a classic in its way. One story, indeed, *Freston Tower*, held the public for a time almost as well as the present book, but I imagine it has ceased

[1] *Public Men of Ipswich and East Suffolk*, by Richard Gowing. Ipswich : W. J. Scopes, 1875.

to command the attention even of the most remote
village library, where indeed it was long ago worn
threadbare.[1]   Essentially our author is a man of one
book, and many adventitious circumstances helped
him here.   It was no small thing that the heroine
should actually have been a native of the very
district in which the writer lived.   She was not merely
a vivid tradition of his boyhood, but had been in
the service of his mother and had stolen from his
father the horse that gave her so unpleasant a noto-

---

[1] The following books by Richard Cobbold are in the
British Museum Library :—

Valentine Verses, or Lines of Truth, Love, and Virtue	1827
A Sermon on Matthew xiv	1829
The Spirit of the Litany of the Church of England. A Poem	1833
The History of Margaret Catchpole, a Suffolk Girl. 2 vols.	1845
Mary Anne Wellington. A Soldier's Daughter, Wife and Widow. 3 vols.	1846
Zenon the Martyr. 3 vols.	1847
The Young Man's Home, or The Penitent's Return	1848
The Character of Woman. A Lecture	1848
A Voice from the Mount. A Poem	1848
A Sermon on Genesis i. 3	1849
Conversations between J. Rye and Mr. Parr	1848
The Comforter, or Short Addresses from the Book of Job	1850
A Father's Legacy. The Proverbs of Solomon in Prose and Verse	1850
Freston Tower, or The Early Days of Cardinal Wolsey. 3 vols.	1850
Courtland: a Novel. By the Daughter of Mary Anne Wellington. 3 vols.	1852
The Union Child's Belief	1855
J. H. Steggall. A Real History of a Suffolk Man	1857
Canticles of Life	1858

riety. Here was a romance ready to hand, which needed but to be set down in passably good writing to attract attention. It might have been worse written than it was by this worthy clergyman and would still have secured readers. How much is truth and how much is fiction in the story will never be known. If Mr. Cobbold had an abundance of documents about this girl Margaret Catchpole and her affairs, inherited from his parents, he must have destroyed them. He claims in the course of the story that, as Margaret three times saved the life of a member of Mr. Cobbold's family, it is not surprising that the records of her life should be so strictly preserved among them. But these records do not appear to exist any longer. It is doubtful if they ever did exist. The author probably worked from family traditions rather than from documents. He possessed, in addition, a genuine imaginative faculty.

Such documents as do exist do not amount to enough to justify the author's declaration that here is "a perfectly true narrative". Mr. Frank Woolnough, of Ipswich [1], courteously informs me that a letter by Margaret Catchpole, written only a few days before she sailed to Australia, and the lyre bird that she sent to her mistress about a year after her arrival, are the two curiosities of the Museum most eagerly inquired after by strangers. Here is the letter in question :—

ipswich May 25th 1801

honred madam

i am sorrey i have to inform you this Bad newes that i am going away on wedensday next or thursday at the Longest

---

[1] The Secretary of the Borough of Ipswich Museum and Free Library.

so i hav taken the Liberty my good Ladey of trobling you with a few Lines as it will Be the Larst time i ever shall trobell you in this sorrofoll Confinement my sorrows are very grat to think i must Be Banished out of my owen Countreay and from all my Dearest friendes for ever it is very hard inded for any one to think on it and much moor for me to enduer the hardship of it honred madam i should Be very happey to see you on tuesday Befor i Leve englent if it is not to much trobbell for you for i am in grat confushon my self now my sorrowes are dobbled i must humbly Beg on your Goodness to Consider me a Littell trifell of monney it wold Be a very Grat Comfort to your poor

unhappy searvent
Margreat Catchpole

How small a matter a sentence of death for horse-stealing was counted in the closing years of the eighteenth century may be gathered from the fact that the contemporary newspaper report of 1797 runs only to five lines, as follows :—

" Margaret Catchpole, for stealing a coach horse, belonging to John Cobbold, Esq., of Ipswich (with whom she formerly lived as a servant), which she rode from thence to London in about 10 hours, dressed in man's apparel, and having there offered it for sale was detected."

Undoubtedly one of the characteristics of the book that give it so permanent a place in literature is the circumstance that it preserves for us a glimpse of the cruel criminal law of the eighteenth century. Hanging for small offences went on for years after this, until, indeed, public opinion was revolted by the case of the young married woman who in Ludgate Hill lifted a piece of cloth from the counter. She hesitated and then put it down again. But she had been seen, and was arrested, tried, condemned, and hanged, although it was clearly proved that her husband had been seized

by a press-gang and that her babe cried for bread.
After this time came a reaction against the death
penalty for theft. Margaret, then, was more fortunate
than that unhappy woman and than the more celebrated Deacon Brodie, who was hanged in Edinburgh,
the city which he had adorned as a Councillor, for a
house-breaking theft which brought him four pounds
or less. She doubtless owed her escape to the powerful
influence of the Cobbolds.[1]

Margaret Catchpole is the classic novel of Suffolk.
That county of soothing landscape and bracing sea
has produced greater books; it has given us more
interesting authors than Richard Cobbold. Within its
borders were written the many fine poems of George
Crabbe, the many attractive letters of Edward Fitz
Gerald. The remarkable paraphrase from the Persian
known to all the English speaking world as *The Rubáiyát
of Omar Khayyám* was composed here. But, although
many latter-day novelists have laid their scenes in
these pleasant places, made memorable by the art of
Constable, not one has secured so fascinating a topic
or so world-wide an audience. Margaret Catchpole is
one of the few heroines of fiction of whom one loves to
remember that she was real flesh and blood.

CLEMENT SHORTER.

[1] The punishment of death for horse-stealing was
abolished in 1832, but in 1833 a little boy of nine who
pushed a stick through a cracked window and pulled
out some painters' colours worth twopence was sentenced
to death. Since 1838 no person has been hanged in
England for any offence other than murder. See
Spencer Walpole's *History of England from the Conclusion
of the Great War in* 1815.

CONTENTS

TO

THE MARCHIONESS OF CORNWALLIS

MOST NOBLE LADY,

Assured that this simple narrative, the most remarkable events of which are still fresh in your Ladyship's memory, will be found far more interesting to the public than many highly-wrought works of fiction, and that to none will it prove more acceptable than to your Ladyship, who for many years resided in this county, beloved and respected by all who knew you, for the encouragement you afforded to every amiable virtue; to you it is dedicated, with sincere respect, by your Ladyship's humble and devoted servant,

RICHARD COBBOLD.

Rectory, Wortham, near Diss, Suffolk.

there she would remain until she was taken off by the same hands which placed her there, and gave her the empty basket to carry home.

" May I come in the evening, father ? " she used to say, as she looked wistfully round the horizon, to see if any appearance of rain forebode an unfavourable answer ; for this request " to come in the evening " contained an imaginative delight, exceeding in its kind the prospect of the fox hunter for a coming run. For Margaret, when she did " come in the evening," used to have the privilege of riding home one of the plough-horses.

This was a singular *penchant* for a female child to imbibe, but with it mingled the pleasure of her father's and brothers' smiles ; and this, after a day of toil, seemed to give elasticity to their spirits, and formed an agreeable change to the unvarying monotony of ploughing straight lines, the clinking of chains, and their rural " *wooah come ather, woree, wooo, jeh !* " sounds as unintelligible to some readers as the language of the savages of the Caribbee islands, when first discovered.

Sometimes the crack of the whip would make the horses start, and the young men, her brothers, who would try to frighten their sister, found, instead of so doing, that it only increased the pleasure of her ride. At length, she began to trot the leading horse home.

After a time, this privilege was extended to riding the farm-horses down to water ; and this appears to have been the very summit of Margaret's delight. She used to take her brother's whip in her tiny hand, drive the whole team before her into the water, keep them in order while there, and then drive them out again, up the sandy lane, into the stable-yard.

It is well known that at such times it is no easy task to sit a cart-horse ; for they will kick, and plunge, and exhibit that rough kind of amusement known by the name of " horse-play," which has as much of shrieking and biting as it has of gambolling in it.

In going out to, and coming home from, water,

horses accustomed to the heaviest labour, if at all well fed, will exhibit no mean share of this species of spirit ; and woe be to the lad without a whip in his hand, or who has not a very steady seat !

Gainsborough and Constable were both lovers of the scenery around Ipswich ; and many are the sketches in the possession of their Suffolk friends, which speak their admiration of the beautiful landscapes which surround the river Orwell.

Had these artists seen Margaret in her equestrian character, they would have immortalized her ; for nothing could have been more appropriate to the spirit of their works.

Margaret was fearless as a Newmarket jockey ; and never was known to have had a single fall. She kept her seat as well as any of the tutored children of the celebrated but unfortunate Ducrow : indeed, it may be fairly questioned if any one of his troop could have managed to sit a Suffolk cart-horse with the same composure.

The fame of our young heroine's exploits reached but little farther than the sequestered farm-house to which her parents belonged, excepting now and then at the Ipswich races, when some of the lads saw an awkward rider, they would exclaim to each other, " Margaret would beat him hollow."

Time flew swiftly on, producing no farther change in the family of the Catchpoles than what may be usually seen in the habitations of the labouring class. Those are generally the most stationary race of all people in a parish, who have constant employment on a large farm : the owners of lands change their places of abode —sell their estates—and leave the country ; the tenants frequently change their occupations ; but the labourer remains to cultivate the soil, and is always found a resident among those " *poor who shall never perish out of the land.*" They have their friends and fellow-labourers, and feel as much interest in each other's welfare as the members of richer or wider-spread fraternities.

The Catchpoles and the Cracknells were two families that principally worked upon the lands of Mr. Denton. Their houses were indeed widely separated; but as their labours were in the same field, their occasions of meeting were frequent, their intimacy became strict, and they were of mutual assistance to each other. One lived near the street at Nacton, and the other upon the farm; so that whenever there was any occasion to go to Nacton, the Catchpoles always had a friend's house to call at, and the Cracknells were as constantly using the Catchpoles' cottage at the entrance of the lane leading down to the farm-house.

This intimacy was productive of especial accommodation on the Sabbath-day; for the Catchpoles, being at a great distance from church, they made use of the Cracknells' cottage, near the street, and used to carry their meals there, with the view of attending the church service twice on that day.

At that time, education was not so widely spread as it is now; and the particular spot in which this labourer's cottage stood being extra-parochial, they had to seek what little instruction they could obtain from the neighbouring parish of Nacton. The Reverend Mr. Hewitt was as attentive to his people as he could be, and was much assisted in his duties by the family of Admiral Vernon, who at that time lived at Orwell Park, and by Philip Broke, Esq., the great landlord of that district, and the father of our deeply-lamented and gallant Suffolk hero, Sir Philip Broke. But education was not considered then so great a desideratum as it is now, though the pious wish of England's patriarchal sovereign, George III, "that every cottager might have a Bible, and be able to read it," was nobly responded to through every densely-peopled district in his kingdom.

The Catchpoles were not an irreligious family, though they could none of them read or write. They were not ignorant, though they were uneducated. The father always repeated aloud the Lord's Prayer every night before his family retired to rest, and the first thing before they went to their work in the morning. They were generally respected by their master and mistress, their friends and acquaintance. They were a well-conducted, orderly family, and were united in love as dearly as those who had the greater zest of education and cultivation to heighten their domestic affections.

Margaret grew up to her thirteenth year, a fine, active, intelligent girl. She had a brother younger than herself by five or six years, of whom she was very fond, from having nursed him during the occasional absence of her mother. Her elder sister was always, as we have stated, of a sickly constitution, and very delicate : she had very little bodily strength, but she had learned to knit and to sew, and in these things she excelled, and was the sempstress of the whole family. She was of a sweet temper, so gentle, so affectionate, and so quiet, that, though a complete contrast to her sister, she nevertheless maintained a just ascendancy over the high spirit of Margaret, which was always curbed by any quiet reproof from the calm wisdom of the invalid.

We have seen something of Margaret's infant spirit : we must now record a simple fact of her childhood, which exhibits a singular instance of intrepidity and presence of mind in a child not yet fourteen years old.

It chanced that her mother one day sent her down to the farm-house to ask for a little broth, which had been promised by Mrs. Denton, her mistress, for poor Susan. Her father and her brothers were all at work on a distant part of the farm ; and, being harvest-time, master and man were every one engaged. When Margaret arrived at the gate, she heard a shriek from a female in the house, and in another minute she was in the kitchen, where the mistress of the house had suddenly fallen down in a fit. In one moment the girl of fourteen exhibited a character which showed the powerful impetus of a strong mind. The two girls in the house were shrieking with fright over their fallen mistress, and were incapable of rendering the least assistance. They stood wringing their hands and stamping their feet, and exclaiming, "Oh, my mistress is dead!—Oh, my mistress is dead!"

"She is not dead!" said Margaret; "she is not dead! Don't stand blubbering there, but get some cold water; lift up her head, untie her cap, loose her gown, and raise her into the chair." Not waiting to see how her words were taken, she did the work herself, and caused the others to help her. She used the water freely, and gave the chest full play, dragged the chair toward the door, sent one of the girls for some vinegar, and made the other rub her hands and feet; and did not slacken her attention until she saw some symptoms of returning animation. When the breathing became more composed, and the extremities more sensitive, she sent off one of the girls to the harvest-field for help; and telling the servant-girl that she was going for Dr. Stebbing, she went to the stable, unslipped the knot by which the pony was tied to the rack; and, with only the halter in her hand, without saddle or bridle, she sprang upon the fiery little Suffolk Punch, snapped her fingers instead of a whip, and was up the sandy lane, and on to the high road to Ipswich, before the other girl was fairly across the first field towards her master. She did not stop even to tell her mother where she was going, but dashed past the cottage.

On she went, and well had she her own wishes answered by the fiery little animal she bestrode. Her heart was up, and so was the pony's, who, feeling a light weight upon his back, and a tight seat over his ribs, gave full play to his lungs and legs, and answered to her heart's content the snap of the finger for expedition. Those who beheld the animal would be astonished, and ask where all the speed could be. But speed there was in his strong and well-knit limbs. So close was he put together, that his action was almost like a ball bounding down the side of Malvern hills. Nothing seemed to check the speed of Margaret or her steed. She passed every cart jogging on to Ipswich market, without taking any notice of the drivers, though she knew many of them well. Her mistress and the doctor were the only things in her mind's eye at this time, and they were four miles asunder, and the sooner she could bring them together the better. She even met Admiral Vernon's carriage just as she turned on to the Ipswich race-course, at the part now called Nacton Corner. The Admiral's attention was called to the extraordinary sight of a female child astride a pony at full speed, with nothing but a halter over his head, and that held as loosely as if the rider wished to go at full speed. The servants called to the child, even the Admiral was sufficiently excited to do the same; but he might as well have attempted to stop a vessel in full sail, with a strong and favourable wind.

Away she dashed, regardless of any impediment. She passed one young farmer from Stratton Hall, who rode what might be termed a high-bred horse. It was a noble turf, and an open course; and the young man, as much astonished as if it were an apparition before him, though convinced that it was flesh and blood, stuck his spurs into his charger's side, and gave him his rein with the full determination to overtake her. But this was not so easy a task as he anticipated. The little nag, hearing the clank of heels behind him, turned his head first on one side, then on the other; and, lifting up his nose like a stag, darted onward with redoubled speed. Not Mazeppa with more sudden bound could have sprung forward with more spirit than this wild little home-bred nag did down the wide turf of the race-course. The youth called aloud to know what was the matter, but Margaret heeded him not; and long before she reached the stewards' stand, she had fairly distanced the young squire of Stratton Hall. At length she reached the end of the race-course, and came on to the common of Bishop's Hill. It is a very deep descent down that hill to the town of Ipswich, which from its summit seems to lie at the very bottom of an extensive pit. But it is a noble expanse that lies before the spectator upon that eminence. The beautiful river flowing to the left, and forming an expanded semicircle bordering the town, and the distant country rising with amphitheatric grandeur beyond the barracks, and above the towers of twelve churches, might induce even a hasty traveller to pause and look upon that sight. But Margaret did not pause. Down she dashed from the verge of the hill into the very thickest part of the back hamlet of St. Clement's. It was market-day, and scores of pig-carts, and carriers' vans, and waggons, stood on one side of the road, taking up nearly half the street. But on through them all at full speed dashed the intrepid girl. From every house people rushed to see the sight—a girl, with her bonnet hanging down behind her, and going like lightning through the crowded thoroughfare, was an extraordinary sight.

People gave way as she rode fearlessly on, and followed her up St. Clement's Fore Street, over the stone pavement across the wash into Orwell Place, where lived the ever humane though eccentric surgeon, Mr. George Stebbing. But not until she reached his very door did Margaret give the first check to the pony.

A passing spectator, who was at the moment opposite the surgeon's door, with an instinctive thought of her errand, gave a violent ring at the surgery-bell, and received such a joyous " Thank you, sir," from the child, that he stopped to see the result.

By this time the street was full of spectators, all anxious to know what was the matter ; but Margaret's eye was fixed upon the door, and the very moment it was opened and the doctor himself appeared, she exclaimed, " Oh, come to my mistress, sir, directly ! —come to my mistress ! "

The gentleman who had rung the bell was Mr. Nathaniel Southgate, of Great Bealings, a rich and excellent agriculturist, and an acquaintance of the doctor's. Having followed him into the surgery, and there learnt the feat the child had performed, he at once resolved to take her into his own service ; and he gave her a crown as a present, telling her, if she was a good girl she should come and live with him· With

the former communication, Margaret, as might be
supposed, was not a little pleased ; but upon the latter
she put a very grave face.

The doctor's gig being by this time ready at the
door, he placed Margaret beside him, and started for
the farm, chatting by the way about her poor sister
Susan, whom she asked the doctor to visit as he
returned from the farm. Once only did she seem to
reflect in an unfavourable manner upon the act she
had done, and said to the doctor, " I hope, sir, if my
master should be angry at my taking the pony, you
will beg of him to forgive me."

On arriving at the farm, the doctor found that the
mistress of the house was much better ; and he then
learned from the servant-girls, that, but for little
Margaret's presence of mind and activity, the apoplectic
fit might have terminated fatally.

Having given the needful instructions as to the
treatment of the invalid, the doctor once more took
Margaret in his gig, and drove to the cottage ; where
having visited and prescribed for poor Susan, he took
leave of the grateful family by telling Margaret, that
if ever she stood in need of a friend to help her, she
had only to " post off again for the doctor."

Numerous were the inquiries concerning Margaret
and her expedition, and she found herself, much to her
surprise and chagrin, extolled for her horsewomanship.
She began, therefore, to be shy of riding the horses at
the farm ; and modesty told her, now that her fame
began to spread, there was something bold and conspicuous in her former pleasures of this kind. So
sensitive was she upon this point, that she avoided as
much as possible all allusion to her past habits, and for
the future carefully avoided the horse-yard and the
horses. Her father and brothers observed this, and
would sometimes say, " Peggy, you will soon forget
how to ride."

" The sooner the better," she would reply, " if I am
to have people staring at me as they now do."

Susan perceived with satisfaction that Margaret,

instead of being vain, and puffed up with the notice of the world, was quite the reverse. Numbers might have risen in their own opinion, and have been giddy from the continual praises of one and another ; but in this case it became a subject of annoyance rather than of congratulation, and her sister began to fear, from finding her so much more occupied in the house, and especially for herself, that Margaret's health would suffer.

It was with some degree of satisfaction that an opportunity was soon afforded for a change of place and action for her sister. Her uncle Catchpole came expressly from Mr. Nathaniel Southgate, of Great Bealings, to treat with her parents about Margaret's going to service ; and matters were so speedily arranged, agreeably to all parties, that she was to accompany her uncle on his return home. All seemed to think it a good thing for the girl ; even she herself, though quite new to the work of a dairymaid, thought she should thus escape the unpleasant observation she had been subject to. This accounted for the readiness with which she complied with her uncle's advice.

When, however, the hour of departure came, never perhaps did a cottage-girl leave home with a heavier heart : tears, unrestrained tears, ran in an honest current over her young face. Oh, how Margaret loved her poor sick sister ! how deeply she felt the grief of leaving her ! nor would she consent to leave her, except under the faithful promise that her father, or one of her brothers, would frequently come and see her, and bring her word of Susan's health.

"Dear sister," she said to Susan, "dear sister, if you should be worse, oh, do let me come and nurse you ! I love to wait upon you, I feel so happy to see you smile."

"God bless you, dear little Peggy ! " was the reply. "God bless you ! Mind and be a good girl, and take pains to do your duty well. Charles, or John, and sometimes little Ned, will walk over to Bealings. I will send for you if I am worse, for I too love to have

you near me ; but it is best for us both that we should
be parted for a time, and especially for you, as you can
learn nothing more at home."

The kiss of filial and parental and brotherly and
sisterly love was given through many tears, and the
little Margaret departed for her first place.

She went with a high character from home, and to
a place where that good character had preceded her,
in the estimation of the gentleman who so promptly
rang the bell for her at the doctor's door. She stayed
a day or two with her uncle in the cottage in which she
was born, and then entered into the service of Mr.
Nathaniel Southgate. At her very first interview with
her new master, she begged of him never to talk about
her riding the pony, and as much as possible to prevent
others speaking of it. This very much raised her in
the good opinion of her master and mistress, for they
had some fears lest she might be too fond of riding to
mind her work. They found her, however, completely
cured of this propensity, nor could she be induced, in
a new and strange place, ever to mount a horse or pony.

How seldom does public praise make mortals shy !
yet where true modesty prevails this is found to be the
case. It speaks highly for this young girl, who, from
an innate distaste to notoriety, shunned a habit which
had once been a prevailing pleasure, and in which, till
the world spoke loudly of her merit, she felt no degree
of shame. How singular that such a being should ever
become so conspicuous, as she afterwards did, in that
very line which she now so sedulously avoided ! Well
may we all say, " We know not what manner of spirit
we are of."

In the situation which Margaret first occupied, her
mistress found her all that she required—she was very
apt at learning to do her work, very diligent in the
performance of it, and always gave satisfaction. She
had plenty of employment, and was stirring with the
lark ; soon understood the accustomed duties of a
dairywoman, and was always praised for cleanliness
and good conduct.

A year passed away rapidly. Margaret, at fifteen years of age, was as tall as she was afterwards at twenty; she was strong, too, though slim. One year makes a great difference in a female at that age—some are almost women at sixteen, when boys are, generally speaking, awkward clowns. She went to service before she had completed her fourteenth year.

Margaret remained a year and a half at Bealings, remarkable for the strict propriety of her behaviour, and for the cheerfulness of her disposition. She had stipulated with her mistress that, in case of her sister's death, or of her requiring her aid at the near approach thereto, she should have full permission to leave. It was on this account that, in the Whitsuntide following, she left her situation, and went to attend her poor sister.

Susan, who was then in her twentieth year, had lingered on, gradually getting weaker and weaker, until she was quite unable to rise from her bed. Her heart always yearned towards her sister; and, as she had promised to let her be with her during her few last days, and she herself thought those days were almost numbered, she now sought her assistance. Margaret's affection answered the sister's call, and she was ready to place all her earnings and all her labours at that sick sister's service. She hesitated not; but, taking a respectful and grateful leave of the family at Bealings, she was, at Whitsuntide, again an inmate of her father's house.

It has been stated, some few pages back, that between the Catchpoles and Cracknells, as labourers upon the same farm, there existed a close intimacy: it was Whitsuntide, and Mrs. Cracknell's baby was to be christened. Poor Susan was to have been one of the sponsors, and the child to be named after her; but "poor Susan was laid on her pillow," and could not answer to the call of her neighbour in any other way than by her prayers. Margaret was therefore asked to take Susan's place, which she consented to do, and went early to Nacton, to render what assistance she might be able to give in the celebration of this event.

Neighbour Cracknell kept a little shop of such goods as might be obtained at the large, red-bricked, coffin-shaped house of Mr. Simon Baker, grocer, St. Clement's Street, Ipswich. This shop divided the fore and back hamlets of St. Clement's, and was the first from the Nacton Road, entering upon the pavement of the town. Master Cracknell and his boys spared what they could for the thrifty wife at home, who had fitted up her closet window with shelves, and placed thereupon a stock of threads, pins, needles, soap, starch, tape, and such like small and least perishable articles, as might make some return in the shape of home profit, instead of working in the fields.

This cottage stood at the entrance of the village, and the shop, if such it might be called, had frequent customers among the poor. A single candle, a small loaf, half an ounce of tea, a halfpennyworth of cheese, a pennyworth of butter, or sugar, or snuff, or tobacco, could here be obtained. Thus Dame Cracknell managed to turn a penny in her own way; contented with small gains, she provided for her rapidly increasing family in a decent and honest manner, and looked forward with hope for more custom. She made no outward show to create opposition, and, had she always done so, might have gone on prosperously; but this joyful Whitsuntide, which found her and her friends so quietly happy, was fraught with untoward circumstances, which neither she nor her neighbours could foresee. She had invited a few friends to partake of her christening fare, and expected her relative, Stephen Laud, from Felixstowe Ferry, to stand with Margaret Catchpole and herself as sponsors for the little Susan.

This Stephen Laud was a famous boatman, and for many years plied at the ferry-boat between Harwich and Langer Fort, now called Landguard Fort. That it required a skilful pilot to manage a ferry-boat, which had nearly two miles to run from the Suffolk to the Essex side, will be easily imagined. As government letters were always conveyed from Harwich to the fort, at that time, the ferryman was in the receipt of government pay, and it was considered a good situation for an active man. Such was Stephen Laud—and not only active, but a man of no common intelligence. He had been left a widower, with one son, William, whose uncle, a boat-builder at Aldborough, had taken a great liking to him. He had bound him apprentice to Mr. Turner, the ship-builder, at Harwich, where the boy had acquired no mean tact at his employment, and grew up a good workman, though somewhat too free a spirit for a settled character. He was very fond of the sea, and, from the joyous buoyancy of his disposition, the captains of the traders to Aldborough used frequently to give him a run.

Mr. Crabbe, a brother of the celebrated poet, with whom young Laud studied navigation, used to say he was the quickest lad as a mathematician he ever knew. He was a merry, high-spirited sailor, rather than a boat-builder. He was very intimate with one Captain Bargood, a master and owner of several ships then trading along the coast, and over to Holland.

So taken was the captain with Will Laud, that he would have persuaded him at once to join service with him. Will was generally liked; and though his uncle wished him to stick to the boat-building, he could not but confess that he would make a far better sailor. He knew, however, that his old father, the pilot, would not approve of his going to sea for a permanency, without his having a voice in the matter; and as Captain Bargood offered to give young Laud a fair share of profits without loss, and Will had such a turn for the sea, he had sent him over to his father, to ask his consent to this change in his course. This was the subject of their conversation, as, upon the Whitsuntide mentioned, they journeyed on foot from Felixstowe Ferry to Nacton, a distance of six miles.

" You speak famously, boy, of this captain : he may be all right, and his offers to you seem to be good. I have heard it hinted, however, that he is not over-nice; and that though, as times go, he may be an honest trader, yet that he can find friends to help him over with a cargo of moonshine, and get a good run too into the country."

"I never heard a word of any such traffic, father, and whenever I have been with him I have never seen him in any suspicious company. He would never persuade me to this work, father. I am the son of a government man, and I hope I shall always prove myself an honest tar."

"I hope so too, my boy; I hope so, too; but when once the block runs, down fall the sails. Take care, my lad; keep your eye ahead."

"Don't be afraid, father; only you give consent, and I shall sail with fair wind and weather."

"I can but wish you well, boy; I can give you but little help. You are now entering your twentieth year, and seem to me determined to go to sea. I shall not persuade you against your own inclinations; so, go; and may the great Pilot above keep you in safety from the dangers of the breakers! I will do what I can for you."

This consent seemed to animate young Laud with most fervent thankfulness, and his elastic spring carried him over every stile he came to. As they neared the village of Nacton he was chatty upon many subjects, but more especially upon the object of his journey.

"I never was at a christening party," said the young man; "whom shall we meet there, father?"

"Your relatives on the mother's side are all poor, William, but honest people. I have long promised to be godfather to one of the Cracknells, and now I am called upon to make good my promise. You will meet their friends the Catchpoles, and one or two others. Perhaps Margaret Catchpole may be there, as her sister Susan, I hear, will never be likely to get out again."

"Margaret Catchpole! Margaret Catchpole! I wonder whether that is the girl whose name I heard so much about two years ago. I was with Captain Bargood at the Neptune, near the quay, as all the people in the street were talking about a spirited girl riding a pony full speed from Nacton to Ipswich for the doctor. The name I heard mentioned was the same you speak of."

"And was the very person we shall perhaps see among the party to-day."

"I am glad of it, for I can easily conceive she must be an enterprising girl; I shall like to see her much. She must be very young still."

"About sixteen. I have heard that she is a very respectable young woman."

Conversation of this kind served to entertain the youth and his father, and to divert the current of their thoughts from the sea, until they arrived at Nacton Street. They descended that ravine-looking village, and, passing the blacksmith's shop at the bottom of the valley, ascended the hill near Admiral Vernon's, passed the church towards the Ipswich road, and arrived at Master Cracknell's cottage. The ever-ready Margaret had been before them to assist, and had made herself useful in many ways. The humble holiday party consisted of the Catchpoles, father and two sons, —the two Calthorpes, Stephen and William Laud, and the no small family of the Cracknells; and last, not least, the heroine of the day, Margaret Catchpole.

The cottage, as the reader may suppose, was full; but welcome were they all to the christening, and joyful that day were all the party. Between the young men and Will Laud a quick intimacy commenced. His character seemed formed for a holiday,—all buoyancy, life, and animation; he could at one time have his fun with the children, another have feats of bodily strength with the young men; tell a good story for the old people, and sing a good song for the whole party.

Laud was greatly prepossessed in Margaret's favour; he had heard much of her at Ipswich, and had been long anxious to see her. When he did see her, she more than answered all his expectations. He thought to see a lively, spirited child, with whom he might joke of her childish but noble act, or romp ; but he beheld a very respectable, decent young woman, who, though active and intelligent, was far from having any childish manners, lively, agreeable, and unaffected, with a quickness and spirit well answering to his own.

As for Margaret, such a bright vision of pleasure had never before entered her thoughts or heart, as stole upon her that day. In short, both William and Margaret may be said to have imbibed a partiality for each other on this day, which ripened into such an attachment as has seldom been recorded among all the host of love-stories which fill the pages of romance. But these pages record no romance of unreal life ; they tell a plain, unvarnished tale,—a tale which, having been continually related in private circles, is now given to the world at large, as a remarkable series of events in

The short and simple annals of the poor.

The merry christening passed away, and the friends parted, but not for a long period. Charles Catchpole, who had been mightily taken with young Laud, agreed to accompany him to his father's. They all left the cottage of Cracknell together, and all arrived in safety at their respective homes ; but not without Will Laud having walked double distance, to show a devotion to our heroine which he, at that time, most sincerely felt.

But they, like all lovers and friends, must and did part. Young William had a long and agreeable soliloquy with himself, as he traversed again that road by night which he had gone in the morning with his father. How different the current of his thoughts ! In the morning he was all raging for the sea, but what a comparative calm as to that desired object now ensued. There was tumult stirring of another kind, which seemed to engross the whole of his thoughts, and centre them upon the land, not upon the ocean.

It is unnecessary to follow this youth through his every day's journey to and from Margaret's cottage. His uncle began to think that his father had succeeded in making a landsman of him; for Time, which flies swiftly on the wings of Love, goes slower and more mechanically with those who have to work hard every day, and whose bread depends upon the sweat of their brow.

Charles Catchpole, though he caught infection from the roving spirit of young Laud, and found in him a love of enterprise which charmed him, did not seem so fond of the sea as to be induced to leave for it his more peaceful occupation. The young men were so far pleased with each other, because Laud endeavoured to entertain Charles, and Charles was only too happy to be so entertained. Yet the young landsman wanted to know more of distant countries than young Laud, who had only been a coasting trader, could tell him. He had once, indeed, been over to Holland, but did not go far into the country; so that all the information he could give related to simply the seaport towns on the coast.

Whence arose this inquiring spirit on the part of Charles Catchpole, no one could determine. The lad had once expressed a wish to be a soldier; and it was the old clerk and sexton of the parish of Nacton who used to read and explain to him that there were strange people in the world; and these notions, which had for some time slumbered, seemed to be awakened by young Laud's company.

Will Laud had idle time to spare, and he devoted a great portion of it to Margaret, and was a constant attendant at Nacton. All the family knew of the attachment, and it was no secret with any neighbour who chanced to come in, all of whom were well pleased with Will Laud, and congratulated their respective friends on the future happiness of the young people. Even the master and mistress, for whom the family worked, were satisfied with appearances; and the maids at the farm, who had never quite forgiven Margaret for her good offices, were not a little jealous at the early prepossession of the young sailor for " the girl," as they called her.

Poor Susan, the sick sister, was the only one of the whole family who did not like Will Laud. There frequently dwells in the sickliest forms the purest love. Susan felt more interested for Margaret's future happiness than did any one else in the family. Through all that weakness of body, there was a strength of mind and of judgement, which those who have for a long time had the prospect of dissolution before them frequently possess. She looked with penetrating eyes upon the young man. She weighed well his spirit, listened to his free conversation, and formed her idea of the young man's character, not from outward appearance, but from the tone of sentiment which came from his heart. She was shocked to find that there was, through all his attentions and general desire to please every one, a levity of expression upon the most serious subjects. She did not say much to Margaret upon this point; but her manner towards her lover was colder, and, in some measure, more repulsive than her sister liked. It is said, that "we can always tell those who love us." It is equally true "that we can always tell those who dislike us."

Poor Susan did not openly rebuke Will Laud. Yet he perceived that she did not approve of him, and said to Margaret—"I do not think your sister Susan likes me." Why should he think this? He had never heard Susan utter a word of rebuke to him. But sometimes, in the midst of his wild vagaries, a glance of that bright eye which flashed, searching into his spirit, would make the young sailor pause and finish his story in a tamer way than he intended. Susan's affectionate disposition would not allow her, in that apparently happy period of the two lovers' intercourse, to speak anything harshly, but the more than usual warmth of her interest was not to be mistaken. That pressure of the hand; that kiss, with a starting tear in the eye, that hope expressed that she might be happy, though a fixed fearfulness of doubt seemed to hover over her mind, whilst she so often prayed for her sister, made Margaret almost tremble, as if Susan foreboded evil.

" Dear sister," said Margaret to her one day ; " dear sister, you look so gloomily on my lover and me ! "

" No, Margaret. I look only with love upon you, and am only, perhaps, too anxious for your future happiness. I am not gloomy. I love you so dearly, Margaret, that I pray that you may live in happiness all your days. I do not like to lose any of your love."

" Nor I any of yours, dear Susan ; but sometimes I fear I either have so done, or may so do. Laud fancies you do not like him."

" It is only that I love you so dearly, that if any one loves you less than I do, it makes me feel unhappy. I like Laud very well as a visitor, and he appears very fond of you, Margaret ; but he seems to me to think too much of himself to be exactly what I wish him to be, for your sake."

" May you not be mistaken, Susan ? I am very young, and it must be years before we marry. Do not you think he may be likely to improve with his years ? "

" I should have thought so, had I not observed that vanity prompts him to boast of his own successes over his uncle and his father. He has got his own will of both, and appears to me to forget the sacrifices they have made for his humour, which he fancies to be for his benefit. But I do not speak against him, Margaret. I only wish him all that can be good, for your sake."

This conversation might have extended much farther but for the entrance of Laud, who came rather in haste to say that he was sent for by Captain Bargood to Felixstowe Ferry. He had been into the field with young Charles Catchpole, and a sailor brought to him an urgent and special message that he would come to the captain, as he wished to see him upon very particular business.

" Margaret," he said, " I must take my leave of you for a short time. I suspect the captain wants me to go a voyage ; but it will not be a long one. I am assured of good pay, in a share, probably, of his profits, without having to sustain the risk of loss."

Whatever present grief Margaret might feel at the departure of her betrothed, she did not give way to any deep lamentation. She knew that Laud must work for his living, as well as she for hers, but she did not despair of success; they were both young, both enjoying health and strength. Regret she might feel, but Hope was ever the bright beacon of Margaret's days. She could only express her hope that they might soon meet again; and as her father and brothers came in from their labour, Laud shook them all by the hand, told them he was going again to sea, and wished them "all health and hearty cheer."

It was with much regret that the old man and his sons found that Laud must leave them, and their honest nature failed not in expressing every good wish for a pleasant voyage. Laud turned to the sick-bed upon which poor Susan lay, and approached to bid her good-bye. He was surprised to see her in tears, and greatly agitated: so much so, indeed, that the bed-clothes shook with such a tremulous motion, that they showed the extent of her agitation.

"Good-bye, Susan," said Laud, and extended his hand.

Susan turned her piercing eye upon him, took his warm hand in her cold, transparent, bloodless fingers, and with great effort spoke to him.

"William, I want to say a word before you go." Here she paused to take breath, and every one who loved her crowded round her bed. "I have observed, William, much in your character that requires alteration, before you can be either happy yourself or can make my sister so. You have a lightness of thought, which you do not blush to express, which appears to me bordering upon infidelity. There is a God, William, Who observes us all, and knows every secret of our hearts, and in His sight piety, parental love, and duty, are qualities which meet His approbation, and the contrary provoke his displeasure. I have observed with pain that you sometimes speak with levity of those whom you ought to love. You may not intend to be wicked, but your language, with respect to the guardians of your youth, is not good. You will forgive my speaking my mind to you now, as I am sure I shall never see you again in this world: but if ever we do meet in another and a better world, you must alter greatly in the sentiments of your heart. We shall never meet if you do not. You want steadiness of principle and firmness of purpose. You may lead those who look up to you; but I can see that you may be very easily led by others, who have only to exercise determination, and they may tempt you to anything. You want, I repeat it, steadiness of principle and stability of purpose. I love my dear sister, and I can foresee that you will make her very unhappy if you do not alter in this respect. Take what I say in good part, and forget it not. I can only pray for your welfare. If ever you are unkind to Margaret, you and I shall never meet in another world. Good-bye, William, good-bye!"

The effort had been too much for her weak state, and she sank back exhausted, hiding her tears upon her pillow.

Youth and health do not dwell long upon the words of sickness, though love cannot fail to produce a powerful effect for the time. Laud returned to Felixstowe, leaving our cottagers to lament his departure, and Margaret to the exercise of those duties to which her nature and inclination made her then, and ever after, so well adapted—the nursing of an invalid. Had she not had these duties to perform, she might have felt more keenly the loss of her lover. She was never of a desponding disposition. She knew that Laud must work hard; and she hoped that his love for her would make him prudent and careful, though it might be years before they both saved a sufficiency to furnish a cottage.

Her duties to poor Susan became every day more urgent, for every day seemed to bring her slowly to her end. Her attentions to this sick sister were of the gentlest and most affectionate kind. Softly, gently, noiselessly, she made every one go in and out of the apartment. Susan wished that all whom she knew

and loved should pray with her, and her good mistress
frequently came up from the farm to read to her. Oh,
how eagerly does the mind of the sufferer devour the
word of God!—the more humble, the more sweet that
precious fruit to the palate of the sick! How does
she desire more and more of the living waters of life,
and lift her eyes to Heaven, and turn them in upon
her heart, to see whence her help might come!

Poor Susan had been too long a sufferer not to have
learned the duties of patience; she had too humble
a spirit to think anything of herself; but when she
thought of her father, mother, brothers, and sister, her
whole soul seemed absorbed in their present and future
welfare.

Oh! what instructive lessons may be learned at the
sick-bed! How wise are the reflections then made
upon life and immortality! Could men only be as
wise at all hours, how happy might they be!

But Susan's hours were numbered, and her end drew
nigh. Scarcely three weeks after the departure of
Laud, she was called away; but her end was so characteristic of piety and love, that, despite of the impatience
of the hasty reader, it must be recorded. On Saturday,
the 24th of June, not long before the family were about
to retire to rest, Susan said to Margaret, "Lift me up,
dear, lift me up—I feel myself going." As might be
expected, a word of this sort called them all around
her. The poor, weak, wasted, emaciated girl, with an
eye as brilliant as the purest crystal, and a countenance
expressive of the calm spirit within, looked upon the
mother bathing her thin hand with tears, and the
affectionate father and brothers a little more composed,
but not less afflicted. Edward, the youngest, knelt
close by her side; whilst the affectionate Margaret,
with her arm and part of her chest supporting the
raised pillow, against which the sufferer leant, held with
her left hand the other transparent one of her dying
sister.

Who shall paint the silver locks of age, and that calm
eye, watching the waning light of a dear daughter's

life ? " Let us pray," said the dying girl; " let us pray." Around the bed knelt six of her relatives, and in deep humility heard Susan's prayer for them all, whilst they could only answer, with a sob, " God bless you ! "

But now came an effort, which seemed to agitate the sufferer beyond all former exertions : the clothes around her poor chest seemed to shake with excess of emotion, as, with a most earnest and impressive look, she half turned herself round, and uttered the name of her sister.

" Margaret," she said, " Margaret, you will never marry William Laud—he will cause you all much sorrow ; but do not forsake the right and honest path, and you will find peace at the last. Margaret, my dear sister, never suffer him to lead you astray ! Promise me, promise me never to be his, except he marry you amidst your friends."

" I never will, dear Susan—I never will."

" Bless you ! God bless you all ! " And with one look up, as if she would pierce the skies, she raised both her hands to heaven, and said, " O blessed Saviour ! " and with those words her spirit took its flight to eternity.

What a thrill, a holy thrill, ran through the hearts of all, as they witnessed this solemn but cheerful end of her they so dearly loved ! That night was, indeed, one of serious reflection among them all : they thought and talked of her, and blessed her, and resolved to follow her advice, and keep the honest path.

CHAPTER II

THE TEMPTATION

LAUD reached Felixstowe Ferry: he had seen his parent, and then went to the shore to meet the captain. There they stand under the cliff, by the shore, opposite the harbour and town of Harwich, whilst the light gleams upon the distant beacon of Walton-on-the-Naze. There is a boat a short distance on the calm wave, and not far ahead a brig is seen standing off and on. The captain is pointing to the brig, and seems very earnest in his conversation; whilst a sort of cool composure is settled upon the firm attitude of Will Laud, as he listens and seems to remain immovable.

Oh! would that he had so remained! Many an afterpang, which the birth of that day's sorrow occasioned, would have been spared.

"Well, Laud, I make you a fair offer," said this artful captain; "I make you a fair offer of the command of the brig: there she is, as tight a vessel as ever cut a wave. I will venture to say, that when you helped to lay her keel with Turner, you little dreamt of commanding on board of her."

"I have no objection to the craft, captain; but I do not like the job."

"No: I suppose you would like to live at home along with the old ferryman, your father; or, perhaps, knock away at boat-building on the Alde. Pshaw, Will, pshaw! this is a tame kind of life. I took you for a fellow of more spirit, or I never should have taken you for my messmate."

"When you took me for such, you took me as an honest man, and all your dealings were above-board. Now you want to make me a smuggler. This is the work, captain, I do not like. My father is an honest man, and under Government—why should I bring disgrace upon him?"

" And does it follow, Will, that I am what you call a smuggler, because I do a little in a free trade ? Where 's the disgrace you speak of ?—and who is to bring it upon us ? Come, Will, there are two sides of a question, and we may hit upon the right as well as the wrong."

" But we shall be cheating the Government of our country."

" As to that, Will, look from the highest to the lowest, and see if they do not all do so as long as they can with impunity."

" I do not see that."

" No, Will, no ; because you shut your eyes. But who pays more tax than he can help, or as much as is strictly due, either for his horses, servants, powder, malt, hops, windows, silk, woollen, or any commodity whatever, upon which a wholesale tax is imposed for the good of the country ? Don't talk, then, of cheating Government. I call mine only a little free trade ; and if I choose to employ a few free hands and pay them well, what is that to anybody ? "

" You may employ them with more freedom in an honest way, than running such risk of life, liberty, and property, as you do. I almost as much grieve that I ever knew you, captain, as I do now at being compelled to leave your service. I have been obliged to you hitherto, but you want now to lay me under an obligation to which I have no stomach."

" This is only since you came to the ferry, and went to the christening. Go back, my boy, go back and turn ploughman. You will like that better than ploughing the waves. You will only be, after all, a lubberly landsman. But I must hail my fellows, and be off. What a pity such a brig should go a-begging for a captain ! Your own work, too, Will. Well, well, I did not think you such a fool. Here, with a silver spoon in your mouth, you would throw it away, and take up with a wooden one. Go, eat your bread sopped in warm water, in a wooden bowl, and leave your old messmates and friends to good fare, an

active life, and cheerful company. Good-bye, Will ;
good-bye."

And the captain turned round to give the signal to
his boatmen to pull to shore ; but without the least
intention of giving up his prey. It was only as a cat
would pretend to let her victim escape to a little
distance, under the idea of having more play.

"Go to your girl, boy ; go to your girl," said he,
as he took a step toward the beach. "She will be
glad to see you without employment, and sick of the
sea for her sake."

"I'll tell you what, captain, my girl's an honest
one, and if you were to make her a disloyal offer, she
would be the first to heave up her anchor, or cut her
cable, and haul to windward and be off."

"I don't make her any offer ; I have nothing to
do with any of her sex, and the less you have to do
with them the better, Will. But if you must have her
in your eye, why not for her sake try to get a comfortable berth for her ? In a very short time, you will be
able to secure enough to make her happy. After a few
runs, you may have a snug cot, near this very cove,
and be as comfortable as you wish to be. But if you
have made up your mind, and are determined not to
accept my offer, why then I must find another who will ;
and I warrant, that I need not go far before I meet
with one who will jump at the chance."

"I say, captain, how many voyages shall I go, before
that time comes you speak of ?"

"That depends upon our luck. The quicker work
we make, the sooner we shall keep our harbour. One
year, perhaps two. At all events, three, and your
berth is sure."

"Well, captain, but how shall it be for share ?"

"Why, there's the brig, and look ye, Will, she's all
right and tight, and everything well provided aboard
her. She is under your command ; your first trip to
Holland ; your cargo, gin ; and as to other goods,
snuff, tobacco, linen, and such things, I let you barter
with for yourself. Only secure me the main chance.

As to risk, that's all mine. You shall receive, say one-sixth of the profit for the first year, one-third for the second; and an equal share after. Now, my boy, but that I know your pluck, and your tact, I should never make you such an offer. There you have it."

"Captain, I'm your man!—I'm your man!"

And so he sold himself to as artful, desperate, and bold a rover, as ever crossed the Channel. How true were poor Susan's last words to him—"You want steadiness of principle and stability of purpose!" From that hour, Will entered upon a course of life which led to his own ruin, and the ruin of others. He was caught in the toils of a smuggler, from which, though he once escaped, he never had sufficient stability to entirely emancipate himself.

Captain Bargood, to whom Will thus sold himself, was a clever as well as a desperate adventurer. He contrived to keep up appearances as a steady trader, and had vessels as regularly chartered as any of England's noblest merchants. His sails visited with proper invoices all the ports along the coast, and he had connexions in every town of the first class of dealers. Yet this man managed to have withal an under-current in the contraband trade, which paid him far greater profits than his regular account.

So well did he arrange his plans, that if a vessel of his was taken by the coastguard, he had always a captain or a mate to father her, and as he always paid them well, his own fair fame was suspected by none but those who occasionally bought goods of him at a price so far below the market, that they were content to let their suspicions subside in their own profits. He was a good judge of men, both of sailors, landsmen, gentry, and men of business. He knew how far to trust them, and how soon to shorten his sail. His ships, captains, and crews, were as well known to him as anything in his own unostentatious cottages at Aldborough, Hollesley, Harwich, or Ipswich; in which he occasionally took up his abode, as business or inclination prompted. But he equally well knew Will Laud,

and foresaw in him the very commander who should
bring him in many a good prize in the shape of spirits
or tobacco, furs or linen. He cared for no man's
success but his own. He could be rough, smooth, hot,
or cool, just as he thought best to gain his end. Money
was his idol, and, as a quick return and enormous
profit for a small outlay, the smuggler's trade seemed
to him the most promising. Laud would, and as the
sequel will show, did prove a valuable servant or slave
to him. This man outlived every one of his captains,
and died about four years ago: namely, in the year
1841.

But the young sailor is arm-in-arm with the captain,
the boat is hailed, the crew, four oars and a steersman,
approach the shore, and the captain calls out—

"Now, Jack, high and dry for your new commander!"

The boat grounds, and Laud and his future master
are seated in the stern.

"Long time bringing-to, captain?" said the gruff
and surly-looking John Luff, a fellow who seemed
formed of such materials as compose a cannon-ball.
He looked like what he was, an iron-hearted and iron-
fisted desperado, whose only pleasure was to serve
a bad man, and to rule every one in the ship who had
a little more feeling than himself.

They were soon on board the brig, and Laud was
duly introduced to the crew, and appointed their
captain.

"Yes, master, yes," said the mate, "we understand.
You need not spin us a long yarn; business, say I, and
the sooner the better. I will take care of him, trust
me. He's a smart boy. He'll do, captain, he'll do."

The mate, John Luff, and the master, seemed to
understand each other. The captain shook hands with
Laud, and bidding him take care of his own craft, he
left them outward bound, and came ashore at Woodbridge Haven.

Let it suffice, for the reader's information, that Laud
was successful in his new career. He made his voyage

pay well, and contrived to send some handsome presents to Margaret, too handsome to be acceptable. Alas! how little did that desperate youth think that he was giving pain instead of pleasure to all those who had any interest in his welfare! How little did he think he was laying the foundation of misery and woe to his father, to the Catchpoles, to the Cracknells, and to every one who knew him!

His first present was received by Margaret at a time when the heart of a true lover is most open to the kind acts of friendship. Poor Margaret and the family had just returned from the funeral of Susan, and were seated in the cottage, talking over the good qualities of their dear departed and beloved friend. Her sayings and doings, her affectionate advice, her patience and resignation, were all topics of conversation, and each had some kind act to record, not one a single fault to mention. One or two of the Cracknells, and a work-man or two on the farm, who helped to carry the corpse, were all of the party who were not relatives. The good mother had prepared the mournful meal, some cake, bread and butter, a cup of tea, and a pint of beer each for the men. They were partaking of this humble meal in a very subdued and quiet spirit, as there came a rap at the door, and young Edward opened it.

"Come in," said the father, and in walked a weather-beaten man, who from his dress might be taken for some honest ploughman, but whose countenance betrayed a very different expression—none of that openness and simplicity which good labourers and countrymen wear, but a shaggy brow, and matted thick black hair. His eyebrows half covered the sockets of his eyes, which peeped from under them with an inquisitive glance, to see if all was safe.

"Does one Margaret Catchpole live here?" said the man.

"Yes, she does," was Margaret's quick reply; "what do you want with her? I am she."

"Oh! you be she, be you? Then I be commissioned

to deliver this here parcel into your hands ; " and, easing his shoulder of a heavy bale of goods, they came with some weight upon the chair which Edward had vacated for the guest.

" From whom does this come ? " said she.

" I don't know who he is. I was at work on the marshes at Bawdsey Ferry, when a young sailor came up to me, and asked me if I knew where Nacton was. I told him I knew whereabouts it was. He then asked me if I would take this here bundle to one Margaret Catchpole, a labourer's daughter, living, as he described, in just this place, which I have found."

" Did he give his name ? "

" No ; he said he couldn't come himself, but that this here would remind you of him."

All immediately concluded who he was, and Margaret asked Edward to bring the packet into the sleeping-room, whilst the countryman was asked to sit down and take a draught of beer.

The parcel was unpacked. There were silks and shawls, caps and lace, ribbons and stuffs, and gloves ; parcels of tea, coffee, tobacco, and snuff ; together with curious-headed and silver-tipped pipes ; in short, enough to stock a small shop. But there was nothing to give pleasure to Margaret. That poor girl's heart sank within her at a sight which she at once perceived was far too costly to be honestly procured. She called to Edward to assist her in tying up the bale again, and removing it into the room where the pretended country-man was seated. As she entered, the fellow roughly accosted her—

" Well ! you find summut there, I dare say, to tempt you soon to put aside these dark-looking dresses which you all wear. I must be going : can I take anything back for you ? "

" Yes," said Margaret—" yes ; you may take the whole bundle back the same way you brought it, and tell the young man who gave it you that I should have valued one single pair of honestly purchased gloves more than all the valuables he has sent me."

There was a twinkle of that small grey eye, and a twitch of the muscles of that sun-burnt face, which showed that even the hardy, rough-looking countryman was startled at such an honest spirit as then addressed him. This person was none other than John Luff, the mate of the *Alde*, who had undertaken to perform this duty for Captain Laud, from a motive, without much love in it, simply because he feared that the captain might be persuaded by his girl to leave off a smuggler's life. He saw in an instant that such would have been the case, had young Laud come with him, or brought the load himself. He had assumed the countryman's dress to avoid any notice from the coastguard, and, until he came to the lane leading to the farm, he had brought the bale of goods in a sack slung over his shoulder, as if it were corn, or chaff, or flour. He was not very easily put out, nor long in giving his answer.

" No, young woman, I have had lug enough to bring it here, and I got a crown for my job ; mayhap, if I were to take it back to the youngster, I might lose half my crown, and so be paid for my trouble. I'm not fond of broken heads for a love-ditty. You may find some one else to take it back : I've done my duty."

" No, you have not," said Margaret ; " you are no landsman, I am sure : your duty is not that of an honest labourer. You are—I am sure you are—connected with the smugglers on the coast. You may take this parcel for yourself. I give it to you, to do what you like with ; but do tell the young man, when you see him, that I hate his presents, though not himself."

" I won't have anything to do with what 's not my own," said the man, " although you tell me I'm not an honest man. I'm off. I was to meet the young chap again to-morrow at the same time and place. If you had any small love-token now, or any words which might not anger the young fellow, why, I shouldn't mind taking 'em ; but if you haven't any, why then I'll tell him you didn't care anything about him or his present. So good-bye to you."

The fellow took up his hat and stick to depart.

"Hold!" said Margaret—"hold!" and taking her father's hat down from its peg, she tore off the crape, and folding it up, she approached the disguised seaman, saying—"Give him this—do give him this—and tell him, I'd rather we all wore the like for him, than the rich things he has sent us. Will you tell him this?"

"No doubt he'll be much obliged to you: but you won't be long in this mind. So, good-bye to you all." And the man departed, leaving that spirited girl to think with pain of the dreaded words of Susan— "Margaret, you will never marry William Laud!"

CHAPTER III

MISFORTUNES

WELL would it have been for the Catchpoles and the Cracknells, had they burnt every bit of valuable stuff which the smuggler had that day brought. What years of anguish would it have spared them!—what miseries! what agonies! Nothing unlawful can long prosper. Sorrow and bitterness follow the days of unjust gain, and whosoever thinks to be happy by the sudden influx of ill-gotten wealth, will find himself grievously mistaken. Wealth gotten by honest industry and fair dealing may enable a good man to soothe the sufferings of others, but even when obtained, men find that it is not the being rich, but the regular employment in a prosperous line of life, that gives the pleasure. Sudden prosperity is too often destructive of a man's peace of mind; but sudden prosperity, by evil means, is sure to bring its own ruin. Had but that first bale of goods been burnt, Margaret might have continued the happy, cheerful child of Nature, respected and received as the honest, good-hearted girl she really was.

It may fairly be said of Margaret, that she had no

covetous hankering after any of the goods which were that day presented to her eye. She told all her friends what they were, and consulted with them what should be done with them. She would have given them up to the government officers, but she saw that it would involve her lover. She would have sent them to Laud's father, but again the idea of causing him distress deterred her. Oh! that she had cast them upon the broad sea, and let who would have caught them! But they were goodly things to look upon; they were costly—too good to throw away. And as Mrs. Cracknell said they might all be serviceable, and it was a sin to waste them, she persuaded Margaret to let her have them.

"Let my good man take them home; we may by degrees get rid of them. I can do the smaller packages up in smaller parcels, in my way; and as to the silks and lace, I can find perhaps a distant customer to take them off my hands."

"You may do what you like with them," said Margaret, "only do not let me know anything more about them."

"You know, Mr. Catchpole," said Mrs. Cracknell, "that we may all want a little help one day, and these things may provide against a stormy hour. At all events, you shall lose nothing by them, though they now bring you no profit."

It did not take much time to persuade these simple-minded people to part with things for which they had no demand and no taste.

Mrs. Cracknell had them conveyed to her cottage, where she had them sorted out, and, as prudently as possible, disposed of them according to the means of her humbler customers.

After a time, she found herself gradually improving in circumstances, and, had she been content, might have gone on improving for years. Her profits were too rapid, however, not to excite a stronger mind than she possessed. She made, of course, handsome presents to the young Catchpoles, and Margaret had the mortification of seeing a smart pipe, and of smelling the fumes of rich tobacco, even in her own cottage, well knowing they were the fruits of her lover's misdoings.

Meantime, that lover's name began to be notorious along the coast. Margaret heard no good of him. The coastguard had set a mark upon him, and it became known throughout the country that Will Laud was the ringleader of as desperate a gang as ever infested the shores of Great Britain.

So frequent were the inroads made at this period upon the commerce of the country, that government had to employ a very active force to stay, though she could not put down, so discreditable a feature upon her coasts.

At this time the shores of Norfolk and Suffolk were most conspicuous for contraband trade. Severe and deadly were the continual actions between the preventive-service men and the smugglers; lives were continually lost on both sides; and dreadful animosities sprang up between the parties upon the sea-shore.

Will Laud and his associates had great luck; and Captain Bargood found in him as bold and profitable a fellow as he could wish. Many were the hairbreadth escapes, however, which he, in conjunction with his crew, experienced. Laud was a tool in the hands of his mate, though he himself was not aware of it; for whilst that fellow had his own way, he always managed to get it through the medium of the captain's permission. He would, in his bluff way, suggest, with all becoming subordination, such and such a scheme, and generally succeeded in the enterprise.

They had observed for a long time a scout upon the beach under Bawdsey Cliffs, and knew that he was one of the Irish cruisers, who had been transplanted to watch their craft: Laud proposed to nab him when he could. He had been ashore one day to meet his employer, and had met this merry-hearted Irishman at the Sun Inn, in a street of that long, sandy village of Bawdsey. Pat was a loquacious, whisky-loving, light-hearted fellow, who, without fear, and with ready wit, made himself agreeable to everybody. He frequented the various inns along the border, and was generally liked for his dash of gallantry, his love of drinking, and his generous spirit; he was a brave fellow, too, and watchful for his honour. He had seen along the beach a man roaming about, and had concealed himself, not far from the fisherman's cottage, on purpose to watch him; but all he could make out was, that the man went to the back of the cottage, and there he lost him. Pat went to the fisherman's cot, found the man and his wife at their meals, searched about the premises, but could spy nothing. Pat had seen this thing several times, and was fully convinced that the man he saw was a smuggler.

In Bawdsey Cliff the smugglers had a cave of no small dimensions. It had formerly been a hollow ravine in the earth, formed by the whirling of a stream of water, which had passed quickly through a gravelly bed, and met with opposition in this mass of clay. It had made for itself a large crater, and then had issued again at the same place, and ran through a sand-gall and gravelly passage down to the sea. This was discovered by a tenant of the Earl of Dysart, who, in sinking a well near his shepherd's cottage, suddenly struck into the opening of this cave. As the springs were low at this season, the cave was almost empty of water, and formed a most curious appearance. It was even then called the Robbers' Cave, and curiosity was greatly excited in the country to visit it. It was so smoothly and regularly formed by the eddies of the whirlpool, that the nicest art could not have made it so uniform. The proprietor sank his well some feet lower, until he came to a good stream; but in making the well, he formed an archway into this curious place, and left it so for the gratification of public curiosity. Time swept on, and the cave became less frequented, and at last forgotten.

A few years, however, previously to this narration, some smugglers had been disappointed of their run, and had thrown their tubs down the well, with the consent of their agent the fisherman, probably a descendant of the old shepherd's, who dwelt in the cottage. This led to the re-discovery and improvement of this famous depôt of arms, ammunition, stock-in-trade, and place of retreat, which was then occupied by Will Laud and his associates, and to which very spot John Luff was at that time bound.

These men had contrived to make the cave as comfortable a berth as a subterraneous place could be. They had ingeniously tapped the land stream below the cave, and laid it perfectly dry, and with much labour and ingenuity had contrived to perforate the clay into the very chimney of the cottage; so that a current of air passed through the archway directly up the chimney, and carried away the smoke, without the least suspicion being awakened. This place was furnished with tables, mats, stools, and every requisite for a place of retreat and rendezvous. The descent was by a bucket well-rope, which a sailor well knew how to handle; whilst the bucket itself served to convey provisions or goods of any kind.

Such was the place into which vanished the choice spirits which poor Pat had seen, and into which Pat himself, *nolens, volens*, was shortly to be introduced. It would be needless to add, that the fisherman and his wife were accomplices of the smugglers.

Some short time after, Pat had an opportunity of discovering the use of the well as an inlet and outlet of the smugglers, and conceived the idea that contraband goods were stowed away at the bottom of it. He had seen a man, after talking to the woman at the spot, descend, and then come up again, and depart.

"Now's my turn," says Pat to himself, as he came out from his hiding-place, and went to the well. As every sailor could let himself down by a rope, and ascend by it likewise, Pat was soon at the bottom of the well, but found nothing. He began his ascent, working away with his hands and feet in a manner which a sailor only understands. He was gaining more daylight, and hoping that he should get out before the woman (whom he concluded had gone for help) should return. He had gained the very part where the archway into the cave was formed, and there found a sort of stay, or bar, at the opposite side, to rest his leg upon. He was taking advantage of this post to get breath, and had just swung off again to ascend, when he felt his ankles grasped by a powerful pair of pincers, as it seemed, and in another instant such a jerk as compelled him instantly to let go the rope, and he came with all his weight against the side of the well. Stunned he was, but not a bone was broken, for his tormentors had taken the precaution to have a well-stuffed hammock ready to break his fall. He was in a moment in the cave, and when reviving, heard such a burst of unearthly merriment, he could think of nothing but that he had arrived at that dreaded purgatory, to escape which he had paid so much to his priest.

In a faint, feeble voice, Pat was heard to exclaim—
" O, Father O'Gharty ; O, Father O'Gharty, deliver me ! "

This caused such another burst, and such a roar of " O, Father O'Gharty ! O, Father O'Gharty ! " from so many voices, that the poor fellow groaned aloud. But a voice, which he fancied he had heard when on earth, addressed him, as he lay with his eyes just opening to a red glare of burning torches.

" Patrick O'Brien ! Patrick O'Brien ! welcome to the shades below."

Pat blinked a little, and opened his eyes wider, and saw, as he thought, twenty or thirty ghosts of smugglers, whom he supposed had been shot by the coastguard, and were answering for their sins in purgatory.

" Come, Pat, take a drop of moonshine, my hearty, to qualify the water you have taken into your stomach : this liquid flame will warm the cold draught."

Pat had need of something to warm him, but had no idea of drinking flame.

" I hope," he said, " your majesty will excuse a poor Irishman."

"No excuse! no excuse! By the saint, your namesake, you shall swallow this gill, or maybe you'll have a little more water to simmer in."

Pat made no further opposition; and one of the uncouth, black-bearded demons, handed him a cup of as bright, shining liquid as any which the sons of whisky ever saw.

"Drink, Pat, drink," said the fellow; "a short life and a merry one."

"Och!" sighed Pat, and the next moment the burning liquid ran down his throat, warming his inside with such a glow, as made the blood circulate rapidly through every vein of his body. Whether it was the pure gin he had drunk, or the naturally aspiring disposition of the man, he began to look around him, and to note the habitation in which they dwelt. Pikes and guns were slung here and there; cables and casks lay about the room; swords and pistols—weapons which seemed more adapted to fleshly men than disembodied spirits—made the reviving spirit of this son of the Emerald Isle bethink him that he had fallen into the hands of mortals. He now looked a little more wise, and began to give a good guess at the truth, when the one who seemed to be the captain of the band soon dissipated all his doubts by saying, "Patrick O'Brien, here's to Lieutenant Barry and the preventive service. Come, Pat, drink to your commander, 'tis the last time you will ever be in such good company."

These words convinced him that he was in the smugglers' cave; and as he knew them to be most desperate fellows, his own lot did not appear much more happy than when he thought himself in the company of evil spirits.

"Come, Pat, drink. You need a little comfort."

Pat drank, and though he foresaw that no good could come to him, yet as the spirit poured in, and his heart grew warm, he thought he would not seem afraid, so he drank "Success to Lieutenant Barry and the coastguard!"

"Now, Pat, one more glass, and we part for ever."

Ominous words—"part for ever!" He heartily wished himself again in his own dear island, ere he had ventured a peep at the bottom of the well. The smugglers—for such he found they were—grinned upon him most unceremoniously, as if they had some horrid purpose in view, and seemed to enjoy the natural timidity which began to creep over his frame.

Pat drank his last glass: John Luff arose, commanded silence, and, in as gentle a voice as such a fellow could assume, said, " Mr. Patrick O'Brien, you are welcome now to your choice of departure."

"Thank ye, gemmen, thank ye, and I shall not forget your hospitality."

Pat rose, as if to depart.

"Mr. Patrick O'Brien, the choice of departure we give you is the choice of death ! "

Pat's heart sank within him, but he did not lose all his courage or presence of mind ; and the latter quality suggested to him that he would try a little blarney.

"Why, gemmen, you wouldn't kill a poor fellow in cold blood, would you ? "

"No, Pat, no ; and for that reason we have made you welcome to a drop, that you may not die a cold-blooded death. Draw swords ! "

In an instant twenty sharp blades were unsheathed.

"Now, Mr. O'Brien, take your choice : shall every man have a cut at you—first a leg, then a hand, then an arm, and so on, until your head only shall remain —or will you be rolled up in a hammock for a sack, as your winding-sheet, and, well shotted, sink as a sailor to the bottom of those waters we have just quitted ? "

"Thank your honour," said the poor victim of their cruelty, " thank your honour ; and of the two I had rather have neither."

There was no smile upon any of the ferocious countenances around him, and Pat's hopes of anything but cruelty forsook him. Just at this moment the bucket descended the well, and in came Will Laud, or Captain Laud, as he was called, who, acquainted with the fact of the Irishman's descent (for he was the very person whom Pat had seen to make his exit, and had been informed by the woman of his being drowned), was a little relieved to see the man standing in the midst of his men unscathed.

He soon understood the position in which he was placed, and, after a few words with his Lieutenant, John Luff, himself repeated the already determined sentence of his crew.

So calm was his voice, so fixed his manner, that the bold Irishman perceived at once that his doom was at hand. Assuming, therefore, his wonted courage, making up his mind to death, he looked the commander in the face, and with the composure of a mind comparatively at ease, said—

"Since I must die, let me die dacently. My choice is made—the hammock for my winding-sheet, the water for my grave, and God forgive you all."

Not a word more did the brave fellow utter, but stood like a hero, or a martyr, ready for execution.

Now to the credit of Laud be it recorded, that in his soul he admired the intrepidity of the man's spirit; and murder, base murder of a bold man, never was his intention.

He whispered to his mate, though in a moment after he exclaimed to his crew, "Do your duty."

Pat was tripped up, rolled up in the hammock, swung upon the chain, heard the whistle, and in an instant found himself, as he thought, descending to the shades below. In fact, however, he was ascending, though consciousness for a time forsook him, and the swoon of anticipated suffocation bereft him of his senses. When he did recover, he found himself at the bottom of a boat, bounding over the billows, and was soon on board a ship. Here he revived, and was treated by the crew with kindness; but after many days he was put ashore on the eastern coast of his own dear isle, with this gentle admonition:—

"Patrick O'Brien, 'all 's well that ends well.' Let well alone for the future, and now farewell."

So ended this spree, which may serve to show the

mind and habits of those men with whom Will Laud
had to deal.

At times these desperate men would be mutinous,
but their common interest kept them together. The
persons of several were known along the coast, and
farmers found it to their interest to wink at their
peccadilloes.

It was no uncommon thing for them to have their
horses taken out of the fields, or even out of their stables,
for a run at night; but they were sure of a handsome
present being left upon their premises—casks of gin,
real Hollands, packets of linen; and, sometimes
learning the thing most wanted by a particular farmer,
he would be surprised to find it directed to him by an
unknown hand, and delivered, without charge, at his
door.

The handsomest saddles and bridles which could be
procured, whips, lamps, lanterns, handsome pairs of
candlesticks, guns, pistols, walking-sticks, pipes, &c.,
were, at various houses, left as presents. Such was
the state of the traffic, that the best spirits could be
always had at the farm-houses on the coast (for all
knew where it might be had without difficulty), only
let the money be left for it with the order. In this
manner was the revenue defrauded; and there were
men in high authority who used to defend the practice
by calling it England's best nursery for seamen.
Seldom, however, were good men secured from these
sources. The generality of smugglers were not such
as England wanted to defend her liberty and laws.

About this time so many presents were sent to
Margaret, and left in such a clandestine manner at or
near the cottage, that although she herself was never
corrupted by any one of these temptations, yet the
effects of them began to show themselves in her family.
Charles, the elder brother, used to find the presents,
and dispose of them to Mrs. Cracknell, and he found
his own gains so rapidly increase that he began to be
idle; would not go to plough; disliked working on
the land; took to carpentering at the old sexton's at

Nacton; learned to read and write; and again encouraged his old *penchant* for soldiering. At length he left his parents and friends, and enlisted in the 33rd regiment of foot, under the fictitious name of Jacob Dedham, at the Black Horse public-house, St. Mary Elm's, Ipswich. He passed himself off as belonging to that parish; and but for the accidental circumstance of a Nacton lad, of the name of Calthorpe, seeing him at the inn, his friends and relatives would have been ignorant of his departure. His regiment soon after his enlistment sailed for the East Indies; and the history of Charles Catchpole, alias Jacob Dedham, would of itself form no uninteresting narrative. He rose in his regiment by great steadiness and assiduity. He became a singular adept at learning Eastern languages and customs. He was taken great notice of by Sir William Jones, the great Oriental linguist, who recommended him to a very important charge under Lord Cornwallis, who employed him in a confidential duty, as a spy, upon the frontiers of Persia. We shall have occasion to contemplate him in a future part of this history. For the present we pass on to some further fruits of the smuggler's intimacy with the Catchpoles.

Robert, another son, in consequence of the unwholesome introduction of rapid profits, took to drinking, smoking, and idle company, and very soon brought himself to an early grave; giving the deepest pangs to his parents, and creating sorrow and suffering to all. He died of delirium tremens, in the year 1791.

James became a poacher, and was shot in a desperate affray with the gamekeepers of Admiral Vernon. He lingered on his brother's bed until December 15th, 1792, and expired in deep distress, and with a declaration to poor Margaret, that it was her acquaintance with Laud that brought him to ruin. The youngest son alone preserved any steady fixed principles, and was the prop of his parents' hopes.

The whole family now fell into disrepute, and the bitterest days of adversity followed. Tales began to be circulated of Margaret's connexion with the smuggler. Sailors were seen to come and go from the cottage; and if they went but to ask for information, the lying tongue of slander was sure to propagate some infamous story. It was true that presents were left about the cottage, and that agents of the Cracknells were ready to receive them; but Margaret never touched a single thing that was so found. She was not insensible to all she saw, and she felt the full weight of Laud's misconduct; but she never forgot to pray for him, and hoped, with that fondness which true love only can know, that he would one day be converted. But she partook of the ignominy which now visited her family, though she assuredly did not deserve it. She recommended her father to take another cottage, and even to seek work under another master. Anything she considered would be better than a place where he met with such continual misfortunes.

It must not be supposed that Mrs. Denton was unkind to Margaret, though her own servants took every opportunity to persuade her that she was a very worthless person—she seemed to think a removal would be best. Accordingly Jonathan Catchpole changed his abode, and, from a regular workman on that farm, became a jobbing labourer wherever he could find employment. He and his family lived at a lone cottage on the borders of Nacton Heath. Edward became a shepherd's boy, and Margaret had serious thoughts of once more going out to service; but where? Alas! she remembered how happy she had been in her first place, and the very remembrance of that happiness made her shrink from having to relate to her former benefactor the then miserable consequences of her first attachment.

Laud's father shared in the general stigma attached to his son's name—he was accused of conniving at the youth's excesses, and lost his situation as ferryman of the government packets from Harwich to Languard Fort. What miseries, heaped one upon the other, now fell with blighting force upon poor Margaret!

But a greater trial just now awaited her—a dreadful conflict took place below Felixstowe beach between the coastguard and Laud's crew. A run was planned and put in execution from the Walton Marshes for Woodbridge—carts were brought to the cliff, the coastguard, as was thought, being attracted to Sizewell Gap, and everything being open before the smugglers. The cargo was landed, and the run began, when the preventive-service men, who had been secretly informed of the intended *ruse* at Sizewell Gap, came out of their hiding-place in a double band, headed by Lieutenant Edward Barry, a brave young sailor, second son of Mr. Henry Barry, a miller and farmer, of Levington Hill. The onset was tremendous, and the resistance deadly; but might and right were on one side, and bore down the stalwart forms of the violent smugglers.

Three of the crew were killed, and the others, unable to stand against the assault, fled as well as they were able. Young Barry and Laud had a severe personal encounter, in which the death of one or the other seemed the determination of both. Laud was the most powerful man, but Barry was the most expert swordsman; but what was the experience of the sword-arm in so dark a night? The two commanders seemed to know each other even in the darkness, for they fought with voices of encouragement to their men. The smugglers had fled, and Laud began to fear he was alone; but the pursuers, too, had gone, and still the two captains were contending. At this moment the contest was most deadly—Laud had wounded young Barry by a thrust. Though it was slight it was felt by the officer, and he determined neither to ask nor to give quarter. Laud had driven him up the side of a bank, and was in the act of giving a thrust at his heart, as Barry, with the advantage of his situation, like lightning gave a cut at his head, which at once went through his hat, and descended upon his forehead. Down fell the smuggler like a thunderbolt, and another moment the sword would have been buried in his side, had not

Barry been compelled to act on the defensive by the opposition of John Luff.

Finding a new antagonist, and being himself wounded, this young man thought best to gather up his strength for a defensive retreat. He was not pursued. Hearing some of his own men he called to them, and, recognizing him, they advanced with him to the spot where, as Barry supposed, Captain Laud lay dead. But Luff had thrown him over his shoulder, and, being well acquainted with the marshes, had carried him over some planks, and so escaped.

CHAPTER IV

DECEIT

MARGARET was seated in her father's cottage, now no longer that happy spot it used to be to her, but a change of abode had brought no rest from the troubles and anxieties of her mind: that very day she had heard of the dreadful encounter between the coastguard and the smugglers, and the report of the death of Will Laud, the notorious commander.

Margaret heard of her lover's death, as may be supposed, with the deepest emotion; but she was not satisfied that the accounts she received were correct, and had serious intentions of going to the ferryman's house to make inquiries for herself, when a rap came at their lone door, and who should come in but the ferryman himself, the father of Laud. The old man seemed to observe the altered state of the family upon whom he intruded himself, and could not help saying, at once,—

"I bring you bad news, Margaret, very bad, and of my poor boy." The old man paused, and Margaret's heart quailed, but in the next moment it revived. "But he would have me bring it!"

"Is he not dead then?" exclaimed the poor girl, as with a bound, she seized the aged ferryman by the arm; "is he not dead?"

"No, not yet—at least he was not when I left him two hours ago, and he would make me come to you, and tell you he wished earnestly to see you before he died."

"Where is he? where is he?" exclaimed Margaret.

"At my poor cot on Walton Cliff; but oh, Margaret, so altered, so dreadfully marked, and so unhappy, that if you do see him I question much if you will know him. But will you come and see him?"

"Will I?—that I will! Only you sit down and eat a bit, and I will soon be ready."

It took but a short space of time for Margaret to make preparation for her journey. Laud was alive, though ill, dangerously ill; still she might be the means of restoring him, if not to health of body, at least to a more healthy state of mind. She is ready, and the old man and Margaret depart together.

"Is he much hurt?" was Margaret's first question, after they had advanced beyond the heath on to the high-road; "is he much wounded?"

"I fear he is. At times he is like a madman, raving at everything, cursing all smugglers and his own misfortunes. The fever is high upon him; he glares wildly at the old woman I have got to do for him—calls her a smuggler's hag; and then he mentions you, Margaret, and the tears roll down his face, and he finds relief. His wound is on the forehead—a deep gash, through the bone; and the pain he suffers from the dressing is dreadful."

"Have you had a surgeon?"

"No, Margaret, no—I dare not: I fear lest he should betray himself. His life would be forfeit to his country's outraged laws, and he would die a more bitter death than now awaits him in my cot."

There ran a sensitive shudder through poor Margaret's frame as she thought of the situation of her lover. Parental affection had been more cautious than she would have been, and she secretly rejoiced. She thought likewise of her own situation; but selfishness had no portion in her soul. Laud might die! The thought was agonizing; but he would die, perhaps, a true penitent. This was surely better than being suddenly sent out of the world with all his sins upon his head. She felt thankful for so much mercy.

"Does he ever seem sorry for his crimes?" she inquired of the old man.

"I cannot exactly say he does," was the reply, "though he speaks so vehemently against his captain. I wish he saw his situation in a more forcible light."

"Time may be given him for that yet, Mr. Laud; at least, I pray God it may be so."

"Amen, say I; amen!"

"How did he find you out? How did he reach home?"

"He was brought here upon a comrade's back, a stout sailor, who came accompanied by old Dame Mitchel, who, if report speaks truth, is well acquainted with the smugglers. She says that John Luff, the captain's mate, brought poor Will to her house; and when he learned that I was living only half a mile off, he persuaded her to come and help me to do for him. He brought him to me at night."

With conversation of this kind, the father and the maiden pursued their course till they arrived at a very sequestered cottage, near the ruins of Walton Castle, close to that celebrated spot where the Earl of Leicester landed with his Flemings in A.D. 1173. "It stood upon a high cliff, about the distance of a mile from the mouth of the Woodbridge haven, two miles from the Orwell. At this time but few stones mark the spot. There is little doubt that it was a Roman fortification, as a great many urns, rings, coins, and torques, have been found in that neighbourhood. It is supposed to have been built by Constantine the Great when he withdrew his legions from the frontier towns in the east of Britain, and built forts or castles to supply the want of them." So says the old *Suffolk Traveller*.

Our travellers arrived at this lone cottage, where a faint, glimmering light from the low window told that the watch was still kept at the sick man's bed. The father entered first, and soon returned, telling Margaret that she might come in, as sleep, for the first time since the night he had been brought home, had overpowered Laud's senses.

By the faint gleam of that miserable light, Margaret perceived how dreadfully altered were the features of her lover. He lay in a heavy, hard-breathing, lethargic sleep, and the convulsive movements of his limbs, and a restless changing of the position of his arms, told that, however weary the body, the spirit was in a very agitated state ; and, oh ! how deadly, how livid was his countenance ! Scarcely could Margaret think it the same she had been accustomed to look upon with so much pleasure : the brow was distorted with pain, the lips scorched with fever—a stiff white moisture exuded from his closed eyelids. A painful moan escaped his heaving chest, and at last he surprised the listeners by a sudden painful cry.

"Margaret, ahoy ! Margaret, ahoy ! Hullo ! hullo ! Don't run away. Here, here ! I want you ! "

And then his limbs moved, just as if he was in the act of running after some one.

The fever was evidently high upon him, and poor Margaret was herself greatly afflicted at seeing his extreme suffering. She gave way to tears, which affected the poor father so much that the old man could not refrain from weeping. The woman alone seemed composed ; as if she had been accustomed to scenes of horror, she exhibited no signs of tenderness or concern. She continued to mumble a piece of brown bread which she held in her hand, lifting up her brows from time to time, and darting her sharp grey eyes, first at the smuggler, then at the girl, and then at the old man, but without uttering or seeming to hear a word, or to feel a single human emotion.

As she looked upon her, a thought shot through Margaret's brain of no very friendly nature toward the singular being before her—she could not help thinking that this Moggy Mitchel was a sort of spy upon her lover. How keen, how quick, how apprehensive is true love!

To prove that Margaret's suspicion was not altogether groundless, that very night the old woman went out of the house, under pretence of seeing what sort of night it was; and as Margaret sat watching by the bedside of Laud, the moon, which was just rising above the summit of the cliff, showed her, through the lattice, two dark figures standing together. She could not, of course, distinguish their features, but the outlines of their forms were very strong, and not to be mistaken —she was sure it was John Luff and Dame Mitchel, and that they were in close conversation on the verge of the cliff.

The old woman shortly returned to the room, and it was evident to Margaret that something had excited her.

"We must get him well as soon as we can," were the first words she uttered; and had not her former coolness and her late meeting upon the cliff awakened in Margaret's mind some sinister motive prompting this speech, she might have been deceived by it.

Margaret had the deepest and purest motives for desiring the young man's restoration to health : she loved him, and she hoped to re-establish his character, and to recover him not only from his sick-bed, but from his state of degradation. But in all her efforts she found herself frustrated by the interference of this beldame, who, as William progressed towards recovery, was constantly keeping alive within him some reports of the successes of the crew, of their kind inquiries after his health, and the hopes they had of soon seeing him among them. Independently of this, there came presents and compliments from Captain Bargood, and these increased as Laud recovered.

Nothing so much stung Margaret's heart as to find

that all her attentions, prayers, entreaties, and admonitions, were counteracted by the secret influences of these agencies; but her object was a righteous one, and she did not slacken in her endeavours to attain it. She found, as Laud gradually recovered, that he was fully sensible of his past folly, and quite alive to the devoted affection she had shown to him; but she found also that no touch of religious feeling blended with his regret for his past conduct.

This gave her the deepest pang, for she would rather have heard him offer one thanksgiving to the Being to whom all thanks are due, than find herself the object of his praise and gratitude.

It was at this time that Margaret wished she had been a scholar. There was a Bible in the cottage, an old black-letter edition, containing the Book of Common Prayer, the genealogies recorded in the sacred Scriptures, together with the Psalms of David, in metre, by Sternhold and Hopkins, with curious old diamond-headed notes of the tunes to each psalm.

Margaret would gladly have read the holy book to her lover, but she might as well have had a Hebrew edition before her, for not a word could she decipher. He could read, and her only way of inducing him so to do was by expressing her desire to hear him read. She found this, however, a difficult and dangerous task, for, independently of the distaste which the old woman had to the Bible, she found her lover very restless and feverish after any exertion of the kind. Where the spirit is unwilling, how irksome is the task!

"How plain is that description you read to me this morning of our first parents' fall," said Margaret one day, when the enemy was absent: "how plainly it shows us the necessity of our denying ourselves anything and everything which God has forbidden us!"

"It does, indeed, Margaret; but no man can help sinning!"

"I doubt that—I think Adam could have done so."

"Then why did he sin, Margaret?"

"You read to me, that the woman tempted him or

persuaded him, and that the serpent beguiled her into sin: so that the serpent was the author of sin."

"Yes: and the woman was first deceived, and then deceived her husband. You must admit that she was the worst of the two."

"I own that she was, and is the weakest; but her sorrows appear to have been the greater, and she has been little better than a slave to man ever since."

"Well, Margaret, well, you have been very kind to me, and I know now that you are a good girl, and wish me to be good. I wish I may be better."

"Do not only wish it, dear William, but pray to God to make you so, and I do think that He will."

"Well, well, I will be better—yes, I will, if I get over this blow on the head; but oh, how it aches! You must not bewilder me too much."

So did this interesting conversation cease, by the man's appeal to his want of strength, when he was asserting a will of his own, which, though bold in words, was but fickle in actions.

Every day, as her patient advanced towards recovery, was poor Margaret more and more convinced that Laud wanted stability of purpose to resist evil,—he was, like every passionate man, self-willed and wicked. Margaret, though at this time uneducated, had been a very attentive listener to all good instruction—she was far from being ignorant of right and wrong. Her principles were good, and through her most eventful years she exhibited but one great error, which was her blind passion for the unhappy man whom she would have made, if she could, a better being; and every day she found a more persevering enemy in Mrs. Mitchel, who counteracted all her salutary influence with Laud. Silent and morose as this woman was at times, she could be loquacious enough when it suited her own purpose.

"I have," said she, one day, "just left a choice set of fellows upon the beach, as merry a set, Will, as I ever saw, and all rejoicing in your improvement. Luff holds your office until you join them again. They have had fine success lately, since young Barry is laid by the leg. I have brought you a box of raisins, and such a choice can of sweetmeats, as a present from the captain."

"Ah! they are all good fellows, but I do not think that I shall ever join them again."

"Pshaw, my lad! this is only a love-fit for the moment." (Margaret was absent upon an errand.) "If that girl does not know what it is to have a high-spirited young fellow like yourself for a lover, without making him a poor, tame, milk-and-water poodle, why then she ought to make herself always as scarce as she is at this moment. I have no patience with the girl —she does not know her own interest. I suppose she would have you stick to the plough's tail, or toil all day at the spade, and bring her home a hard-earned pittance at the week's-end. Pshaw! Will, you are formed for better things."

"But she's a good girl, Moggy," said Will.

"Oh, aye! the girl is well enough, and decent too. I don't mean to say she would not make a chap a good sort of wife either, but she's not the sort of girl for you, Will. She's no spirit about her. She don't see how a young fellow like you can do better by her, in a bold, dashing way, than by such tame, dull, plodding industry as her family use."

"No; but then she wishes to see me happy, and I might be popped off the next skirmish."

"You always look on the black side of things. Here are your fellows making their fortunes rapidly, and you talking of drudging on, in a quiet, stupid way, with the chance of being informed against and executed for your past doings. Young Barry won't easily forgive you."

"Nor I him, either," was the significant reply, with a clenching of the fist and a grinding of the teeth, which proved how artfully the hag had worked upon Laud's worst feelings.

Margaret, on her return, could perceive that her

absence had been taken advantage of to effect a purpose adverse to all her hopes.

Against all these disadvantages, however, Margaret combated with some success, and by degrees had the happiness of seeing her patient get the better of his sufferings. The wound would have healed sooner and better, had Laud's mind been kept free from feverish excitement. It did heal up, though not so well as Margaret wished—a frightful scar extended over the *os frontis*, directly to the high cheek-bone. For a long time the eye seemed as if it had perished, but as the fever abated its sight returned.

It will be sufficient to record, that in due time Laud perfectly recovered, and the services of his nurses became no longer necessary.

If at this time any situation had offered itself by which Laud could have gained an honest livelihood, he would, probably, have accepted it, and become an honest man ; and in talking with Margaret of his future life, he promised that she should never again hear of anything against him. He would go to sea, and earn an honest livelihood, even if he was obliged to serve a foreigner.

"Well, Laud, I will trust you again," said Margaret, on the day she took her leave of him : "I will trust you again, William, though my heart aches bitterly at parting with you, whilst you have no regular employment, but I shall pray for you wherever I am. I shall probably go to service soon, for I do not like to be a burden to my friends."

They parted affectionately, for Laud felt that he owed his life to her care ; and she, that all her hopes of future comfort in this life were centred in his welfare. Yet that very night did William Laud meet his former comrades, and was persuaded to join their crew at the Bawdsey Cave, to assume the name of Hudson, and to become again neither more nor less than a desperate smuggler.

We will not follow him through his career of guilt : suffice it to say, that he contrived to send word to

Margaret that he had entered into the service of a Dutch trader, and was promised a future share of his ship. He pretended to have quitted the society of the smugglers, who at that time so infested the eastern coasts of this country; and as she heard no more of his name, and received no more suspicious presents, she suffered her heart to cherish the fond hope of his reformation.

The anticipation of days to come, and the promised pleasure of those days, are always greater than are ever realized by mortals. It is, however, one of the greatest blessings of life to anticipate good. The hope, too, of another's welfare, and of being the humble instrument of promoting the interest of another, is the sweetest bond of woman's cherished affection. Truly may such be termed man's helpmate, who would do him good, and not evil, all the days of his life.

Poor Margaret found, that the more she hoped for Laud's amendment, the more constant became her attachment, the more she excused his past life, and the more deeply her heart became engaged to him.

CHAPTER V

WILD SCENES

MARGARET, true to her intentions of going to service, found a kind friend in Mrs. Denton, who recommended her to Mrs. Wake, of the Priory Farm, Downham Reach. Here, in September, 1792, she took up her abode as servant-of-all-work. The whole farmhouse was formerly the priory of a small body of Augustine Monks, and was known by the name of the Alneshbourne Priory. It is surrounded by a moat of considerable depth and breadth, and was formerly approached by a drawbridge from the southern side.

The site of this old house is still a most romantic

and sequestered spot. In front of it, along a pleasant green slope to the shore, runs a rippling stream, which having passed through the moat, meanders along the meadow down to the Orwell, whose broad waters look here like a magnificent lake.

On either side of the valley rise the rich woods of Downham Reach; and behind the house, in the green meadows, may still be seen, though now covered in with a roof and used as a barn, the chapel of this sequestered fraternity.

Lofty elms overshadow the summit of this ancient house, though they grow upon the open space beyond the moat; and the woods of the owner of the present house and the district, Sir Philip Broke, stand conspicuously towering on the sides of the hills. The lover of peaceful nature could not fail to be struck with the tranquil yet picturesque scenery around this spot. Here Gainsborough, who, in his younger days, was much encouraged by Dr. Coyte of Ipswich, loved to roam, and catch the ever-varying tints of spring and autumn. Here Constable,—the enthusiastic, amiable, but pensive John Constable, one of the best of England's landscape-painters,—indulged himself in all the hopes of his aspiring genius; and Frost, a native of Ipswich, one of the best imitators of Gainsborough's style, and whose sketches are at this day most highly esteemed, used to indulge himself in the full enjoyment of his art.

At the period we write of—the year 1792—the Orwell's waves went boldly up to the port, as new and briny as in the days of the Danish invasion. Now they no longer wash the town. A wet-dock, with its embankments and its locks, shuts out the ebb and flow of waters, and may be convenient to the inhabitants of the place; but sadly interferes with the early associations and recollections of those who, like the writer of this narrative, passed their boyish years upon the banks of the Orwell.

But we must no longer wander from our narrative. Margaret, as servant at the Priory Farm, conducted herself in so exemplary a manner, that she soon gained the good will of her master and mistress, and the good word of all the labourers upon the farm. Amongst these latter was a young man who was particularly acquainted with Margaret's history, and whose name has occurred in a previous chapter. This was no other than John Barry, the elder brother of young Edward Barry, who so gallantly led the attack upon the smugglers on the night in which Will Laud was supposed to have been killed. John was well aware of Margaret's attachment and engagement to Will Laud; and he knew the part his brother had taken in the conflict; and believed, as Edward told him, that he had slain Margaret's lover. Whether it was the sympathy which arose toward the poor girl under these circumstances, or the real pleasure which he felt in her society, it is certain that he became so deeply enamoured as never to be able to root out of his mind this his first and last attachment.

This young man was a contrast in every respect to Will Laud. John Barry was the elder son of a small farmer and miller at Levington, who, having a numerous family, was anxious they should all be employed. John, as was customary in that day, sought employment away from his parents' house. He had asked their permission to let him turn his hand to farming for a year; and as he was already a good ploughman, and understood the various methods of culture, he readily found an employer. He was also as good a scholar for that period as could be found in any of the adjoining parishes. Added to this, he was a good-principled, steady, persevering, industrious young man. His father was not badly off in the world for his station. He it was who first discovered the use of crag-shells for manure. His man, Edmund Edwards, finding a load or two of manure was wanted to complete the fertilization of a field which Mr. Barry cultivated, carried a load or two of the crag, which lay near the mill, to make it up. He observed, that in the very place which he thought would prove the worst crop, on account of the seeming poverty of the soil carted, there arose the most luxuriant produce. Next year Mr. Barry used it more freely, and found a more abundant recompense. He then opened immense crag-pits, supplied the country around, and shipped a large quantity at Levington Creek. By these means he became known as an enterprising man. His second son took to the sea, and became active in the service of his native coast. Another son went out to America, and did remarkably well.

John went as head man to Mr. Wake, of the Priory Farm. When he left his father's house, the worthy miller gave him one guinea, with this advice—

"Many a man, John, has entered into the world with less than that, and by industry, integrity, and good behaviour, has risen to usefulness and respectability; and many a man, John, who has entered upon life with thousands and thousands of those shining coins, has sunk to worthlessness and degradation. Go, boy; be honest, sober, steady, and diligent. Keep your church and God's commandments, John, and you will prosper. But should misfortune ever visit you, remember that whilst your mother and I live you will always find a welcome home. God bless you, boy! God bless you!"

John left home, with a guinea in his pocket and with love in his heart. He did well, even in his first situation. He lived in the farm-house with Mr. and Mrs. Wake, about seven miles from his father's house. He did not then dream that he should ever visit any distant shore connected with his native country. His dreams were of home, industry, and peace. He had enough—was contented—was well respected; had good health and full employment, and was a burden to no one. From his constant habit of witnessing the energy, and activity, and good disposition of the youthful Margaret, and from a certain knowledge of her past misfortunes, he imbibed a delicacy of interest in her behalf, which was shown to her by repeated acts of respect, which others on the farm less delicate did

not care to show. Margaret herself perceived these
attentions, and felt grateful to him for them. Whilst
some would now and then relate what they heard of
the wild adventures of Hudson the smuggler, John
Barry always carefully concealed any mention of
matters which he could see gave her pain. So cautious
had been his advances towards a more intimate acquaintance with Margaret, that no one on the farm suspected
that John Barry, the son of the well-to-do Mr. Barry,
of Levington, was in the least captivated by the humble
maid of the Priory. Margaret, however, suspected
and dreaded that such might be the case ; and she
avoided him as pointedly as she could, without offence
to one whom she so much respected. Barry, however,
was too honest to conceal his feelings from the only
person he wished to know them. Returning one
evening from work along Gainsborough's Lane, he
met Margaret, who had been to Sawyer's farm upon
an errand for her mistress.

"Margaret, you know I love you," said the young
man, " though I do not believe that any one upon the
farm besides yourself has any idea of it."

"I feared you did, John, and it grieves me very
much to hear you say so."

"But why should it grieve you ? I love you honestly,
and will alway do my best to make you happy."

"Yes, John, I do not doubt you in anything you
say, and I feel very grateful to you for your kindness ;
but I cannot return your love."

"Why not, Margaret ? Why should you not learn
to like me ? I am not indeed like your former lover,
but I think I love you quite as well."

"That may be also, John ; but when I tell you that
it is impossible for me to suffer you to cherish such
feelings, you will, I hope, not be angry with me."

"I am not angry : I know your past attachment ;
but I hope that you do not intend to live and die single
because Laud is dead."

"No ; but whilst he lives, John, I neither can nor
ought to give encouragement to any other."

" But he is dead ! "

" I would let any one else but yourself suppose so."

" My brother Edward told me himself that he saw him fall."

" Yes, John, and your brother Edward thought that he gave him his death-blow; but I am happy, for his sake and for Laud's, that it was not so."

" Are you sure of this ? " sighed the youth, as if he half regretted that his brother had not done so. " Are you sure of this ? "

" Quite so—quite so ! To no one else would I speak it, but I am sure of your goodness. I know you will not betray me."

" Never, Margaret, never ! "

" Well, then, these very hands healed the wound which your brother gave him. I myself nursed him through his dangerous illness ; and I know at this time that he is in a respectable foreign merchant's service, and as well as ever he was."

This was a tremendous blow to the young man's prospects ; an answer which he did not in the least expect, and from which he could find no encouragement. He begged Margaret's pardon for what he had said, which was freely given, and a promise made on both sides never to divulge that day's secret. Alas ! this promise was broken by both, as we shall presently see, at the very same moment.

But where is Laud, and what is he doing at this time ? While the honest-hearted girl is denying all attachment to any but himself, and living upon the hope of his future welfare and well-doing, what is *he* about ?

He is standing at the Green Cottage, as it was called, on account of the green shutters which used to shade its casements, close to Butley Abbey. The dark-frowning ruin of this seat of the black canons of St. Austin, formerly so grand and extensive, was then in a state of crumbling desolation. Here, close against that magnificent old gateway, seemingly in mock grandeur, was a very fine arch, surmounted with the arms of Michael de la Pole, the third Lord Wingfield,

Earl of Suffolk, who was slain at the battle of Agincourt with Edward Plantagenet, Duke of York.

Not far from these ruins, with a mind somewhat partaking of the darkness of that desolation, stood Laud and Luff in close conversation; the subject of which was no other than Margaret Catchpole!

Luff had found out Laud's deep-rooted fancy for the maiden, and, villain as he was, was proposing a deep-laid scheme for the destruction of the poor girl, who at that very time was undergoing a severe trial of her affection.

"I'll tell you what, Laud, the thing is easily to be done. We have nothing to do but to run the cutter, at the beginning of our next voyage, into Harwich Harbour, at the fall of the evening, when the mists hide us from the shore; you and I can run up the Orwell in the gig, and soon carry off the prize. Once on board, and she is yours as long as you like."

"I think I shall leave the service and marry."

"And get a halter for your pains! No, Will; no, my boy; you are made of sterner stuff than that. What! for the sake of a girl whom you may have for many a cruise, and who will like you all the better for your spirit, would you consent to run the land-robber's risk of being hanged? You will soon have a new cutter, and your old crew; and though we may have a long voyage, surely it will be far better to have your damsel with you, though she may be unwilling at first, than to be living ashore in continual fear of the officers of justice."

"But Margaret supposes me at this moment in a foreign ship, and in an honest trader."

"Let her think so still. Only once get her on board the *Stour*, and never trust me if we don't quickly run over to Holland, get you decently married, and you may settle with her on shore in a short time."

"Well, Luff, I think it might be done, and fairly, too; and if it be, you shall have half my share of the prize upon the next run."

"'Tis a bargain—'tis a bargain! and when we next

meet in Bawdsey Cave, our first trip shall be for the harbour. In the meantime, let us enjoy ourselves as we can."

The Green Cottage just mentioned, was one of those places hired by Captain Bargood, on the eastern coast, which was always kept neat, and ready for his occupation, by a dame whom he permitted to live in it rent-free, and paid her something extra too for housekeeping. This was a place of resort for his captains when out of immediate employ, when his ships were repairing or building, at home or abroad. The method he took to secure their services, and to keep them in readiness for the sea, was to initiate them into the mysteries of poaching when on land.

So well did this bold fellow play his cards, that his men seldom wanted employment.

Game they always had, in season or out of season—no matter—they stuck at nothing! If they wished for a good custard at Whitsuntide, and made of the richest eggs, they would have pheasants' and partridges' eggs by hundreds. In fact these smugglers were as well known for poachers by many of the people on the coast, as they were for dealers in contraband goods. They, too, enjoyed the keen zest of the sportsman in a tenfold manner, if the excitement of the field, the danger of the enterprise, and the success of the sport, be any criterion by which the pleasure of such things may be estimated.

Tame, indeed, they considered the turn-out of the Marquis of Hertford, with his green-brogued keepers, and their double-barrelled guns and brushes, for a walk, or rather a stand, at the end of a plantation, where the pheasants rose in a shower, and were killed like barn-door fowls. They often saw the noble sportsmen turn into those coverts, against which they knew they had been such successful poachers the very night before.

If hairbreadth escapes, contests with keepers, making nets, snares, and gins, were amusements to these fellows, they had enough of them. They could, upon occasion, bribe an unsteady keeper, or make him drunk, and go his beat for him. All manner of desperate adventures were their pleasures. Sometimes their society was courted by farmers and others, who chanced to know, and would occasionally entertain them. Their knowledge of all that was going on in and out of the country made them welcome visitors to others ; and in a very dangerous period of our struggle at Flushing, when an order from the coast was to be carried in spite of danger and difficulty, the intelligence and spirit of these men were made use of by some in power, who could never countenance them openly.

One instance of a singular kind of frolic may here be mentioned, which might have been of serious consequence to a young man of fortune.

This gentleman resided in his own house, and upon his own estate, not far from Hollesley Bay ; and though possessed of many broad acres, abundantly supplied with every species of game common to that country, yet, singularly enough, he was an exception to that prevalent habit of all country gentlemen—the being a sportsman. The writer of these pages has often heard him narrate the following facts :—

Laud, or rather Hudson, as he was then called (for Laud was generally supposed to be dead), met this young man at the Boyton Alms-houses, when the following conversation arose :—

" Good morning to you, captain. But little stirring at sea, I suppose ? "

" We're ashore awhile upon a cruise."

" So I suppose. What tack do you go upon to-night ? "

" That I know not, sir ; but not hereabouts. We shall probably run down to Orford."

" I know you are all good hands. I never went sporting in my life, and never saw any poaching. Now, captain, it 's no use being qualmish upon the subject, but upon my word I should like to see how you poachers manage to take your game. You need not fear that I should inform against you, or take advantage of your secrets—for I am no sportsman, as you know, and care as little about game as any man; but I have heard so much of your adroitness, and of the methodical manner in which you proceed, that I really should like to see it. Come, what shall I give you to take me with you to-night?"

The smuggler looked at him with a very significant countenance, as much as to say, "Are you in earnest? May I trust you?" It was very few he thought he could trust; but there was a simplicity and honesty, a straight-forward singleness of mind, and such a real, truthful heartiness of character about the young man, that a far less shrewd man than Laud could see there was no danger in him. So far from ever intending evil to any one, he was kind even to a fault: witness his very treatment of such a man as Laud. He had often seen him about his marshes, or along the river's side, or in the village, or upon the heath. He knew what Hudson was; and like many others in that retired country, became an occasional talker with him, even upon the subject of smuggling. He knew that his own horses came in for a share of night-work, as well as his neighbours'; but he always found himself well treated by the smugglers, and frequently acknowledged the receipt of some acceptable present. He knew the habits of poaching which these seamen enjoyed ashore, and he never interrupted them. His own lands were always abounding in game for his friends, and he never knew that they were poached.

"Well, captain, what say you? Will you take me?"

"That I will, with all my heart. Where will you meet me?"

"Where you like. Where shall it be?"

"Suppose my messmate and I call you at eleven o'clock? We can take a glass of grog with you, and perhaps use your own cart and horse. We shall most likely go to Iken or Orford. But I will see my mate, and have everything arranged, and be with you by eleven."

H.M.C.   D

The honest bachelor who had made this appointment with Laud and Luff, had no idea of his temerity and of the danger of the deed. He saw only, for the time, a certain mystery, which he wished to see unravelled, and forgot all the penalties the law attached to it.

Our worthy bachelor received his two promising visitors at eleven o'clock, having first sent every servant to bed, and parted with an aged mother, who was ignorant, blessedly ignorant, of her son's movements at such a time of night ; Laud and Luff were let into the house ; they came, partook of his good cheer, and then opened upon the subject of their campaign.

They told him their intention to have a drag over some of the stubbles of the Marquis of Hertford's estate, between Iken and Orford, and they instructed him in the plan of operation. Five men were to meet them in the lane leading down into Iken Wood : they carried a net capable of covering four furrows. Not a single word must be spoken. Five would drag in front, and three behind ; one was to hold the checkstring, by which an alarm was conveyed to every one who had hold of the net. In case of a sudden jerk at this string, each person dropped his hold of the net, and ran for the nearest hedge, where he concealed himself until he heard the signal to join forces again, which signal was for that night the crowing of a cock. When by sundry kicks in the net they found that game was enclosed, they were to drop the net, at the sound of a small reed whistle, so low as only to be heard by those who were at a short distance. As the young host was only a novice, it was proposed that he should take his station between Hudson and Luff, his two visitors.

After all proper hints had been repeated, and these worthies had sufficiently regaled themselves, they all went to the cart-lodge ; took out the market-cart, harnessed the old chestnut gelding, something between a cart-horse and a roadster, and off they started for as novel an expedition as ever any man of fortune undertook.

Will the reader believe that a man of good character —aye, and as honest, upright, good-natured, kind-hearted, and benevolent a man, as any of his rank and condition—a man of an intelligent and unwarped mind—and one who through life was looked upon as good a neighbour as could be—should so forget himself as to trust his reputation, his honour—his very life and happiness (for at that time the Game Laws were very severe), between two as great rascals as ever stole a head of game, or shot a fellow-creature, in the frenzy of their career ?

The reader must imagine a man far above all want, and with every blessing which an abundant fortune could supply, without any idea of intending an affront to the lord of Orford, or any of his affluent neighbours, seated in his own luggage-cart, with his very name written in large letters, X. Y. Z., Esq., with his place of abode upon it ! He must imagine such a man, trusting himself between two notorious characters merely for the spree of the moment, and purely for the sake of curiosity running the risk of losing his character and his liberty, and yet without a thought of his danger. Yet the tale is as true as it is strange. Had not the writer heard the subject of it often declare the fact, he should have believed it impossible.

They are off, however, and Luff is the driver. As if acquainted with his horse, and the horse with him, they went at a rate which astonished even the owner of the animal. He had said, "Let me drive, for I understand his humour"; but he found that another understood his own horse as well as himself. This brute was like a donkey in one respect. Except you gave him a jerk with the rein, and at the same time gave a rap on the sides of the cart, you could not get him to move. What, then, was the surprise of the Squire to find that a stranger could make the old horse go as well as he could. But not a word was to be spoken— so in silence he brooded over the singular knowledge of his coachman, and gave him credit for his driving, which he richly deserved. It was evident the old horse had been in his hands before that night. On they went through Boyton, Butley, the borders of Eyke, to the lane leading down to Orford. Here at a certain gate they stopped, and on the other side of the hedge were the five men with the net. The old horse was tied to the gate, the net unrolled, spread out, and, without a single word being spoken, each man took his station.

It was just the dawning of the morn, when they could hear the old cock pheasants crowing to their mates, to come down from their perches to feed. A rustling wind favoured the work ; a large barley stubble was before them, lying with a slope up to the famous preserve of Iken Wood.

As they proceeded onward, sundry kicks in the net told of the captured game, which was regularly and dexterously bagged, by the leading man passing on to the net to the place of fluttering, and wringing the necks of the said partridges, pheasants, hares, rabbits, or whatever they were ; then passing them along the meshes to the head of the net, whence they were safely deposited in the different game-bags of the foremen.

That this sport was as much enjoyed by these men as that enjoyed by the best shot in the land ; that these fellows were as expert in their movements and as experienced as Colonel Hawker himself, and as bold as any foxhunter in the country, is quite true.

There was one in that party whose courage was soon put to the test, after a fashion which he little calculated upon, and never forgot.

After having bagged a considerable quantity of game, and swept several acres of stubble, they were ascending the middle of the field, toward the covert, when a sudden violent check of the alarm-string, which ran from one to the other, told that they must drop the net, and be off. Off they ran, helter-skelter, as fast as they could, to the nearest fence.

The Squire's heart was in his throat, and his courage

in his heels, as, with unwonted speed, he ran for his life to the fence. Into brake and briar, amidst nettles and thistles, brambles and thorns, dashed the hero of the night, with his top-boots sticking plounce into the mud, and, for the life of him, not daring to extricate them, for fear of his being heard and taken by the gamekeepers. The water oozed coolly over the tops, conveying a gentle moisture to his feverish skin, and proving no small consolation for his exertions.

There he lay in a dreadful fright, expecting every instant some stout keeper's hand to seize him by the shoulders, and lug him out of his hiding-place. Then it was for the first moment that he felt the awkwardness of his situation. Reflection told him his danger. Though he durst scarcely breathe, he felt his heart beat tumultuously against his chest, at the thought of his folly and the possibility of detection.

" Oh, what a fool I am," thought he, " to run the risk of transportation for such a freak ! My name is on my cart ; it is my horse, and the fellows will swear they were in my employ. On me will be visited the vengeance of the law. Lord Hertford will never forgive me. I shall have all the magistrates, squires, noblemen, gentlemen, gamekeepers, and watchers up in arms against me ; and all for what ?—for a foolish curiosity, which I have thus gratified at the expense of my character. Oh ! if I get out of this scrape, never, never will I get into such a one again ! "

In the midst of these painful impressions, the Squire's heart was gladdened by the cheerful sound of " bright chanticleer." Never did cock crow with a pleasanter sound than that good imitation, which told that the coast was clear.

Some time did the Squire hesitate whether he should join the sport again, and a still longer time did it take him to extricate his boots from the mud, for he came out of the ditch minus the right leg covering, and, after sundry tugs, and, when out, sundry shakings, &c., to turn out the water, and then, as may be supposed, no small difficulty in getting it on again, he managed to join his companions, who had almost felt persuaded that he had totally decamped. The cause of this alarm was a poor unfortunate jackass, which had strayed from the lane into the stubble, and which, standing with his head and ears erect, had presented to the foreman the appearance of a determined game-keeper.

A few more acres were dragged, more game secured, and the party once more safely seated in the cart. Two sacks of game lay in the bottom of the vehicle, which were both deposited (saving one bagful for the host) at the Green Cottage at Butley Moor. What a happy man was that host, when, after all his dangers, he found himself again within his own doors ! happier still, when, after entertaining his free companions, whose jokes upon his expressions of joy at escape were amusing enough to them, though painfully interesting to himself ; happier still was he, when, at four o'clock in the morn, he let them out of his house, and bade poachers and poaching good-bye for ever !

Nineteen beautiful cock pheasants were hung up in his larder ; but so ashamed was the Squire of their being seen there, that, before he retired to his own bed, he put them all into a box, with hay, &c., and directed them to Mr. Thomas Page, his wine-merchant, in London. His *spolia opima* were not mentioned till years had in some measure worn off the rust of danger, and then he gave his friends and neighbours reason to rejoice in his adventure, and that he had escaped transportation.

CHAPTER VI

HARVEST-HOME

IT was the evening before Harvest-Home, September 29, 1793, that a sailor called at the back-door of the Priory Farm, Downham Reach, to ask for a draught of fresh water. It was no uncommon thing for sailors to call for such a purpose. Downham Reach was the nearest point at which ships of large tonnage would usually anchor, and shift their cargoes in lighters for the town of Ipswich, whence it was distant about four miles. The crews of vessels frequently had to walk up to the town from this spot; so that it was no uncommon thing for them, upon landing near the Priory Farm after a voyage, to be glad of a sparkling draught of clear water. The desired draught was handed to the sailor by the ever-ready hand of Margaret Catchpole, who always took an interest in men belonging to the sea.

"Is dis de Priry Barm?" asked the man, in broken English.

"This is the Priory Farm," was the quick and eager reply of Margaret.

"How bar to Gipswitch?"

"Four miles to Ipswich. What country are you from?"

"Mynheer be brom Hamsterdam. I lept me bessel in de harber. Mynheer de Captan did 'mand me up to Gipswitch. 'E 'mand me 'top at Priry Barm to tale von Margaret Catchpole dad 'e vou'd come up 'ere to-morrow, at nine o'clock in de eve."

"What is your captain's name?"

"Von Villiam Laud."

The reader need not be told the rest of the conversation, which of course related to the Captain. How he was? How he got on? Whose service he was in? How he would come up? And where Margaret was to

meet him? It was all arranged that she should be
upon the shore at nine o'clock, and look out for a small
sail-boat, which should come up the river and run
ashore against the creek : that the watchword should
be "Margaret," and that punctuality should be
observed.

Margaret's quick understanding soon construed all
the sailor said into proper English, though she could
not perceive that the man only feigned a foreign accent
and manner. He was indeed one of Laud's crew, an
emissary sent on purpose to decoy the poor girl on to
the strand, that he might carry her off to a foreign shore,
against her own determined purpose.

It is not to be wondered at that she should be a little
agitated. Whose heart would not have been so under
similar circumstances? The expected arrival of some
fashionable and insinuating man of fortune into the
saloon of fashion has not agitated the heart of an
amiable and interesting young lady more sensibly than
poor Margaret felt herself fluttering within at this
peculiar time. It is a great question, however, whether
any high-spirited damsel could prevent the exposure
of her high feelings with more effect than this poor girl
did hers, who not only had her own interest to induce
her so to do, but her lover's also.

The last day of September came, and with it all the
bustle and pleasure of Harvest-Home. No small share
of work fell to Margaret's hands, who had to prepare
the harvest supper for fourteen men, besides women
and children.

At that time of day, all the single men lodged in the
master's house, and were expected to conform to all
the rules, regulations, hours, and work, of a well-
regulated family.

Once in a year, the good farmer invited the married
men, with their wives and families, to supper ; and this
supper was always the Harvest-Home. This was the
day on which the last load of corn was conveyed into
the barn or stack-yard, covered with green boughs,
with shouting, and blowing of the merry harvest horn.

All the labourers upon the Priory Farm were assembled at six o'clock in the evening : nine married men, and five single ones ; the wives, and those children who were old enough to come to the feast, together with the boys, four in number, who had to work upon the land.

A picture fit for the hand of Wilkie was exhibited in that ancient farm-house. It is surprising that no good artist should have painted The Harvest Supper. The Rent-day, Blindman's-buff, The Fair, The Blind Fiddler, or any of his celebrated works, could scarcely afford a more striking subject for the canvas, or the printseller, than The Harvest-Home. Such a scene may have been painted, but the writer of these pages has never seen it described, though he has often witnessed it in real life, and has shared with innocent pleasure in its rustic joy.

Margaret received great assistance from some of the married women. One pair of hands could not, indeed, have prepared sufficient eatables for such a party :— smoking puddings, plain and plum ; piles of hot potatoes, cabbages, turnips, carrots, and every species of vegetable which the farmer's lands could produce— beef, roast and boiled, mutton, veal, and pork, everything good and substantial ; a rich custard, and applepies, to which the children did ample justice, for all were seated round this well-furnished table in the old kitchen, celebrated for its curious roof and antique chimney-piece.

The lord of the feast, or head man in the harvestfield, took his station at the head of the table, whilst the master of the house, and his wife, his sister, and even his daughter, were the servants of the feast, and took every pains to gratify and satisfy the party.

Poor labourers are not the only class in England fond of a good dinner. There are hundreds and thousands, with half the appetites of these joyful sons and daughters of the sickle, who glory in a feast. How often is the rich table spread with every delicacy, and at an enormous cost the greatest rarities provided, and

a group of lords and ladies seated thereat ! Things just
tasted and dismissed, and all due ceremonies performed,
the company rise without any satisfaction, and return
to their homes grateful to nobody ; sometimes hungry
and dissatisfied, moody and contentious ; disappointed,
disaffected, tired, and palled by the very fashion of the
thing, in which there has been no enjoyment and no
thankfulness.

It was not so at this rustic feast. Simplicity and
pleasure sat upon each face. Fathers and mothers,
sons and daughters, felt thankful to God for their
master's prosperity, and received his attentions with
unaffected gratitude.

After the feast, and a flowing jug or two of brown
ale had been emptied, the wives and children were
invited into the best parlour to tea and cakes, whilst
the merry reapers were left to themselves, to enjoy in
their own way the stronger harvest ale, which was just
broached by the hand of their master.

Margaret had done her duty well, and was busily
engaged washing up the dishes as fast as she could,
that she might, in the midst of this bustling evening
get her work sufficiently forward not to be missed,
should she run down to the shore.

" Boy, take the can to the girl and have it filled " ;
for the master had deputed Margaret to draw whatever
ale was called for.

This was soon done, and the boy returned just as
the old clock struck eight.

Margaret heard with a fluttering heart the songs,
according to custom, commencing ; and getting her
work well forward, she resolved, after the next can of
ale was replenished, to be off.

Accordingly, she ran up the back stairs, and brought
down her bonnet and shawl, which she left behind the
staircase-door, and anxiously awaited the moment to
be off duty. She had put every plate in the rack, laid
all the iron spoons in the drawer, cleaned the spit, and
placed it, bright and shining, over the chimney-piece.
All the skewers had been strung, all the knives and

forks washed and wiped, boilers, saucepans, gridirons, and the rest of the culinary utensils cleaned, and placed in their proper places ; in short, scarcely any one would have believed that they had that day been used. Clean they were, and cleaner the well-washed face and hands of the active girl, who had finished her work, and prepared herself for an interview with one whose image had been graven on her mind through every period of her short service.

At last she heard that welcome sound, more enchanting to her ear than any song which the young men had sung : "Boy, take the can to Margaret!"

It was soon replenished ; and scarcely was the kitchen-door closed, ere the bonnet and shawl were put on, the latch of the door lifted up, and the bright rising moon shining gloriously in at the door. Happy moment! what pencil could portray the features of that face upon which the moon so clearly shone on that September night?

Poor girl! 'twas a breathless moment of long anticipated pleasure to thy good and honest heart, such as many a one, like thee, may have experienced ; but such as none, be she who she may, could have more anxiously endured.

At last, Margaret is off.

The pleasure of the feast continued ; and, as the foaming ale went round, the spirits of the youths arose, and each bachelor who could not sing had to toast his favourite lass.

There were singular disclosures made at this season, which generally indicated the future destiny of the bachelor. It was amusing enough to hear those who did not choose to tell their lover's name attempt to sing, as "the lord" called upon him for a toast or song.

"We haven't had Jack Barry's song," said a sly fellow of the name of Riches, who himself was one of the best singers in the party. "Please, sir" (for such the lord of the feast was styled that night), "call upon Jack for his song."

Now, the labourer at the head of the table knew that Jack could not sing. He did not suppose, either, that he had any favourite lass; for no one had seen Jack flirting, or directing his attentions towards any favoured individual. The lord, however, was bound to do his duty, when so urged; he therefore said, " John Barry, we call upon you for a song."

" I cannot sing, master: I wish I could," was the reply.

" Then you must give us a toast; and you know what it must be—' Your favourite lass.' "

Jack hung down his head in solemn silence, for he felt extremely awkward. He *had* a favourite lass; he felt he had; and no one knew it but himself; and if he should toast her, he felt that he should be laughed at. He remained in a state of painful suspense, between doubt and fear. A thousand thoughts revolved in his mind, whether he should not give a fictitious name, or some one whom he had heard of, or only knew by sight; but then appeared the certainty of some of them congratulating the person he might happen to mention, and so bringing him into a scrape. He thought also of dissimulation, and a lie, at which Jack's honest nature revolted. But if he should really tell his sweetheart's name! He felt for her, he felt for himself, and he remained a long time without uttering a word.

" Come, Jack, my boy, what's the matter? Give us your favourite lass! What makes you flinch, my lad? "

Jack remained silent, until some began to think he meant to shirk the subject. The fact is, that Jack had really some notion of bolting, and once or twice he cast a sidelong glance at the door, with the full intention of an escape; but Will Riches, perceiving this, most unceremoniously bolted the door; and, as the jug stood close by him, he declared he would know Jack's sweetheart before another drop should be drunk.

" Come, Jack," says he, " why not give us at once the girl you love best? "

"Because she does not love me," was Jack's quick reply.

Here was a most significant glance from one to another round about the room; and more than one whispered to his neighbour, "Who is it?" Not a soul could tell, for no one had the slightest idea who the girl could be who would refuse so honest a fellow as Jack Barry. Some began to think that Jack had stepped out of his latitude, that he had dared to aspire to the master's daughter; some, that it was Matilda Baker, the grocer's girl; others set it down as Lucy Harper, of Stratton. But, be the damsel whom she might, Jack's speech had set such a spirit of curiosity a-working, that the married men hoped to know for their wives' sake, and the single ones for their mistresses' amusement. Jack had got further into the mire by his floundering, and every one saw that he was struggling all he could to escape.

"Well, Jack, who is she? Who is she? Do we any of us know her?"

"Yes, all of you."

Here they were all out at sea again.

"It must be the master's fair daughter," said Ned Palmer to his neighbour.

"I don't think it," was the reply; "but he is not willing to tell us, and it's hardly fair to press him."

"It's a law, a positive law—I've told mine," says John Ruddock, "and I don't see why he should flinch from the name. I must have it."

"The name! the name!" exclaimed one or two resolute fellows.

A tear stood in Jack's eye. This might be a good joke to some; but the elders of the party, who saw it, especially honest Tom Keeble, the lord of the evening, felt for the young man that respect which induced him to make a sortie or parley, in the hope of giving him relief.

"Riches," said he, "as the jug stands by you, I shall call upon you for a song. Our young friend may, by the time you have entertained us, have recovered himself ; and, after your song, I shall order the jug round to drink your health, if we do not get the lass.''

Now, Will prided himself upon his vocal powers, and was a bold, forward fellow. He had no objection to sing, nor had any of the company any objection to his song ; and, truth to tell, all hoped the jug of brown ale would not be stopped long, either for the song or for " the favourite lass." So Will sang his song.

" I'll sing you a new song," says he. " I'll sing you one in which you can all join in chorus in the house, as you have often done in the field. I'll sing you—

'HALLO LARGESS.' "

Accordingly, he lifted up his voice, and sang this truly happy and appropriate harvest song :—

> Now the ripened corn
> In sheaves is borne,
> And the loaded wain
> Brings home the grain,
> The merry, merry reapers sing a bind,
> And jocund shouts the happy harvest hind,
> Hallo Large ! Hallo Large ! Hallo Largess !
>
> Now the harvest 's o'er,
> And the grain we store,
> And the stacks we pull,
> And the barn is full,
> The merry, merry reapers sing again,
> And jocund shouts the happy harvest swain,
> Hallo Large ! Hallo Large ! Hallo Largess !
>
> Now our toil is done,
> And the feast is won,
> And we meet once more
> As we did of yore,
> The merry, merry reapers sing with glee,
> And jocund shout their happy harvest spree,
> Hallo Large ! Hallo Large ! Hallo Largess !
>
> Now the feast we share—
> 'Tis our master's fare,

May he long, long live
Such a treat to give,
And merry, merry reapers sing with joy,
And jocund shouts the happy harvest boy,
    Hallo Large! Hallo Large! Hallo Largess!

Now we join in song
With our voices strong,
And our hearts are high
With our good supply,
We merry, merry reapers joyful come
To shout and sing our happy Harvest-Home,
    Hallo Large! Hallo Large! Hallo Largess!

The spirit of this song is in the chorus, which is peculiar to the eastern counties of this kingdom. So "Hallo Largess!" may be well understood here, but in many parts of the country is quite unknown. At the time of harvest, when the men are reaping down the fields, should their master have any friends visiting his fields, the head man among the labourers usually asks a largess, which is generally a shilling. This is asked not only of friends and visitors, but of strangers likewise, should they pause to look at the reapers as they bind up the sheaves.

At evening, when the work of the day is over, all the men collect in a circle, and Hallo, that is, cry, Largess. Three times they say, in a low tone, "Hallo Large! Hallo Large! Hallo Large!" and all, hand in hand, bow their heads almost to the ground; but, after the third monotonous yet sonorous junction, they lift up their heads, and, with one burst of their voices, cry out, "Gess!"

Varieties of this peculiar custom may exist in some districts. Sometimes the man with the most stentorian lungs will mount an eminence and lead the rest, who join in chorus. They generally conclude the ceremony with three shouts, and then "Thank Mr., Mrs., Miss, or Master" (as the case of the donor may be) "for his largess." Whence the origin of this practice, is not now easily to be ascertained. It was much more common than it is. The habit of dividing the gains, too, at the harvest frolic, is going fast out of fashion ; nor is its substitute an amendment.

At the period here mentioned, and in the Priory Farm, it was customary for the lord to divide the largess among the men, women, and children ; which formed a species of family nest-egg, to provide against some urgent necessity. The custom has now degenerated into an ale-house revel, and the money is all drunk out for the benefit of no one but the publican.

" Will Riches, your health ! " said the lord, as, at the same moment, he turned the contents of a canvas-bag upon the table, which exhibited a very good aspect of liberal contributions. The reader may suppose that every master-tradesman who visited the farm had to give his share, and that the lord had not been unmindful of his solicitations, when, upon counting the contents of the bag, there were found one hundred shillings and sixpence. This exactly gave five shillings a-piece to the fourteen men, half-a-crown ditto to the nine women, and two shillings each to the four boys.

The division of this sum gave great satisfaction ; and our persecuted friend, Jack Barry, had almost unperceived accomplished a successful retreat in the interesting moment of pocketing the cash. But the watchful songster had him in his eye ; and, as he rose to thank the company for the honour done him in drinking his health, he intercepted Jack in the act of drawing back the bolt of the door.

" I think this is the best place I can speak from ; and, as Jack is so anxious to be off, perhaps to see his sweetheart, I hope he'll give me the opportunity of proposing her health in his absence, for not until he has given us her name shall the bolt be drawn."

The poor fellow had counted on his escape, but little thought of the extremity of ridicule he was thus bringing upon himself. At length, urged on all sides, he could resist no longer, but, in a kind of ludicrous despair, he exclaimed—

" Well, then, I'll toast the health of Margaret Catchpole ! "

The pencil of Wilkie could alone describe the wild burst of unrestrained glee at this declaration.

" Margaret Catchpole ! " was as suddenly responded in surprise by men, women, and children ; and such grinning countenances, and coarse laughter, and joking congratulations, were beginning to show themselves, that Jack, no longer able to endure their gibes, bolted to the door, and, finding no resistance to his will, made his exit, amidst the roars of his companions, who vociferated, with a cheer, " The health of Margaret Catchpole ! "

Jack fled precipitately from this scene of tumult and confusion, and, as he passed the little foot-bridge over the stream from the moat, he still heard the rude merriment he had excited. The moon rose brilliantly over the little chapel in the dark background, and was reflected upon the water in a line with the bridge, and showed Jack's figure in darkness crossing the light plank ; but he was soon in the shadow of those lofty trees, which darkened the footpath towards the game-keeper's cottage. He had instinctively taken this path because it led to Levington, his father's house ; and he then remembered that parent's parting words—" If ever you feel yourself unhappy, my boy, remember you have a home here, in which, as long as your mother and I live, we shall be happy to give you a welcome."

Jack was really unhappy, and he had some cause for feeling so, though he felt that it lay not with himself. He knew that he had spoken the truth, though it had cost him a severe pang ; and whilst he felt much grief at the thought of the jeers and quizzings he should meet with, and the annoyances he might occasion the poor girl whom he really loved, he had still spoken the truth, which he was not ashamed to confess. He was arrested in his progress by the voice of John Gooding, the old gamekeeper of the great Squire of Nacton—Philip Broke.

" Who goes there ? " was his question.

"John Barry," was the reply.

"Where now, Jack—where now?"

"What, Mr. Gooding, is it you? Has the tide turned? Can I walk along the shore to Levington?"

"The tide has only just turned; but, if you take the wood-path for a while to Nacton, you may then, if you like it, keep the shore along Orwell Park, and pass the old Hall to Levington. But what makes you leave good company at this time o' night?"

"I have left them all very merry at the harvest supper, but I had a mind to see my friends."

"Well, Jack, had it been any other man upon the farm, I should have been suspicious of you as a poacher; but I know you well, and can believe you. I should not trust some that you have left behind. I was just going down to the Priory, to see how you lads fared to-night."

"Well, Mr. Gooding, you will find them all very glad to see you, and no doubt they will make you welcome; but will you trouble yourself to let master know where I am gone to-night, that he may close his doors without expecting to see me?"

"That I will; and, when I get there, I will propose your health, Jack, during your absence."

"Do so, Mr. Gooding; and tell them all, they have my hearty good wishes for their health and happiness."

"Good-night."

"Good-night."

CHAPTER VII

THE CONFLICT

BUT where is Margaret all this time ? She is on the shore, casting an anxious eye upon the waters. The moon is shining with such perfect brightness, that she can see across the river, though it be nearly two miles from the strand at Downham Reach to Freston Tower. She looks towards the dark shades of Woolverstone, and with a lover's anxious eye, fancies she can descry a sail. A sail there was ; but it came very slowly on, though a breeze reached the spot where poor Margaret was standing.

In that old vessel, seated at the helm, was as extraordinary a character as ever sailed upon the waves of the Orwell ; and as he will be no insignificant actor in some succeeding scenes of this work, he shall be here introduced to the notice of the reader. He is thus described in the *Suffolk Garland.*

" The ancient fisherman whose character is here portrayed is not a mere creature of the imagination, but an eccentric being, once resident in the parish of St. Clement, Ipswich, by name Thomas Colson, but better known by the appellation of Robinson Crusoe. He was originally a wool-comber, and afterwards a weaver ; but a want of constant employment in either of these occupations induced him to enter into the East Suffolk Militia. Whilst quartered at Leicester, he learned, with his usual ingenuity, the art of stocking-weaving, which trade he afterwards followed in this county. But this employment, in its turn, he soon relinquished, and became a fisherman on the river Orwell. His little vessel (if vessel it might be called, for every part of it was his own handiwork) presented a curious specimen of naval patchwork, for his extreme poverty did not afford him the means of procuring proper materials. In this leaky and crazy vessel, it was his constant custom, by day and by night, in calms and in storms, to toil on the river for fish. His figure was tall and thin ; his countenance meagre, yet striking ; and his eye sharp and piercing. Subject to violent chronic complaints, with a mind somewhat distempered, and faculties impaired, he was a firm believer in the evil agency of wizards and witchcraft. . . . His mind was so haunted with the dreams of charms and enchantments, as to fancy that he was continually under the influence of these mischievous tormentors. His arms and legs, nay, almost his whole body, was encircled with bones of horses, rings, amulets, and characts, verses, words, &c., &c., as spells and charms to protect him against their evil machinations. On different parts of his boat was to be seen ' the horse-shoe nailed,' that most effective antidote against the power of witches. When conversing with him, he would describe to you that he saw them hovering about his person, and endeavouring by all their arts to punish and torment him. Though a wretched martyr to the fancies of a disordered imagination, his manners were mild and harmless, and his character honest and irreproachable. But, however powerful and effective his charms might be to protect him from the agency of evil spirits, they did not prove sufficiently operative against the dangers of storm and tempest. For, being unfortunately driven on the ooze by a violent storm on the 3rd of October, 1811, he was seen, and earnestly importuned to quit his crazy vessel ; but relying on the efficacy of his charms, he obstinately refused ; and the ebb of the tide drawing his bark off into deep water, his charms and his spells failed him, and poor Robinson sank to rise no more."

The writer of these pages knew Colson well. He has often, when a boy, been in his boat with him ; and always found him kind and gentle.

The old man who sat at the helm of his crazy vessel, now toiling up the Orwell, was a perfect fisherman, patient, quiet, steady, active, and thoughtful. He had enough to employ his mind as well as his body, and too deeply was that mind engaged. The whole legion of evil spirits seemed to be his familiar companions, or rather his incessant enemies. He knew all their names, and their propensities; how they visited and afflicted men; and his great study was, how to prevent their malice taking effect upon himself or any one else. He would converse with them, and parley with them; he would seem to suffer when any of them took him by surprise and found him off his guard. The loss of any one of his numerous charms was sure to occasion the visit of that very demon from whose attacks it was supposed to defend him. He has often been tried by intelligent persons, anxious to discover if he really invented a new tale for each spirit; notes were kept of the name and the peculiar temper he attributed to each; and, months afterwards, he was questioned again and again upon the same points, but he never faltered—never attributed a wrong direction to any one—but was as accurate and certain as on the first day he spoke of them.

The whole purport of these attacks was to persuade Robin to do some wicked deed, at which his mind revolted; and when they could not prevail against him, they used to seem, to his suffering mind, to torment him, sometimes to pinch him, sometimes to pelt him, at others, to burn or scald him, pull his hair off his head, to pull his ears, his nose, or his arms; and, under all these seeming attacks, the old man's countenance would exhibit the species of suffering resembling the agonies of one really under such torture. No one could persuade him that it was imaginative; he would shake his head and say, ".I see them plainly—take care they do not visit you!"

He was a very kind friend to many who were afflicted; and never saw a person in distress whilst he had a fish in his boat, or a penny in his pocket, and refused to help him.

From the great encouragement he met with, and the friends who were always kind to him, it is supposed

that he might have laid by a sufficiency for his latter
days, for at one time he had amassed enough to have
purchased a new vessel, but in an evil hour he was
induced to lend it to an artful villain, who represented
himself in great distress, but who ran off with the
whole.

It was curious to see the old man whilst repairing
his boat, which was, when given to him by Mr. Seekamp,
but a wreck, as it lay upon the mud near Hog Island.
It was curious to see him, whilst plying his hatchet,
suddenly stop, seat himself on a piece of timber, and
hold parley with one of the demons, who, in his frenzy,
he fancied attacked him. After searching about his
person, he would suddenly catch up a talisman, which
shown to the enraged spirit would send him off, and
leave the tormented in peace. His delight was visible
in the chuckling joy of his speech, as he returned
triumphantly and speedily to his accustomed work.

Colson, who sat at the helm of his vessel, which
creaked heavily under the breeze as it sprang up, was
in one of his moods of reverie, when, stooping down
and straining his eyes to windward, he saw a sail. It
was a small boat, which seemed to have got more wind
in her canvas than Robin could obtain.

On came the boat; and the breeze began to swell
the many-coloured sail of the bewitched barque; but
Robin's canvas was heavy compared with the airy
trimming of the feathers of the little duck that followed
him. Like a creature of life, she skipped along, and
soon overtook the old fisherman of the Orwell.

"What ship ahoy! What ship ahoy!" exclaimed
a gruff voice from the boat below, as Robin, leaning
over the stern of his clumsy craft, looked closely into
her with an eager eye.

"It's only old Robinson Crusoe," replied the other.
"You may speak long to him before you know what he
means, even if you get any answer at all."

"Ahoy! ahoy!" was, however, the old man's reply.
"You've got the foul fiend aboard. What are you up
to, Will ? I know that's Will Laud's voice, though

I haven't heard it lately. Whither bound, Will? whither bound?"

"Confound the fellow!" muttered Will. "I never heard him say so much before. The foul fiend always sails with him. But give him a good word, John, and a wide berth."

"Heavy laden, Robin? heavy laden? You've a good haul aboard. Crabs, or lobsters, or crayfish—eh, Robin? turbot, plaice, or flounders? soles, brill, or whiting? sanddabs, or eels? But you've got plenty, Bob, or I mistake, if not a choice. The tide is falling: you'll never reach the Grove to-night."

"I shall get up in time, Will. You've lightened my cargo. You've got a pleasant companion aboard. You've got my black fiend on your mainsail. There he sits, pointing at you both, as if he had you in his own clutches. Take care he don't drive you aground. He sticks close to the sail, Will."

"Heave ahoy! heave ahoy! Good-night!" and away bounded the boat, which was then passing Pin Mill, in the widest part of the river, and steering towards the shades of Woolverstone. The obelisk rose high over the dark trees, pointing to the clear, moonlit sky, its pinnacle still tinged with the last red light of that autumnal evening.

But the breeze freshening, the little skiff darted along the side of the greensward, which sloped to the water's edge; and, as she passed, the startled doe leaped up from her repose, and stamped her foot, and snorted to the herd reposing or browsing on the side of the hill.

Woolverstone Park, with its thick copses and stately trees, whose roots reached, in snaky windings, to the very shore, was now the range along which the barque skirted till it came opposite the white cottage, which stands on a small green opening, or lawn, slanting down to the river.

The park boat was moored against the stairs, and a single light burned against the window, at which a white cat might be seen to be sitting. It was a favourite cat of the gamekeeper's, which had accidentally been killed in a rabbit-trap, and, being stuffed, was placed in the window of the cottage. Visible as it always was in the same place, in the broad day and in the clear moonlight, the sailors on the river always called that dwelling by the name of the Cat House; by which it is known at the present day. High above it might be seen the mansion, shining in the moonbeam, and many lights burning in its various apartments—a sign of the hospitality of W. Berners, Esquire, the lord of that beautiful domain.

But the two sailors in the boat were little occupied with thoughts about the beauty of this scene, or the interest that might attach to that side of the water. Their eyes were bent upon the opposite shore; and, as they sailed along, with a favourable wind, they soon passed the boathouse and the mansion of Woolverstone.

"Luff, do you think we shall be lucky? I'd venture my share of the next run, if I could once safely harbour the prize from yonder shore."

"Why, Will, you speak as if the Philistines were to meet you. Who can prevent your cutting out such a prize?"

"I know not; except that she is too difficult a craft to manage."

"Pshaw, Will! her cable may be easily cut; and once we have her in tow, with this side-wind upon our sail, we shall be back again as quickly as we came."

"Maybe, maybe, John; but I do not like being too desperate. I'll fulfil my word, and give you more than half my share, which you know is a pretty good one, if you will lend me an honest and fair play."

"I'll do nothing, Bill, but what you tell me. I'll lay like a log in the boat, and stir not without the boatswain's whistle; and as to an honest hand, I'll tell you what, Will, 'tis something as good as your own—it will do by you as well as your own would do by me."

"Say no more, say no more! But look, John—I do believe I see her by the shore."

"I see something white, but that's the cottage in the Reach."

" No, no, John ; keep her head well up ; my eyes are clearer than yours—I see her flag waving in the wind. You may take your tack now, John—we shall run directly across. Ease out the mainsail a bit, and I'll mind the foresail. Bear up, my hearty ! bear up, my hearty ! "

With such words of mutual encouragement did these men of the sea, the river, and the land, after passing Woolverstone Park, steer directly across, towards Nacton Creek, that they might hug the wind under Downham Reach, and move more rapidly, in shallow water, against the tide.

Any one would imagine, from their conversation, that they were intent upon cutting out some vessel from her moorings, instead of a poor, defenceless girl, who, trusting to nothing but the strength of true love, stood waiting for them on the shore.

There stood the ever faithful Margaret, with palpitating heart, watching the light barque, as it came bounding over the small curling waves of the Orwell. In her breast beat feelings such as some may have experienced ; but, whoever they may be, they must have been most desperately in love. Hope, fear, joy, and terror, anxiety, and affection—each, in turn, sent their separate sensations, in quick succession, into her soul. Hope predominated over the rest, and suggested these bright thoughts—

" He is coming to me, no more to be tried, no more to be disapproved, but to tell me he is an honest man, and engaged in honest service."

What a picture would she have presented at that moment to any genuine lover of nature ! Who could describe that eye of expectation, swelled as it was with the animating hope of happiness to come ! Who could describe that heaving heart, answering as it did to every heave of the little boat which came bounding to the shore ! And what words shall speak that sudden emotion, as the welcome sound of the grounding keel, and the rush of waters following it, told that the boat was ashore, which conveyed to a woman's heart all

that she had so long looked for, hoped, and feared—
her lover's return !

The watchword, "*Margaret*," was spoken, and in
another moment her joy and grief, and love and hope,
were, as it were, embodied in the embrace of him she
loved. Moments at such time fly too rapidly—an hour
seems but an instant. There is so much to say, to
express, to ponder upon, that the time is always too
short. In honest love there seems to be no fear,
no death, no time, no change—a sort of existence
indescribably happy, indefinitely blissful, hopeful, and
enduring.

In the heart of Margaret, the poor Margaret Catchpole, love was her life ; and as she stood upon that
strand, and first welcomed her William, she felt the
purest, happiest, and holiest feelings of joy, rectitude,
and honesty—such as she never before had felt to such
extent, and such as she knew but for a few short
moments, and often wished for again, but never, never
afterwards experienced.

Since his absence from Margaret, the character of
Laud had become more and more desperate, and to
say that the same pure feeling burned in his breast as
did in Margaret's would not be true. No man who
leads a guilty life can entertain that purity of love in
his heart which shall stand the test of every earthly
trial ; but Margaret, like many real lovers, attributed
to him she loved the same perfection and singleness of
attachment which she felt towards him. Had she
known that this pure flame was only burning as pure
and bright in the honest soul of Jack Barry, she would,
it may be, have rejected Laud, and have accepted
him ; but she knew not this. She was not blind to
the faults of the sailor, though she was blinded to his
real character. . She expected to find a love like her
own, and really believed his affection to be the same
to the last.

"Now, Margaret," he at length exclaimed, "now's
the time : my boat is ready, my ship is at the mouth
of the river. A snug little cabin is at your service ;

and you will find more hearts and hands to serve you than you ever had in your life."

" But where am I to go, William ? What business have I on board your master's vessel ? He would not approve of your sailing with your young wife. I thought you came to tell me you were prepared to marry me from my own dear father's house, and to be a comfort and a blessing to my aged mother."

" Margaret, you say you love me. My time is short. I am come here to prove the sincerity of my love, and to take you, in an honest way, to a country where we may be married ; but if you send me away now, we may never meet again."

" If you are true, William—if, as you say, your prospects are good, and you have spared sufficient from your lawful gains to hire a cottage and to make me happy, why not get leave of absence, and come and marry me in dear old England ? "

" I may not be able to get leave for a long time ; and what difference does it make whether we are married here, or in my employer's country ? Marriage is marriage, Margaret, in every place, all the world over."

" Yes, Will ; but I have heard that marriages solemnized in some countries do not hold good in others ; and whether they did or not, I should like those who first gave me birth to give me to you, William. My consent, they know, is a willing one ; but I should not be happy in mind, if I were to leave my parents without their knowing where I was gone."

" What will it matter if they do not know it till we return ? I almost think you would like another better than me, Margaret."

" If you, William, were, in some respects, other than you are, I should like you full as well ; but, as you are, I love you, and you know it. Why not come ashore, and marry me at our own church, and in the presence of my own parents ? As to any other, William, though another may like me, I cannot help it, but I can help his having me."

" Then there is another that does love you !—is
there, Margaret ? "

A blush passed over Margaret's face as she replied,
" Another has told me so, and I did not deceive him.
He thought you dead, or he would never have ventured
upon the subject. I told him he was mistaken, that
you were not dead, and that I still loved you, William."

" Then he knows I live, does he ? "

" Yes."

" And you have betrayed me ? "

" No : I have not told any one but him ; and as he
pressed his suit, thinking that you were no more, I felt
it to be only due to him to tell him you were alive."

" And who is he, Margaret ? You would not have
been so plain with him if he had not had somewhat of
your confidence."

" He is an honest young man, and of very good and
respectable parents—he works at the Priory Farm ;
and seeing him, as I do, daily, I can form sufficient
judgement of his character to believe he would never
betray any one."

" Upon my word, Margaret, he must be a prodigy
of perfection ! Perhaps you would like him to be
bridesman upon our wedding-day ? "

" I would, indeed, if he would like it, and you had
no objection."

" What is his name ? "

" John Barry."

" What ! of Levington ? "

" Yes."

" His brother is in the coastguard. It was he who
gave me this, Margaret, this cut upon my forehead—
this, that you took such pains to heal."

" And it is healed, William ; and your heart, too,
I hope."

" No, no, no !—I owe him one ! "

" Consider me his creditor, and pay it me ; for I
healed that wound, and it brought with it reformation."

" I would not give you what I would give him."

" No, William ; but you ought not to bear malice.

His brother has been very kind to me. I may say, he is the only one who never reproached me with having been the mistress of a smuggler." (There was a fearful frown upon the smuggler's brow at this moment, and a convulsive grasp of the poor girl's hand, that told there was agony and anger stirring in his soul.) "But you are not a smuggler now, William. I did not mean to hurt your feelings. All reproach of that name has long passed away from my mind."

William was silent, and gazed wildly upon the waters. One hand was in his bosom, the other was in Margaret's hand, as she leaned upon his shoulder. There might be seen a strange paleness passing over his face, and a painful compression of his lips. A sudden start, as if involuntary, and it was most truly so. It told of a chilliness on the heart, that seemed to freeze the blood in his veins. He actually trembled.

"William, you are not well."

"No, I am not; but a little grog, which is in the boat, will soon set me right again."

"Shall I run and fetch it?"

"No, no,—wait a bit, wait a bit. Hold—I was a smuggler! Yes, you said I was a smuggler! The world despised me! You bore the reproach of my name! Well, Margaret, the smuggler comes home— he comes to marry you. Will the world believe him to be altered? Will they not call you, then, the smuggler's bride?"

"No, William, not if you are really altered, as you say you are. I wish you were in the British service; seamen are wanted now, and the smuggler would soon be forgiven, when he once sailed under the flag of Old England."

"'Tis too late, 'tis too late, now, Margaret! I will not say I may not ever sail under our gallant Nelson. You might persuade me to it, if you would only sail with me to Holland, and there be married to me, Margaret."

"You have heard me upon this point: do not urge it any more. I have now stolen away from duty,

William, to meet you here, and I hope I shall not be missed. Let me only hear you say you will come again soon, to marry me at home, and I shall return to my service happy."

"I would if I could, but I cannot."

"Why not, William? why not?"

"Do not ask me why. Come, Margaret, come to the boat, and share my fate. I will be constant to you, and you shall be my counsellor."

"Nay, William, do not urge me to forsake all my friends, and put all this country in terror as to what has become of me. I cannot go on board your boat. I cannot give you myself until God and my parents have given me to you. So do not think of it; but, come again, come again!—yes, again and again!—but come openly, in the sight of all men, and I will be yours. I live for you only, William, and will never be another's whilst you live."

"But how can I live without you, Margaret? I cannot come in the way you talk of; I tell you I cannot. Do, then, do be mine."

"I am yours, William, and will ever be so; but it must be openly, before all men, and upon no other terms."

"Then it will never be!"

"Why so?"

"Because I am a smuggler!"

"You have been such, but you are not so now. You have long forsaken the gang; you are forgotten, and supposed to be dead. You may change your name; but being changed in your life, it will only be known to me."

"And to Barry, too, Margaret; and then to his brother, and to numbers of others, who will know me. I was recognized this very night."

"What, if you change your name?"

"My name is changed, but not my nature. I am a smuggler still!"

"No, William, no—you cannot be! You are in the service of an honest man, though a foreigner."

"No, Margaret, I am not. You see before you the notorious Hudson. I am a smuggler still!"

It was now poor Margaret's turn to tremble, and she felt more than language can speak. She had heard of Hudson—Captain Hudson, as he was called—but had no idea that her lover was that, or such a man. She felt a revulsion amounting to sickness, a giddiness overcame her, and she felt as if she must fall to the earth. Half carried, half urged, half pulled along, she was unconsciously moving, with her eyes fixed fully upon the boat, and approaching it, and she had no power to resist—a sort of trance-like senselessness seemed to overpower her; and yet she felt that hand, knew that form, and saw the waters and the boat, and had no energy or impulse to resist. Her heart was so struck with the deadliness of grief and despair, that the nerves had no power to obey the will, and the will seemed but a wish to die. We cannot die when we wish it, and it is well for us we cannot. Happy they who do not shrink when the time comes appointedly; thrice happy they who welcome it with joy, and hope, and love!

Margaret revived a little before she reached the boat, and resisted. The firm grasp of the smuggler was not, however, to be loosed.

"You do not mean to force me away, William?"

"I must, if you will not go."

"I will not go."

"You shall—you must—you cannot help it! Do not resist."

"Shame, William, shame! Is this your love?"

"It is, Margaret, it is. I mean you fair."

"Your means are foul. Let me go, William! let me go!"

"Yes: you shall go on board my boat."

"Not with my life, William. I will go overboard!"

"Then will I follow you; but I cannot parley longer. Come on!"

The poor girl's struggles now became so violent, and her efforts to escape so powerful, that Will Laud's utmost strength could not drag her along the sand. Her fears, too, were increasing with his cruel violence ; and these fears were greatly increased by Laud giving a loud, shrill boatswain's whistle. This awakened her to the sight of the trap into which she had been beguiled, for, in another moment, she saw a man spring from the boat, and hasten towards her. He came along with rapid strides to join them, and soon, with horrid voice, exclaimed,—

" Your signal, Laud, is late indeed, but better late than never."

That voice was too well known by Margaret : 'twas the hated countryman's—'twas John Luff's.

This fellow seized her in his arms, and, as a tiger would swing a fawn over his back, so poor Margaret was swung over his shoulders in an instant. The last effort a defenceless female can make is the shriek of despair ; and such a one was heard, as not only sounded through the woods of Downham Reach, but reached the opposite shores of Woolverstone Park.

That shriek was heard by one whose heart was too true to nature to resist the good motives which it awakened. Young Barry, as the reader knows, was journeying toward the gamekeeper's cottage on the cliff, and had just entered the wood in front of that dwelling, as the piercing shriek struck upon his ear. He sprang over the paling in an instant, and by the broad moonlight beheld a man carrying a female towards a boat, and the other assisting to stop her cries. He leaped down the cliff, and seizing a strong break-water stake, which he tore up from the sand, rushed forward to the man who carried the female. It was a good, trusty, heart-of-oak stake which he held, and which in one moment he swung round his head, and sent its full weight upon the hamstrings of Luff. The fellow rolled upon the sand, and over and over rolled the poor girl into the very waves of the Orwell.

It was no slight work which Barry had now in hand. It was a bold deed to attack two such daring villains, both well armed, and he with nothing but a stake.

But the consequences he neither foresaw nor dreaded; the cause was a good one, and he left the issue to God. As quick as thought he had already dashed one foeman to the earth; the other stood aghast, beholding Margaret fallen into the water, and his comrade rolling on the shore. He flew to help Margaret, and raising her up, determined not to relinquish her, but stood opposed to the dauntless Barry.

"Villains, release the girl!" was his exclamation.

"It is Barry's voice!" shrieked Margaret. "Help, John, help!"

There was a strange opposition of feeling in all the parties at these words. The blood curdled in the veins of the smugglers, whilst it seemed to burst with over-powering fullness upon the forehead of the young man who now attacked them. He fought for the prize of true love—they for revenge. The moment they heard the name uttered by the girl they seemed to think no more about her; but the fallen man sprang up, and Laud let Margaret go, and both rushed, like enraged wild beasts, with full force against young Barry. He, with true heroic daring, committed himself at once to the encounter. He was a fine athletic young man, a head taller than either of the sailors, but odds were fearfully against him. Luff was a stout, stiff, sturdy seaman; and Laud young, active, cool, and desperate.

A smuggler is seldom without a weapon of offence and defence. Luff seized his pistol from his girdle, and fired at his brave antagonist; it missed its mark, and the stout oak arm was not long in thundering a blow upon his head, which again sent him sprawling upon the ground. It was Laud's turn now to take his aim, which he did in the most cool, determined manner, with as much ease, and as steady a hand, as if he were firing at a holiday mark. It was a cruel aim, and rendered the contest still more unequal. It took effect in the young man's left shoulder, and rendered that arm useless.

None but such a frame and such a spirit could have stood against that pistol-shot. It made him stagger for the moment; but he had presence of mind to ward off the next blow of a cutlass with his good oaken staff. And now might be seen the most desperate conflict for life or death between the rivals. Barry and Laud closed and parted, and struggled fiercely with each other, though the former had but one arm to act upon the defensive with. His right hand, however, was powerful enough to dash the sword of Laud at least ten yards into the wave; and with such dexterity did he handle his weapon, that had not Luff come again unexpectedly to the encounter, the contest must have been speedily terminated in favour of Barry: Luff recovered his feet again, and rushed at Barry with such rage, that again his other pistol missed its aim.

Barry had now to act entirely upon his own defence, with only one arm against four. He had this advantage, however, that they had no time to load their pistols, and had only their short butt-ends to fight with, whilst he had a good long arm.

But assistance—unexpected assistance—was at hand. A tall, gaunt figure strode along the strand, armed with a long fisherman's pike, or hook, a weapon commonly used to take codfish off the fishing-lines. His was a sinewy arm, which few could resist or disable.

When such a man was aroused, harmless and peaceable as was his general character, his appearance became truly terrific; and his firm and steady step, and determined resolution, told that he was a soldier of cool courage, not easily to be beaten.

It was old Colson, or poor Robinson Crusoe, who, as it has been stated, was making his way with fish up the Orwell.

He and young Barry, now side by side, beat back the smugglers to their boat. Desperate was the contest; but there was no opposing the unearthly-looking being, with his bones, perforated plates, and charms dangling about his person. Well was it that he came so opportunely, for without his help the fate of young Barry had been sealed for ever. It was bad enough as it was. The smugglers retreated, and jumped into their boat. Laud, seizing a carabine, levelled it at

Barry, whilst Luff pushed off the boat from the shore.
" Let fly at him, Will ! let fly at him ! Revenge yourself and my fall ! "

A flash and loud explosion followed this advice.
The smoke cleared off in a second, and the pirates saw
but the stately form of Robin standing upon the shore.
Young Barry—the generous, brave, and faithful Barry
—lay stretched upon the sand.

Meantime Margaret had escaped. She had reached
the Priory Farm ; and rushing into the room where
the harvest-men were assembled, fell down exhausted,
with just strength of voice to say, " Fly—fly—fly to
the shore ! Barry will be murdered ! "

The gamekeeper was off before Margaret arrived,
having heard the report of the pistols ; and he went
into the wood. The young men ran off to the shore,
and soon found the old fisherman supporting the head
of the poor young man. The blood was flowing fast
from his wounds, and he was in a swoon like death,
though his heart beat, and he breathed painfully. They
formed a double row ; they lifted him up, and carried
him along as gently as they could ; but the poor fellow
groaned with the agony of his shattered arm and
wounded side.

Robin followed them, muttering curses against the
foul fiend, and every moment pointing to the departing
boat of the smugglers with a clenched fist, exclaiming,
" The foul fiend be with you ! He'll consume you yet,
ye cowards ! "

CHAPTER VIII

DISAPPOINTMENT

THERE is a sad and fearful void in the disappointed heart.

Poor Margaret! but one short hour past and thy prospects were as bright as the broad moonlight that shone upon thy path. Yea, they were as bright to thine eye as that beautiful orb in the most brilliant night; for thy love was pure, true, and abiding.

How great was the reverse our heroine experienced when she quitted her lover, and returned to the Priory Farm worse than desolate! Had she never seen him again, *her* disappointment could not have been so great. Time might have taught her to consider him lost at sea, or taken by the enemy, or killed in battle, or as having died a natural death. But as it was, the tide had turned so suddenly; the change from the full flow to the very lowest ebb was as instantaneous as if some gulf had swallowed up the river, and left the channel dry. Clouds, black clouds intervened between her and her lover. She had received a blight to all her hopes, save one, and that was the last and best that any one could cleave to; it was, " that God would change his heart, and one day make him see the error of his way."

She little thought how distant that day was. But it seemed that her sister's words were at this time true: " Margaret, you will never marry William Laud."

Margaret was in the little parlour of the Priory Farm, in all the agony of terror and the perturbation of confessing her faults to her master and mistress, when the murmur of returning voices told that the good farmer's men were coming from the shore. Her soul was so full—her heart so anxious—her confession so open, so sincere—that even they who were most angry with her could not find it in their hearts to be angry and severe towards her at such a moment of distress. She was so full of terror that she dared not to stir ; she had no power to rise and make inquiries upon the dreadful point upon which she wished to be most satisfied. She heard the footsteps approach ; and as the parlour-door stood open, looking into the kitchen, she saw the young men bringing in the heavy body of the youth, to whom, perhaps, she then owed her existence ; for her resolution had been formed, to have plunged into the waves sooner than be taken away, against her will, by the smugglers. Certainly she owed her present safety to the intrepid boldness of that wounded man. She saw them bring him into the kitchen, pale, bloody, and, as she first thought, lifeless ; but a heavy groan, as they laid him down upon the floor, by the fire, made her start up, and feel the first spring of joy in her desponding heart, that he was not murdered. But the joy that Laud was not his murderer was as great as that the youth was not dead.

Her mistress's voice, calling to bring water and assist her, restored her to a consciousness of her duties. Here might be seen the benefit of active employment in diverting her mind from its most painful feelings, rousing it to think, and turning it away from tormenting itself.

The surgeon was sent for immediately ; and after a short delay in preparing a bed in a room by itself, the young man was carried up by his companions. Never was there a more melancholy change from the mirth of " harvest-home," to the misery of a house of woe. To look into that kitchen, which so shortly before was resounding with the cheerful voices of merriment, and to see the long faces, to hear the whispers, and the questions, and the remarks made upon the circumstances, presented a scene so different and so painful, that description would fail to express it. There sat the ancient fisherman, silent and thoughtful, his left hand upon his forehead, and his right clutched convulsively with his inward emotion. There stood the foreman of the field, with his fellow-labourers,

anxious to know who it was that had given the wound ;
for they had as yet only been told that two men in
a boat had fired upon Barry, and wounded him.

Meanwhile the old fisherman, who had witnessed the
scene, was so absorbed in his own reflections, that he
did not seem disposed voluntarily to afford them any
information.

At last one of them addressed Robin.

" Who was the fellow that fired the gun, Robin ? "

" The foul fiend ! " said Robin ; " I saw him in the
boat."

" What foul fiend ? was he devil or man ? "

" He was a demon, who left me for a moment to torment others. I knew mischief would come of him as
soon as he left me. He is always stirring up infernal
broils ; and would bring a host of enemies against me,
if it were not for this charm. Look here," and taking
from his side a perforated bone, he held it up, saying,
" this is the rib of Margery Beddingfield, who was
gibbeted on Rushmere Heath for the murder of her
husband. When I show him this, he will soon be off.
This is so strong a spell, he cannot touch me. But look !
there he is ! there he is ! " and the startled hinds closed
round their lord, and looked fearfully in the direction
of the door, to see if the murderer was coming.

" Aye, look at this, thou false fiend ! Dost thou
remember how thou didst stir up Margery, and Richard
Ringe of Sternfield, her paramour, to murder John
Beddingfield, the farmer, near Saxmundham ? Thou
couldst inflame their hot young blood to mischief ;
but what dost thou come here for ? Off ! off, I say !
Look here ! thou hadst better go to the officers of
justice. Ha ! ha ! he is gone ! " and the old man
smiled again, as if he had defeated his foe, and was
congratulating himself on the victory.

These things were very unsatisfactory to the minds
of these plain-thinking countrymen. They again and
again put questions to him, but could get no other
answers than incoherences about the foul fiend.

" But what had Margaret Catchpole to do with it ? "

"Ask her yourself: the foul fiend always finds an easier prey in a woman."

At this time Margaret came into the room; and ignorant as she herself was of Robin's efficient aid, she could not help asking him if he had seen the fight.

"Did *you* see it, young woman? I saw you long before I saw the fight."

Margaret did not ask any more questions; for in another minute several asked her who had been fighting, what it was for, and what she had to do with it. She knew too well to speak would be to betray herself; and she was glad to find they were in ignorance of the real perpetrator of the deed. She was called into the parlour just then, and rejoiced to escape the inquisitive demands of her fellow-servants.

"That's a clever girl," said old Robin, as she left the kitchen,—"that's a clever girl. Which of you boys would like her for a wife?"

"Ask Will Simpson," said a sly fellow.

"Ask poor Jack Barry," said another; "'tis my belief Jack got his blow from a rival in Margaret's love."

"What fiend told you that, young man? 'Tis seldom any of 'em speak the truth? But, perhaps, you know who he is that rivals Jack?"

"No, not I—not I. I know who he would be, if he was alive; and just the sort of fellow, too, to give Jack a nab. But he's dead and gone long ago, and maybe his bones are at the bottom of the sea, for he was killed on Felixstowe beach."

"Who's he? who's he?"

"Why, Will Laud, the smuggler. Don't you know him, Robin?"

"Yes; but I never knew that he was dead."

"Oh, yes, he's dead enough. I saw a fellow who told me he helped to bury him in the sands at the foot of the cliff."

"Then the foul fiend has brought him back to life again, for I have seen him many times; and I spoke to him this very night, and he to me. Not only so, I know him well; and I wish all the fiends had him before he had given that brave lad his death-blow."

"What! Will Laud? you do not mean to say Will Laud was on the shore to-night?"

"Ask Margaret Catchpole: she can tell you as much as I."

Margaret returned just as this was said; and Will Simpson, perhaps as much in spite (for Margaret had upon some occasion of his rudeness given him such a specimen of her dexterity with a frying-pan, as left a memorial on his head not easily to be forgotten or forgiven) as for inquisitiveness, put this question—

"I say, Peggy, who met you upon the shore to-night, eh?"

"What's that to you? A better man than you."

"Perhaps a better Will, too; eh, Peggy? One who will have his will of you, too, before you die, and tame you, my dear."

"Perhaps he may; and should it be so, he will make a ' will o' the wisp' of you, Simpson."

"He'll be hanged first, Peggy, take my word for that. He'll not be shot, nor drowned: he's born to be hanged."

"And what are you born for, you coward, that, at such a time as this, you should be quarrelling with me?"

"I'm born to be his informer; and, before long, I'll have you both up before the Squire, for all this piece of work."

Margaret did not like this banter; it looked as if they already knew that Will Laud was the intruder. She was somewhat less ready at her replies than usual, and felt too great a fear that she might commit herself. She tried, therefore, to turn the subject.

"My master, Robin, desires me to give you some supper."

"Thank your master, but I have had mine; and, but that I hoped to hear what the doctor said to the poor young man upstairs, I should long ago have been on board my boat."

The greatest cowards are not easily silenced when they find themselves able to browbeat an adversary with impunity, and that adversary a woman.

"Well, Margaret, if you won't tell me, I'll tell you whom you met upon the shore. You met one whom Robin says the foul fiend has raised to life again."

Margaret turned very pale, and staggered to a chair. But Simpson still went on.

"O Peggy, Peggy, you have a guilty face! I don't wonder at your feeling shame. You've managed to hide the smuggler, have you? If you don't take care, both you and Will Laud will come to a bad end."

Margaret rushed into the parlour, and fell at her master's feet, imploring him to interfere and stop the reproaches of his men, who were treating her in a way she did not deserve. Her mistress made her sit down in the keeping-room; and, speaking a few words to her husband, he left them. He remonstrated with his men, and was in the act of insisting upon their departure to their homes, as Dr. Stebbing arrived. He was desired at once to go into the parlour; and there he recognized that high-spirited girl who, in the cause of humanity, had, in her childhood, galloped the pony to Ipswich for his aid. She rose and curtseyed; but her feet gave way under her, and she sank to the floor. The memory of her dear sister, the doctor's former patient, her own happiness at that time, and her present misery, were too much for her to bear, and she was quite overcome. The good doctor raised her up, and, with his cheerful voice, tried, in his usual kind way, to comfort her.

"Come, come, my girl, what's the matter? what's the matter? Are you the patient I'm come all this way to see? I thought I was sent for to see a young man. But what's the matter with you? Ah! is it so, my lassie?" (for his sagacity gave him a glimpse of the truth). "Come, cheer up, cheer up; we'll go and see the lad. I dare say he'll soon be better. Cheer up, cheer up."

"Come, my good sir, let us have a light, and go

upstairs," said the doctor to the master of the house. "Now, my dear, go and fetch us a towel and some warm water. Come, bestir yourself; I know it will do you good."

This was the best medicine for Margaret, with whom to be told to do anything, and not to go and do it, was almost an impossibility, so much had she been accustomed to obey.

All that could be done for the youth was to lay him in as easy a posture as possible; for he was in too much agony even to have his clothes removed. One of his companions sat and wiped the cold perspiration from his brows, whilst another washed his hands and face. He breathed quickly and heavily, with shuddering fits that shook the bed violently, and he was evidently in great pain.

"Come, my lads, come, lend me a hand—let us see —let us see! where is the hurt?—where is the wound? —what's the lad's name?"

"John Barry, sir."

"John, my lad, let's look at you!" but John took no notice of the doctor.

"I think, sir, his arm is broke, for it dangled by his side all the way we carried him."

"Let us see, my boy, let us see! 'Tis broken! high up too, too high up. But we must strip him. Gently there—gently there, my lad"; and the groans of the poor fellow told his agony. The work was done with great care, and by slow degrees. But it was done, and then the frightful nature of his wounds became conspicuous: a gunshot wound from the middle of the arm to the shoulder. The ball had struck the humerus, and broken it, glanced over the head of it, and passed between the scapula and clavicle, and it might be easily felt lying in the external portion of the trapezian muscle. It was so near the skin that it was easily extracted; the difficulty was to get away those parts of the clothing which had been carried into the wound. Such was the effect of the first shot.

The second was the most severe. It had pierced

through the long dorsal muscle, and the ball lay directly against the lumbar vertebrae. This wound was the more agonizing because it had pierced the strongest muscles of the human frame, and bruised the stoutest part of the backbone.

After the doctor had examined his wounds and ascertained that they were of the most serious nature, he said—

"This will be a work of time. Get some stimulants —put warm flannels on his feet—his extremities are icy cold. He has had violent exertion—all his muscles are hard and stiff. Put his hands in warm water. Wash his temples with warm vinegar. There, there ; come, my poor fellow, come ; consciousness will soon return."

He opened his eyes, looked at the doctor, then at his master, then at his friends, and at last at Margaret, who was putting warm flannels to his feet. He looked earnestly at her, spoke not, but a tear stole down his face as he closed his eyes again.

His wounds were now probed, cleaned, and dressed, as carefully as if he had been one of the wealthiest squires or nobles of the land, and he was then left for the night, attended by two of his fellow-servants, in case he should need assistance or restraint.

"There, there, good-night, John, good-night. I think you'll do now. Come, come, he feels a little easier. He breathes better " ; and patting his cheeks in his good-humoured way, Dr. Stebbing left him, and went down into the parlour.

There is always a little chit-chat with the doctor after the usual labour of his profession is over, and he is quietly seated with the family. It is then he judges of what is best for his patient, for at such times the secrets of most families come forth ; and if love or law, if loss of stock or money, if cruelties, injuries, or any causes whatever have been acting upon the patient's mind, the doctor is sure to be made the confidant.

If the faculty could find out the means of supplying all their invalids with such things as they really wanted, they would soon get well, but in default of such means medicine and good advice—very necessary articles in their way—are supplies in which the faculty seldom fail.

"Doctor, will you take anything to-night? you have had a cold ride, and will have another on your way home—shall my mistress give you anything warm?"

"I care not if she does. A little nutmeg in a little warm brandy-and-water, and just one slice of your nice harvest-cake, and I shall be comfortable."

The first question asked of the doctor was, "What he thought of his patient?"

Why, he has got an ugly wound that will take months to heal. He will not be able to be moved for six or seven weeks. Where do his parents live?"

"At Levington," was the reply. "His father is tolerably well to do in the world, though he has a large family. I have not a steadier young man on my premises, nor a quieter, soberer, or better behaved lad, or a better workman belonging to me."

"So much the better. But what does the old fisherman do in the kitchen? I thought he never sat down in any house, but always kept to his boat?"

"He is only waiting to speak to you, doctor. At least, he said he should stop to hear your report."

"I should like to have one word with him."

"I'll go and tell him so"; and off trotted the worthy farmer for Robin, with whom he soon returned, and then, beckoning to his wife, they left him and the doctor alone together.

"Well, Robin, what an odd fish you are! I can never persuade you to come into my kitchen, and here you are, hail fellow well met, with the farmer's men at Harvest-Home. How is this, Robin? I shall tell my daughter of you, and leave her to set some of your foul fiends to work upon you."

"They've been at work pretty well to-night, doctor, or else I'm wofully mistaken. One of 'em has done a pretty job of mischief here; and it's well if he don't do more before he's done."

The doctor understood his dialect, and knew how to get out of him what he wanted.

"Who did the foul fiend work upon? who was his victim?"

"He left my boat, and went aboard Will Laud's."

"What! the smuggler? I thought he was shot long ago."

"So others thought, but not I; for I saw him and a sturdy villain of his pass my boat, with all their sails set; and when my Infernal Broiler left me, and sat grinning on his mast, I knew he was up to mischief."

"What mischief, Robin?"

"Why, look ye, doctor; you must ha' seen the mischief. Ha'en't you dressed the young man's wounds?"

"Yes, Robin; but how came your imp to be the cause of this?"

"Nay, that you must ask the girl here; for seldom do my imps fail to make mischief among the sex."

"Was it a love affair?"

"Nay, it didn't appear much o' that." And here Robin, in his quaint language, well understood by the doctor, told his own tale as it happened.

"Well, Robin, all I can say is, that but for you, one of the finest young fellows in the land would have lost his life; and there's a guinea for you."

"No, no, master; give me a guinea for my fish, but don't give me a guinea for doing no more than I ought to do. Give it to the poor boy for loss of time. I've got some good fish, and you may have some to-morrow morning; but the fiends would torment me all night, if I went to my hammock with a guinea for my reward. No, doctor, no. I thank you, too; but tell me the boy will do well, and I'm well paid for my pains."

"He will do well, I think, Robin, if his mind be not disturbed."

The doctor felt, as perhaps the reader will, that the honest old fisherman, bewitched and bewildered as he was, had more good feeling about him than many a man of clearer head and a less scrupulous conscience, who would have crept along the mud to pick up a guinea for his dirty pocket.

"Well, well, my boy, I shall not find such an odd fish in your boat as your own self. You may bring up your basket to my door, and my daughter will deal with you. Instead of a guinea, I must give you any charm that you can ask me for."

"Keep to that, doctor, and I'll ask you soon to give me one that I stand much in need of, and which you only can furnish me with. You are surgeon to the gaol, and I want something out of that place. I'll tell you, one of these days, what it is. My boat is now high and dry upon the shore. You might ask some of the landsmen here to lend me a hand to get her off. I shall be in Ipswich as soon as yourself."

No sooner was the request made than it was granted ; and Robin and five or six good stout fellows were on the shore, and soon shoved the boat off, which, quicker than the men could walk upon the sand, moved on her native element to the well-timed stroke of the able fisherman.

The doctor's first introduction to the flying Margaret is well known to the reader. His knowledge of her under those circumstances made him feel for her ; but there were some questions he wished to put to her, as his curiosity had been excited by what Robin had revealed. The farmer had already given him some hint about her confessions ; but the doctor wanted to find out whether, after what had taken place that night, the tide of her affections might not have turned a little toward his patient. It was a delicate question to ask, but he thought he would find it out by another plan ; so he desired to see Margaret in the parlour before he left the house.

"I did not half like your look, my girl, when I first saw you to-night. Come hither ; let me feel your pulse : let me look at your tongue. Your pulse is quick, and you've some fever hanging about you."

"I thank you, sir, I shall be better to-morrow. I'm very sorry for what has happened."

"You could not help it, my girl—you could not help it; it was not your fault."

"I don't know that, sir,—I don't know that. I blame myself much; but—but—"

"But you don't like to blame anybody else, Margaret; I know you."

"Well, sir, that's the truth; but yet he was to blame."

"Who? Barry?"

"No, sir, no; but he who shot him."

"Yes, he was a cowardly fellow. What induced him to do it?"

"Because Barry's brother shot *him*. I suspect he was excited at the remembrance of his own sufferings, and urged on to desperation by the fellow that was with him; and, in a moment of madness, thought to revenge himself."

"This was not right, Margaret; it was still very cowardly."

"Why, yes, it was; but—but, I do not defend him, sir."

"What then, Margaret? what then?"

"Why, I was to blame, sir!"

"Why so?"

"Because I told him Barry loved me, sir."

"Ho, ho! a little jealousy, was it? Was it so, Margaret? Well, well, he will be more jealous now."

"I'm sorry for it, sir. Had I not thought he would have known my preference for him, I should not have told him this. It is this I blame myself for, as much as I do him. I hope Barry will do well, sir."

"Your hopes may be disappointed, Margaret. His is a very bad case; and, if he dies, Will Laud will be hanged."

"Then you know all, sir? Oh, pray save him if you can, sir!"

"Who?"

"John Barry, sir,—John Barry."

"Margaret, do you love him?"

"No, sir; yes—yes, sir. I think he is a very good

young man, and he would be a great loss to his parents."

"More so than to you, my girl ? "

"Oh, yes, sir, yes. I'm sure I wish him well, and shall always feel grateful to him for his kindness to me. I do hope he will recover, sir, for Laud's sake."

This was enough ; the doctor now knew all. He saw that his patient was in love with Margaret, but that Margaret loved another. He was in possession of the whole secret. He promised to do all he could ; he dismissed the girl ; and, after a few minutes' further chat with the master and mistress of the house, and strongly advising them to send for Barry's parents in the morning, he took his leave. His little bay pony soon rattled up Gainsborough's Lane, through the open fields towards the Race-course, and over Bishop's Hill, to the town of Ipswich.

Barry's parents were not long in coming to their son, nor long in learning the real state both of his mind and body. It is the happiest time to die when a parent's tender care is round you. Then the agony of suffering is greatly relieved, and the heart can open its most inward thoughts. It turns, with such filial respect and thankfulness, towards those whom it does not like to grieve, but who are always the most quick-sighted to see our wants and to relieve our distresses. So gentle is a mother's love—so delicate, so soothing, so healing to the youthful mind, that nature almost decays with pleasure before her soft attentions. Nor is a father's manliness and feeling less sensibly experienced at such a time. He may not have a woman's gentle-ness, but he has a firmness and a quietness of action which are seldom seen at other times, and which make a sick room seem more calm and sufferable. He has quite as deep feeling, though it is more subdued. Who that ever has been ill in his youth, and has seen the kindness of parental love, but has thought that he never could die happier than when his fond parents were near him ?

So thought young Barry when his parents were by

his side ; and not only thought so, but plainly told them that he wished to die.

" I hope not yet, my boy," said his father. " The young sapling may get a blight, but it soon recovers, and springs up vigorously ; but the old trees naturally decay. I hope to go first, my boy."

" Yes, father, such may be your hope and natural expectation ; but Heaven avert it ! You have others to live for ; may I never live to see your death ! "

" Come, John, do not give way to such feelings. You know not yet what the good God may have in store for you."

" He has, indeed, been good to me, father, and has left me nothing more to wish for in this world."

" Perhaps not for your own benefit, John ; but we are not always to die just when we wish it. Neither are we to live merely for ourselves. We are called upon to live for others ; and more may be expected of us on this account than upon our own. We are not to be such selfish beings as to think, ' The wind blows only for our own mill.' "

" I meant not to find fault, father ; but I am disappointed, and feel therefore useless."

" I know your disappointment, boy ; but I would not have you take it so to heart as to let it prey upon your spirits. There are others far better and more worthy of you, who may esteem you, John, for your good conduct and character ; and one of such may make you an excellent companion for life."

" Father, I know I am not so wise as you are. I have not your experience ; yet this I feel and say, that I hope you will never find fault with that poor girl."

" I will not, John, in your presence ; but how can a father help feeling hurt and angry with a girl who prefers a smuggler to an honest man ? "

" That may or may not be a fault ; but you just now told me we should live for others, and not be so selfish as to think only of ourselves. Now, I do believe that Margaret lives only in the hope that Will Laud will become an altered man."

" He never will !   A lawless villain, who will revenge a blow upon the innocent hand that never gave it, has a heart too reprobate and stony ever to change."

" You will not say it is impossible ? "

" I did not mean to say it is a thing impossible with God ; but you seemed to think that, by Margaret's influence, such a change might be effected.   This, I say, will never be.   Laud may influence her, and may corrupt her mind ; but, take my word for it, the man whose love is swallowed up in the violence of passion, as his is, will never produce anything good.   He will be a selfish villain even towards the poor unfortunate victim of his choice."

" Oh, father, would that you could persuade Margaret of this !   She is indeed a good girl, and a warm-hearted one ; and, had she received any education, would have been as good and respectable as my own dear mother."

" All this may be, John ; but, if I could persuade you out of this fit of fancy, I then might have hope that I should have some power of persuasion with Margaret.   Till then I shall stand no chance.   For, if I cannot root the weeds out of my own ground, how shall I be fit to work for others ? "

The young man sighed deeply, and could answer no more.   He felt the force of the superior wisdom of his father ; and, owning to himself that there was much truth in the remark, felt how difficult it would indeed be to conquer in his own heart his hopeless attachment.

In due time, Barry's wounds progressed towards recovery, and it was agreed among his fellow-labourers that, before the cold weather should set in, they would form a corps for carrying him home to Levington. Twelve undertook the task ; and, one fine October day, they managed to place him and his bed upon a frame, made for the occasion, to which were attached shoulder-pieces, and so conveyed him to his father's residence, where all things were made ready by his mother's hand for his reception.

CHAPTER IX

EVIL WAYS

ONWARD went the boat to the haven at the mouth of the river, and the two guilty souls in her felt that they had narrowly escaped capture, and that, if the law of the land should ever lay hold upon them, they would both have to rue the foul deed they had committed. But the law of the land had long been set at defiance by them ; and they owned none but those of the wind and weather, which compelled them to run for foreign ports, and to slink into those of their own country at the dead of night.

After various congratulations upon their luck in getting off, and making many remarks upon the late encounter, they turned to their duties as sailors, kept their boat trim, and scudded along, with all sails set, toward the *Alde*, which now lay in the shade of Felixstowe Cliff, moored, as if waiting wind and tide to carry her up the river. They were well acquainted with the spot, and bore away through the bright moonlight, reached the mouth of the river, and were at length lifted up by the rolling waves of old Ocean, which came tumbling in from the harbour's mouth.

" The light burns low by the water's edge, and is hidden from the sentinel on Landguard Fort. All's right ; we shall be on board presently."

Soon did they run along the side of the dark cutter ; and giving the signal, " Aldeburgh ", were well understood by the dark-looking sailor who kept watch upon the forecastle of the ship. All was right ; and when the captain came on board, all hands were had up, the sails quickly set, and the anchor weighed. Luff took the helm, the captain retired to his cabin, and in a short time the boat was hoisted in, and away they dashed to sea.

The dark dreams of the captain were mingled with

the visions of his past failure, and disturbed with the
jealousy and hatred of all the Barrys.   The phosphoric
lights upon the sea, as the vessel glided through the
waves, made it look like a boiling ocean of flame, like
burning waters ; and the spray which the waves gave
off resembled smoke.   They were fiery spirits who lived
on board that vessel, as ardent as the liquid flame they
bore in their tubs, and about as productive of good.
Could the history of every one on board the *Alde* be told,
it would make the blood curdle in the veins of many
a stout landsman.   They were pirates as well as smugglers.   Secrecy and crime went hand-in-hand with
them.   Daylight and honesty were things scarcely
known amongst them.

The chief employer of these men lived, as the reader
knows, in tolerable repute, sometimes at one place,
sometimes at another.   He had many vessels at sea,
and Captain Bargood was as well known on the opposite
side of the German Ocean as on this.   He accumulated
riches, but he never enjoyed them.   He lived in a kind
of terror, which those only who have felt it can describe.
He outlived, however, all his ships and all his ships'
companies ; and looked, to the day of his death, an
old weather-beaten log, which had outstood storms
and tempests, and come ashore at last to be consumed.
He prided himself, in his old days, upon the many
daring captains he had made, and the manner in which
he had secretly commanded them.   He had a regular
register of their appointments and their course, how
many trips each ship had taken, how she paid, how she
was lost or taken, and what became of her and her
crew.   That fearful log-book could tell of many a
horrid tale.   It would also serve to show the enormous
extent of illicit traffic carried on at that period by one
man alone.

We must now return to the *Alde*.   While dashing
through the sea, past the sand-bank, or bar, at the
mouth of the Deben, those on board saw a solitary
light burning in Ramsholt Church, a sign that she
might send a boat on shore in safety.   Luff undertook

to go. He did so, and found a messenger from Captain Bargood to land the cargo at the Eastern Cliff, as the coastguard had received information that a run was going to take place at Sizewell Gap, and they had therefore drawn away their men, that their force at that point might be strong enough.

The work was soon done, and the desperate crew betook themselves to the cave, to spend a night of revel and carouse, such as spirits like theirs only could delight in.

To the surprise of many, Will Laud remained on board, and preferred taking a cruise, and coming in again the following night for the ship's company. The fact, however, was, that he was afraid of the land. The consciousness of his guilt, and the fear of the revenge of Barry, should the coast-guard hear of his attack upon young Barry, the brother, acted upon his nerves, and made him think himself safe only on the broad sea.

A certain number of men always remained on board to take the vessel out of sight of the land until the night, and then only were these free-traders able to near the shore. The lives of these men were always in jeopardy, and none of them ever turned out good husbands or friends. When they were compelled to leave off the contraband traffic, they generally took to poaching, and led fearful and miserable lives ; which, if traced to the close, would generally be found to end in sorrow, if not in the extremity of horror.

John Luff had an interview with Captain Bargood, and then told him of Will Laud's awkward situation upon the banks of the Orwell.

"A lucky fellow to escape as he did ! " exclaimed Bargood. "He might have been at this moment in Ipswich gaol, and from thence he would only have escaped through the hangman's hands."

"We must keep him out of the way, sir. We must again report him killed, and change his name from Hudson. He is already known as Will Laud, and his fame will spread along the shore."

" Well, he is a lucky fellow. He should go round the world. I'll send him, ship and crew, a good long voyage. Something may be done in the fur-trade this winter. I have received a notice that I might send a ship, and cheat the Hudson's Bay Company of a good cargo of skins. What shall we dub the captain ? "

" Let 's call him Captain Cook ; I'll tell the crew it 's your desire to have the captain honoured for his success by giving him the title of the great navigator."

" That will do, John—that will do. Take these orders to Captain Cook. Give these presents to the men. Tell them to disperse themselves upon a visit to their friends, and meet again at the Cliff on the 12th of next month, for the purpose of making a long voyage. In the meantime do you and the captain contrive to get the ship into friendly quarters abroad, and if you like to run ashore yourselves, there is my cottage at Butley Moor, and you can take possession of it. But keep yourselves quiet. Five of the crew belong to Butley, and I know what they will be up to. Do not let Captain Cook go up the Orwell again, if you can help it, and steer clear of the coastguard."

" Aye, aye, master, I'll manage " ; and, leaving the old commodore, he returned to the cave, and reached it at the precise moment when the hardy fellows were drinking " Long life to Jack Luff ! "

" I'm just come in time, boys, to make you all return thanks instead of me. I wish you all long life and good luck. I've got you all near three weeks' run ashore. So here 's your healths ! But I say, boys, the commodore approves our young captain, and has appointed him a good voyage next turn ; and as he is to sail across the Atlantic, he wills that you all should join in calling him Captain Cook."

" With all our hearts ! With all our hearts ! " exclaimed several of the crew. " But what were you saying about the three weeks' run ? "

" Why, that you must all be here by the 12th of October. In the meantime, if you want to see me or the captain, you will find us after next week at the green-windowed cottage at Butley. Till then, my boys, follow your own fun. Here's your pay, and a present besides for each."

A noisy shout issued through that dark and dreary cavern. They were not long in obeying their employer's orders. By twos and threes they dispersed, some to Boyton, some to Butley, some to Shottisham, Ramsholt, Bawdsey, Hollesley, Felixstowe, one or two as far as Trimley, Nacton, and Ipswich.

The country was too hot for some of them, who, being suspected of being concerned in the attack made upon young Barry, were looked after in order to be prosecuted for attempt at murder. All pains had been taken ; rewards offered, their persons described ; and so nearly did some of the crew resemble the description of their companions, that they had to cut their cables, and run for the furthest port in safety. John Luff and the captain took up their quarters again by Butley Moor, and employed themselves, as before, in the dangers, and to them familiar sports, of poaching.

The 12th of October came, and the smugglers returned to their places of meeting, and the captain and his mate met them at the cave. Two only did not come to the muster, and these two were always suspected of being rather " shy cocks."

" I say, captain," said one of the men, " I had like to have suffered for you, and Tim Lester for Jack Luff. Two fellows laid an information against us, and swore that we were the men who attempted to murder young Barry. The hundred pounds' reward would have made them stick to it as close as a nor'-wester to the skin. We cut our cables, and ran off and escaped. The country around is hot enough after you both, so the sooner we are on board the better."

Accordingly, stores were soon shipped, anchors, cables, spars, and rigging carried on board, orders given, and " far, far at sea they steered their course."

CHAPTER X

THE PARTING

UNAFFECTED was the joy with which the parents and family of young Barry received their brave son into their peaceful cot. The good miller and his wife welcomed the pale and dejected youth with that quiet, composed, and affectionate interest which at once soothes and comforts a sick soul.

The young man had more upon his mind than he chose to speak of, and a heavy weight upon his spirits, which not all the cheerfulness of his brothers and sisters and parents could allay. His wounds gradually healed; but his weakness continued, and he appeared to be suffering some internal torture which prevented his sleeping at night. He read, and tried to improve his mind; but it availed nothing. His sisters, too, sought every opportunity to afford him diversion; but the languid smile and forced expression of thankfulness told that, although he felt grateful, he did not relish their mirth. He looked intently into the newspaper, especially into all matters connected with the coast and coastguard; and when he read of any skirmish with the smugglers, he was feverishly anxious to know who they were. He also expressed a particular wish to see his brother Edward.

Though the miller could not say exactly when Edward might be expected home, he resolved to send to the stations where he might be found, and urge him to obtain leave of absence.

It was not long before that leave was given, and he returned to visit his parents and his invalid brother. The young men mutually rejoiced to see each other, and were not long in comparing notes upon their separate adventures.

"I prophesy I shall catch him one of these days,"

said Ned; "and if I do, he shall never remember his last escape. We know him well when we see him, but the fellow changes his name as often as he does his place, so that our information is frequently contradictory. If once I have a chance of changing shots with him again, Jack, he shall pay me for those cowardly wounds in your side."

"Nay, Ned, I had rather that the sea swallowed him up, than that you should shoot him."

"How then would you know he was dead, Jack? His ship might be lost, and the wreck driven on shore; but we should not know it, and he might or might not escape. There's nothing like a bullet for certainty."

"But you would know him, if you saw his body cast ashore?"

"Yes, that I should; and I would soon let you know it, too."

"Well, if I must hope for his destruction, I would rather it were in this way than by your hand."

"For your sake, Jack, I should be satisfied with it so; but, for my own part, I have no compunction in shooting a desperado like him, who lives upon the vitals of others, and fights against his king and country, and sets at defiance all laws, human and divine. He would kill any man that opposed his nefarious traffic; and, as I am one that he has sworn to attack by land or by sea, whether in war or peace, I see no reason why I should not defend your life and my own, even though it may cost the taking away of his."

The sufferer did not argue the point any further; and especially as there were reasons of a private nature which had a powerful influence upon his mind. He revived very much during his brother's stay, and seemed to be more cheerful than at any former period of his illness. He even assisted in the labours of the mill, and by little and little began to pick up strength. His brother's leave of absence, however, expired; and the two were seen to walk away together over the hill, arm-in-arm, in the most earnest and deep conversation.

"Never fear, Jack; I will keep your secret honestly.

and render you all the help in my power. I will let you know our movements."

" And take care of yourself, Ned, and do not risk your life for my sake. If you should fall, what should I feel ? "

" I hope you would feel that I fell in a good cause, brother. At least, I do feel it so myself, or I should not be a happy man. No man can be happy, John, who even thinks that he is doing wrong."

" God preserve you, dear brother ! Farewell ! "

The two brothers parted, one to his duties at Dunwich, where his station then was, the other to his home and thoughts.

Anticipation is the greatest quickener of mortal spirits. There is something so lively in the expectation of things upon which the heart is fixed, that even time passes quickly by during the period in which hope is so vivid. But there is a point at which the tide turns, and as gradually operates in a reverse manner, when the heart sickens, desponds, and grows gloomy.

Young Barry returned from his parting walk with his brother in high spirits, elated with hope, and better both in mind and body. He assisted his father in his work, and was at times playful with his sisters. So much did his health improve at this time, that his parents began to hope that the ensuing spring would see him perfectly restored.

And where, all this time, was she, the unfortunate cause of all his misery, and the most unintentional marplot in this history ? She was as great a sufferer as he could possibly be. Nothing could equal her distress of mind at the turn affairs had taken. A bodily affliction might have proved a comfort to her. She felt, after all that had taken place, that the indulgence of her kind master and mistress should be rewarded with more than usual exertions on her part. She had stirring employment for her hands, as well as much exertion for her mind.

It would have been a pleasant thing for her could she have been absent when the sharp gibes of her fellow-servants would torment her with insinuations. There is dreadful cruelty in that man's heart who delights to torment a creature which cannot defend itself. Poor Margaret felt that she had no defence to set up, and no friend to defend her. To hear the hopes expressed that Laud might be soon taken, and the reward talked of for his apprehension, and the wishes expressed by some that they might have the opportunity of handling the cash : these things, coming from those whom she met every day, made her present position very uncomfortable.

More than once, one would announce at dinner-time that the smuggler had been seen on shore and captured. Again, it was stated that he was taken in an open boat at sea. And if a sailor chanced to call at the house, Margaret's heart was in a flutter lest he should be seen by some of the men, and she should be ridiculed. These things kept the poor girl's heart in a constant state of apprehension, and evidently affected her health ; whilst the accounts brought to the farm, from time to time, of young Barry's protracted sufferings, were anything but satisfactory to her. Her master and mistress were uniformly kind to her, or she could not have borne her sufferings. As it was, she found herself so uncomfortable, that she resolved to give her mistress warning, and to leave her as soon as she could suit herself with another servant. She begged her mistress not to think that she was dissatisfied with her or with her work : she told her plainly that she suffered so much from the taunts, and even the looks, of the men upon the farm, that she could not live there, and she was resolved to go home to her parents.

About the latter end of the ensuing November, Margaret returned to her parents ; and if she did not live quite so well as she had done, she lived, at all events, in peace.

It was at this moment of her utmost poverty that Margaret's love and fortitude were put to the severest trial. In the depth of the winter, she received an unexpected visit from young Barry, who, claiming as he did a more than common interest in her fate, and a more than passing share of her acquaintance, well knew that he should not be denied admission into her father's cottage. He entered, looking extremely pale and thin ; but Margaret was glad to see him ; and more especially as he declared that he had walked all the way from Levington. She dusted a seat for him ; and placed it by the crackling fagot-fire, requesting him to rest himself after his walk. It was about half-past two o'clock in the afternoon ; her father was cutting fagots on the heath ; her mother, who had been unwell, had gone upstairs to lie down ; her youngest brother was attending the sheep ; and she was alone at the time young Barry entered. He seated himself, and answered her kind inquiries after his health, and received her grateful expressions of thankfulness for his kindness to her upon former occasions, and especially upon that day when he had received his wound.

Barry heard this with that true modesty which a good man always feels. He said it was only his duty ; he regretted the conduct of his former friends and fellow-labourers, which had driven Margaret from her place, and he asked her if she intended to go to service again. She replied, " Not in this part of the country. I hope soon to go and stay with my Uncle Leader at Brandiston, who, though he has a large family of his own, has yet kindly consented to take me in, if I should want a home."

"Margaret," said the young man, fixing his eyes upon her intently, " are you in want of a home, and are there any circumstances in the world that will ever induce you to share mine with me ? I am come over for no other purpose than to ask you this question. Give me a hopeful answer."

It is impossible for any woman, with a woman's heart, not to feel grateful to an honourable man, who, regarding not the poverty and reverse of circumstances which she may have experienced, renews those earnest vows which once, in happier days, he had before offered. Margaret felt young Barry's kindness, and owned it with the deepest thankfulness, if not in words of eloquence, yet in words of such simplicity and earnestness, as spoke the noble resolution of a good and honest, though, alas, mistaken mind !

"I do not say, John, that there are no circumstances under which I might not be induced to accept your kindness, and for which I might not endeavour to render you the service and obedience of my whole life ; but there is one circumstance which would utterly preclude my acceptance of your offer ; yet forgive me if I say, I hope that one circumstance will for ever exist."

"What is that one, Margaret ? Name it."

"Nay, John, you know it well. I have told you before, that as long as I know that Will Laud is living, or at least until I know that he is dead, I will never marry any other man."

"But you must know, Margaret, the dangerous life he leads, and the precarious tenure by which that life is held, subject as it is to all the perils of the sea."

"Alas ! I know it well ; but there is a God who governs and directs all things for good, and I hope still that the day of grace and penitence may arrive, in which, though fickle as he now is, he may be altered and improved. Nothing is impossible ; and as long as life lasts, so long will I have hope."

"But your hopes, Margaret, may be blighted—it may be that the sea itself may devour him."

"It may be so. It will require something more than the bare report of such a calamity to convince me of the fact, even though years should bring no tidings of him."

"But if you should have the truth asserted by one who should chance to see him perish, would that be sufficient proof ?"

"No, sir, no ! Except I know from my own sight, or from the most positive evidence of more than one, I could not trust to it."

"But if you were at last convinced of his death, might I then hope ?"

"It will be time to speak to me of that if God should grant me life beyond that dreadful time; but, now that I think of your kindheartedness, and know how unwilling you are to give unnecessary pain, I begin to fear that you have some melancholy tidings to communicate. Speak, John, speak!—your manner is unusual, and your conversation is too ominous. Have you heard anything of Laud? Pray speak, and tell me at once."

This was more than the youth could at once perform. He had been so carried away by his own passion, that he had not foreseen the effect which his own unwelcome tidings might occasion. He now heartily wished that he had left it for others to communicate. He hesitated, looked painfully distressed, and was disconcerted at his own precipitancy.

"I know, John, by your manner, that you have something to tell me, though you seem afraid to utter it. Tell me the worst, tell me the worst!"

"Margaret, I own that I have been too abrupt. My own hopes have made me overlook the shock I know you will experience; but I had really no intention of giving you pain. The worst is, that which I have often thought would come to pass—Will Laud is dead!"

"How do you know that?"

"I saw him myself this very morning."

"Where? where?"

"At Bawdsey Ferry."

"How knew you it was Laud?"

"My brother saw his boat coming ashore in the gale last night, saw it driven upon the rocks inside the bar, and smashed to pieces. Laud, with three others, was cast on the shore quite dead. My brother sent me word with the morning's light. I would not even trust to his report, so I went to Bawdsey and saw him. I then hastened to be the first to convey the intelligence to you. Forgive me, Margaret, that my selfish thoughts should have made me forget your feelings."

"I can forgive *you*; but I never should forgive myself, if I did not go directly and judge from my own sight if it be really so. I have long made up my mind to hear unpleasant tidings; but I have never been without hope that something would alter him."

"I fear that he was too desperate ever to reform."

"I did not think he could reform himself. I lived in hopes that some severe blow might bring him to his senses; but I must go and see. In the meantime let me request you not to mention those matters to me again; at least, let me have time to think of the past and consider of the future."

"You will pardon me, Margaret, and attribute to my regard for you the precipitate step I have taken upon this occasion."

"Where lies the body of poor Laud?" said Margaret, without seeming to hear what Barry had last said.

"It is in the boat-house at Bawdsey Ferry, together with the three others."

"I will go there to-day." And she immediately prepared to fulfil her resolution.

"How will you go? Will you let me drive you there? I can obtain a horse and cart; and I think you know me well enough to be persuaded of my care."

"I do not doubt it, sir, but I had rather not go with you. I have no objection to be your debtor for the horse and cart, but my youngest brother will drive me."

"It shall be here in half an hour. May I offer you any other aid?"

"None, sir, whatever. You have my thanks; and I so far consider your honesty and truth deserves my esteem, that, by to-morrow at this time, if you will pay us another visit, I shall be glad to see you."

"It is all that I could wish or hope. Till then, Margaret, good-bye."

Young Barry left with a heart somewhat easier, though touched with pain for the poor girl. He had, however, seen the only being who stood between him and his affections laid a helpless corpse upon the boat. Hope took the place of despair—he soon obtained the horse and cart, and sent them to their destination.

Barry's anxiety was greatly increased as the day wore away, and a night of feverish suspense succeeded. Sleep was quite out of the question—every hour he heard the clock strike in the room beneath him. He saw the grey dawn approach, and beheld the gradually increasing light clearer and clearer shining, and throughout the whole livelong night he dwelt but upon one theme—that theme was Margaret !

He rose next morning, looking, as his friends declared, like a ghost. He ate no breakfast—he could not talk—he could not work ; but could only walk about, lost in abstracted meditation. The dinner-hour came with noon, but he could eat nothing—he had neither appetite, speech, nor animation. No efforts of his parents could call forth any of his energies—they knew he had been to see his brother ; but they could not get him to declare the purport of his visit. He said that his brother was well ; that nothing had happened to him ; that he had seen him quite well ; and that he was promoted a step in the service ; and that he was constantly employed. It was evident to them that something was preying upon the young man's mind which he would not disclose. They did not, however, distress him with questions ; and after dinner, he departed from the house, and was observed to walk toward Nacton.

He found Margaret returned, and seated by the fireside, as she was the day before when he visited her. She looked very pale and thoughtful. The young man took this as a necessary consequence of the shock she had received at the sight of her lover's corpse, little dreaming that at that very moment she was actually feeling for the distress of him who then stood before her.

"Well, Margaret, I am come, according to your appointment."

"I am very grateful to you for your assistance. I should never have forgiven myself had I not gone. I saw your brother, sir, and he was very kind to me. Through his permission I obtained a sight of the bodies in the boat-house, and he told me concerning the melancholy wreck of the schooner ; but—but both you and your brother, sir, are mistaken."

The heart of the youth was so stricken, he could not for a time utter one single word—he sat all astonishment, all dismay, all agony, all despair. There was no joyful congratulation for Margaret, there was no apology for his mistake—feelings too deep for utterance overpowered him.

Margaret saw and felt, in the midst of her own hope, the painful disappointment of his, nor could she summon courage to utter more. After the most afflicting silence, John Barry, as if he could not doubt his own and his brother's eyes, said—

" Are you sure I was mistaken ? "

" Quite," said Margaret ; " quite."

" And my brother, how could he be so deceived ? he knew Laud so well."

" Few knew him better, but I convinced him that he was mistaken. I asked him where the wound was upon the forehead, which he had given him, and which I had such difficulty in healing. It certainly was very like Laud, and, had I not well considered him, I also might have been deceived ; but I am glad I went. Your brother is quite satisfied upon the point, but very much hurt to think of the grief he has occasioned you. He felt very sorry, also, for the pain which he kindly imagined I must have felt, which, however, was greatly relieved by the joy I experienced in proving to his satisfaction that he was mistaken. He declared that, for my sake, he would never injure Will Laud if he could help it. Oh, how I wish that Will could have heard that declaration ! I am persuaded that they would have been good friends from that time. I think you will find your brother at Levington upon your return, for I know he asked permission of Lieutenant Brand to let him visit his father for a day upon very urgent business. I suspect this is but to see you, and explain to you his mistake."

" Margaret, I ought to have felt more for you than for myself. I wish you well—I scarcely now can hope.

I am indeed wretched, but it is my duty to strive against these feelings—I know it is. But here in this country I cannot remain—I must go abroad. I must see if I can get a grant of land in Canada—I cannot live here; but I shall never forget you, Margaret, never! —and may I hope that you will sometimes think of me ? "

"I can never forget you; and, depend upon it, wherever you may be, I shall never cease to be grateful for your past kindness to a poor unfortunate girl like myself. God will prosper you, sir—I am sure He will. I am far too unworthy your notice. At all times I will pray for your happiness."

"I know not where I shall go, Margaret. I will see you but once more before I go; but now good-bye."

They shook hands and parted—each felt a sincere wish for the other's welfare. One felt that the hopes of his life were blighted; the other, that her vows of attachment were unalterable.

Young Barry returned home, and found, as Margaret had supposed, his brother Edward, who had been there some time before his return. It needed but a look to tell what each felt. They took a turn round the fields, and were seen arm-in-arm together. They were mutually satisfied with each other.

Edward Barry saw and admired his brother's choice, for until then he had never been prepossessed in her favour. The warmth of feeling which she betrayed when looking at the countenance of her supposed lover, as he lay in the boat-house, and the pure and simple joy at discovering the mistake; the very sensible manner in which she proved that she could not be mistaken; the gratitude she felt, and the exemplary manner in which she conducted herself, all conspired to give him a high opinion of the character of this young woman, and made him feel that, notwithstanding the strong wish he had entertained for Laud's death, for he had even counted upon being opposed in deadly skirmish with him, he never could take his life without giving a deep wound to one innocent and deserving heart.

Young Barry became another being—his health improved rapidly; he began to work, and to talk of future days with cheerfulness.

CHAPTER XI

THE LAST INTERVIEW

ABOUT this time a new settlement was projected at New South Wales, and Government had already sent several convict ships to Botany Bay and Port Jackson; but the unruly state of the people, and the necessary military government of the colony, made it very desirable that some respectable settlers should be induced to go out. Accordingly, whenever store-ships were sent, a premium was offered for farmers' sons or farming men to emigrate. One hundred acres of land for as many dollars were granted: still very few could be induced to go. It was not for some years that any regular settlers' ship went out with free passengers.

Young Barry conversed with his father upon this subject, and found him quite disposed to let him have double the above-named sum, and even encouraged the idea in the youth's mind.

It so happened that Captain Johnson, who commanded one of the earliest store-ships which was sent to that colony, was acquainted with Lieutenant Brand, and had written to ask him if there was any young farmer who would like to go out with him from Suffolk. It was through him that young Barry got an introduction to Captain Johnson, who promised him a good berth, and every convenient accommodation. It was soon resolved that John Barry should forthwith get a grant of land; and, being furnished with all requisite particulars, he went to London to see his ship, and make arrangements with his captain.

All his family now felt a double interest in him because he was going away, to leave them, perhaps, for ever—at all events for a very long period. His sisters worked hard to make him such changes of linen as should last him for years ; and every hand they could muster in the village, capable of doing needle-work, was fully employed. Presents of various kinds flowed in ; and, upon his return home from town, he found himself master of more stock than he could possibly have got together for his own use in England, though he had laboured for it for many years. He was very cheerful, and even told his sisters that as he might, perhaps, marry soon in the new settlement, they might make him some sets of female apparel ! They laughed with astonishment at this request ; but, as they found him earnest, they each spared something from their own wardrobe for his most eccentric request. Little, however, did they surmise the real motive of his heart.

The day was fixed for the vessel to sail, and John must be, with all his goods and chattels, at London in a fortnight. The last Sabbath-day that he spent with his father, mother, brothers, and sisters, was memorable for the deep-rooted power it ever after retained over his mind. The clergyman's sermon was upon the universal providence of God, and, as if he preached it on purpose (but which was not the case, for he was ignorant of the intended movement of the young man), he discoursed upon the unity of the Church of Christ in every place—the communion we had even with our antipodes in the worship of the same God. He instanced the especial interest which the Church had with all the colonies of the mother country, and spoke of the joy to be felt when that reunion should take place at the resurrection of the just. The preacher spoke as if even the poor benighted aborigines of Van Diemen's Land were his brethren, and showed how necessary it was for us to extend to them our helping hand to bring them to Christianity.

After service, the worthy miller told his pastor that his son was going to that very country, and that the young man had said he never should forget that discourse. The clergyman went home with the family, and spent that Sabbath evening with them. He fully entered into the prospect before the young man, and pointed out to him the sure path to heaven, through the strait gate, and inspired him with many hopes of doing good. He joined with them in prayer, and gave them his blessing. He promised to send him a valuable present of books, which he performed the next day. Bibles, testaments, prayer-books, homilies, tracts, *The Whole Duty of Man*, together with a work on planting, farming, horticulture, and seeds, and one on natural history and botany, all which prôved of the greatest utility to the worthy and honourable young man upon whom they were bestowed.

The day of parting at length came—the last sad day—and the young man remembered his promise to Margaret, that he would see her once more before he departed. He found her at home on the Monday, that very day upon the eve of which he was to take the mail from Ipswich for London. He came to take a long and a last farewell. And why did he torment himself and the poor girl with this last interview ? Was it with a lurking hope that he might persuade her to accompany him ? He had really and truly prepared for such an event, could he have brought it about. In his chests were presents which his sisters had made at his request, in case he should marry in the new settlement. He had suggested this ; but his heart had to the very last a lingering thought that perhaps Margaret might be induced to embark with him. Upon what small last links will not true love depend !

" I am come, Margaret, to take my leave of you," said he, on meeting her. " I am going to a colony the farthest off our own dear country of any known island in the world."

" Indeed, sir ! if so I wish you well, and pray God to bless you ! "

" Before I go, Margaret," resumed he, " I must tell you that as long as life holds in this poor heart of mine,

I shall never love any one else. I may prosper—I may be rich—I may be blessed with abundance—but I shall never be blessed with a wife."

"Oh, sir, say not so! you grieve me very much to hear you talk in that way. You are a young man, and the path of life, though it may not be without thorns, has yet many blessed plants for your happiness. Why should you speak so despondingly? Change of place and occupation will make you feel very differently."

"You may think it may be so with me, Margaret; but if there be any truth in this last doctrine which you have yourself divulged, it will hold good in yourself as well as in me. If you change your place of abode, and go with me, Margaret, will not you think very differently to what you do now? Oh, that I could persuade you! Oh, that I could induce you to join your lot with mine! Shake off that wild attachment to the smuggler, and go with me. I will marry you to-morrow morning before we sail. I have even hinted the matter to my captain. He has promised to be bridesman, and has even taken out the license, and will be ready to-morrow at ten o'clock. No preparation will be necessary for you: I have prepared everything. Your bridal dress is even ready; and our honeymoon will be kept on board the *Kitty*, which is to sail to-morrow from London. Margaret, hear me! I am sure that your present connexion will end in ruin. What is Will Laud but a desperate fellow who cannot and, believe me, will not protect you? What sacrifice can it be to leave a man who would have taken you away without your consent, for one who, with your consent, will unite all his interests with yours as long as he lives?"

There was a pause—an awful pause—after this declaration, such as beings feel who are held in the most agitating suspense, between life and death. Painful—very painful—was the situation in which Margaret was placed. There was a flood of overwhelming agitation. The tears stole down her cheeks.

Her dark eye shone like the sun through the midst of a watery cloud, and told that it longed to burst through the mists of darkness, but could not find an opening for its beams. Faster and faster fell the big drops—heavier and heavier dropped the clouds of the eyelids, till, like a flash of lightning, burst the words from her lips—

"Oh, leave me! leave me, sir! I never can alter the pledge I have given! I never can be unfaithful! Though I may be unhappy in my choice, yet it is a choice to which I feel so bound, that nothing but death can part us. Oh, that Laud were as good as yourself! I feel, I own, the contrast; but I hope he may be better. Oh, do not urge me, sir—do not urge me to desert the only chance left for the restoration of a young man to honesty and life!"

"Margaret, hear then my last words, and if they fail I will leave you. I do not believe that Laud loves you as he ought to love. Did I think there was one chance for your happiness with him, I would not urge my present suit a moment longer. Believe me, he is not worthy of you. You compel me to say he is a villain. He will betray you. He will desert you. He will bring you to want, misery, and ruin. I know you love him. Your early feelings have all been engaged in his favour; but which of those has he not disappointed? which of those feelings has he not wounded? Yet you cling to him, as if he were a safe-ground of anchorage. Believe me—believe me, Margaret, the anchor you cast there will not hold; it will suffer you to drift upon the rocks, upon which you will perish. Say in one word, will you, or will you not, consent to my offer?"

"John Barry, on my knees (and she suited the action to the word) I thank you, and bless you; but I do not —I cannot—accept your offer!"

"Margaret, farewell!" exclaimed he, as he raised her from the ground, "a long, a last farewell. Nevertheless, take this; it is a gift, which may some future day be of service to you. You will not refuse it, as it

is the last gift of one who will never see you again.
I know you cannot even read it now; but the time
may come when you may be enabled so to do, and
I had counted in my long voyage of teaching you so
to do. It was a present to me from my mother; but
I have many more like it, given me by our clergyman.
Take it—take it—it can never do you hurt; and,
with God's blessing, it may be the means of our meeting
in another world, though we never meet again in this.
God bless you, Margaret! farewell!"

He placed a small clasped Bible in her hands, in the
opening and the closing leaf of which were two five-
pound notes; small sums perhaps apparently to us
in this day, but magnificent compared with the means
of an early settler in a strange land. This ten pounds
paid poor Margaret's rent, and all her parents' debts,
at a subsequent time, when the deepest distress might
have overwhelmed her. But Barry returned to his
parents with a noble consciousness of an upright mind.
His parting with them was not, comparatively speaking,
of so passionate or stirring a nature as that which he
had so recently undergone, but it was purely affectionate and loving.

The hour of parting is over; and John Barry, as
honest and worthy a young man as ever left the shores
of Old England, was soon on board the *Kitty*, 440 tons;
and with some few others, who like himself had a mind
to try their fortunes in a foreign land, he sailed for
that colony, once the most distant and unpromising,
now becoming renowned, and which probably will be
the most glorious island of the Eastern world.

CHAPTER XII

THE WELCOME VISIT

THERE is no greater misery upon earth than to be left alone ; to feel that nobody cares for you—nobody is interested in you ; and that you are destitute as well as desolate ! Poor Margaret at this time felt something akin to this sensation. She had a regard for the youth who had driven himself into voluntary exile on her account. She was not, however, to blame for this, though many a one accused her of being the cause of it. She was shunned by those of her own sex, on account of the disreputable character of her lover, with whom it was believed that she still held secret correspondence, although for a long time she had heard nothing of him. The men cared little about her, because she cared nothing about them ; but kept herself quietly at home, attending to the sick-bed of a rapidly declining mother. Occasionally she ventured to the Priory Farm, to ask for some few necessaries required by her aged parent. Her former mistress was uniformly kind to her ; and not contented with affording the assistance which was asked for, this good woman visited the sick-bed of poverty, and ministered to the wants of the aged and infirm.

Gratitude is very eloquent, if not in the multitude of words, yet in the choice of them, because it speaks from the heart. Margaret's gratitude was always sincere. She was a creature of feeling without cultivation, and imbibed at once the very perfection of that spirit which all benevolent minds wish to see ; but which if they do not see, they are so accustomed to the world that they are not very greatly disappointed. Their surprise is rather expressed in that pleasure which they imbibe in seeing the feeling of a truly grateful heart. An aged female, on a bed of poverty and sickness, is but too frequently left to negligence and want. When their infirmities are the greatest, and their cares always the most anxious, then is it that the really charitable aid of the benevolent is most needed.

Margaret felt her own inability to assist her aged mother, beyond the doing for her to the best of her powers in all attendances as nurse and housewife. She herself earned no money; but she made the best possible use of all the earnings of the family, as at that time she had not discovered the munificent present of poor John Barry; for, not being able to read, she had carefully laid up the treasured book, unconscious of the generosity and self-denial of the donor.

At this time Margaret appears to have suffered much privation. She felt that she was dependent upon the kindness of richer friends for those little delicacies which she required to support her mother's sinking frame; and never was heart more sensitively grateful than this poor girl's when she received some unexpected trifle of bounty from the table of her indulgent mistress. She wept with joy as she bore the present home to her affectionate but fast-sinking parent.

She had not very long to continue her nursings. Early in the year she lost her mother. Nature could not be suspended; and she sank to rest, with her head supported by the arms of an affectionate daughter and a good husband.

The death of her mother was felt by Margaret very keenly. It reminded her of her own early affliction; and a singular occurrence took place at the funeral, which more forcibly reminded her of her sister's death. A stranger entered the churchyard at the time of the ceremony, and stood at the foot of the grave, and actually wept with the mourners. No one knew who he was, or where he came from; nor did he speak to any one, but he seemed to be much afflicted at the scene of sorrow. He remained some time after the mourners had departed, and saw the grave filled up again; and when the old clerk had neatly patted round the mound with his spade, and was about to leave it, the stranger asked him if he did not mean to turf it.

"Why, I don't know ; I don't think they can afford to have it done properly ; but, at all events, I must let the earth settle a bit first."

"How long will it take to do that ? "

"That depends upon the weather. Come rain, and that will soon settle ; but if frost, and dry weather continue, it will be some time first. They cannot afford to have it flagged and binded."

"What will that cost ? "

"I charge one shilling and sixpence extra for that, as I have to get the turf from the heath ; but I shall have some time to wait before I am paid for what I have done. Time was when that family was well off ; but no good comes of bad doings."

"What do you mean, my man ? what bad doings have these poor people been guilty of ? "

"I see, sir, you are a stranger in these parts, or else the Catchpoles, especially one of them, would be known to you by common report."

"Which one is that ? "

"Margaret, sir."

"Well, what of her ? has she been unfortunate ? "

"If she has it has been her own seeking, no one's else. She might have done well, but she would not."

"What might she have done ? and what has she done ? "

"Why, sir, she might have married an industrious young man, who would have done well by her ; but she chose to encourage a vagabond smuggler, who first set her up with high notions, and then ruined and left her to poverty and shame."

"You do not mean to say that the young woman is a depraved and abandoned character ? "

"No, no ; I mean she don't like any honester man, and so no one seems to care anything about her."

A tear stole down the stranger's cheeks ; and, whoever he was, he seemed to feel a little relief at this information.

"Is the young woman living at home with her family?"

"Yes; because nobody will hire her. She is laughed at by the females, and the men don't care anything about her. If they could catch her lover, and pocket a hundred pounds reward for his capture, they would like the chance."

"How are the family supported?"

"Why, I suppose the father earns eight shillings a week, the youngest son one-and-sixpence; but they must have been hard run this winter, and it will take them some time to get up their back-rent and present expenses."

"What is the amount of their present expense?"

"Why, I must get, if I can, sixteen shillings, some-how or another. I dare say I shall have it; but it will take them some time to pay it. There is ten shillings for the coffin (for I am carpenter, clerk, and sexton), three shillings and sixpence digging the grave, one shilling for tolling the bell, and one shilling and sixpence for the clergyman; that will exactly make the sum."

"You say it will take one shilling and sixpence extra for turfing and binding: that will be seventeen shillings and sixpence. How much do you think they owe at the shop?"

"I know that it cost them three shillings and sixpence for flannel; but I know it is not paid for yet."

"There's a guinea; that will exactly pay you all, will it not?" and the stranger pitched a guinea against the sexton's spade.

What a wonderful thing is a golden guinea in the eye of a poor parish clerk! how reverential it makes a man feel, especially when a stranger pays it for a poor man! He might have got it; but he must have waited the chance till after the next harvest.

"That it will, sir—that it will. I'll call and pay

the bill at the shop. Are you coming to live in these parts ? "

"Not for long—not long ! " sighed the stranger.

"Why, you look very healthy, sir ? You are not ill ? "

"No, no, my man ; I do not mean to give you a chance of getting another guinea by me, at least for the present. I only meant to say my stay in this village would not be for long. But where do these poor people live ? "

"Not in the same place they used to do in the days of their prosperity and respectability. Their house now stands at the corner of the heath, sir : shall I go with you and show it you ? "

"I can find it ; there are not many cottages there. Do you go and pay the bill at the shop ; and then if you have a mind to bring the receipt, instead of giving me the trouble to call at your house for it, you will find me at the cottage of these poor people ; and hear me, old man, do not talk to any one about this matter. You may as well bring a receipt, also, for your own work at the same time."

"You are quite a man of business, I see, sir. I will not fail to be at the cottage this very evening with a receipt in full."

The old sexton placed the guinea carefully at the bottom of his pocket, and, shouldering his spade and mattock, marched off towards the village shop. The stranger walked round Nacton churchyard. He stood sometime attentively reading the inscription upon Admiral Vernon's mausoleum ; and, taking another look at the humble, new-made grave of Margaret Catchpole's mother, he took the highroad to the heath, and saw the cottage, known by the name of the Shepherd's Cot, at the verge of that wild waste.

Meantime the following conversation was going on in that cottage :—

"I wonder," said Margaret to her father, as the old man sat by the log-fire in the chimney-corner, "whether our brother Charles is alive or dead ? "

"I can just remember him," said the boy; "he used to be very fond of me, and said I should make a good soldier."

"I have never heard of him," said the father, "since he went to Ipswich, and enlisted in another name, at the Black Horse, in St. Mary Elms. I understood that his regiment went off to India almost immediately after he enlisted."

"I wonder if he is alive?"

"I cannot tell, my dear; the chances are very much against it. He was a quick, intelligent, lively boy; and, when he was at work in the fields, used often to say he should like to be a soldier. The old clerk taught him to read and write, and used to say, 'If Charles had a chance he would be scholar enough to succeed him as parish clerk.' He left us at the commencement of our misfortunes; God grant he may meet us again in happier days!"

Poor Margaret sighed; for she too well remembered the origin of all their sorrows not to feel for her dear parent. That sigh was answered by a sudden knock at the door, which occasioned a start. The latch was lifted up, and in walked the stranger who had attended the funeral. His entrance gave a change to their conversation; and Margaret placed a chair for him, in which he quietly sat down opposite to the old labourer. Care had worn the countenance of the venerable man more than years and work. The only mourning of an outward kind which met the eye, was an old piece of crape round the equally old hat which hung upon a peg in the wall. Nothing else could be afforded; but their countenances betokened the state of their hearts. They were really melancholy. It is not in the outward pageantry of a funeral that real sorrow is to be seen; and the real grief of the Shepherd's Cottage surpassed all the pageantry of the palace, and was viewed with calm and respectful silence by the stranger.

He was a tall, pale, thin young man, with a scar upon the side of his face: he looked as if he had undergone much sickness or misfortune. He was dressed in a plain suit of black, which hung rather loosely round him. He asked Margaret if the youth beside her was her youngest brother, and whether she had any other brothers living. She replied that it was, to the best of her knowledge, her only brother living. He then made inquiries concerning the illness of her late mother; and after various other domestic matters, he looked very earnestly at Margaret, and in a seemingly abstracted manner said, "Where is Will Laud?" It was as if an electric shock had been given to all in the room; for all started at the question, and even the stranger was greatly moved at his own question, when he saw Margaret hide her face in her hands, weeping.

"I did not mean to occasion you any grief. I only asked after a man whom I once knew as a boy, and whom the old clerk informed me you could tell me more about than any one else."

"And do not you know more of him than we do, sir?" said the old man.

"I know nothing of him, and have heard nothing of him since I was a youth; my question was purely accidental. I am sorry to see your daughter so afflicted by it. Has the man been unkind to her?"

"No, sir! no!" said Margaret. "If you are here as a spy, sir, indeed we know not where he is."

"A spy!" said the stranger; and the stranger started and muttered something to himself. Margaret herself now began to feel alarmed; for the stranger seemed to be deep in thought; and, as the flame from the log of wood cast its light upon his face, she thought he looked ghastly pale.

"A spy!" said the stranger; "what made you think me a spy?—and what should I be a spy for?"

"I did not mean to affront you, sir; but the question you asked concerning one for whose apprehension a hundred pounds is offered, made me think of it. Pray pardon me, sir."

"I am sorry that he has done anything to occasion such an offer from the Government. Has he murdered any one?"

"No, sir; but Will is a wild young man, and he attempted to kill young Barry of Levington, and wounded him so severely, that a reward was offered for his apprehension."

"Has Barry recovered?"

"Yes, sir; and he is gone out of the country to Canada, or some more distant land."

"Then never mind if Laud be caught. Government will never pay a hundred pounds for his conviction when the principal evidence cannot be obtained. Never mind! never mind!—that will soon be forgotten."

Such words of consolation had never been uttered in Peggy's ear before. She began to feel very differently toward the stranger, as the tone of his voice, and his manner, together with his words, became so soothing.

"Thank you, sir, for your good wishes; you make my heart joyful in the midst of my mourning."

"I only wish I could make it more joyful by telling you any good news of your lover, Margaret; but though I know nothing of him, and only wish he were more worthy of you than he is, yet I bear you tidings of some one else of whom you will all be glad to hear."

"Our brother Charles!" both she and the boy at once exclaimed, whilst the old man remained in mute astonishment.

"It is of your brother Charles; and first, let me tell you that he is alive and well."

"Thank God for that!" said the father.

"Next, that he is in England, and it will not be long before you will have the pleasure of seeing him."

At this moment the door opened, and in walked the old clerk, who, seeing the stranger, made his bow, and gave him a piece of paper containing a receipt for the guinea which he had received. To the surprise of all, the stranger rose, and taking a little red box made in the shape of a barrel, which stood on the wooden shelf over the fire-place, he unscrewed it, and put the paper in it; and, replacing it, seated himself again.

"You were just telling us of our brother Charles," said Margaret.

" What ! " exclaimed the sexton, " is Charles alive ? My old scholar ! Where is the boy ? I have often thought of him. Oh ! what a pity he took to drinking ! He was as good a reader as our clergyman, and beat me out and out."

" He is not addicted to drink now, and is as sober as a man can be."

" I am glad of that. Then he will succeed in anything he undertakes. But where has he been these many years ? "

" You shall hear if you will sit down ; for, as I knew him well, and was his most intimate friend, he made me his confidant in everything. He was always of a restless spirit ; and when he left his father and friends, he had no settled plan in his mind. He enlisted in the 33rd regiment of Foot, which was then going out to India ; and that his relatives and friends might not grieve about him, he gave his name to the parochial authorities of St. Mary Elms, at Ipswich, as Jacob Dedham, the name of a boy who, he knew, was not alive. The parish-officer gave him a shilling, and he took another shilling of the recruiting-officer.

" He was sworn in, and took his departure with many others for Portsmouth, at which place he embarked for India, and joined the 33rd regiment at Bombay. He was always of an aspiring and inquisitive turn of mind. He became an active and orderly soldier, and assisted the sergeant-major in all his writings and accounts. He soon became an adept in all the cunning and customs of the various castes of natives in India ; was remarkable for the quickness with which he mastered the different idioms of the different territories of the East ; and at length became so noticed by Sir William Forbes, that he introduced him to Lord Cornwallis, who employed him upon the frontier of Persia.

" Here he became a spy, and was actively engaged for that highly honourable and intelligent Governor-General. He readily entered into his lordship's views ; and, receiving from him a purse well stored, to provide himself with disguises, he assumed the garb of a Moorish priest, and with wonderful tact made himself master of all the requisites of his office. I have here a sketch of him, in the very dress in which he travelled through the country."

Taking out a roll from his coat-pocket, he unfolded the canvas wrapper in which it was enclosed, and presented it to Margaret, asking her if she recognized her brother.

With eager and interested glance she looked at the sketch, but not a feature could she challenge. She then looked up at the stranger, and, as she did so, said—

"It is much more like you, sir, than it is like my brother."

"I think it is full as like me as it is like him. But, such as it is, you have it; for he commissioned me to give it to you, together with a sketch of a fortress in which he resided a long time as the priest of the family. This is Tabgur, on the frontiers of Persia. His master and family are walking on the rampart-garden of the fort."

Here the old clerk could not help bursting out with an exclamation of astonishment at the wonderful talent of his former pupil.

"I always said he would be a wonderful man, did I not, Master Catchpole,—did I not? Did he teach himself this art, sir?"

"Indeed he did; and many others he learned, which did him equal credit. He was a very quiet man in appearance, though he was alive to everything around him. Many were the hairbreadth escapes he had; but his self-possession carried him through all. He had to conceal all his drawings of the different fortresses, all his calculations of the inhabitants, of their forces, and their condition; but he contrived to wrap them about his person, so that they could not be discovered.

"Once, indeed, one of his papers, written as close as pencil could write, was picked up in the fort-garden at Tabgur, and he was suspected for a spy; but he quickly changed their suspicions; for, observing that his master had a bad toothache, he told him it was a charm to prevent it. Every person, he said, for whom he wrote that charm, would be free from the toothache as long as he kept it secreted in his turban; but it must be one expressly written for the purpose, and for the person; and that, during the time of its being written, the person must have a piece of rock-salt upon that very tooth which was aching at the time. The charm was only of use for the person for whom it was written; and, as that one was written for himself, it could do the Persian warrior no good. This answered well; for he got back his valuable paper, and wrote one immediately, in the presence of his master, who, placing a piece of rock-salt upon the tooth, found that, as he wrote, the pain was diminished; and when he concluded, it was completely gone.

"But the next day, your brother, the Moorish priest, was gone also. He passed over into Hindostan, changed his Moorish dress, and soon made his way to head-quarters, where he delivered such an accurate account of all that befell him, and of all that was required of him, that he received a most ample reward. He called himself Caulins Jaun, the Moorish priest.

"He has been sent to England by Lord Cornwallis, to deliver some despatches to the government, relating to the Mysore territory and Tippoo Saib's conduct; and, having accomplished his mission, he has asked permission to visit his poor friends at Nacton, in Suffolk. His leave is very short, as his services are again required."

"And when may we expect him here?" exclaimed Margaret. "Oh, how I long to see him!"

"I expect him here this night; for, as I was his companion, and am to go back again with him, so I am his forerunner upon this occasion."

"I could almost set the village-bells ringing for joy," said the old clerk. "I wonder whether he would know me."

"That I am sure he would."

"Pray, sir, how do you know that?"

"Because the description he gave me of you is so accurate that I could tell you from a thousand. Do you remember the sketch he made of an old woman throwing a cat at her husband?"

"That I do. Did he tell you of that?"

"That he did; and of the scratch he got from the cat's claws, as you bopped your head, and puss lit directly on his face."

Here the old man could not help laughing.

"But did he tell you nothing else about the sketch?"

"That he did, and with such feeling, that I almost fancy I see now the scrub-brush belabouring his head for his pains."

"Oh, dear! oh, dear! I thought he had forgotten all that."

"No; he thought of it at the very time he was sketching the forts of his enemies' country. Had he been caught in such freaks as those, he would have had a severer punishment than what your good dame gave him."

"But if my old dame could see him now, how rejoiced she would be; for notwithstanding his roguery, he was a great favourite of hers!"

"She will see him to-morrow."

"That will be news for the old woman. But shall I see him this night? I would not mind waiting till midnight for such a purpose."

"That you may. But I do not think that even you would know him, were you to see him."

"Why not? Would he know me?"

"He would: but youth alters more in countenance than age, especially where a foreign climate has acted upon the constitution."

"I should know him from two things," said Margaret. "He once so nearly cut off the end of his little finger with a sharp tool, that it hung only by a piece of skin: it was bound up, so that it adhered and grew together; but somehow, the tip got a twist, so that the nail of the finger grew under the hand : it was the left hand."

" And what was the other mark ? "

" It was a deep scar on the back of the same hand, caused by imprudently cutting off a large wart."

" Now tell me," said the stranger, drawing the glove off his left hand, " were the scars you mention anything like those ? "

" Exactly," said the clerk, who looked at him again and again with amazement.

" Why, you can't be he ? Are you Master Charles ? "

" Can you doubt it ? "

" The hand is his."

" And the hand is mine. Therefore the hand is the hand of Charles."

The old man rose, and coming forward said, " I do believe you are my son ; I have been thinking so for some time, and I am now satisfied that it is so. God bless you, my boy ! You are come at a seasonable hour, for the Lord gives and takes away as He sees best."

A hearty embrace and affectionate recognition took place. The stranger (now no longer such) soon convinced them of his identity ; and though no one could really have known a single feature of his countenance, yet he gave them such internal and external evidences of his relationship, calling to mind so many circumstances of such deep interest to them all, that he was soon acknowledged to be their relative.

Happiness comes unexpectedly in the days of mourning. The wild recruit had returned, after many days, to cheer an aged parent and a forlorn sister, who needed the hand of some one to help them in their troubles. The old man's heart revived again ; and it was a pleasure to witness the joys of the few days which then visited the Catchpoles, and the congratulations which they received from the old clerk and his wife upon the bright prospects of a hopeful son. Reports spread like wildfire that Charles Catchpole had come home, and that he had returned from India as rich as a Nabob. Reports are generally exaggerated, and they were not a little so in the present case; for although Charles might be comparatively rich, his fortune, as the world terms it, was anything but made. He had a few guineas to spare; but he had to return to India, and to pursue a very hazardous course of life, before he could even hope to gain that independence which had been promised to him. A few guineas, however, made a great show in a cottage. He paid his father's debts; made a present to the old clerk's wife; bought his sister a new gown; his younger brother, Edward, a new suit of clothes; paid one year's rent in advance for the cottage; left a present with the sexton to keep his mother's grave ever green; and announced his departure to his family after staying one short week after five years' absence.

"I shall see you no more, Charles!" exclaimed Margaret, at parting. "I fear that I shall see you no more! You are going through a dangerous country, and the perils you have already escaped you must not always expect to avoid."

"Fear not, Peggy, fear not. God sent me in a proper season to comfort you, and if you trust in Him, He will send you some other friend in need, if it be not such a one as myself."

"Oh, let me go with you, dear brother! I should like to accompany you," said Edward, his brother.

"That cannot be, Edward. You must remain at home to help your father and sister; you are not able to undertake a march of many thousand miles, under a sun burning your face, and a sand scorching your feet. I have a good friend, however, in Lord Cornwallis, and I have no doubt that some time hence I shall be enabled to do you some service. I do not recommend you to be a soldier; but if you wish it, when I see his lordship I will ask him to help you. You shall hear from me in the course of a year or so; in the meantime make all the progress you can in reading and writing with the old clerk, and be industrious   I must be in London to-morrow, and shall soon sail for India. I shall never forget any of you."

"God bless you all!—good-bye," were the parting words of Charles Catchpole. There is in that short sentence, "Good-bye," a melancholy sense of departure which the full heart cannot express.

"Good-bye!—good-bye!" and Margaret gave vent to her grief in tears, whilst the old man clasped his hands in silent prayer.

The fond brother and affectionate son is gone; and never did Margaret see that brother again. She was shortly to change her place of abode. Her uncle Leader, who lived at Brandiston, and who had a young family, and was left a widower, sought the assistance of his niece; and though her father could but ill spare her, yet as there were so many children, and Margaret was so good a nurse, he could not refuse his consent. There was another feeling, too, which prompted the good old man to spare her. Though he loved his daughter's company, he knew that she deserved to be thought better of by many who disregarded her in her own neighbourhood, and he thought a change would be good for her. It might produce in her a change of mind towards Will Laud—a thing he most earnestly wished for, though he would not grieve her by saying so. It would at all events remove her from many little persecutions which, though she professed not to feel them, he knew weighed heavily on her spirits; and come what might, even should Laud return, he was not known there, and he might be a happier man. Under all these circumstances, he not only gave his consent, but urged her going. She left her father's roof on the Monday with her uncle.

CHAPTER XIII

POVERTY AND PRIDE

On the evening of the very day on which Margaret quitted her father's roof for that of her uncle, as the old man was sitting pensively at his cottage fire, a knock at the door announced a visitor. The door opened, and in walked Will Laud, together with his friend, John Luff.

"Good-evening, father," said Will. "We are come now from the shore. Our boat is once more moored to the rails at the landing-place, by Orwell Park, and we are come across the lands to see you. We had some difficulty in finding out your berth. You have changed your place of abode."

"Say that you have changed it for us, and you will be nearer the mark. For ever since we knew you and your companion, we have known nothing but changes, and few of them for the better."

"Things cannot always change for the worse, surely."

"I wonder you are not afraid to be seen in this part of the country. There are many here, Will, that would be glad of a hundred pounds, the price set upon your head."

"And yourself foremost of that number, I dare say," said the gruff smuggler who accompanied Will Laud.

The old man looked at him with a placid but firm countenance, and said, "That is the language of a villain! Do you think I am so fond of money as yourself; or that I would sell my daughter's lover for a hundred pounds? The door you have just opened is not yet closed, and if such be your opinion, the sooner you take your departure hence the better."

"Humph! humph!" said Luff. "You need not be so crusty, Mr. Catchpole—you need not be so boisterous. We have not seen the inside of a house

for many a long month, and if this be the first welcome
we are to have, it is rather ominous."

"What welcome do those men deserve who cause
the ruin of others ?"

"We have not intentionally caused your ruin,
father," said Laud ; "but we come in peace ; we
wish to abide in peace, and to depart in peace."

"Then you should teach your friend to keep his foul
tongue still, or it will cause you more trouble than you
are aware of."

"I miss the principal ornament of your house, Master
Catchpole," said Will. "Where are all the females
gone ?"

"Some are gone where I hope soon to join them ;
the one you feel most interest about is gone to service."

"I was told, not an hour ago, that Margaret lived
at home with you."

At this instant the door was opened, and young
Edward Catchpole entered. He had been to put his
sheep safe into fold, and came whistling home, with
little thought of seeing any strangers in his father's
cottage.

"Boy, do you know me ?" was the inquiry made by
Will Laud.

"Not yet," said the younger ; "but I can give a
shrewd guess ; and I can tell you something which
will soon prove whether I guess right or not. As I came
over the heath, I met two sailors, who appeared to me
to belong to the preventive service. They were on
horseback. They stopped and asked me if I had seen
a cart, and whether it was going fast, and which road
it took ; whether it went across the heath, or along
the road. I told them plainly it was before them,
and that it had turned down the road towards the
decoy-ponds. They then asked me if I had met
two sailor-looking men walking. To this, of course,
I said No. But I suspect they must have meant
you."

"How could that be ?" said Laud. "We came not
along the road."

"No; but you might have seen some one who was going to Nacton Street, and they might have been inquired of."

"That's true, indeed. We had to ask where your father lived, and our curiosity concerning your family has led to this pursuit of us."

"One of the men I think I have seen before, and, if I mistake not, it is the same Edward Barry that my sister and I went to see at Bawdsey boat-house."

"Your sister went to see Edward Barry! What on earth for, my lad?"

"Nay, don't be jealous, Laud. There was a report that you were drowned, and that your body was cast on shore. The bearer of that report was your rival, John Barry. Margaret would not believe that report, unless she should see your body. So I drove her there, and Edward Barry, who had the key of the boat-house, permitted her to see the bodies, which satisfied her that the report was unfounded."

The two men looked significantly at each other, as much as to say, "It is time for us to be off."

"I have one question more to ask," said Laud. "Where is Margaret?"

"She is gone to service at her Uncle Leader's, of Brandiston. It is no great place for her, but she will be out of the way of reproaches she has suffered, Laud, on your account. Moreover, she has refused the hand of a most respectable young man, whom I should have been glad that she would have accepted. But he is gone to a distant land, and neither you nor I, Will, shall see him again. John Barry has sailed, as a free settler, either to Van Diemen's Land, or to Canada, I know not which."

These words were most welcome to the listener's heart. He had not heard any which sounded so joyful to him for a long time. He made no reply, however, but tendered a purse to the old man.

"No; keep your money to yourself, Laud, and make an honest use of it. I would not touch it, if I was starving. But you may rest here if you please, and such cheer as my poor cot can afford you shall be welcome to, for my dear daughter's sake!"

"No, no, I thank you. We must be on board our ship again to-night. Our bark is in the river, and if the enemy catch us, he will show us no quarter. So good-night, father, good-night!"

"I do not wish to detain you, but hear me, Laud. If you have a mind to make my poor girl happy, leave off your present life, and this acquaintance too, this man's company."

"Come on!" said Luff, impatiently—"Come on! We've got no time to lose. Our boat will be fast upon the mud. Good-night, old man, and when you and I meet again, let us be a little more friendly to each other."

It was well for both of them that they departed as they did; for, shortly after they were gone, the tramp of horses along the road told of the return of the coast-guard.

They stopped at Catchpole's cottage, and calling aloud, young Edward went out to them.

"Hold our horses, young man, will you? we want to light our pipes."

"By all means," said Edward, coming to the little garden-gate. Both men alighted, and he could see that they were well armed. They walked directly to the door; and seeing the old man seated by the fire, one of them said—

"We want to light our pipes, Master Catchpole. It is a blustering night. Have you a tobacco-pipe, for I have broken mine rather short?"

The old man took one from his corner and gave it to young Barry, whom, from his likeness to his brother, he could distinguish, and simply said, "You are welcome to it, sir."

"Your son sent us on a wrong scent to-night."

"I do not think he did so knowingly. I heard him say he met you; and he told me he directed you aright."

"We saw nothing of the cart. We have reason to

believe that a rich cargo of goods has been landed at Felixstowe, and that the last cart-load went along this road to Ipswich. Have you had any of your old seafaring friends here ? Are there any here now? You know who I mean."

" You may search and see for yourself. Every door of this house will open at your trial. If that is sufficient answer to your question, you are welcome to take it. Nay, I wish most heartily that you and your brother had been my friends long before the one to whom you allude had ever darkened my door."

When the young man remembered his brother's attachment, and the really worthy object of it, there was a grateful feeling which came over his mind, notwithstanding the disappointment which his brother, himself, and his family had experienced, which made him feel respect for the old man.

" I thank you, Master Catchpole—I thank you. Had such been the case, you might have had a good son, and I should not have lost a good brother ; and in my conscience I believe I should have gained a good sister. But there is no accounting for a woman's taste. I tell you honestly, Master Catchpole, that for your daughter's sake I wish her lover, or the man she loves, were a worthier character."

" I know that both she and I wish it so—she with hope—I, alas ! confess that I have no hope of that. As long as he lives he will never alter, except for the worse."

" I wish it may be otherwise. But come, my mate, it is no use our waiting here, we must go on to Felixstowe. If at any time, Master Catchpole, I can be of service to you, you have nothing to do but to send a messenger to Bawdsey Ferry, and the brother of him who is now far away will do what he can to help you. Goodnight, Master Catchpole ! "

They returned to their horses, mounted them again, and telling Ned that he might drink their healths whenever he pleased, gave him sixpence, and rode off.

" Father," said Edward, when he was again seated

by the fire, " I do not—I cannot like that fellow Laud ; and how Margaret can endure him is to me strange."

"She knew him, my boy, before he became the character he now is."

" I am sorry to lose my sister ; but she will at least be better off where she is, and far away from reproaches. We must make out without her aid as well as we can. Our old sexton's sister has promised to come and do for us ; so we shall have some help."

So father and son consoled themselves ; and after their frugal meal returned to their straw-stuffed beds ; and slept upon their cares.

Meantime it was no small task that Margaret had undertaken. She was to be as a mother to seven young children, and to keep her uncle's house in order, and to provide everything to the best of her power. But her spirit was equal to the undertaking ; and the new life which came to her through change of place and people soon animated her to those exertions necessary to her position—a situation so difficult and arduous.

Place a woman in a domestic station, where the power of a mistress and the work of a servant are to be performed, and see if she cannot show what a quantity of work may be done with one pair of hands. A good head, and a kind heart, and a willing hand, are virtues which, as long as industry and honesty are praiseworthy, will be sure to succeed.

Her uncle was but a labourer, earning twelve shillings a week at the utmost, and that by working over-hours. At that time of day such wages were considered very large ; and where the housewife was active with her loom, or the aged with her spinning-wheel, labourers used sometimes to lay by something considerable, and not unfrequently rose to be themselves masters. The wages which Mr. Leader earned were sufficient, in the hands of this active girl, to provide every necessary for the week, and to lay by something for rent.

She soon made the eldest girl a good nurse ; and gave her such a method of management as saved herself much trouble. In the first place, she began her rule with a most valuable maxim of her own inculcation : " A place for everything, and everything in its place." Another of her maxims was : " Clean everything when done with, and put it up properly and promptly." Also, " Whenever you see anything wrong, put it right." " Everything that is broken should be either mended or thrown away." She would not admit of waste in anything. Among her good old saws was also :

Early to bed, and early to rise,
Makes a man healthy, and wealthy, and wise.

She would never suffer a bill to stand beyond the week at any shop. The Saturday night, at nine o'clock, saw her and her uncle's family out of debt, and the children all clean washed, with their white linen laid out for the Sabbath-day. And to see, on that holy day, with what quiet, hushed little feet they entered, four of them at least, the village church of Brandiston, with their foster-mother, was a sight which caught the attention of every well-disposed person in the parish. Master Leader's luck in a housekeeper was soon spoken of ; and many a parent pointed out Margaret as a good chance for a poor man.

Up to this time Margaret could not read a single word : but she was very glad when the vicar's lady undertook to send two of the children to the village-school. She encouraged them to learn their daily tasks, and made them teach her in the evening what they had learned at the school in the day ; and in this manner she acquired her first knowledge of letters. The children took such pleasure in teaching her, that they always paid the greatest attention to their lessons.

Margaret was now comparatively happy in the performance of her duties ; and felt relieved from the restraint and reproach which at Nacton, where her father lived, had been attached to her character, on account of William Laud. How long she might have continued in this enviable state of things it would be difficult to surmise ; but she seemed fated to encounter untoward circumstances over which she could exercise no control. She conducted herself with the greatest propriety. The children loved her as they would a kind parent; and all who knew her in the village of Brandiston esteemed her for her able conduct of her uncle's family. Had that uncle himself been a wise man, he would never have given occasion for Margaret to leave him: but no man is wise at all hours; and Mr. Leader, though a very honest, good labourer, and a steady man in his way, in an hour of too little thought, perhaps, or of too superficial promise of happiness, chose to take unto himself a new wife; a fat buxom widow of forty, owner of two cottages, and two pieces of land in Brandiston Street, and a little ready money besides, with only one little daughter, engaged his attention. He, poor simple man, thinking he might better his condition, save his rent, and add to his domestic comfort, consented, or rather entreated, that the banns might be published for his second marriage.

Had the woman herself been a wise one, she would have seen how requisite Margaret's care was to the family. But she became mistress, and must command every one in the house—her house too! and she was not to be interfered with by any one. She would not be dictated to in her own house. No! though her husband had a niece who might have been all very well, yet he had now a wife, and a wife ought to be a man's first consideration—a wife with a house over her head, her own property.

Men may have notions of the greatness of their possessions; but a weak woman, when once she has an all-absorbing and over-weening idea of her own great wealth, becomes so infatuated with the possession of power which that property gives her, that there are scarcely any bounds to her folly. Money may make some men, perhaps many, tyrants; but when a woman exercises the power of money alone, she becomes the far greater tyrant. Her fondness for wealth makes her more cruel and unnatural in her conduct; she forgets her sex—her nature—her children—her friends—her dependents—and, alas ! her God !

And soon did the new Mrs. Leader make a chaos of that family which had recently been all order and regularity. The management of household affairs was taken out of Margaret's hands. Bills were left to be paid when the new mistress received the rents of her cottages and land. The children were foolishly indulged ; turned out to play in the street ; taught to disregard Margaret, and to look upon her as a servant ; her daughter was never to be contradicted ; in short, every one in the house was to bend to the will of its new mistress.

Such a change had taken place in the comforts and conduct of the house, that Margaret, with all her care could manage nothing. She was thwarted in all she did—eyed with jealousy on account of the praise bestowed upon her—taught continually to remember and know herself and her station—and to behave with more respect to her betters, or else to quit the house.

Margaret had a sweet temper, and really loved her uncle and the children, or she could not have endured so long as she did the waywardness of this purse-proud woman.

Matters had been going on in no very pleasant manner in Mr. Leader's cottage, and Margaret had found herself in a very uncomfortable situation. She had been quite removed from her honourable station, as governess of the family, and had been treated as a very unworthy menial by her ignorant aunt.

While things were in this state, it so happened, that one evening in the month of April, Margaret was sent from her aunt's cottage to the village shop to purchase some article that was wanted for the morrow. It was late when she went out, and the shop stood completely at the end of the village. It was one of those general shops, half a good dwelling-house, and half a shop, where the respected tenant carried on a considerable business without much outward show.

A lane branched off from the main street leading

down to the vicarage, called the Church Road. It was, properly speaking, the Woodbridge Road from Brandiston. At the moment Margaret was passing over this crossway towards the shop, she was accosted by the familiar voice of one asking where Mr. William Leader lived. Margaret replied:—

"I am now come from Mr. Leader's. He is my uncle. Do you want to see him?"

"No, Margaret, it is yourself I am in search of. Do you not know my voice?"

It was William Laud!

The reader must conceive the joy, the astonishment, the surprise, the fear, or all these sensations combined in one, which Margaret, the persecuted Margaret, felt in being thus accosted by her lover. Did it require any great persuasion to induce her to turn aside at such a moment, and walk a little way down the Church Road, past the Old Hall, with one she had not seen or heard of for so long a time; one whom, with a woman's faithfulness, she still loved with all the strength of her mind and heart?

"I have been very ill, Margaret," said Laud, "since I came ashore and saw your father and brother. It was the very evening of the day you left home. Had you left one day later, I should have seen you, and, perhaps, I might have been spared a fever which has reduced me to the verge of the grave."

"It is so long since I have seen or heard of you, William, that I began to think you had forgotten me."

"I have never forgotten you, Margaret, and I never shall, till I cease to remember anything. In storm and tempest, in calm and sunshine; in the midnight watch, or under the clear blue sky; in danger or in safety, in health or in sickness; in the hour of boisterous mirth, or in the rough hammock of the seaman, when the dash of waves and the whistling winds have swept by me, Margaret, I have always thought of you; but never more than in those moments of fever and anxiety, when I have been suffering from the extremes of pain and sickness. Then, Margaret, I remembered your soothing kindness; and then I bitterly felt your absence. But have you forgotten and forgiven my rough conduct, when we last met, a long time ago? I am alone now, and but a poor creature."

"I have not forgotten, William, because I cannot forget; but I have always forgiven you. Much, much have I suffered on your account; shame, reproach, and poverty, have visited me through you—loss of kindred, friends, and companions; but God has enabled me to bear all, with the hope that I should one day see you an altered man."

"Yes, Margaret, yes; and so you shall. I am altered much—I long to leave my present line of life and to settle in some place where I never was known. Captain Bargood has given me his word, that, after one more voyage, I shall be released, with prize-money sufficient to settle anywhere I please, and to give me a free passage to that place, be-it where it may."

"I can only say, William, I wish that one voyage was over. I hate your companions and your employment. I fear to lose you again, William. Oh, why not get some honest work on land, and let me toil for and with you?"

"Margaret, I am here upon my word of honour to the captain, that I would go one more run for him. I have been a long trip this last time, across the Atlantic, and I am promised a different tack the next time. But it will soon be over, and then I will renounce them all. The captain has nursed me in his own house, and though a rough fellow and a poor comforter for a sick man, yet I believe he did his best, and I am bound to be grateful to him."

"I wish your duty taught you, Will, some better obligation. My heart misgives me for you; and I can never sanction a day in unlawful pursuits. I grieve for you. But time steals away, William, and I have forgotten my own duty. I have not a very kind mistress in my new aunt; but my duty is obedience. I have to go to shop now, and I fear it will be closed if I delay any longer. When shall I see you again, William?"

"I fear me, not until this last voyage is over. I hope that will be a short one. I shall just go into the King's Head, refresh myself, and start again for the coast by daylight."

"Well, William, you have my prayers and my love, and I hope you may one day claim my duty. At present, that duty is due to my uncle. So we must part!—Take care of yourself.—How did you catch that fever?"

"By over-exertion in returning to my boat by Orwell Park, the night I left your father. We struck across the country, as we heard of our pursuers, and came to the shore greatly heated with our run. The wind was fair for us, and I had nothing else to do but to sit still. I covered myself with a piece of damp sail and fell asleep, and when I awoke I found myself as stiff as a mast—I could not move a limb. But I will take care of myself for your sake, Margaret, for the future."

By this time they had just arrived at the vicarage palings, upon their return, where the angle of the street branched off, and for a moment they paused to take the farewell salute which faithful lovers ever appreciate.

They little thought who was near to hear their last parting words, and to witness that love which they thought no one but themselves beheld. The farewell was spoken, and Laud departed. Margaret stood a moment, with affectionate heart and tearful eye, to watch his receding form, and then, turning round the corner to go to the shop, she encountered the enraged Mrs. Leader. She could only walk on in passive silence through the village, whilst her aunt's voice, rising higher and higher as she approached her own domicile, made the neighbours peep out of their windows to learn the cause of such a disturbance. At last they arrived at home, and Mr. Leader, with a thousand exaggerations, was informed of his niece's atrocious conduct.

She eyed the poor girl with such malignant satisfaction, as if she had already seen her condemned, by judge, jury, counsel, and all the court. Poor Margaret! she had not attempted to speak; she felt for her uncle—she felt for his children—she felt for her lover; but for herself, nothing. She knew her own heart, and felt keenly the cruelty and injustice of her aunt's spiteful accusations; but that did not wound her so much as to see the crestfallen distress of the master of that cottage, who, but a short time before, never addressed her but in thanks or praise.

Margaret sighed, looked at her uncle, and briefly explained her accidental meeting with William Laud.

This only caused Mrs. Leader to break out into a fresh passion. She abused her husband, abused Margaret, her lover, her father, her brother, and every one connected with her. The base reflections she heard cast upon her family roused the poor girl's indignation, and, after telling the enraged woman a few home truths, expressed her determination to quit the house.

"I shall leave you now—yes, before another hour is gone. I shall only kiss the children, pack up my little bundle, and then I take my departure. Uncle, I have done my duty by you, and I sincerely wish you happy. I have had nothing of you, and have nothing to leave behind me, but my humble blessing for yourself and your children. Give me your hand, uncle; let *us*, at all events, part good friends. You know that I do not mind the night. A journey to me at this time, under these circumstances, is no more than a journey would be by day. As to you, aunt Leader, whether you shake hands with me or not must rest with your own self. I would not part even with you in malice. Good-bye, aunt Leader. Good-night!"

Mrs. Leader had heard enough; she had met with a spirit which, when roused, was equal to her own; and though she looked as if she could have dashed the poker at the poor girl before her, she dared not stir an inch: the fury fell back from her seat, and went off in a fit.

Margaret stayed that night, but not another day.

The next morning she set her uncle's breakfast out, saw the children dressed, and sent to the school, and then went upstairs to pack up her own bundle. Before doing so, however, the Bible, which had been given her by John Barry, attracted her attention. It was a small clasped book, and, from being unable to read it, she had never made any outward parade of her possession of it. On now seeing it, she mechanically unclasped the book, and in the first page there lay a £5 banknote, and in the last page another of the same value. What a treasure was here! How did her heart bless the noble generosity of the youth who, at a time when money was of the greatest value to him, thus sacrificed a great share of his riches to the welfare of one who could never personally thank him for it!

Margaret had made up her mind, however, to seek a situation for herself in Ipswich. She remembered the kindness of the worthy surgeon who had attended her sister in her childhood, and poor John Barry when he was wounded, and she resolved to seek his aid. With a full heart, she carefully replaced the notes as she found them, resolving to store them up against a time of need. And, with more consciousness of independence than she had ever before felt, she packed up her little bundle, and went to take leave of her uncle and aunt.

With five shillings, the gift of her uncle, a half-guinea, the gift of her brother Charles, and a bundle, not a very weighty one, Margaret Catchpole departed from Brandiston. But, fearing her aunt's displeasure, and that she would send strange reports to Nacton, and that her own presence under her father's roof would give some countenance to these malicious falsehoods, she determined not to return home, but to take the road to Woodbridge.

At that time, Noller's wagon, from Ipswich to Woodbridge, Wickham Market, and Framlingham, passed her upon its return; and the driver asking her if she would like to ride, she gladly accepted the offer. They arrived at Ipswich about two o'clock

in the afternoon.   Margaret determined to seek a place
immediately, and for that purpose brushed the dust
off her gown, and made herself as decent as her poor
wardrobe would allow, and arrived at the door of
Mr. George Stebbing, under very different circumstances from those which had formerly brought her
to the same spot.

CHAPTER XIV

A CHEERFUL CHANGE

HE was a merry, cheerful man, the active surgeon,
who lived in the tall, red-bricked house, in Orwell
Place. His practice was good, extending from the
best families in the town and neighbourhood of Ipswich,
to that which is always the most benevolent part of
a surgeon's duty, the dispensing medicine and advice
to the poor. George Stebbing was an early riser, and
a very active practitioner ; he was skilful and attentive ; and it was truly said of him, that he never
neglected a poor patient to attend a rich one. He
had his rounds before breakfast, among his poorer
patients ; next his town practice ; and his country
visits in the afternoon. He generally contrived to be
found at home from nine to ten o'clock in the morning ;
and from two to three in the afternoon, always dining
at one.

There was one passion, if it may be so called, which,
at certain seasons of the year, made the doctor break
through all his rules and regulations, and to which
he so willingly gave way, as to cause him serious loss
of practice among family patients, who could not
make allowances for his neglect,—namely, a passion
for shooting. He was an excellent shot, delighted
in the exercise, and enjoyed it as much in his old days
as he did in his youth. His figure scarcely ever altered
through life. He never grew corpulent, never inactive ;

but retained his zest for his gun, with a steady hand, to a good old age.

But for this passion for shooting, the doctor might have secured for himself a more extensive and lucrative practice. It certainly was a kind of passport among many great landed proprietors, who liked his shooting and his society, and for a good day's shooting, come it when it might, many of his patients were neglected. He was of a very generous nature, and sometimes felt keenly the reproaches of those whom for the sports of the field he deserted ; and there were times in which his own conscious neglect made him sorrowful ; but it did not cure him of his favourite propensity. At all other times, he was as regular as a well-cleaned clock.

Margaret arrived at this gentleman's door, and was shown into the surgery just as he was preparing to go into the country. The surgery was a lofty room, though of small dimensions ; the window looked down a neatly paved area, beside the offices of the house ; and flower-stands, filled with geraniums and other green-house plants, stood against the side of the wall opposite the kitchen. All was neatness within and without the walls of his house.

She had scarcely been seated in the surgery a minute, before in came the merry man, with his cheerful smile and ready address. "Well, young woman, what's the matter with you, eh ? What is it ? A bad tooth ? let us see—let us see. It can be nothing else. You look the picture of health ! What's the matter ? "

"Nothing is the matter, sir," said Margaret, rising and curtsying.

"Then what do you want with the doctor, my girl ? "

"I am come to ask you, sir, if you could help me to a place."

"A place ! " cried the doctor ; "why, whom do you take me for ? Did you think my surgery was a register-office for servants ? What have I to do with places ? Who on earth sent you to me ? "

"No one sent me, sir; I came of my own accord, because you are the only person that I know in Ipswich."

"Well, they say a great many more people know Tom Fool than Tom Fool knows. I don't recollect ever seeing you before. I know not who you are in the least."

"What, sir! do you not remember when you lifted me off the pony at your door, ever so many years ago, and called me a brave little girl, and told me, when you left me at my father's, that if ever I wanted a friend I should find one in you?"

"What! are you the girl that made the pony go? Can you be Margaret Catchpole, the heroine of Nacton Turf?"

"I am Margaret, sir; I left my uncle's, at Brandiston, this morning, and am come to Ipswich in search of a place. I have lost my sister, my mother, and two brothers, and, knowing no one in Ipswich but you, I thought, sir, as you promised to help me, you would not be offended at my asking. I only want to work and live without being burdensome to any one."

"Well, and what place do you want, my girl?"

"I can do any kind of plain work, sir, from the cow-house to the nursery."

"Nursery! nursery! do you know anything about the care of children?"

"I am very partial to children, sir, and children are very fond of me; my uncle had seven little ones, and only me to look after them until he married again."

"Humph!—Well, go into my kitchen, my girl"— and here the kind-hearted man opened his door and introduced her to his cook. "Sally, this is the girl that rode the pony for the doctor, see and take care of her. Where is your young mistress?" But suddenly turning round as if a thought struck him he said, "Margaret! Margaret! my girl, stop one moment, I must know if you have quite recovered from that complaint you had before you left the Priory Farm ? "

" Dear me, sir, I never was ill there."

" Oh! yes, you were, Margaret; if you remember, I had to feel your pulse and prescribe for you; your heart was very bad ? "

" Oh! no, sir, I hope not."

" Let me ask you one question, Margaret—Have you done with the smuggler ? Because, though I should be glad to serve *you,* I should be sorry to run the risk of introducing bad acquaintances into any respectable family where I might recommend you."

This was another terrible blow for poor Margaret, and how to answer it she knew not; she remained silent and abashed, and the worthy surgeon was touched more by her silence than if she had spoken ever so much; it told him at once the state of the case.

" Well, well, my girl, I see how it is; but you must not encourage him to visit you when you are at service. Go! go! I will talk to you another time."

And Margaret was again an inmate in that kind man's house, who always was a steady and sincere friend to her throughout her eventful career. He had at that very time made up his mind to write a note of recommendation to a lady who lived at the Cliff, upon the banks of the Orwell; but he delayed it for a day or two, on purpose to hear what report his own domestic gave of her. And here Margaret remained in the humblest and purest enjoyment of peace and quietness that she had felt for many years.

It was a lovely evening in the latter part of the month of May, when the mackerel-boats were coming up the Orwell, being unable to reach the mouth of the Nore, that old Colson (better known to the reader as Robinson Crusoe) rowed his little boat up to the landing-place, close to the Cliff Brewery, and startled some young children who were watching the tiny eels playing about those large dark stones which formed the head of the landing-place. Here a stream of fresh water, gushing from beneath, formed the outlet of the canal stream which turned the great wheel in the brewery of John Cobbold, Esq.

The eels from the river, especially the young ones, used to be incessantly playing about this outlet, striving either to get up into the fresh water, or else feeding upon the animalculæ which came from the canal, and tried to get back again out of the salt water.

The old man lifted up some small sand-dabs for the children, all alive and kicking, and gave them to them, with which they soon bounded up the Cliff steps, and ran joyously to a lady, who, with two gentlemen, sat sketching under the lime-trees which then fronted the small dwelling-house adjoining the more lofty buildings of the brewery.

The lady was Mrs. Cobbold, and the two gentlemen were her friends, and both eminent artists in their day. One had already greatly distinguished himself as a portrait-painter, and vied with Sir Joshua Reynolds in his own particular school of painting: this was Gardiner, a distant relative of the lady. He was a singular old gentleman, in every way a talented original; his family groups, in half crayon, half water-colour, gained general admiration; and to this day they stand the test of years, never losing their peculiar freshness, and remain as spirited as on the first day they were painted. The other was indeed but a boy, a fine intelligent lad, with handsome, open countenance, beaming with all the ardour of a young aspirant for fame: this was John Constable, who was then sketching the town of Ipswich from the Cliff, and brushing in the tints of the setting sun, and receiving those early praises from the lips of that benevolent and talented lady which became a stimulus to his exertions, before he was raised to the eminence of a first-rate landscape-painter.

Gardiner delighted in the buoyant group of children, who, with their flapping fish, came bounding up the Cliff. "Look here! look here! see what old Robin has given us."

The artist's eyes dilated with glee as he quickly noted down their jocund faces and merry antics for some future painting. If he had experienced pleasure in the character of James, Thomas, George, Elizabeth Ann, and Mary, what a fine master-figure was now added to the group in the person of old Robin, the fisherman, who, with his basket of mackerel and soles, stood behind the children in front of the happy party!

Gardiner's picture of the "Fisherman's Family" was taken from this group, and it was one which in his mature years gained him much celebrity.

"Well, Robin, what fish have you got?" said the lady, "and how do the witches treat you?"

"As to the first, madam, here are mackerel and soles; as to the latter, they treat me scurvily?"

"What's that? what's that?" said Gardiner; "what's all that about the witches?"

Old Colson looked at him a minute, and partly believed he was a brother sufferer; for Gardiner never was what the world has since denominated a dandy, he was never even a beau; he was careless in his dress, and very abrupt in his address,—extremely clever and extremely eccentric.

"Why, this is it," said the old fisherman, "if the foul fiend treats you as he does me, he makes us both such hideous objects that nobody can bear to look at us."

There was no little colour in the artist's face at this moment: he had met with a light and shade, an odd mixture upon his palette not easily defined, and he looked himself rather vacant upon the fisherman.

"I see how it is," said Robin; "they have been at work upon you, and have put your robes out of order; but give them a blast of this ram's horn, and you will soon get rid of them."

Here the old man presented a ram's horn to the astonished artist.

"What does the man mean, Mrs. Cobbold? what does the man mean?"

This was rather a delicate point to answer; but the little shrewd Mary, who perfectly well knew what the old man meant, said at once with the most perfect innocence—

"Oh, Mr. Gardiner! Robin means that you look so dirty and shabby that you must be bewitched."

At this moment a servant brought a note to the lady, which, on opening, she read as follows:—

"MY DEAR MADAM,

"You mentioned to me some time since that you wanted a good strong girl who could assist in the double capacity of a laundress and a nursery-maid; the bearer of this is Margaret Catchpole, whom I have known from her infancy. My cook tells me she is very quick at learning, and very handy at any work that may be required of her; she also states herself to be very fond of children. She lived servant-of-all-work at the Priory Farm, and has since kept her uncle's house, where she has had the care of seven young children. Mr. Notcutt, who knew her when she lived at service at Bealings, speaks highly of her character. I think you will find her a very useful servant; and if you have not engaged one, I really think you will be satisfied with this young woman. Wishing that such may be the case, believe me to remain, my dear madam, yours faithfully,

"GEORGE STEBBING.

"Orwell Place,
"May 25th, 1793."

As Mrs. Cobbold opened the note, the artists retired; and she told the footman to send the young woman round to the front of the house, and she would speak to her there. She then kindly addressed the old fisherman:—

"I wish, Robin, I could find a charm which would drive all these fiends away from you at once, that you might become a believer in a more blessed agency than in such unhappy beings."

"Ah! bless you, lady! bless you! If your wish could but be gratified, I should soon be at liberty; but it will never be so: they have taken up their abode with me, and as long as they can torment me, they will. I knew last night that there would be a storm, and, sure enough, there was one; but my old barque rode it out, though many a tighter craft went to the bottom. My foes, though they love to punish my flesh, will not let me perish."

"That is but a vain hope, Robin, which will one day deceive you: you trust too much in your crazy barque, and to a no less crazy imagination; and, when too late, you will own your self-delusion."

His benefactress could not succeed in arguing him out of his belief, and had just told him to leave the fish at the back-door, as Margaret made her appearance before her future mistress.

She started back when she beheld Robin, and again thought that some evil genius had determined to oppose her wherever she went.

"Ah! is that you, Peggy? It's many a long day since I've seen you. Have the fiends played you any more tricks?"

Margaret made her curtsy to the lady, but dared not reply to the salutation of the old fisherman, lest he should betray the secret of her heart. She was evidently confused.

"You need not be so proud either, young woman, as to forget a friend; but you are like the rest of the world:—'Those whom we first serve are the first to forget us.' Now, to my mind, you're a fit match for Will Laud, and he's about as ungracious a chap as any I know."

The tear started into Margaret's eye, and she could not utter a word. In the accents of kindness, however, the lady addressed the trembling girl.

"You must not mind all the wanderings of old Robin, you will be better acquainted with him here-after."

"And so will you, ma'am, with her before long.

The foul fiend has long dwelt with her and hers, and you'll soon find that out. I've known her almost as long as I've known you, ma'am; and if she's a-coming to your service, why, all I can say is, there will be pretty pranks a-going on in your house."

Here the poor girl could refrain no longer from tears; she sobbed as if her heart would break, and the scene more than commonly interested the benevolent lady.

"What has Robin known of you, young woman, that he should speak so harshly against you? How have you offended him?"

"I never offended him, ma'am—never that I know of! He was very kind to me, and once, ma'am— once——" and here Margaret paused, and could not finish her sentence.

Robin now quickly saw he was mistaken, and going close up to the girl, he said,—

"I ask your pardon, Peggy! I thought you were proud—I see how it is! I see how it is!—Forgive me! forgive me, ma'am! She's a good girl; aye, she's a clever girl! I thought she was a bit proud, so the fiend made me bark at her, that's all;" and, making his bow, he went with his basket of fish to the back-door.

The lady evidently saw there was a mystery; but, well knowing the sudden changes of the bewildered mind of the fisherman, although she always found a shadow of truth about all his ravings, she placed no faith in any of his prognostications. She did not again question Margaret upon that subject, but spoke to her about her duties. She found her fully sensible of what she might have to do, and quite ready to undertake the place. She agreed to give her, progressively improving wages, and told her that as Mr. Stebbing had given her a recommendation, she should try her. Mrs. Cobbold desired her to come on the morrow, and wished her good-evening.

The next day saw Margaret an inmate of that family where her name will never be forgotten; where she spent so many days of real, uninterrupted happiness ; where she became respected by her mistress and family, and was a very great favourite with all her fellow-servants. Margaret came to her new place with a good character ; with youth, health, hope, and a willing mind for work. By the advice of the doctor's old servant, she came (by means of John Barry's generous gift) with every article clean, new, and decent, and had the sum of six pounds left for a nest-egg.

CHAPTER XV

THE NEW PLACE

THERE is no class of persons in society so much neglected as domestic servants, none who are placed in more responsible stations, to whom more confidence is given, and from whom more is expected ; yet there are none who are less instructed, except in the duties of their stations, and even these they have to learn as they can. The law visits no one with severer penalties for any dereliction of duty ; and the world makes fewer allowances for their faults than for those of any other class.

The excellent lady in whose service Margaret was placed was one who felt this truth, and took every opportunity she could to improve the minds of all who came under her roof. She was one of the most enlightened of her sex, with a mind cultivated to the highest degree, and acquainted from her infancy with many of the leading persons of the day, in art, litera-ture, and science. And she was not less domestic than enlightened. The writer of these pages knew her well, and loved her dearly. He admired her with deep and reverential love. He was not able, indeed, to appreciate the full extent of her benevolent character till years had snatched her away, and left him " never to look upon her like again." This he can truly say, that, in the course of twenty years' acquaintance, he never knew what it was to have a dull moment in her company. Lest any may think this is saying too much, let some of those who now occupy public stations of importance, and some of whom were her domestic servants, say, how much they were indebted to her instructions. Let some, even of a higher and more independent class, who have since attained the pinnacle of their professions, tell how much they were indebted to the first encouraging advice of her, who saw and prized their talents, and rejoiced in their development. She was a most kind benefactress to all who needed her advice or assistance, and to none was she a greater friend, and by none was she more deeply loved, than by the poor girl whom she took into her service, as a sort of general help in the humblest station in her family.

At the Cliff there was not a single individual in whom the mistress did not feel a deep interest. None were beneath her notice; none came near her whom she did not strive to improve. Though she commanded the hearts of many highly distinguished persons in the drawing-room, she commanded the affections of her family, and of every servant under her roof. Poor Margaret appeared to her an object of peculiar interest. Ignorant as she found her in letters, and in many things relating to her situation, there was in her a capacity, which this lady discovered, to require nothing but instruction to perfect it. Readily did she comprehend when the kindness of her mistress was shown in condescending to teach her, and rapid was the progress she made in everything explained to her.

Margaret had a difficult situation to fulfil even in the household arrangements of this excellent lady; for she was under-nursemaid in the morning, and under-cook in the evening; two very different stations, but both of which she discharged with fidelity, and at length rose in that family to fill the head place in both stations at different periods.

Her mistress had married a gentleman who had fourteen children living at the time, and she had every prospect of seeing the number increase. It required a woman of energy to direct the household affairs of such a numerous family, as well as a woman of method and management in the nursery. Well did Margaret second the work which the head nurse had in hand. No one could be more indefatigable in her duties—none more constantly employed.

It was Margaret's especial province to walk out with the children, to carry the young ones, and to lead now and then an elder one. A retired and pleasant walk it was at the back of the Cliff to Sawyer's Farm, either along the river's side to the Grove, or Hog Island, or through the farmyard, up the sandy hill, from the top of which Ipswich and its environs were so conspicuous. In all the innocent enjoyments of children, Margaret took particular delight. She would make chains of dandelions, whistles of cats' tails; collect lords and ladies, string ladies' hair; make whips of rushes for the boys, and cradles for dolls for the girls. Her eyes were ever watchful, her hands ever useful. The children loved her, and bounded to her with pleasure, whenever the order was given for a walk. She was equally dauntless in their defence, whether it was against a dog, or the geese, or the cattle of the field, or the gipsy, or the drunken sailor.

During this service, an occurrence took place of a singularly providential nature, which showed the sagacity of this poor girl, and her presence of mind in so striking a light, that it is well worthy to be here recorded. The children were all going for a walk, and Master George and Master Frederic were listening at a rat's hole, under the foundation of a building, where the workmen were making some alterations, and had taken away a great deal of the soil, upon one side of the brickwork. As Margaret came up with some half-dozen of the young fry, the boys exultingly called to her to come and hear the old rat gnawing something in the hole.

Margaret approached, and with that natural quickness of perception with which she was so gifted, saw danger in the situation of the children. Listening one moment at the hole she was convinced that the creaking sound she heard did not proceed from a rat. In another instant she seized the children by their arms, and exclaimed, with a terror that communicated itself to them all, "Come away! come away! that wall is settling!" Scarcely had she ran with the children half a dozen yards from the spot, when down came the wall in a mass of ruin that must have buried them all beneath it but for the providential sagacity of this young girl. To this day the circumstance is remembered by the parties interested in it, and is looked upon as the interposition of their good angel, in making use of this humble instrument for the preservation of their lives.

Margaret, by this time, could both read and write; for the lady, who superintended the whole management of the nursery, had her regular school-hours in the morning devoted to the minutiae of progressive improvement. It was at one of these morning lessons that she discovered Margaret's abilities. Hearing the children their lessons in history, and examining them in the chronology of the kings of England, she was surprised to hear Margaret prompting Miss Sophia, in a whisper, when the child was at a loss for the right date. And when she came to question Margaret, she found that this poor girl had been, though unknown to her, her most attentive scholar. This induced her to take pains with her, and to let her be a participator in all the most useful branches of a nursery education. She was taught to read and write, and understand the Bible history and the Gospel scheme of redemption; in all which studies she became as well informed as any of the children. Soon after this, she rose to be the head nursemaid.

As the winter came on, the walks became more circumscribed; and though she occasionally saw the old fisherman, with his basket of soles and plaice, yet from him she could gather no tidings of her lover, good or bad. To hear nothing may be better than to hear bad tidings; but some may even think that bad news is better than none at all. The certain knowledge of any catastrophe, if it has taken place, at ever so great a distance, is always more satisfactory and consoling than years of agonizing suspense.

Perhaps some such ideas might have passed in Margaret's mind; but she had been so accustomed to hear nothing that was good of her lover, that she began to construe the long interregnum of his non-appearance into the hope of some permanent amendment.

The Orwell, at the period of our narrative, and during the winter season, was famous for its wild-fowl. At some particular times, when the decoy-ponds around were frozen over, the birds used to come into the channel of the river in prodigious flights, covering hundreds of acres of water with their varieties of plumage. Millions of black coot used to darken the waves, whilst the duck and the mallard, the diver, the pin-tail, the bar-goose, and even the wild swan, used to be seen in such numbers, as in the present day would seem to be incredible. Those, however, who can remember this river only fifty years ago will fully corroborate this account. Some live at Ipswich, at this day, who can well remember the time in which they have made dreadful havoc among the feathered tribes of the river. Now and then a solitary flight may here and there be seen visiting the river in the evening, and departing with the dawn. Since the port of Ipswich has so rapidly increased its shipping, the traffic of winter, as well as summer, has been so constant, that the birds have sought some quieter feeding-ground than the ooze of the Orwell.

It was at the time when these birds were most frequent, that the young fowlers of the port used to have extraordinary tales to tell of the numbers they had killed, and the escapes and adventures they had met with in the pursuit. One of Mr. Cobbold's younger sons had a great *penchant* for this sport, and, though

quite a lad, would venture upon the most hardy enter-
prises with the weather-beaten sailors, who had been
long accustomed to the river. He was a good shot,
too, for a boy, and would bring home many a duck
and mallard as the fruits of his own excursions.

It was about four o'clock, one winter evening, when
this young gentleman was seen descending the steps
of the Cliff, with the oars over his shoulder, and his
gun in his hand. He looked at the cloudy sky, and
thought he should have good sport upon the river
before the morning. His sisters, Harriet and Sophia,
saw him stealing down the Cliff, and he requested of
them not to take any notice of his absence. He un-
locked his boat, and shoved off into the channel alone,
rejoicing in the thought of the *spolia opima* he
should expose next morning at the breakfast-table.

At tea-time, all the numerous party seated themselves
round the table, before piles of hot toast and bread and
butter ; and the venerated father came from his own
private room to take his seat with his affectionate wife
and children. He cast his eye upon the party, and
looked round the room, evidently missing one of his
children. " Where 's William ? " he inquired. The
sisters, Harriet and Sophia, began to titter. " Where 's
William ? " again asked the anxious parent ; and the
lady, who had been reading some new book, which had
absorbed her attention, had not until then missed
the boy.

Mr. Parkinson, the confidential clerk, a distant
relative, replied, " Master William has gone out in
his boat to shoot wild-fowl."

" What ! on such a night as this ? How long
since ? "

" Two hours or more, sir."

The worthy parent rose from his seat, summoned
the clerk to follow him immediately, and, with a fearful
expression of countenance, which communicated terror
to the whole party, he said, " Depend upon it, the
child is lost ! "

It was a night on which no reasonable man would

have suffered even the stoutest and strongest sailor to go down the river for such a purpose. The tide was running out fast, and the ice was floating down in great masses, enough to stave a stout boat. A piercing sleet, the forerunner of a snow-storm, drifted along with the wind. Altogether it was as dismal as darkness and the foreboding anxiety of a fond parent's heart could make it. Yet Master William, a mere stripling, was upon the waters, in a boat which required at least two stout men to manage her, and at the mercy of the storm. Had not his father by mere chance missed him, and made inquiries about him, he would not have been heard of till the next morning, and then they would have spoken of his death. As it was, the sequel will show how nearly that event came to pass.

The brewhouse men were summoned, two stout fellows, who were put into the small boat, and it then came out that Master William had taken the oars belonging to the little boat, to manage a great, heavy craft that was large enough to hold a dozen men.

Mr. Cobbold and his clerk went along the shore, whilst the two men in the skiff, with great oars, shoved along the edge of the channel. Occasionally the parties communicated by voice, when the lull of the waves and winds permitted them to do so ; but no tidings of the lost boy could be obtained.

What agony did that truly good father endure, yet how mild was his censure of those who ought to have prevented such a lad incurring such danger !

In the midst of these anxieties, there was one who shared them with as much earnestness as if she had been the mother of the child ; and this was Margaret Catchpole. No weather, no winds, no commands of her master's, could overrule that determined activity of mind which this girl possessed, to lend a helping hand in time of danger. She had thrown her cloak over her head, and followed her master with the hope that she might be of some service.

The party on the shore could no longer hear even

the voices of those who were in the boat, as the channel
took them round the bed of ooze to the opposite shore.
Still did they pursue their course, calling aloud, and
stopping to listen for some faint sound in reply. Nothing
answered their anxious call but the cold moaning of
the wintry wind. They stretched their eyes in vain;
they could see nothing: and they had walked miles
along the shore, passing by the Grove, Hog Island,
and the Long Reach, until they came to Downham
Reach. No soul had they met, nor had any sound,
save the whistling of the curlew and the winds, greeted
their ears. The anxious father, down whose cheeks
tears began to steal and to stiffen with the frost, gave
his dear son up for lost. He had lived so long by
the river, and knew so well its dangers, that it seemed
to him an impossibility he should be saved; and he
turned round just by the opening to the Priory Farm,
and said to his clerk, "We must give it up;" when
Margaret said, "Oh, no, sir, not yet; pray do not
give it up yet! Let us go on farther! Do not go home
yet."

Thus urged, her master turned again to pursue the
search, and she followed in his path.

About a hundred yards onwards, under the shade
of the wood, they met a man.

"Who goes there?" was the question of the anxious
father.

"What 's that to you?" was the rough uncourteous
reply, strangely grating to the father's heart at such
a moment.

In those rough sounds Margaret recognized Will
Laud's voice. She sprang forward, exclaiming, to
the no small astonishment of her master, "Oh, William!
Mr. Cobbold has lost his son! Do lend a hand to find
him."

It is needless to dwell upon the mutual surprise of
both parties at such a rencontre. Laud was equally
astonished at Margaret's presence at such a time,
and Margaret herself felt an indescribable hope that
her lover might render some effectual service.

"I beg pardon, sir," said Laud, "but I did not know you."

"My son went down the river in a boat some three or four hours since, and I fear he is lost," said Mr. Cobbold.

"I came up the river as far as I could, and have seen no boat. The floats of ice were so troublesome, that I resolved to come ashore, and walk to Ipswich. Had there been a boat between Harwich and the Nacton shore, I must have seen it. I landed close by Cowhall, and I know there was no boat on the river, at least so far."

At that moment they thought they heard some one call. They listened, and plainly heard the men hallooing from the boat.

"Ahoy! Ahoy!" called out Will Laud.

They then listened again, and recognized the voice of Richard Lee, one of the brewing-men, who called out,—

"We have found the boat, but no one in her."

"Aye, sir," said Will Laud, "then the young gentleman has got ashore!"

"I fear not!" said the father; "I fear he is lost!"

Laud feared the same, when he heard that the young lad had taken no mud-splashers with him: "But," he added, "if the youth knew the river, he would get out of his boat, and walk by the edge of the channel till he came to this hardware, and then he might get ashore."

"What is that dark spot yonder, by the edge of the water?" said Margaret, as she stooped down to let her eye glance along the dark level line of the mud.

"It is only one of the buoys," said the father, "such as they moor ships to in the reach."

"There is no buoy in that part of the river," said Will. "Margaret sees something, and so do I now. I don't know what it is, but I soon will though."

And without more ado, he stepped on to the mud and was soon upon all-fours, creeping along, and dragging his body over the softest places of the ooze, where he must have sunk into the mud up to his waist, if he had kept an erect posture. As he advanced, he evidently saw something lying close to the water's edge, and, after great toil, he came up to it. True enough he found it to be the stiff body of the poor youth they had been in search of. Lifting himself up, he called aloud, "Ahoy! ahoy! Margaret, you are right;" words of such joy as were never forgotten in after years by any of that party.

Laud lost no time in hoisting the poor boy on his back, and, tying his stiff hands round his own neck with his handkerchief, he crept upon the mud again toward that shore where stood those anxious friends awaiting his approach. The boy was, to all appearance, stiff and lifeless. The hair of his head was one matted mass of ice and mud; his limbs were stiff and frozen; one leg seemed like a log of hard wood, the other they could bend a little. He had been up to his neck in the mud, and had evidently been overcome with the exertion of extricating himself. His clothes were drawn off his back, and had been used as mud-splashers, until exhausted nature could make no further effort, and he had sunk, unconscious, upon the ooze. Death seemed to have done his work.

The only plan now was to get him home as soon as they could. Laud soon constructed a carriage for him, of a hurdle, upon which he laid his own jacket, the father's great-coat, and over him he threw Margaret's cloak. Each of the four persons taking a corner of the hurdle upon their shoulders, they made their way, as fast as possible, along the shore. In this way they proceeded at a good round pace, until they reached the Grove-side, where they met the other servants, coming in company with the two brewhouse-men, with blankets and brandy, in case Master William should be found. Their arrival was very opportune, as it enabled the exhausted party to transfer their burden to the new comers. Mr. Cobbold expressed his gratitude to Laud, and asked him to come on to the Cliff, and rest himself that night, and he would endeavour to repay him in the morning.

"I thank you, sir," said Laud; "I was coming to see Margaret, and if you would only grant me a word or two with her, it is all the favour I ask."

"As many as you please, my man; but it would be better for her and you, too, to be at the kitchen fire such a night as this, than to be talking upon the banks of the Orwell."

Laud seemed to hesitate; at last he said, "Well, sir, I will come."

Soon afterwards the thoughtful Margaret said to Mr. Cobbold, "Had I not better run forward, sir, and prepare the slipper-bath, and get the fire lit in the bed-room, and have warm blankets ready, and send off for Dr. Stebbing?"

"Right, Margaret, right!" was her master's reply; "run, my girl, run! It will be good for you, too. We shall soon follow you."

On went the damsel, and soon passed the men carrying their young master, and was the first who brought the joyful tidings that Master William was found. In all her plans, however, she was anticipated by her ever-thoughtful mistress. The amber room was prepared, as being the quietest in the house. The bath, the hot water, the salt to rub his benumbed limbs, were all ready; for it was concluded, that if he was found, he would be in such a state of paralysation, from the effects of the weather, as would make it a work of time to recover him. The boy was sent off immediately for Mr. Stebbing. The whole family were in a state of hushed and whispering anxiety. The two sisters, especially, who had seen their brother depart, and had not spoken a word about it, were deeply bewailing their own faults. In short, all was anxiety, all was expectation, almost breathless suspense. Margaret's description to her mistress was clear, simple, and concise. Her meeting with a sailor, whom she knew when she lived at Priory Farm, and his acquaintance with all the buoys on the river, all seemed natural and providential. She gave orders immediately for a bed to be prepared in the coachman's room for the sailor, to whose exertions they were so indebted for the restoration of the child, dead or alive, to his affectionate parents.

Voices were soon heard coming up the road from the shrubbery, and the first who entered the house was the father, supporting the head, whilst the others raised the body of the poor boy. Every exertion was now used, but for some time no symptoms of life could be observed in him. The doctor arrived, and he perfectly approved of the steps which had been taken. He opened a vein, from which the smallest drop of blood exuded. This he counted a good symptom. He then ordered a bath, at first merely tepid, and by degrees made warmer. The blood began to flow a little faster from the arm, and the doctor felt increased hope that the vital functions were not extinct. With joy he noticed the beginning of a gentle pulsation of the heart, and a few minutes afterwards of the wrist, and pointed out these favourable symptoms to the anxious parents. A little brandy was now forced into the throat. The lips, which had hitherto been livid as death, began to show a slight change. At length, in the midst of anxious exertions, the chest began to heave, and the lungs to obtain a little play ; a sort of bubbling sound became audible from the throat ; and, shortly afterwards, a moan, and then the eyelids half unclosed, though with no consciousness of sight. Convulsive shudders began to creep over the frame— an indication that a warmer bath would be judicious. This was soon effected. As the warmth circulated through the veins, the hands began to move, the eyes to open wider, and to wander wildly over the space between them. At length they seemed to rest upon the face of Margaret, who stood at the foot of the bath, and down whose cheeks tears of hope literally chased each other. A faint smile was seen to play upon his lips, which told that recognition was returning. He was then removed from the warm bath to his warm bed.

An hour afterwards, and their unwearied exertions were rewarded with hearing Master William pronounce the name of "Margaret." Though so weak that he could not lift his hand, yet his tongue whispered her name, as if he felt she had been his preserver.

He shortly afterwards interchanged smiles with the doctor and his sisters, and presently afterwards, with his father's hand clasped in his, he fell asleep.

CHAPTER XVI

BRIGHT HOPES

IT is not surprising that Laud, as he stood by the kitchen-fire, and scraped off the mud, a mixture of clay, weeds, and samphire, which were clotted upon his coarse trousers, should be considered by the tenants of that part of the house as a person worthy of all admiration. He had signalized himself in more than one pair of eyes. The master of the family and the head clerk had beheld his prowess, and had spoken most highly of him. They had given orders that whatever he required should be furnished for him. No wonder, then, that in Tom's, John's, or Sally's eyes, he should shine with such increased lustre. In Margaret's he was beheld with those feelings of love, and hope, and joy, which anticipated rapid improvement after long drawbacks, and she saw the object of her attachment at the most happy and propitious moment of her existence. The joy of that evening was unalloyed. Master William was recovering. The grateful father made Will and all his servants enjoy a hearty supper together, before they retired to rest, and took care the social glass was not wanting to make them as comfortable as possible.

The whole establishment sat around the well-spread table before a cheerfully blazing fire, and were descanting upon the dangers of the night and the perils which

Mr. William must have encountered. At this moment the doctor entered.

His curiosity had been excited by the account he had heard of Will Laud. He easily distinguished that dark swarthy being, with his blue jacket, changed, by the drying of the mud upon it, to a kind of dun or fawn-colour. His black hair hung down over his shaggy brow with his long man-of-war pigtail; and his whiskers, scarcely distinguishable from his black beard, fulfilled the idea of the weather-beaten sailor which the doctor had previously entertained. He was fully satisfied in his own mind with what he saw. He came, he said, to report to Laud the state of his patient; and after asking him a few questions, and making some remarks upon his bravery, he wished them all a good-night, and returned to the parlour, to encounter the entertaining queries of the intelligent family at the Cliff.

His report brought them another visitor. The door again opened, and their mistress stood before her servants. They all rose as she entered, and Laud above the rest; but whether from the strangeness of his situation, or from the belief that the lady was about to speak to him, the moment that his eye met that intellectual and penetrating glance of inquiry, it became fixed upon the ground. The voice of thanks reached him, as well as the words of praise. If they did not gratify *him*, they did at least the heart of the poor girl who stood close by him. She looked in her mistress's face, and in her heart blessed her for her kindness.

"Can we be of any service to you, young man?" said the lady. "We are anxious to prove ourselves grateful to you: and in any way that you may claim our future service, you will find us ready to repay you. As an immediate help, Mr. Cobbold sends you this guinea, an earnest of some future recompense."

"Thank you, ma'am! Let Margaret have the guinea, and the thanks too; for she first discovered the young gentleman."

This was spoken by Laud without looking at the lady, or once lifting up his eyes. Was it timidity, or was it shame ? Perhaps Laud had never been interrogated in the presence of a lady before that time.

He was truly relieved, when Mrs. Cobbold, hoping, as she said, that he had been well taken care of, and again thanking him for his assistance, wished him a good night's rest, and took her departure.

The opinion of the parlour was not so favourable to Laud as that of the kitchen, as the character of the bold smuggler was estimated very differently in each place. Mr. and Mrs. Cobbold, however, were not aware that Laud was in the British navy, having been seized in his boat by a pressgang, and been bound to serve his majesty three years on board the *Briton* man-of-war, then cruising off the coast of Holland.

Such was the want of British seamen just at this period of the breaking-out of the long war, that many smugglers received not only their pardon, but good pay for joining the navy ; and even those taken by the pressgang were only punished, if it may be termed so, by a three-years' well-paid service. Laud had been thus taken, and had been so well received on board, that his captain, on the night in question, had granted him permission to come up to Ipswich. He had offered him a crew, but Laud said he knew the river, and would rather go alone, if the captain would only lend him one of the small boats and a pair of oars. He had promised to be on board again the next day. The request was granted ; for the captain was pleased with Laud's confession of his object in undertaking to go alone—so, in spite of wind and weather, ice and snow, he had rowed himself up the river Orwell as far as Nacton Creek.

These facts Will had already communicated to Margaret, who, rejoicing in his present honourable position, overlooked the dangers of a three-years' service in defence of his country. She felt more proud of his presence that night at the Cliff than she had ever before done since the day of his first entrance into her father's cottage. She did not indeed experience that thrilling warmth of devotion which she once felt when he visited her on the shores of Downham Reach; but love, through all its shocks, was much more firm and really hopeful than even at that enthusiastic period.

Though Margaret became acquainted with the fact of Laud's admission into the British navy, and he spoke openly in the kitchen of his ship and her commander, yet these things were unknown in the parlour, where, as has just been stated, his personal appearance and character stood at a heavy discount. In the kitchen he was a hero, in the parlour a desperado.

The doctor found Master William in a sound and apparently refreshing sleep; and retired to a couch prepared for himself in an adjoining room, in case his services might be required in the night. The servants soon after parted for their respective dormitories, and Laud took leave of Margaret for the night.

It is scarcely possible to believe that Margaret, after all her fatigues and anxieties, should have refused to retire to her room. She actually begged permission to sit up all night with Master William. Vain were all attempts at persuasion. She said she knew that if she went to bed she could not sleep, and as she begged so hard to be permitted to sit up, the request was granted.

Hope is a sweet comforter to an anxious heart, and presented a vision of future bliss to the wakeful spirit of the maid, which afforded her occupation for the night, presenting to her the prospect of days to come, when Laud should obtain an honourable discharge from his country's service, where he was now numbered among the bold, the brave, and the free, and in which the same Providence which had preserved him to perform the good act of that night would, she hoped, still preserve him for many more good deeds. In pleasant reflections the night passed away; nor was there one in that family who did not join in the general thanksgiving to God for the signal preservation of the youth, who was wrapped in a profound and refreshing

sleep, watched by the ever-constant and faithful
Margaret. The tempest of the night had swept along,
and was succeeded by a calm and glorious sun-rising,
which shone upon the glittering fields of snow. The
fir-trees were weighed down with the weight of the
ice and snow lodged upon their branches, whilst the
beams of the sun made the drops of pendent icicles
fall with a smart sound to the earth. The sailor
came down from his bedroom refreshed after a sound
sleep; and, after he had partaken of a hearty breakfast, he shook hands with all the servants, and took
a more tender leave of Margaret: leaving his best
wishes for the young gentleman, he returned to his
boat some miles down the river, and thence to his ship.

He was gone before the Cliff party assembled at the
breakfast-table, but he took with him the best prayers
of all, and most especially those of the girl of his heart,
for his future safety and prosperity.

Master William gradually recovered, and took
warning from this narrow escape not to venture any
more upon such dangerous excursions. Though fond
of boating, he lost the zest for wild-fowl shooting, and
left it for others to pursue who had not purchased
experience at so dear a price.

CHAPTER XVII

ALTERATION AND EXPLANATION

It was not long after these occurrences that Mr.
Cobbold and his family removed from the Cliff to a
house in the town, a large family mansion, formerly
the property of C. Norton, Esq., on St. Margaret's
Green, which he had purchased, and thither he and his
family would have earlier removed but for some repairs
which were not completed until that time. It was
a fine old mansion, fronting the town, with its entrance
porch, and lofty windows, with numerous attics;
whilst its drawing, dining, and breakfast rooms, faced

the beautiful green fields which then skirted the town towards the hills upon the Woodbridge Road.

Mrs. Cobbold took the first favourable opportunity of questioning Margaret respecting her attachment to Will Laud, of whose character she spoke freely. Margaret spoke warmly in his defence, while she acknowledged the truth of much that had been advanced against him, and as warmly expressed her conviction he would reform. Sincerely did the lady hope that all her poor servant's favourable anticipations might be confirmed.

Upon Margaret's spirits, however, this conversation, which was broken off suddenly by the entrance of one of the servants, produced a depression which greatly affected and afflicted her. Her mistress did not appear in her eyes either so amiable, or so kind, or so just, or so considerate, as she had always previously done. She began to suspect that she was prejudiced even against her on Laud's account. She fancied herself not so much beloved by her as she used to be, and that she did not estimate her services as highly as, by her manner, she used formerly to show that she did. Words which Margaret would never have thought anything about at other times, when now spoken by her mistress, seemed to import something unpleasant, as if her attachment was the reason of their being uttered. She was never admonished now but she thought it was because of her unfortunate acquaintance with Laud. Mrs. Cobbold did not revert, in the least degree, to the past matter of confidential conversation. Indeed, after her most devout aspirations had been made for her servant's future comfort, she did not think about the matter. But in Margaret's eyes every little thing said or done seemed to have a peculiar meaning, which her own warped mind attached to it. In fact, she became an altered person—suspicious, distrustful, capricious, and, in many things, far less careful than she ought to have been. And all this arose from that well-intentioned conversation, voluntarily begun on the part of her mistress, but which had created such a serious disappointment in Margaret's mind.

A circumstance arose about the time of the removal of the family, which, though simple in itself, tended very greatly to inflame that disquietude in Margaret's breast, which only wanted to be stirred up to burn most fiercely.

Many of the things had been removed to St. Margaret's Green. Part of the family had already left the Cliff, and were domesticated in the mansion. Several of the children, especially all the younger ones, had become familiarized with their far more extensive nursery: Margaret was with them. The footman had been sent, together with the gardener, as safeguards to the house; and even the old coachman, though frequently engaged driving backwards and forwards from one house to the other, considered himself, horses and all, as settled at the town-house.

The Cliff began to be deserted, and in another day the master and mistress would leave the house to those only who were to live in it. Mrs. Cobbold and one or two of the elder boys were still at the Cliff. The faithful old dog, Pompey, still kept his kennel, which stood at the entrance of the stable-yard. Mr. Cobbold had been superintending the unpacking of some valuable goods until a late hour, and his lady, at the Cliff, was anxiously awaiting his return. It was a clear frosty night, and the snow was upon the ground; but the gravel path had been well swept down to the shrubbery gate. Pompey had been furiously barking for some time, and had disturbed Mrs. Cobbold, who was engaged with her book—some new publication of that eventful time. The two elder boys sat by the fire. She said to them—

"I wish, boys, you would go and see what Pompey is barking at."

"Oh! it is nothing, I dare say, but some sailors on the shore."

The young men, for so they might be called, had taken off their boots or shoes, and had put on their

slippers, and very naturally were little disposed to
put them on again, and to move from a nice, comfortable
fire, into the cold air of a frosty night.

Mrs. Cobbold finding, however, that she could not
get on with her book for the increasing rage of the dog,
determined to go out herself. She was a person of
no mean courage, and not easily daunted. She thought,
moreover, that if she moved, her sons would leave their
backgammon-board and follow her, and, if not, that
she might probably meet her husband. She put on
her thick cloak, threw a shawl over her head, and sallied
forth. As the door opened, Pompey ceased his loud
bark, but every now and then gave a low growl, and
a short, suppressed bark, as if he was not quite satisfied.
Mrs. Cobbold walked down the gravel path toward the
gate, and, as she proceeded, she saw a man go across
the path and enter the laurel shrubbery directly before
her. She went back immediately to the parlour, and
told the two young men what she had seen; but,
whether it was that they were too deeply engaged with
their game, or that they were really afraid, they treated
the matter very lightly, simply saying, that it was
some sweetheart of the cottagers, or that she must
have fancied she saw some one. At all events, they
declined to go out, and advised her not to think anything more about it.

This neither satisfied the lady nor old Pompey, who
began again to give tongue most furiously. Finding
that she was unable to make them stir, the lady
determined to investigate the matter herself; and,
telling the young men her intention, she again went out,
and advanced to the very spot where she had seen
the man enter the shrubbery. The traces on the
snow convinced her the man was in the shrubbery.
In a firm and decided voice, she cried out—

"Come out of that bush—come out, I say! I
know you are there; I saw you enter; and if you
do not immediately come out, I will order the dog to
be let out upon you! Come out! You had better
come out this moment."

The bushes began to move, the snow to fall from the leaves, and out rolled a heavy-looking man, dressed as a sailor, and apparently drunk; he looked up at the lady with a villainous scowl, and staggered a step towards her.

"What do you do here? Who are you?" she said, without moving.

"My name's John Luff. I—(hiccup)—I—I do no harm!"

At the sound of his voice, Pompey became so furious that he actually dragged his great kennel from its fixture, and as his chain would not break, it came lumbering along over the stones towards the spot.

As the fellow heard this, he began to stagger off, but at every step turned round to see if the lady followed him.

This she did, keeping at the same distance from him, and saying, "Be off with you! be off!" She then saw him go out at the gate, and turn round the wall, to the shore.

Farther than her own gate she did not think it prudent to go; but when she got so far, she was rejoiced to see her husband at a distance returning upon the marsh wall to the Cliff.

Old Pompey had by this time come up to the gate with his kennel behind him, and evidently impatient to be let loose.

She was engaged in the attempt to unloose the dog as her astonished husband came up to the gate; he soon learned the cause of this appearance, and immediately undid Pompey's collar; the animal sprang over the gate, and ran along the shore till he came to the cut where boats occasionally landed, and was closely followed by his master, who plainly saw a man pulling into the channel in a manner which convinced him he was no inexperienced hand at the oar.

In the meantime an exaggerated report reached St. Margaret's Green, that a sailor had been seen lurking about the premises at the Cliff, and that he had attacked their mistress.

Of course, the tale lost nothing but truth by the telling; and it was affirmed in the kitchen that it was Will Laud himself.

Some told Margaret the fact; she felt greatly annoyed, and was much surprised that when Mrs. Cobbold came to the house the next day, she did not speak to her upon the subject. She resolved that if her mistress did not soon speak to her, she would broach the subject herself; but Mrs. Cobbold put this question to her the next day:—

"Margaret, do you know a man of the name of John Luff?"

"Yes, madam," she replied; "I do know such a man, and I most heartily wish I had never known him."

"I wish the same, Margaret," said her mistress, and then related her recent adventure.

"He is the man," said Margaret, "who perverted all Will's naturally good talents, and induced him to join his nefarious traffickers. He is a desperate villain, and would murder any one! Did he threaten you with any violence? I am glad, indeed, that you escaped unhurt from the fangs of such a monster."

"He did me no injury," answered the lady.

Another long conversation then followed between Mrs. Cobbold and Margaret, in which the latter complained bitterly of the change she fancied had taken place in her mistress's behaviour towards her. The lady denied such change had taken place, and endeavoured to convince her servant that the alteration was in her own disposition.

CHAPTER XVIII

THE RECONCILIATION

WHETHER it was that Margaret's fame had reached the village of Brandiston, or that Mrs. Leader repented most bitterly the loss of her assistance, or that her rents of the land and cottages began to be in arrear and to fall off, and she herself found that poverty crept in upon her, certain it was that something sufficiently powerful in its nature prompted her to speak kindly to Margaret, whom she accidentally met that very day as she was going across the Green towards Christ Church Park. She had arrived at Ipswich with her husband, and was passing over the Green just as Margaret with the children, all wrapped up in cloaks and muffs, were going to see the skaters on the Round Pond in the Park.

The meeting was much more cordial than could have been expected ; but Mrs. Leader was a changed woman. After the interchange of mutual civilities, Margaret said that she should be home by four o'clock, and if her uncle and aunt would call, she knew that her mistress would have no objection to their coming into the house. Mrs. Leader even shook hands with her, and promised to pay her a visit.

What a wonderful change ! thought Margaret, as she hastened on with the little ones to overtake two or three of the impatient party, who were looking behind from the Park-gate.

The Park at Ipswich is a beautiful place in summer : twice a week were its gates thrown open by the liberal proprietor of the domain to the inhabitants of the town, who rambled along the shady chestnut walk to its utmost bound. Many were the happy walks that infancy, delighting in the sunny flowers of the mead, took in that lovely place ; and many the more tender and animating rambles which fond hearts and faithful

lovers in the days of youth enjoyed. Parents and
their children breaking away from the cares of business,
delighted to stroll in holiday attire, and repose themselves beneath the branches of those stately trees which
everywhere adorned the Park. There they heard the
first notes of the cuckoo ; there they watched the
green and spotted woodpecker ; observed the busy
rooks ; heard the nightingales, the thrushes, and the
doves, and spoke of all the innocent pleasures of
nature.

The spotted fallow deer crossed their path in a long
line of rapid flight, and assembled in a herd in the
valley ; the pheasant and the partridge roamed about
in pride and beauty ; whilst the hare and the rabbit,
familiarized to the sound of children's voices, lifted
up their long ears, or stood up upon their hind legs
to gaze upon them as they passed.

In the winter, the stragglers in the Park were comparatively few, excepting at that period when the
pond was frozen over, and became the fashionable
resort for company to view the skaters ; thither the
young party whom Margaret had the care of resorted,
to see the dexterous movements of Counsellor Green,
or some of his majesty's officers from the barracks.
The company that day was numerous, and the scene
such as would delight thousands, even were it in the
gay metropolis ; it would have induced many of the
fashionables to leave the warm, soft cushions by the
fireside, and to wrap themselves in furs, and to put
on their snow-shoes, and to enjoy the healthy, though
frosty, air of Christmas.

Many in the busy town of Ipswich left their labours
and their cares for a few hours' recreation ; fair ladies
ventured to lean upon a brother's or a lover's arm and
try the slippery ice ; sledges, too, were in requisition.

Though the skating was good, and all the young
people enjoyed it, Margaret's thoughts were upon her
uncle and aunt, and she was the first to remind her
young people that the old Christ Church clock had
struck four.

Home they went, gratified and satisfied, talking of the frightful cracks and heavy falls, and well-contested races, which they had mightily enjoyed; when they came into the house they gave a lively account of all they had seen.

With Mrs. Cobbold's permission, Mr. and Mrs. Leader were invited to take tea in the housekeeper's room, and Margaret was allowed to have a long talk with them.

She found her uncle much more chatty than her aunt, for sorrow and coming poverty had cast their shadows before Mrs. Leader, and wonderfully softened the asperity of her former purse-proud disposition; she let her husband speak of all the family troubles, and did not once interrupt him. Margaret soon learned that all their property was mortgaged, and for its full value. She learned that the children were barefoot, and neglected; that it would require steady management indeed ever to bring them again into a prosperous or a comfortable state; she felt for them all, and not only felt, but did all she could to ameliorate their condition. She offered advice, which was taken in good part by the now crestfallen aunt.

A strange effect had that comfortable reception in the housekeeper's room upon the nerves and manners of Mrs. Leader, she looked up to Margaret as if she was a person of considerable consequence in that family; she asked Margaret if she might also see the children; nothing could have given Margaret greater pleasure.

All in the nursery were delighted to see a visitor; and Mrs. Leader very soon discovered that where management, cleanliness, and strict attention are paid there will grow up order, regularity, and comfort; she stayed some minutes with the happy family. As she returned to the housekeeper's room, she sighed when she said to Margaret—

"I now wish I had never provoked you to leave us! I did not like to own it, but, very soon after you were gone, I felt your loss; I hope you will be able to come and see us in the summer, and should you ever be tired of service, and wish for a home, you will find us very altered in our manner to you, and more grateful for your services."

Margaret could forgive all that her aunt had ever said or done to her ; she felt so happy in having been reconciled to her, that she could not refrain from telling her so. She gave a portion of her wages for the schooling of the children, and thanked her uncle and aunt for their kind invitation. She even hinted that the time might come when her hopes of settling in Brandiston might be realized, should Laud obtain his discharge ; in short, she promised to see them in summer, as she had no doubt that she could obtain leave from her kind mistress.

The day was gone, and the moon was high, and the sky was clear, and the happy Margaret would have had them stay all night. She had received a message to the effect that the pony might be put in the stable, and that her uncle and aunt might sleep in the house ; they prudently declined, lest a deep snow might fall and prevent their reaching home ; so off they went, happier than they had been any day since their affectionate niece left them, and this happiness arose from the reconciliation.

It was a lucky thing for Mr. and Mrs. Leader that they went home as they did that very night, for not long after their arrival home began that severe winter and deep snow which formed one of the most remarkable features in the history of the climate of England.

It would be foreign to the present narrative to dwell upon the events of that particular season, further than to refer to the great exertions made by persons of all ranks and conditions, above actual distress, to support the famishing poor. Houses were established in different parts of the town of Ipswich for the public distribution of soup, coals, and blankets, and various families agreed to furnish supplies for the various days of the week.

Margaret was now as busy in the kitchen as she had been in the nursery, for at this time the cook of the family returned home ill, and no one else could be found so apt as Margaret to supply her place.

It was at this memorable season that her aptitude for this situation was discovered, which led to such a change in her condition, as future pages will record. A servant was soon found for the nursery, who supplied her place, and she became the active cook of the family. In such a large domestic establishment as that of Mr Cobbold, the cook was a person of the utmost consequence; and although there was a regular housekeeper who acted as an intervening link between the parlour and the kitchen, yet Mrs. Cobbold was by no means so unacquainted with the proceedings of her house, as to be found negligent of a due supervision over every department.

In the new place Margaret had undertaken at the earnest request of her mistress, her active powers of benevolence were now called into existence. The feeling manner in which she represented to her fellow-servants the destitution of thousands around them, and the great sin there was in the least waste; the strong necessity now became a duty in every one to deny themselves some portion of their daily bread, that those who were starving might have a share; made a powerful impression upon the domestics of that establishment. At this time, though a greater allowance was made on account of the provisions given away by this affluent family, yet such was the economy in the kitchen, and the honest, self-satisfactory privation exercised by the whole house, that not the least waste was made, and the accustomed expenditure was very little increased. The poor, however, were bountifully supplied, and Margaret's name was as justly praised below stairs, as, in past days, it had been above. Little did she think that her activity, economy, and management, which a sense of duty and charity had called into action, would fix her in the kitchen at such an increase of wages, as, comparatively, seemed to her like coming into a little fortune. She had now become the head of all the domestics, from having been the servant of all. She had an increase of toil, but she had a help under her. There was dinner for the nursery, dinner for the kitchen, dinner for the parlour, and that which is now almost obsolete, a hot supper for all the house. But what is work to one who is strong and willing, and ready and desirous of giving satisfaction?

Time, fully occupied, passes on rapidly, and Margaret was now looked upon with respect by the whole house. What a pity that that respect should ever have been blighted, or that any circumstances should have interfered with that peaceful enjoyment which she seemed at this time to experience, and which in after years she never forgot! In leaving the nursery, she left that frequent intercourse with her mistress, and consequently that continued mental improvement which she had gradually imbibed. She was not now under her immediate eye; she seldom heard that sweet voice of approbation, pleasing beyond all expression from such a mistress.

It was one of those singular coincidences which happened in her eventful life, that on the celebrated 1st of June, 1794, her lover, William Laud, distinguished himself in Lord Howe's victory over the French, and was one of the seamen appointed to bring home a splendid prize to Portsmouth; and that Margaret herself, on the very same day, distinguished herself in an aquatic feat, which would have been no disgrace to a British seaman to have performed, and which exhibited a degree of courage and presence of mind, truly wonderful in a female.

In the garden belonging to the mansion at St. Margaret's Green was a very deep pond, with turfed sides, which were sloping and steep, so that the gardener had to descend to the water by a flight of six steps. Formerly it had been a handsome square pond, with edges neatly kept, and surrounded by alpine strawberry-beds. At the period of this tale, one side opened into the adjoining meadow, and half of that extensive garden was laid down to grass. To this day, the two stately weeping willows may be seen dipping their pensile edges into the pond, though time has lopped off many an arm, and somewhat curtailed them of their beauty. At that time, when Margaret was cook at St. Margaret's Green, these trees were the ornaments of the exterior of the town, and to have made a sketch from the hill, on the Woodbridge Road, without including them, would have been to have robbed the town of Ipswich of one of its most prominent and pleasing features of landscape beauty. They were very lofty, though pendent, and in the month of June, might be justly styled magnificent. Hundreds of their boughs kissed the water with their thin, taper points. The girl who had the care of the children had been often warned not to go near the edge of the road.

On this 1st of June, 1794, Margaret had entered the garden to gather some herbs, and had scarcely closed the gate before she heard a sudden shriek of distress. The voices of the children struck upon her, from the centre of the garden. She ran down the path, and there she saw the whole group standing and screaming at the edge of the pond, and the nursemaid completely at her wits' end with fright. Master Henry had been running away from his sisters, who were pursuing him down the path, and having turned his head round to look at them, he did not perceive his danger. His foot caught the edge of the grass border which surrounded the pond, and he was precipitated headforemost into the deepest part of it. In a moment he was seen plunging and screaming for help, but all his efforts only tended to carry him still further towards the middle of the pond : he must inevitably have been drowned, had not Margaret at that moment providentially entered the garden.

Margaret's astonishing presence of mind enabled her to resolve in an instant what it was best to do, and her heroic courage caused her not to shrink from doing it ; she ordered the nurserymaid to run with all speed to the stables for a ladder and rope, and then creeping along the strongest arm of the weeping willow that spread

itself over the centre of the pond, and going as far
as she could towards the child, she grasped a handful
of those pendent branches which dipped themselves
into the water, and swinging herself by her right
arm, into the pond, and stretching out her left to the
utmost, she seized the child by the collar of his little
jacket, and held him above the water until the assistance she sent for arrived.

It required both nerve and presence of mind, as well
as bodily strength to support herself in this position
only for a few minutes. She gradually drew the child
nearer to her, and though in great danger herself, her
first words to him were, " Don't be afraid, Master
Henry ; I have got you ! Keep still ! keep still !
don't struggle ! "

The gardener and the coachman had by this time
arrived with the ladder and a rope, they let it down
from the arm of the tree, resting the upper stave just
against its branches. The gardener descended a few
steps, and Margaret gave him the child, whilst she
herself remained with the boughs in her hand, until
the boy was safe. She then requested them to throw
her the rope, that she might leave go of the willow
and be drawn to the side of the pond. She put the
rope round her waist and took hold of it, doubled,
with both hands, and in this way was dragged through
the water to the bank.

Thus was Margaret Catchpole, for the third time,
the providential instrument in preserving the life of
a member of Mr. Cobbold's family. It will not, then,
be a matter of surprise, that the records of her life
should have been so strictly preserved among them.
If there had been any former coolness or misunder-
standing between her and any of the domestics of the
family, this event completely reconciled all differences.
It was felt by one and all, that a woman who could
risk her life to save another's, in this manner, was
worthy of their united respect. She was, at this time,
at the very summit of her reputation. A few days
more brought the news of that celebrated victory over

the French fleet, which added so much to the naval glory of Old England. In that victory more than one Ipswich man partook, and returned to speak of the engagement. One poor fellow, in particular, was sent home, desperately wounded, who, for many years, became an object of respect, as well as charitable attention, to many families in the town and neighbourhood. This was poor old Jack, whose friends kept the Salutation public-house, in Carr Street, who always went by the name of "What Cheer?" When he first returned to his aunt, the landlady of the house, he had his senses perfect, and could speak of the engagement with such clearness and precision as delighted the seamen who frequented the house. He was on board the same ship as Will Laud, and on the 1st of June they fought side by side.

Margaret heard of this, and used to go down to the public-house in question, to hear from Jack all she could of one who was as dear to her as her own life. He was desired by Laud to tell Margaret that he was coming home with plenty of prize-money as soon as he could obtain his discharge. It was this which gave her spirit such joy, and made her so anxious to hear all she could of the battle; and, of course, of that part which her lover took in it. Poor Jack's intellects, however, from the severity of his wounds, and consequent attack of fever, became irretrievably impaired; and though he recovered his health, and became a constant visitor at St. Margaret's Green, yet he never could afterwards give any connected account of the battle.

CHAPTER XIX

THE ALTERATION

WE left our heroine, in the last chapter, esteemed of every one who knew her, and looking forward to what was to her the height of human felicity—the reformation and return of her sailor-lover. No less true than strange is the fact, that when we reach the highest pinnacle of this world's happiness, some giddiness of the head is apt to make us fall. So, at all events, it proved with the female who gives a title to this book. It became matter of deep concern to every member of Mr. Cobbold's family, to behold in her an alteration which no previous circumstances in her life had prepared them for. There was nothing in reason, and consistent with their own happiness, that her grateful master and mistress would not have granted her. Any situation she wished to attain, either for herself or for her friends, would have commanded every exertion they could have made in her favour. She stood so high in their opinion, and in every one's else who knew her, that it scarcely seemed possible for her to forfeit it. Apparently she had nothing to complain of ; no cause for dissatisfaction ; no inducement whatever to alter her disposition. Yet an alteration did take place, and one which became evident to every one.

Where the heart is unsettled, things seldom go on well. There wants that peace and security which can alone make the discharge of our daily duties a daily pleasure. Margaret's early impressions of religion had been of a very desultory kind, and here was the root of all the evil that afterwards befell her. The want of fixed religious principles early instilled into the young mind has caused many a good dis-

position to give way to those changes and chances
which happen in life, and to create an alteration even
in the brightest prospects. In the earliest days of
this child of nature, an innate humanity of disposition
had been cultivated and increased by her attendance
on a sick and afflicted sister and an aged mother,
both of whom had constantly required her aid. Her
natural qualities were, as the reader has seen, up to
this moment of the noblest cast. Still, in the absence
of any strong religious sentiment, the best dispositions
are at the mercy of violent passions, and are subject
to the most dangerous caprices. The reader must
have observed that, in the midst of all her good qualities,
Margaret Catchpole evinced a pertinacity of attachment to the object of her affections, even in his most
unworthy days—an attachment which no circumstances whatever, not even the warning of her sister's
death-bed, could shake. She had built upon a vague
hope of Laud's alteration of life, and his settlement
in some quiet occupation. She had been accustomed
to very great disappointments and vexations; and,
with a spirit above her years, she had borne them all,
and had shown an energy of mind and activity worthy
of better things. How weak are all qualities without
the support of religion! At a time when promises
seemed most fair, when an unexpected reconciliation
had taken place with her uncle and aunt Leader, when
Laud's return was daily expected, and all the favours
of a generous family were heaped upon her for her
good conduct,—at such a time an alteration of her
disposition took place, which embittered her existence
for many years. She became peevish and irritable,
discontented and unhappy, moody and melancholy.
She thanked nobody for assistance, asked nothing
of any one, and gave no reason to any of her fellow-
servants for this sudden alteration. Such would not
have been the case, had religion taught her, as it now
does many in her station of life, how to feel supported
in prosperity as well as in adversity. It is a trite
saying, that "we seldom know when we are well

off." We are not content to "let well alone;" but
too often foolishly speculate upon the future, and fall
into some present snare.

Nothing had been heard of or from Laud, except that
a sailor, who had served with him in the glorious
battle of the 1st of June, had visited the town, and
told Margaret that Laud was appointed to come home
in one of the prizes taken by Lord Howe; and that,
probably, he was then at Portsmouth, waiting until
he should receive his prize-money and his discharge.
Margaret occasionally stole down in the evening to
the Salutation public-house, where the sailor was
staying, to speak with him, and to hear the naval
news. She was here occasionally seen by other sailors,
who frequented the house, and learned where she lived.
They understood the bearings of her history, and some
of them used to fabricate tales on purpose to get an
introduction into the kitchen at St. Margaret's Green,
where they were sure to be welcomed and well treated
by Margaret. She was, at this time, very anxious to
hear tidings of her lover, and day after day exhibited
symptoms of restlessness, which could not long be
passed by without notice. The frequency of sailors'
visits to the kitchen began to be rumoured through
the house, and stories injurious to the reputations of
the inmates were circulated in the neighbourhood.
Moreover, the housekeeper missed various articles;
and meat, and bread, and stores, began to be un-
accountably diminished. Inquiries were instituted,
and it was found that Margaret had certainly given
such and such things to sailors; and without doubt,
some things were stolen.

Under these circumstances, it became high time for
the mistress of the house to take notice of these things;
and, in as gentle a manner as the circumstances of the
case would permit, she spoke to Margaret alone on
the subject. She regretted to hear from all quarters
the alteration which had taken place in her manner.
She spoke to her most feelingly upon the result of such
a change, and with great kindness contrasted the

pleasure of the past with the sorrow which her late conduct occasioned.

"I cannot," she added, "permit sailors of every kind to be incessantly coming to the house at all hours with pretended news of Laud, and so deceiving you by playing upon your disposition, and then robbing you and the house. Reports of a very unpleasant nature have reached my ears injurious to your character and that of my establishment. I cannot submit to these things; and, though I most sincerely regard you, Margaret, yet I must make you sensible of the danger you incur by listening to the artful tales of these men. I strongly recommend you to have nothing to do with them. Your own character is of much more consequence to you than their nonsensical stories. If you wish it, I will write for you to Portsmouth to make inquiries about Laud; and, rather than you should be in doubt and affliction, and in any uncertainty about him, I am sure that your master will send a trustworthy person to search him out and ascertain the cause of his detention.

"Let me see you henceforth what you used to be— cheerful and contented, thankful and happy, and not over-anxious about matters which in the end will all probably come right. You have my entire forgiveness of the past, even though you do not ask it; but let me not be imposed upon for the future. Go, Margaret, go; and let me hear no more of these complaints."

Margaret heard all that her mistress said in perfect silence. She neither defended herself, nor yet thanked her mistress, as she used to do. She seemed sullen and indifferent. She left the presence of that kind lady and most sincere friend with scarce a curtsy, and with such a pale, downcast countenance, as deeply distressed her benefactress. Then was it the painful reflection occurred, that her servant's religious principles had been neglected; that her duty as a servant had been done from no higher motive than that of pleasing man; and that when she had failed to do so, and received a rebuke, her spirit would not bear it.

These reflections pressed themselves upon the kind lady's mind, and she resolved to do her best to correct for the future that which appeared so deficient.

Margaret returned to the kitchen unaltered, saving in feature; she was silent, pale, and restless. She did her work mechanically, but something appeared to be working upon her in a very strange way. She could not sit still a moment. Sometimes she put down her work, and sat looking at the fire, as if she was counting the coals upon it. At one time she would rise and appear to go in search of something, without knowing what she went for. At another time she would bite her lips and mutter something, as if she were resolute and determined upon some point which she did not reveal. Her fellow-servants did not lay anything to her, and took as little notice as her strange manner would permit. They all considered that something very unpleasant had occurred between herself and her mistress. Some surmised that warning had been given; others that she would leave of her own accord; but all felt sorry that one who had been so highly esteemed should now be so perverse.

One evening, in the midst of these domestic arrangements of the kitchen, when all the servants were assembled, a knock was heard at the back-kitchen door; the girl who opened it immediately called out, "Another sailor wants to see you, Margaret!"

Without rising from her seat, as she was accustomed to do with alacrity upon such occasions, Margaret petulantly and passionately replied, loud enough for the sailor to hear her through the door of the kitchen, which now stood open, "Tell the fellow to go about his business! I have nothing to do with, or to say to, any more sailors. Tell him to be off!"

The sailor stepped one step forward, and pitched a canvas bag in at the kitchen-door, which fell with a loud chink upon the bricks. He had heard the words of Margaret, and was off in a moment.

The reader will doubtless surmise that this was none other than Will Laud. He it was who, at this unfortunate moment, returned, with all his prize-money, on purpose to give it to Margaret, for whom he had kept it, intending to purchase a shop at Brandiston, or one of the neighbouring villages, where she might like to live. The bag had a label, directed

" To Margaret Catchpole,
John Cobbold's, Esq.,
Cliff, Ipswich."

Had this unfortunate girl been in a different mood, she might have recognized the voice, as she once did on that memorable night when Mr. William's life was saved. She heard the rap, and the inquiry for her ; but knowing her mistress's commands, and believing the visitor to be one of those whom she had styled impostors and thieves, she had, with considerable energy and irritability, spoken those cutting words, which sent him away in despair.

What agony now struck upon the heart of Margaret ! She started at the sound of the bag as it fell at her feet ; she looked bewildered for one moment ; the truth burst upon her, and she rushed out of the house with such a wild shriek as pierced the heart of every one who heard it. She ran into the street. The night was growing dark ; but, on the opposite side of the green, against the garden pales, she saw a sailor standing and looking at the house. She ran to him, seized his arm, and exclaimed, " Laud, is it you ? "

He replied, " Yes—hush ! "

" Come in, then ; come into the house ; I am sure you may come in."

The sailor walked on, with Margaret by his side. He did not speak. This Margaret naturally attributed to her late repulsive words, and she now said, soothingly, by way of apologizing for her harshness—

" I did not intend to send you away. I have lately had several sailors to speak to me about you, and I was only too glad to hear them ; but my mistress gave orders to me this day not to have anything more to do with them. I am sure she did not mean to send you away—neither did I intend it. Come back, come back!"

"Come on, come on!" said the sailor, in as soft accents as he could. And, by this time, they had approached the old granary wall, at the back of the park stables. Opposite to these stables was a cow-keeper's yard, with the dwelling inside the gates. The gates stood open: they might rather be termed folding-doors, for, when shut, no one could see through any part but the keyhole. The sailor turned in here with Margaret, as if he knew the premises, and immediately closed the gates. A light glanced from a window in the cottage, and fell upon the sailor's face. In an instant Margaret recognized the hated features of John Luff.

The poor girl was paralysed; she was completely in the tiger's claws; she could not speak, her heart so swelled with agony. She thought of this monster's cruelty, and believed him to be capable of any desperate deed. She recovered sufficient presence of mind, however, to be resolved to grapple with him, should he have any evil purpose in view. She retreated a few steps toward the gates. He suspected by this that she had discovered who he was, and he threw off the mask in a moment.

"You know who I am, I see; and I know you. I do not want to harm you; but I want to know something from you, which, if you tell me truly, you shall receive no injury; but, if you do not tell me, I tell you plainly that, as you are now in my power, so you shall never escape me. You spoke just now of Will Laud. Now, no tacking about; bear up at once, and come to the point. Tell me where he can be found."

"I do not know," replied Margaret.

"No lies, girl! You do know. You were expecting him from Portsmouth this very night. I knew he was coming home with his prize-money; so did you. I don't want his money, but I want him. I have sworn to take him, dead or alive, and have him I will. You have seen him: I have not. Now tell me where he is, and I will let you go; but if you tell me not, down you shall go headlong into the well at the bottom of this yard!"

The truth burst upon the poor girl's mind, that this fellow was watching Laud to murder him. She was now convinced that it was Laud who came to the back-kitchen door, and that he must have gone over the garden palings towards the Woodbridge Road, instead of going into the street. With a woman's heart beating high at the danger of her lover, she inwardly rejoiced, even at this dreadful moment, that her sudden words had perhaps saved Laud's life. She forgot her own loss, and her spirit rose to reply firmly and boldly to the cowardly rascal who threatened her—

"I do not know where Laud is. I wish I did; and I would let him know that such a villain as you are ought to be hanged."

The monster seized her, gagged her mouth with a tow-knot, and tried to pull her away from the gate. She had seized hold of the long iron bar, which was fastened to a low post, and fitted into a staple on the door. She thought she heard voices outside the gates, speaking of her. Just as the villain lifted her from the ground to fulfil his determined purpose, she swung the iron against the door with such force, that the servants outside were convinced something was wrong. They called, but received no answer. They heard footsteps receding from the door, and called to Smith, the cowkeeper, to know what was the matter. They did not receive any immediate answer, but a light streamed under the door, and in another moment they heard a scuffle, and Smith's voice calling for help.

With their united force they burst the gates open, and ran down the yard. The candle was burning on the ground, and Smith prostrate beside it. In a moment after, they heard the bucket of the well descending with rapidity, and then a sudden splash, as if a heavy body had reached the bottom of it.

Smith recovered quickly from his fall, and declared he saw a sailor-looking man, carrying a female in his arms, and he firmly believed that she was thrown down the well. He got his lantern, and directed the men to take down the long church ladder, which was hung up under the roof of the cowhouse, and bring it after him. The ladder was put down the well, and Smith descended with his lantern, and called out that there was a woman in the well.

"Unhank the bucket: tie the rope round her body, and ease her up the ladder; we can help you to get her out so."

This was done: and when she was drawn up, the servants recognized the features of Margaret Catchpole.

Smith was quite sure the man he saw was in sailor's dress. It was a providential circumstance that the very act of gagging had prevented the water getting to her lungs, and so saved her from drowning. She breathed hard, and harder still when the gag was removed, and was very black in the face. She had received a severe blow on the head from her fall against the bucket, the iron of which had caught her gown, and was the cause of its descending with her to the water. She might have had a severer blow against the sides of the well but for this circumstance. She was quite insensible, and in this state was carried home, where she was laid between warm blankets, and the doctor sent for. She was quickly bled, and was soon restored to conscious animation.

As she revived, she refused to communicate anything on the subject of the disaster; and it was thought best, at that time, not to say much to her about it. Conjectures were much raised, and the matter was much talked over. The bag, which was opened by her master, was found to contain one hundred and thirty guineas in gold and silver coin. Mr. Cobbold took charge of it, and sealed it with his own seal. From all that could be learned, it seemed that a sailor, whom all now conjectured to be Laud, had thrown the money in at the door, and Margaret had rushed out after him; that she had overtaken him; and that some violent altercation had taken place between them, which had led to this most extraordinary act. The whole affair seemed to be fraught with reckless desperation. Could anything be more so than to throw such a sum of money at a person's foot, and then to throw that person down a well? Why do such a deed? Was he jealous? Had he heard of the many sailors who had lately made Margaret's acquaintance? It might be, thought some, that he had suddenly returned, and hearing of her conduct, had put the worst construction upon it; and, in a desperate state, had been foolishly generous, but too fatally jealous to hear any explanation. These ideas passed through the minds of more than one of the family.

Margaret slowly recovered from the fever which had settled in her frame, and greatly reduced it. She kept her bed for several weeks; she kept her tongue, too, as still and as free from communication with any one as she possibly could under the circumstances. She did not say anything of her own accord, even to her anxious and beloved mistress.

It was soon circulated about that an atrocious attempt at murder had been made in the parish of St. Margaret's, and the authorities of the town took it up, and made inquiries into the matter. Understanding that the young female was in too weak a state to have her deposition taken, they did not visit her, but a reward was offered for the apprehension of the man, and his person was described by the cowkeeper.

There was but one person to whom Margaret opened her lips willingly upon the subject, and that was her old friend and medical attendant, Mr. Stebbing. He learned from her, that it was not Laud that had thrown her down the well, but a fellow named Luff, one of his former evil companions. She told the doctor her belief that Laud was the person who had unintentionally been driven away by her on that unfortunate night; "And I fear," she added, "that he will be induced by my seeming harshness to return to his old courses. He will never forgive me—I know he never will! Oh, that I could have had one word with him! If I could but get well, I would try and find him. Oh, doctor, I am so anxious to get well! Pray, help me!"

"This is the plain reason, my girl, why you are so slow in recovering. I knew you had something upon your mind that you kept back; and now that you have told me thus much, let me speak to you in my own way. I tell you honestly, Margaret, I never should think a man worth having who took himself off in that kind of way. If, as you say, you refused to see a sailor who did not give his name, the man ought to have been pleased, rather than displeased, if he really loved you. If he was not a fool, he would naturally think it would be the very first thing a girl with any proper feeling would say. Take my word, Margaret, and I am somewhat more experienced than you are, that if Laud is worth your having, he will soon be here again. But don't you think of running after him. If he comes back in a few days, well; but if not, I wish I might be able to persuade you not to think of him at all. What could induce Luff to attempt to murder you?"

"He threatened, that unless I told him where Laud was, he would throw me down the well. I imagine that Laud having escaped from the gang of smugglers, this villain was sworn either to be revenged upon him for some quarrel, or else he had promised Captain Bargood, his employer, to bring him back again. I was determined not to tell him that Laud had been to the house, and the fellow took this desperate revenge on me. But, thank God, his purpose is frustrated! You know Laud, doctor, as well as I do. I can conceive that my speech took him so completely by surprise, that, after he had been saving up all his money for me, and had been congratulating his mind upon my joy at his change, my words must have cut him to the quick, and have driven him away in desperation."

"I wish I could think so, Margaret; but my idea is, that if he had been the altered man you picture him, he would never have conducted himself in that way. I tell you plainly, that I should be much more apt to think he liked somebody else better than you; and that he threw down the money merely because his conscience told him he had wronged you; and made him feel that he ought to make you some recompense. If he does not come back in a few days, I shall be confirmed in this opinion."

The poor girl had never looked at the matter in this light. She felt a strange sensation creeping over her mind, and, in the weak state she then was in, she had a superstitious dread of her sister's last words—"Margaret, you will never marry William Laud." The words seemed to tingle in her ears, and to come, at this moment, with redoubled force; she shook her head, sighed, and thanked the doctor for his good advice.

"I shall explain these matters to your mistress, Margaret," said Mr. Stebbing. "It will remove all erroneous ideas, and may spare you some pain and trouble. You must rouse yourself; the magistrates are daily asking me about you; I have told them that you have too virulent a fever upon you at present to make it safe for them to see you; and, depend upon it, they will not be over-anxious to run any risk."

"Pray, sir, could not you take down what I have said, as well as having any other person to do it?"

"If I do, Margaret, it must be read to you before two justices of the peace, and you will have to swear to it."

"Well, sir, so it must be then."

And the good doctor left his patient, and gladly explained the exact state of the case to her mistress.

It was not very difficult for that lady to form her own conclusions now. She was of Margaret's opinion, that Laud's first step would be to rejoin the smugglers.

She thought that he would become a more desperate character than ever. Instability of purpose was always Laud's failing. When Margaret got about again, her mistress, having considered all the circumstances, thought it best that she should go home to her parent's roof for a time. "As you are so much better," said she to her one day, "and have been so much shaken lately, and your deposition has been taken before the magistrates, I would strongly recommend a little change for the benefit of your health. The doctor thinks it advisable. You can go and stay a while with your uncle and aunt Leader, or you can go and see your father and younger brother. You may go when you please. Remember that there are one hundred and thirty guineas in your master's hands, to be appropriated to your use. Your father or your uncle may wish to consult us for your benefit. We shall be happy to see them for such purpose at any time. If you wish to enter into any business, you shall have our best advice and assistance. I think change will do you good. If you do not settle in any way for yourself, and still prefer service, we shall be glad to receive you amongst us again when you have recruited your health and spirits."

"I do not," Margaret replied, "want anything beyond my wages. I do not consider that money my own, and shall never appropriate any of it to my own use. It belongs to Will Laud. I feel very much obliged to both my master and yourself for the interest you have always taken in me, and for your offer of future assistance. I will consult with my friends. I certainly do not feel so happy as I used to do."

Her kind mistress did not choose to remind her of the great alteration of her temper and conduct of late, because she did not wish to revive old grievances. And, as she was about to leave for a time, with a possibility of some chance of settlement without service, she let the matter rest.

Margaret, shortly after this conversation, took leave of as good a mistress as a servant ever had.

If she did not feel quite the warmth of attachment to her that she had formerly done, the fault lay in herself, not in that benevolent lady, who at that time and ever after, manifested for her the sincerest kindness.

CHAPTER XX

CHANGE OF SCENE AND CHANGE OF PLACE

Soon after Margaret's recovery, and the taking of her deposition before Colonel Neale, Mr. Gibson, and Mr. Seekamp, justices of the peace, she took leave of the affectionate friends she had gained in the family at St. Margaret's Green. She had permission to go and stay as long as she felt necessary for the recruiting of her spirits, and accordingly she went to Nacton. She found her aged father and her younger brother living in the same cottage, and in better work and condition than when she had left them. They gladly welcomed her, and she spent a peaceful quiet time with them, though painful thoughts intruded themselves upon her mind. Old and joyful, as well as joyless, associations crowded upon her; she thought of her career of fortune and misfortune, with many a deep and painful sigh. Oh! had religious instruction then fortified that mind as it did years afterwards, what comfort might it not have gained even in this moment of adversity—what pain might it not have turned aside! Her father soon perceived that disappointment was gnawing at Margaret's heart, the more keenly, as it found stronger food to feed upon, from the past revival of warm hopes, now severely blighted. The old man sought her confidence, and found that, by conversation with her, he lightened the heaviness of her load.

Margaret told her father the exact state of her mind, and did not conceal anything from him.

"I much fear," said the old man, "that he has

returned to the coast again, and perhaps to his former vicious companions. Not that I have heard anything of him; but I know that the coastguard are as active as they ever were in the discharge of their desperate duty. I cannot think of any other method of ascertaining the fact, than by sending your brother Edward down to the coast for a time, and let him learn what he can. He is a very sharp young fellow, and I can tell you, Margaret, that for activity of head, heart, and limb, not one of my boys ever exceeded him."

"I think the scheme might answer," replied Margaret: "at all events, it is worth trying. I shall feel more satisfied, let the result be what it may. I will give him part of my wages, so that he shall lose nothing by the trip."

In the evening the plan was proposed to the young man, who readily entered into his sister's views upon the subject. He would ask his master for a week or ten days, or a fortnight, if required.

Margaret gave him strict charge to explain to Will Laud the circumstance of her having so hastily uttered those words which had given him such offence; that it was her mistress's command that she should see no more sailors. "Be cautious," she added; "avoid that villain Luff; for in his clutches you would be no more than a lamb beneath a tiger's paw. You must visit all the different places along the coast from Felixstowe to Aldeburgh. If any of the coastguard speak to you, tell them honestly who you are; and if you see young Edward Barry, you may tell him all the truth. He will help you, as he promised to befriend me, should I ever require his aid. If any private opportunity of speaking to Laud should occur, tell him his money is all safe, and shall be employed according to his directions. I consider it his property, though directed to me. Go, Edward. I shall spend many a restless hour until you return."

Edward Catchpole was soon on his road to Felixstowe. His first attempt was to find out the old ferryman, Laud's father, and ascertain if he knew anything of him. But he learned that the old man had quietly departed this life, soon after receiving the news of his son's engagement with the French, in Lord Howe's victory of the 1st of June. The only thing like a footmark of Laud was in the report given by some of the neighbours, that a sailor had been there some weeks ago, making inquiries about the old ferryman ; who, ascertaining, however, that he was dead, went away, and no one heard anything more of him.

Edward next went on from Felixstowe to Bawdsey Ferry, and took up his quarters at the Sun Inn. Here he seemed as one come to the seaside for health ; for he was to be seen wandering along the shore, and talking whenever he could with the sailors. But he could gain no tidings, directly or indirectly, of the person he sought. He shifted his position from the Sun to the Old Beach House, at the mouth of the river Alde, now known by the name of the Life-Boat public-house, then kept by Jacob Merrells, a pilot.

Great preparations were then making for building forts and Martello towers along the coast, to oppose any invasion. Numbers of surveyors, and workmen in the employ of Government, frequented the Beach House. The conversation sometimes turned upon smuggling, and young Catchpole's heart beat high at such moments, with the hope of some clue to Laud. Nothing, however, could he elicit, except that, as so many Government men were about at that time, the smugglers were not likely to be carrying on a very brisk trade. Still it *was* carried on, and Captain Bargood was, it was said, as busy as ever.

He next visited Boyton and Sudbourn, and Orford. He lodged at the Mariner's Compass, then kept by an old weather-beaten sailor, who often put him across from the quay on the banks of the Alde, to the North Vere ; and here he used to spend so many hours, that the coastguard, who kept a watch upon his movements, suspected that his countryman's dress was only a ruse to hide some sinister intention. They observed, however, that he did not avoid them, but rather sought opportunity for their acquaintance. A more dreary place than this North Vere is scarcely to be found on all the coast of Great Britain. It is a mass of shingle nearly twenty miles long, in some places nearly a mile broad, in others, only a few hundred yards. This wall of pebbles separates the river Alde from the ocean. The bank reaches from Hollesley Bay to Aldeburgh. The sea and the river are very deep along the shelving banks on either side.

Thousands upon thousands of sea-birds build, or rather lay their eggs, upon this desolate bed of shingle. A few wild, straggling plants of seakale, and very long, thin, sickly spires of grass, occasionally shoot up through the stones; but there is no other vegetation, except here and there in some few hollows in this desert of stones, where a little clay, mixed with the sea-fowl dung, formed a green patch. These spots used to be much frequented by smugglers, which, from their sunken situations, used to hide both them and their goods from view. Nothing prominent can be seen for miles round this coast, except the Orford lights, which stand conspicuous enough about midway between Hollesley and Aldeburgh.

The poor fellows who acted as preventive-service men in the coastguard had no sinecure in this dreadful situation. The sun burnt them by day, and the wind, from whatever quarter it blew, and especially in the winter nights, was cutting and cold; and from the exposure between two waters, the sea and the river, it roared like the discharge of batteries. In some of the hollows these poor men used to construct huts of such rude materials as came to hand; old pieces of wrecks, or broken-up boats, which they covered with seaweed, collected after a storm. These served to break the east winds which blew over the German Ocean, in their terrible night-watches, which they were forced to keep pretty constantly, as they were watched, though they were watchers. Many were the desperate struggles upon this wild beach between these brave men and the smugglers, in which hard fighting, and too often death-blows, told the desperate nature of the service.

"Well, my man, what brings you upon this coast ?" said one of the officers to Edward Catchpole, as he was sauntering lazily along the seaside.

"Oh," replied Edward, "I have got a holiday, and I wish to spend a day or two by the seaside."

"A day or two! Why you have been here six days, and you have been staying at Hollesley, and Boyton, and Felixstowe. Come, come, young man, you are up to some work which may get you into trouble. You had better take my advice, and sheer off."

"I have no unlawful calling; if I had, I might deserve your scrutiny. You think, perhaps, that I am connected with smugglers, and am here for the purpose of giving them information. I am, however, much more desirous of receiving than of giving information. I never saw a smuggler's boat in my life. You suspect me, I see; but what of ?—tell me."

"I ought to be suspicious of the truth of what you tell me. But I never saw you before, and your looks do not betray deceit."

"Are you sure you never saw me before ? Perhaps you may be mistaken. I have seen you before to-day, and have spoken to you before this day. I know you, if you do not know me."

"I certainly do not know you, and assuredly have never spoken to you till now. My memory is pretty accurate as to persons and faces, yet neither the one nor the other are familiar to me in you."

"Your face is familiar to me. I never saw you more than twice, and then you spoke to me, and very kindly too."

"You certainly puzzle me. What is your name, and whence do you come ?"

"You are Edward Barry, and I am Edward Catchpole. Do you remember the lad that drove his sister down to the boat-house at Bawdsey ?"

"Yes, I remember you now, though you are greatly changed. But what brings you here ?"

"That which keeps you here night and day ! I am upon the look-out for the smugglers."

"You may look a long time if you are looking for Will Laud. Do you not know that he is in the British navy ?"

"I knew that he was so, but I do not know that he is. My sister told me if I met you to make you acquainted with her trials, and to ask your assistance."

Here the young man told him the events which had taken place, and her fears that Laud had returned to his old career.

"I do not think he has. His old companions are as active as ever ; but I heard that he had split with them, and that, when he was taken by the pressgang, he was quarrelling with Luff, who, as I understood, escaped, and swore to finish his work upon Laud whenever he could catch him. There is not a man among us but would run any risk to deliver that fellow up to justice. We have had orders from Government to secure him if we can, and the reward is extended to us. He is a daring wretch, and knowing, as he must do, our determination to take him, it is my conviction that he will never be taken alive. But, if you wish to see a bit of sharp work, we have got information that he is now off this coast, preparing to land a cargo on the Vere. If you have a mind to lend a hand to take him, you can be of great service to us, without running much danger in work that you are not accustomed to."

"That I will do gladly."

"Well, now listen. You cannot walk five hundred yards along the brow of the beach without meeting one of my men. They are all upon the shore in readiness, and have had their eyes upon you, though you have not seen them. Look along the line of the coast against the upper ridge of shingle at the spring-tide mark,—you see nothing. If you walk along that line five hundred yards from where you stand, you will see a head pop up from the shingle and salute you. They are placed there, and have buried themselves in the shingle on purpose to watch your motions. You are suspected to be the person appointed to hoist a white flag, opposite Havergate Island, as a signal that the boat may come ashore. I implicitly believe what you have told me of yourself, and, if you will assist me, I will in return render you all the assistance I can in search of your object."

"I will do anything you appoint me to do within my power."

"I ask nothing of you, but what you can easily perform. Remember the watchword which I now give you. It is 'King George for ever,' an expression you must use if any of my men salute you. What I want you to do is, to pass along the whole line in the direction of the spring-tide mark, which is the highest point that the tide reaches. Every five hundred yards you will find yourself spoken to by one of my men, who will say, 'Who goes there?' Do you reply, 'King George for ever!' They will say 'Hurrah! pass on.' You will find fourteen men, which will tell you that four miles of this coast is strictly guarded to-night. Pass along the whole line; but note when you come to the seventh man, and lay this pole, and white flag which is bound to it, about twenty yards on this side of him. You will observe that, at that point, a tall poplar tree in Sudbourn Grove, on the horizon, will be in a direct line with you and the Shepherd's Cottage on Havergate Island. Leave the flag-pole there until you return from going the whole line. Take this keg over your shoulder, and replenish every man's can as you pass along, for they will have sharp work to-night, and it is cold work lying in suspense. As you come back from the line, unfurl the flag, and fix the staff strongly in the ground. The wind blows off-shore, and will soon carry it streaming outward. It will then be your duty to take up your position at a respectful distance from the spot, and see that no one from the land removes the flag. I strongly suspect that the old shepherd, who lives in the Red Cottage on Havergate Island, is the man who will come to remove it if he can. If you can secure him without our aid, so much the better; but if not, just put your lips to this whistle which I give you, and assistance will be close at hand. At all events, the old fellow must be secured, and carried back to his cottage, and be bound to his bed. And you must remain with him until night draws on. Then put the old man's light, an oil lamp, which you will find standing under the bed, into the little window looking towards the sea, which is at the gable-end to the east.

"Then you must come over again with his boat, and mind and shove her the full length of her moorings into the water before you fix her anchor on the shore, or the falling tide will leave her high and dry. Then return to the place, where you can bury yourself in the shingle. If I mistake not, as soon as the moon is high, you will see a boat come ashore with a cargo. There is a dell not far off the flag, to which they will probably carry all their tubs. You must not be seen by them. You will easily see how my men manage to hide themselves. Now be very particular in noting what I tell you, or the lives of many may be forfeited. After the men have landed their goods, two of them will go across to the river, to see if the shepherd's boat is moored ready for them. When they come back, you will hear them say 'Up! all's right!' They will then each take up his burden, and proceed with it to the river's side. I expect there will be ten or twelve of them. As soon as they are all fairly out of the dell, do you give a good loud long whistle. By this time, my men, who will have seen the boat coming ashore, will be getting on their hands and knees close up to you. The smugglers will throw down their loads, and hasten to their boat; we shall be ready to receive them. But, whatever you do, lie still, and you will be out of danger; and if you have a mind to see what a battle is, you will have a good view of it. I do not ask you to risk your life, you will probably see some of us killed, and should I be among the number, just remember, that in the bottom of my cartridge-box there is a letter to my sister, which I will get you to deliver. Do you think you fully understand me ? and are you now willing to help us ? It is singular that I should find in you the very instrument we wanted. I was about to have you secured, and to perform the part myself ; but ten to one if the old shepherd saw me, but he would smell powder, and keep at home ; but, seeing you a country youth, he will not mind you, but will come to the scratch. You see how much depends upon your courage."

Young Edward Catchpole had long made up his mind, notwithstanding all the danger, to run any risk sooner than give up the enterprise ; like his sister he possessed great personal courage, and was quick, intelligent, and active. He also looked upon the cause as a good one ; it was for his king and country, and for a sister whom he loved. He had given up the idea of meeting with Laud, and thought only of securing the vile assassin whose crimes had reached such an enormous pitch. He entered upon his commission immediately, pursued his career along the high-water mark of the beach, and, true enough, about every five hundred yards, a head popped up from the shingle, with, "Who goes there ?" "King George for ever ! " was the answer ; and " That 's right, my hearty, we'll drink his health if you please," was the hint for the young man to replenish the brave sailor's can. He noted the seventh man ; there he left the flag and staff, and proceeded on the whole length of the line. As he returned he placed the pole firmly into the deep shingle, and unfurled the white sheet, which soon formed a most conspicuous streamer in the air. He then quietly secreted himself in the manner he had been shown by one of the men, by working his body into the shingle, and letting the larger stones fall over him until he was completely covered, save his head. It was not long before a sail, which had been seen in the distance, now kept standing off and on in the offing. But now came his own work.

About an hour after the flag had been unfurled, Edward plainly heard the bleating of sheep, and saw

a shepherd driving a score of sheep leisurely along
towards the flag, apparently watching his sheep
cropping the scant herbage of the North Vere. As
he came whistling on, and approached the staff, looking
cautiously around him, Edward thought it was time
to commence proceedings, especially as the old man
laid hold of the flagstaff to unship it. He jumped
up, and called to the shepherd,—

"I say, old boy, let that bell wether of mine alone,
will you?"

The shepherd started, and left the staff, and approached the young man.

"What do you put that flag there for, young man?"

"Because such are my orders."

"But suppose I wish to have that flag for a sheet
for my bed to-night, who shall prevent it?"

"I will."

"Why, I could lick half a dozen such fellows as you,
with one arm."

"Maybe so—but come, now, let's have a fair trial of
strength. Lay down your crook between us, and see
if you or I can pull the other over it. If you succeed,
then take the flag. If I, then you must take yourself
off how you can."

"Done," said the shepherd—"it shall be a bargain;"
and he threw his crook down on the ground. "Now
for it, young man."

Accordingly, they approached each other. Young
Edward saw that he had a formidable antagonist to
contend with, a brawny, sinewy frame, full of compact
strength, and more than an equal match for his youth;
but he resolved not to give the whistle, if he could
overcome the man any how by himself.

"Stop," said Edward; "you have laid the crook
so as to give yourself the upper hand: that is not fair.
Lay it down from sea to river, so that we both have the
same chance in the slant. I'll show you what I mean."

And the young man showed him in a moment what
he meant; for, taking up the crook, and stooping down
to place it as he had said, with a shepherd's dexterity

(for the reader will remember that the youth was also a shepherd) he swung it round the ankle of the old man, and at the same instant gave it such a jerk, as pitched him backwards upon his head, which came with such violence upon the stones, that he was completely stunned. Edward was for a moment fearful that he was dead; but conjecturing, very wisely, that he might revive, he took out of his wallet the old man's sheep-cords (strong thongs which shepherds use when they dress their sheep, or such as sheep-shearers use when they clip them), and, without more ado, he tied his hands and legs together behind him, so that he was completely pinioned.

It was well that young Catchpole had taken this advantage and precaution; for, upon searching the inner pocket of the wallet, he found a brace of pistols, primed and loaded, which would have made the contest very uneven. As the old man shortly began to revive, he called out most lustily for help.

"Hold your tongue," said Edward, "or I will shoot you dead with your own pistols! Lie still, and no one will hurt you. What should an honest man, in your calling, do with such weapons as these?"

The old fellow was soon convinced that he had to deal with as good a hand as his own; and one as expert at catching a ram, too. His arms and legs were tied in such a scientific manner, as convinced him that the young man was a shepherd. He thought it best, therefore, to bear his present condition silently.

"Come along, old boy," said the youth, as he stuck the shepherd's crook under the cords, and began dragging him along towards his boat; "I'll ease you down to the river."

"Take care you are not eased down yourself," said the old man. "I have friends, who will give you your deserts before long, and ease me of these clutches."

"I'll tell you what you deserve, old man; and what, if the coastguard suffer to-night, you will receive. You deserve to be thrown into the river as you are; and if I have many words with you, and you refuse

to give me a plain direction and answer to whatever
question I put to you, you may depend upon it I will
do it myself; and that will soon settle all disputes
between us. You have had in your wallet, pistols;
your crook would make a flagstaff; and I find, upon
dragging you along, that, as your jacket buttons give
way, you have half a sheet round your body. Tell me,
when did you intend to give the smugglers the signal?
It will do you no good to tell me a lie. You have seen
enough to be convinced I understand what you are.
You had better tell me the truth at once, or a cold
salt-water bath will compel you to do so."

"Not to-night!—not to-night!"

"Why not to-night?"

"Because the coastguard are upon the watch."

As they proceeded on their way, Edward asked the
old man, "Do you expect Captains Laud or Luff to-
night? You may as well tell me; for you must be
pretty well convinced, by this time, that I know what
is going on."

"Well—I expect Captain Luff. Laud is dead."

The young man fairly dropped the crook, as he
repeated Maud's words—"Laud is dead! Laud is
dead!—How do you know that?"

"If you will unbind me, I will tell you all about it."

"Perhaps I may, when you tell me how and where he
died, and show me what proof you have of his death."

"Will you unbind me then?"

"Yes; when I think you have been bound long
enough."

"These thongs cut me sore."

"How can that be? they are too broad to cut;
and if you do not attempt to draw your hands asunder,
you know, as well as I do, that the knot is tied so that
they cannot hurt you. I see, by your keeping your
hands close together, that they do not hurt you."

They had now arrived at the river's side, where a
large ferry-boat, such as is used to carry stock over
from the mainland to the island, was moored against
the shore. Edward lifted the old man into the broad-

bottomed craft, and laying him down upon the boards, pulled up the anchor, and shoved off towards the island. The old man soon perceived that Edward was no sailor, by the manner in which he managed, or rather mismanaged the boat; and truly this was the hardest work the young man had yet to perform. He had been so taken up with the thought of doing everything he was commissioned to do, and in his pride so determined to do it all himself, without help, that he had overlooked his greatest difficulty, and forgot that he should want assistance to row the boat. He still did not use his whistle; but, with very great exertion, and very awkward management, contrived to bring the boat to the island, and to shove her along the side of the marsh wall, to a creek, close by the shepherd's house. He then lifted the old man out of the boat, and dragged him up the mud wall, and laid him down at his cottage door. The door was locked; and, in the scuffle, the key of it had fallen out of the old man's pocket; and Edward was obliged to make his way in at a low window behind the house; when, having forced back the bolt, he pulled the old man in, and lifted him on to a bed, which was in the room adjoining, and took a seat by his side.

" I'm both hungry and thirsty after all my exertions; have you any refreshment of any kind in this comfortable dwelling ? "

" You will find plenty in the closet by the fireplace. I wish I could eat and drink with you."

" So you may, and I will feed you as if you were my cosset lamb."

He soon found that the shepherd's cottage contained sufficient to recruit the spirits of any man whose stomach was not too proud for wholesome food. There was a slice of cold boiled bacon, and bread and cheese in plenty. There was brandy, too, but very bad water; and it required something stronger than tea to take off the brackish taste; brandy alone could make it palatable for man. The cattle sometimes suffered by drinking it. The young shepherd fed the old one,

whose muscular limbs were now as powerless as an
infant's; not from second childhood, but from the
dexterity with which they were bound together.
There was something of kindness in the young man's
manner, though he was justified, in self-defence, to
take the advantage he had done.

"Now," said he, "tell me how you know Captain
Laud is dead ? "

"Captain Luff told me so."

"And is that all you know of it ? Have you no
other proof ? "

"Yes ; I have the captain's watch, which Luff gave
to me, and the case of it has his true-love's name engraved in the inside. The watch is in the old plum-
tree box, in the cupboard."

The young man eagerly examined the spot. He
found the box, and in it the watch, with both names
engraved on the inside of the case, shining as bright,
and the engraving as sharp, as if it had been executed
only that very day. "William Laud and Margaret
Catchpole," round the interior circumference, and
" June 1st, 1794," with a wreath of victory surrounding
it, in the centre.

"All this is correct, as you say ; but how did he
die ? "

"Well, I will tell you all I know. Captain Luff
(if you do not know him, I do) is a most desperate
fellow ; a price is set upon his head, dead or alive, so
that it be but taken. Well, he murdered the poor
girl whose name is written in the watch ; and I firmly
believe that he murdered Captain Laud too ! Towards
the close of the last year I was upon Sudbourn Heath,
keeping my sheep, and who should I meet but Captain
Luff, who accosted me with this question :—

" ' Have you seen my young commander, Captain
Laud, pass this way ? '

"Well, it was a curious question, and quite natural
too ; for about six o'clock that very morning, as I was
taking my sheep out of the fold, who should pass by me
but the gallant young fellow whom he inquired after ?

Singularly enough he asked after Luff, and whether I knew if he was upon the coast. I told him that I had not had any signals lately; but that some of the crew were ashore, and were staying at the Mariner's Compass, at Orford. Well, I told Luff the same as I now tell you; and he no sooner received the intelligence, than with all the eagerness of a blood-hound when he touches upon the scent of his victim, he was off for Orford in a moment. Well, I thought this was all for old acquaintance' sake, or for business; so I rather rejoiced in the adventure. That very night I had made an appointment to take some game; and as I went up the Gap Lane, leading to the Heath, I heard angry words, and soon found the two captains at variance. I had no wish, as you may suppose, to interfere with their strife, so I quietly laid myself up in the ferns. It was a dreadful sound to hear the thunder of those two men's voices. How they cursed each other! At length I heard the report of two pistols, and one of the balls passed within a yard of my head; but as for blows, I could not count them. They fought each other like two bull-dogs, I should say for near an hour, till I heard the snap and jingle of a broken sword, and then one of them fled. I found the broken part of the blade next morning close to the spot. It was red with blood; and the marks of feet in the sand were as numerous as if twenty men had been contending. I found drops of blood sunk into the sand all the way down the lane, until you come to the marshes: here I lost the track. I have seen no more of Laud since. But what makes me think that he was killed by Luff on that night is the after-behaviour of the captain. About two months after this occurrence I received a signal from the North Vere; and who should it be but Luff. Well, he came home to my cottage, and as we sat together I said, by way of a sounder, 'Where's Captain Laud?'

"'What makes you ask that question?' says he, hastily and fiercely. 'Have you any particular reason for asking me after him? Speak out at once,' says he,—' speak out; have you heard anything about him?'

"The terrific glare of the fiend's eye fell upon me so cruelly that I dared not tell him I had witnessed the fight, so I said, 'I have not seen the captain for so long a time, that I did not know where he was.'

"'Ho! ho! that's it, is it?' says he. 'Have you seen him since the morning you fed your sheep on Sudbourn Heath?'

"'No,' says I; 'he was then anxious to see you. Did you find him?'

"'Yes, I did; and I have reason to think he was lost at sea that very night; for he agreed to come on board, and we have seen nothing more of him, nor two of our crew, since that very time. Two of my men were in the river boat, but I have seen nothing of them since. They were to have joined the crew off the head of the North Vere, but we never saw them again.'

"'That's very odd,' says I; 'but how did you join the crew?'

"'I got a cast down the river in Master Mannell's boat, the old fisherman of Boyton.'

"Then, after a pause,

"'Here, Jim,' says he, 'I'll make you a present of poor Will's watch. I do not like to wear it; it grieves me when I look at it. We used to be such friends.'

"Now I thought this very strange, and it confirmed me in the opinion that his conscience would not let him rest. I took the watch, and you have now got it in your hand."

"What shall I give you for this watch?" said Edward.

"What you like; for ever since I have had it, it has appeared to me as if I was an accomplice in Captain Laud's murder."

"I will give you half a guinea."

"Well, it is yours."

"I will put the money into the box in the cupboard. Time now wears away. What are all these pieces of wood for?"

" They are tholes for the boat, when the smugglers use it."

" With your permission I will take them with me. Have you any oars for them also ? "

" No ! the smugglers bring their own oars."

" Well, I must be moving ; and now since you have told me the truth, and I have every reason to thank you, I will candidly tell you who I am : I am Margaret Catchpole's brother."

" You are a shepherd, then ? "

" I am a shepherd."

" I was sure of it by the manner in which you used these thongs. May I ask, is your sister dead ? "

" She is not dead. How many men do you expect from the lugger when they land ? "

" Ten, with the captain."

" Well, lie you still now. I must, for the sake of fulfilling the orders of my commander, fasten your cords to the bedstead, or I may be blamed. So : that will do. Now, should the captain himself come to see you, he will be convinced that the foul play was not your part ; and if he does not come to-night, I will. But time presses, and I must do my duty. Where is your lamp ? "

" I see by your question," said the old man, " that all is discovered. You want the lamp to put in the window upstairs ; you will find it under the bed."

There it was, and was soon lighted and put in its proper place : a joyful signal of success to the brave and patient coastguard, and a fatal lure to the desperadoes on board the smuggler.

" Now then, old friend, good-bye," said Edward. " If success attend our scheme you and I may be better acquainted ; you may be glad that you have told me all the truth. Farewell."

The youth was soon on board the ferry-boat ; and with much labour brought her to the same spot where he had before unmoored her. The tide had fallen some feet, and was near its last ebb, so that he very wisely drew her up as high as he could on to the shore, concluding that if he anchored her in the water when the tide flowed again, which it would soon do, it would cover the anchor on the shore. He drew her up far enough just to place her cable's end at high-water mark; and having put the tholes in their proper places, he then walked across to the white flag. Just before he passed the dell, who should lift up his head but young Barry!

"I began to think our plan had not succeeded. Is all right?"

"All is as you could wish it, and more; but I will tell you all another time."

"We can see the lugger," said young Barry, "standing off and on: our white flag is successful. You must go to the right, so as to lay yourself in such a position as to command a view of this little dell and the river. Bring yourself to anchor full a hundred yards from this hole, for I suspect the fight will be here; keep your head below the ocean mark when you give the signal, or a few bullets may whistle about your ears."

Only those who have had anything to do with the preventive service can tell the dangers and difficulties which the poor fellows who defend our trade have to encounter; how much toil and anxiety, and how seldom sufficient honour or reward do such men gain in discharging their onerous duty. It is a life of feverish vexation. Fancy fourteen men collected and stationed along four miles of coast the whole day, buried in the pebbles, and waiting on a cold night for the approach of the smuggler. They all saw the vessel reconnoitring and sailing about the offing: the least want of circumspection on their part would thwart the scheme which up to this moment promised success. Even the men accustomed to this kind of work shook with the anxiety of suspense; but what must have been the sensations of the young landsman who had to give the signal for the onset, in which more than one might fall? To say that he did not suffer severely, enough almost to make him wish himself at home, would not be true; the thought, however, that he might be instrumental in bringing the villain Luff to justice for all his crimes, and the singular manner in which he had discovered his treachery to Laud, made the young man some amends for the truly painful task he had undertaken.

Night now began to draw on, and the sea-birds left off their screaming; the tern and the dottrell hastened to their resting-places; and the last of all the feathered sea-shore tribe, the one which goes to roost the latest, the grey curlew, bent his rapid wing toward Havergate Island, and gave a mournful note as he flapped over the head of the young watchman. As the moon arose the wind began to blow a little fresh, and the ocean to roar upon the beach. The smugglers rejoiced at this, as it would enable them to land their cargo with less chance of being heard. The flag still streamed and flapped in the wind; the light shone like a star in the shepherd's cot; and the time drew near for the contest.

Not a sound could be now heard save that of the wind. The vessel, however, might be seen in the moonlight, approaching the shore; and now a heavy eight-oared boat was seen to leave her: she was heavily laden, even to the gunwale. The boat lurched through the breakers like a log. On she came, with her helmsman, John Luff, who laid her broadside on to the shore. Now for an anxious moment. Not a word was spoken. The wind preventing any sound along the shore, nothing could be heard even of the grounding of the boat's keel upon the beach. Dark figures of men were seen getting out of the boat. They were expert sailors, up to their work; as the sea heaved the boat up, they dragged her higher on the shore, until they could more conveniently unload her. This was done as expeditiously as possible; each man carried a sack heavily laden. They went to the very spot that Barry had named, deposited their load, and again returned to their boat. Twice they performed this work; and now the two last men, carrying the eight oars, brought up the rear. The eight quietly seated themselves on the sacks, whilst the other two went forward with the oars; they returned, and, as young Edward concluded, must have said, " All's right."

By this time the coastguard were drawing their lines closer to the spot, each man taking up his brother, or calling on him as he passed him, until the whole fourteen were within the space of ten yards from the flag; breathless, on their knees did they await the shrill whistle which, like the trumpet's sound, was to give the word for the charge.

Young Catchpole saw the smugglers emerge from the dell, with each man his sack upon his shoulder; for an instant he thought he ought to wait until they came the second time, but as his orders did not say so, and he judged that if they once stowed away half their cargo they would make quickly for the river, he deemed it best to give the signal at once; so drawing in his breath, he gave the whistle such a long, shrill blast, that had the wind lain that way it might have been heard to Orford. He did not raise himself up, and it was well he did not, for over his head whizzed a ball, and flash—flash—flash went the pistols. As was predicted the men dropped their cargoes, and ran for the pit, but here stood the coastguard ready to receive them, young Barry having brought his men down below the horizon of the sea, that they might not be exposed to the sight of the smugglers, whilst the river lying lower, and they ascending from it, became a visible mark against the moonlit water for their fire.

Dreadful was the contest that ensued. The smugglers formed a close line: the coastguard line was more measured, and with some spaces between each two men, so that their danger was the less. The firing, as they approached each other, was awful; two men of the smugglers fell. They closed nearer, and swords clashed and sparkled in the moonlight; and the uproar at length became more audible than the noise of the wind and waves. At last there was one sudden, tremendous yell from the boat's crew, and then the cry for quarter; some fell, others fled, not to the boat but along the coast. It was the object of the coast-guard not to pursue them so far as to separate from each other ; and as three fled one way, and two another, they merely sent flying shots after them, and cleared a passage to the boat. The shout announced the leader of the smugglers to be shot, and two more were lying by his side, and two surrendered, and were disarmed and guarded, whilst but one of the coast-guard had fallen.

As the enemy was dispersed young Barry mustered his men, and missed his comrade. They found him near the two smugglers who had first fallen. Close to them lay the captain, his arm nearly cut in two, shot in the side, and severely wounded on the head. Young Edward, who had seen the fight, now came forward to render further assistance. The two smugglers were dead ; but the preventive-service man and the captain of the crew were not dead, though both were severely wounded.

The two wounded men were taken to the shepherd's cottage. Four men, with Barry and young Edward, rowed across to the island, whilst ten men were left to guard the prisoners and the cargo, and to secure the smugglers' boat. The whole proved to be a most valuable prize.

The captain, as the reader may suppose, proved to be no other than the hated John Luff. The old shepherd was released by young Catchpole, and from cramp and pain from his long doubled-up position he could scarcely stand. The two wounded men were placed upon his bed, presenting such a contrast of feature, expression, and character, as the ablest artist in the world could not have justly delineated. Luff, with his dark brow, haggard eye, and hairy face, looking like a dying hyena, looked up and saw before him, Barry, Catchpole, and the shepherd ; and with the scowl of revenge (a strong passion to exhibit in such agony), he muttered a dreadful curse upon them all. The poor coastguard man, with his pale but placid countenance, though suffering severely from his wounds, extended his hands to his commander, and implored him to let him be carried to another bed, to let him lie on the floor in the other room, or anywhere but head to head beside the demon who lay shuddering and cursing by his side.

The bed of the shepherd's daughter, who was at that time staying at Orford, was brought down and laid in the keeping-room beside the fireplace, and the poor fellow was laid upon it. Luff's death-hour was evidently at hand. It was a fearful thing to see him in his horrible tortures, and to hear him, in his groans and moans, proclaiming himself the murderer of Will Laud. Whenever he opened his eyes he saw nothing but the evidences of guilt before him, as he raved in wild frenzy,—

"There! there! there! I see him! He is not dead!—no! no! no! There's Laud and Margaret Catchpole! Look! they laugh at me!"

At last, with one wild scream, his spirit, like an affrighted bird, fled away. Never did those who stood near him witness such a death. A cold shudder crept over their flesh, and they owned one to another that they should never forget that awful sight.

When it became known that the notorious smuggler, John Luff, was killed, numbers came to see him; and few that saw his body but owned that he was a fearful fellow when living. Government paid the reward over into the hands of the coastguard, who all subscribed liberally towards the comfort of their wounded messmate. Edward Catchpole was included among those who shared the reward, and this enabled him to pay all his expenses without any recurrence to his sister's purse.

When young Catchpole returned to Nacton with the eventful tidings of his journey, and related all the particulars to Margaret, stating his full belief of Laud's death, she pondered for a while over his statement, and then expressed her dissent from her brother's conclusions.

"I see no certain proof of Laud's death," said she.

"The old shepherd and the wretch Luff, may both have supposed him dead; but there is a mystery not yet cleared up which fills me with strange hopes—I mean the sudden disappearance of the two sailors with the boat that very night. Luff made no mention of them in his dying moments. I really think these two men are somehow connected with the safety of Laud; and I yet have hope."

She rejoiced, however, that Laud was not found in company with his former band, and especially with that bad man Luff; and drew conclusions, in her own mind, favourable to his character and conduct. She was very grateful to her brother; and not long afterwards she proposed to return to her place. She had certainly been very remiss in not communicating with her mistress once since she left her. So taken up was she with her thoughts of Laud, that she forgot her situation; and, until her brother's return, had never spoken of going back to Ipswich. Her mistress not hearing of or from her, sent over to Brandiston, and there learned that she had never been to see her uncle and aunt, nor had they heard anything of her. A man was sent to Nacton, and, unfortunately, the cottage was locked up, as Margaret had been that day to spend a few hours with her first mistress, at the Priory Farm. These strange circumstances made her mistress at Ipswich conclude that she was gone in search of Laud; and consequently she engaged another servant. When Margaret returned to St. Margaret's Green she found her place filled up; and her mistress reproached her for her neglect in not having had some communication with her. Margaret felt hurt and disappointed. She stayed a short time at one or two places, but was extremely unsettled and dissatisfied. She was in the habit of frequently visiting St. Margaret's Green, and of being asked to go and see the children. About eight months after a vacancy unexpectedly occurred in Mrs. Cobbold's establishment, and Margaret entered a second time into the service of her former mistress, in the capacity of cook; but her stay this time was short. She was now as unlike as possible to the Margaret of former days. She was not happy. Her temper had been soured by disappointment, and her spirit made restless by rumours of Laud being alive. She became impatient towards her fellow-servants, careless in her dress and manner, and negligent in her work—a complete contrast to her former self, who had been a pattern of order, decency, and regularity. At the end of one year, it became her mistress's painful duty to give her a final warning. It was a real heart-felt sorrow to that benevolent lady to be compelled, for the sake of example to her other servants, to discharge Margaret. But she could not do otherwise.

Here was a painful duty discharged conscientiously. Let not the reader think that it made no impression. It fell with full force upon Margaret's mind. Margaret wept most bitterly when she found that she must now break off all connexion with that family in which she had once been so happy. She merely asked permission to remain till the end of the week, and that in such a subdued tone and supplicating manner, as touched her mistress's heart. It is needless to say that her request was granted.

The morning of departure arrived, and not a servant, no, nor a child in that house, could say " Good-bye " without tears. Her mistress, when handing over to her the money directed to her by Laud, made Margaret sit down, and conversed with her upon her future prospects. She also gave her some good books for a remembrance, expressed a hope that she would read them, and told her she should forget all but her good deeds, and be ever ready to serve her.

Then, with tears rolling down her cheeks, Margaret tottered to the cart which had been provided to take her to Brandiston, and left that house never to enter it again, and never to look upon it without terror.

The author cannot help introducing at the close of this chapter an authenticated document, which has been sent to him from Reading, in Berkshire. It is the testimony of a man still living, who has never forgotten Margaret Catchpole: and the reader will say he had good reason to remember her. This man now lives in the service of Mr. John Snare, No. 16 Minster Street, Reading; and, since the publication of the former edition of this work, has made known to his master a providential escape which he had in his infancy, through the intrepidity of this extraordinary woman. Poor Margaret! it is with inexpressible pleasure that the author transcribes this tribute to her memory; for it proves to him, that whatever was the cause of her unsettled state of mind, her noble spirit was still as prompt to hear the cry of the helpless as in her days of confidence and comfort with her beloved mistress. The author is indebted to the Rev. John Connop, Bradfield Hall, Reading, for the original document, which he now gives to the public; and which he is happy to add, is fully confirmed by persons now living at Ipswich.

The Declaration of William White, of Reading, in Berkshire.

"My parents lived on St. Margaret's Green, St. Margaret's parish, Ipswich, about five doors from the house of John Cobbold, Esq. Margaret Catchpole was then living in Mr. Cobbold's service as cook. About the middle of the spring of 1797, I, being then a child about six years of age, was playing on the Green with many of the neighbours' children; and in the midst of our sport, a mad bull rushed most furiously towards us, directing his attack upon our little group to the precise spot where I stood. Paralysed by fear and surprise, I saw no hope of safety in flight, and must have fallen a victim to the assault of the infuriated beast, had not my companions set up a cry of alarm. At this critical moment, Margaret Catchpole rushed out of Mr. Cobbold's house, to ascertain the cause of the disturbance, and had the courage to fly in the face of the bull, just as he was in the act of tossing me. Indeed I was slightly gored by him, and must inevitably have been severely injured, had not this courageous woman snatched me up, and carried me into Mr. Cobbold's kitchen, taking every care of me until my parents arrived.

"I was not seriously hurt, but I have been told that my bruises and scars did not disappear for several weeks ; and during this time I was visited by Margaret Catchpole and Mrs. Cobbold, who both took great notice of me, and evinced great anxiety for my recovery.

"I remember that this courageous act of Margaret Catchpole's was much talked of at the time, and the Rev. Mr. Fonnereau, the rector of St. Margaret's, took much interest in the affair ; so much, indeed, did he think of it, that on my marriage in 1817, he, being still the rector, and performing the ceremony, reminded me of the extraordinary circumstance which had occurred in my childhood, and of my providential escape from an early grave.

"My uncle, Samuel Bayley (my mother's brother), was cooper and brewer to J. Cobbold, Esq., being in his employment at the Cliff Brewery, near Ipswich, at the time the above occurred.

"WILLIAM WHITE.

"READING, February 18th, 1847."

CHAPTER XXI

GUILT AND CRIME

THE reader will be anxious to know what really was the fate of Will Laud, and will not be surprised to learn that Margaret's idea was quite in accordance with the fact. When Luff quitted the old shepherd upon Sudbourn Heath, in search of Laud, he was prepared to find him at the Compasses at Orford, and there he did find him, and he pretended to be glad to see him, and to be very friendly with him. All former ani-

mosities seemed to be extinct; and Luff quickly
wormed out of him the secrets of his heart. He asked
after Margaret with as much apparent indifference as
if he had heard nothing of her.

"I have left her for ever," said Laud. "I will
have nothing more to do with her. Some more
powerful enemy than I have ever contended with has
at last prevailed over me, and pulled down the proud
flag I had hoisted in her love. I heard her say, almost
to my face, that she would never see another sailor,
though she must have been expecting me home, for
I sent her word by an old messmate that I was coming;
and what could she mean, but to let me know flatly
that she preferred some lubberly landsman (perhaps
some powdered footman) to one of Lord Howe's
Britons? I could stand it no longer, so I just threw
all my prize-money overboard; and here I am, Jack,
ready to join your crew again. Have you forgotten
our last rub? Come, give us your hand, Jack."

Luff put out his blood-stained palm, and pretended
all the peace of a restored friendship. Grog was
ordered; and the two easily struck a bargain to go
on board again in the service of Captain Bargood.
But Luff was too determined a villain to forgo that
opportunity, which now offered itself, of fulfilling the
deadly purpose he had often sworn to his crew that
he would accomplish, "to bring Laud a captive, dead
or alive, on board the brig." The treacherous fellow
had left no stone unturned to bring about this plan.
It was he who pursued such a system of fraud with
regard to Margaret as led to her disgrace. He hired
sailors to deceive her with false tales, and to learn
what they could of Laud, that he might the more
easily wreak his vengeance upon his victim. And
now at last here was the object of his hatred, trusting
to him as he would have done to the most tried friend.
He was as loud and artful in his ridicule of Margaret
as a determined monster of envy could be. He had
heard, he said, many tales of her; and that she was
at last going to marry one of the brewhouse men

Such were the inventions of this hollow-hearted villain, to inflame the irritable mind of Laud. There were two of the crew present, to whom Luff had given the wink, and made them to understand he had trapped his man.

"Let us take a bit of a cruise, and have a look at the port," said Luff to his pretended friend; and then turning to the others, he said, "We shall be in again presently, and go on board to-night."

"Aye, aye, master," replied one of the men, "all right! —I say, Sam," observed he, when the two captains had left the room, "what a shocking fellow our captain is! I'll wager now that he either puts a bullet through Laud's head, or a dagger in his heart, or shoves him overboard at night!"

"Aye, Jim, I don't mind a brush with the coast-guard, but I don't like such cold-blooded work as this any more than you do. Don't let us wait for the captain; but, as soon as we have finished our grog, let's be off for the boat."

"With all my heart, Sam; and let us drink our young captain's health, and good luck to him."

Luff had enticed his captain to a longer walk than he expected; and no sooner had they entered the Gap Lane than he began a quarrel, and presently attacked him, sword in hand. Laud defended himself with great dexterity, until his sword was broken, and he himself disarmed. He fled towards the marshes, but was overtaken, cut down, and cast for dead into one of those deep marsh ditches which abound in the neighbourhood of Orford. After Luff had thus wreaked his vengeance, he crept stealthily towards the town; and as he went picked up Laud's watch, which had fallen from his pocket. It made his blood, already heated with exertion, grow cold with conscious horror. He was too great a villain, however, to have much thought of mercy, pity, or repentance. He entered the Compasses and called for a strong north-wester, and inquired for his men, and learned they had been gone to their boat some time. He gave them some

coarse malediction for their pains, and sat down to his
strong potation.

The two men were at that time crossing a plank
over the very dyke which Laud had been cast into,
and were startled by his groans. On looking about
them they observed a man's head just out of the
water, beside the bank; they pulled him out, and found
to their horror that it was Laud. Having decided on
taking him to his uncle's, they lifted Laud up and
carried him across the marshes, and laid him as carefully as they could upon some old sails at the bottom
of the boat; and instead of going down the river to
Hollesley Bay, they rowed directly up the river with
the flood tide. They arrived at Aldborough just as the
tide turned, and had the precaution or prudence,
directly they landed, to send their boat adrift; which,
getting into the channel, was carried down the river,
and was cast upon a sand-bank, within a few yards of
the smuggler's cutter, by which means it was supposed
that the two men had perished; for at daybreak,
when Luff came on board, he was the first to discover
the boat, keel upwards, upon the bank.

"It served them right," said the captain, "for
leaving their commander behind them."

They had safely conveyed Will Laud to the Jolly
Tar, which then stood close to the river's side. His
uncle was sent for, who came, attended by Mr. Nursey,
at that time the skilful and highly esteemed surgeon
of Aldborough. He found him dreadfully wounded;
but at length, by strict attention and consummate
skill, succeeded in effecting a cure. That uncle had
always loved his nephew, and in some measure considered himself responsible for the waywardness of
his seafaring propensities; and he took him to his
home, and treated him in every respect as a lost son
restored.

Here, then, was an opportunity—a golden opportunity—for reformation. Laud's former character had
been cancelled by his service in the British navy; and
his gallant conduct on the glorious 1st of June had

obtained for him a free discharge, with prize-money, and certificate of character in the service. He was now placed in a situation calculated to restore him to independence. In the years 1795 and 1796 he served his uncle faithfully; and such were the hopes entertained of his steadiness and attention to business, that at the end of that year, when his uncle died, he left him all that he possessed.

It may seem strange that Laud should never have sought for Margaret Catchpole during all this time, or that she should not have made further inquiries about him. Had they met at this period, and come to a mutual explanation, they might both have been spared from that misery and remorse attendant upon a degraded character. But it was otherwise decreed. He had always brooded over his imaginary wrongs at the hands of Margaret; had learned to think little of her; and never to have forgiven her for that unfortunate speech the night he left Ipswich. And when he became a master and a man of substance (as above related), he did not appear to be settled or happy. The news of Luff's death might have been supposed to take away from him any hankering after the illicit pursuits of his youth; but the escape of some of the crew, and their strong attachment to Laud, induced him to listen to their proposals of service, and to employ a ship in the trade; and he actually sent out smugglers, though he would not head them himself; so that, very soon after the decease of his uncle, Laud became deeply engaged again in the illicit traffic of the coast.

But what was Margaret doing all this time? She returned to her uncle and aunt Leader, and became their assistant. She undertook once more the management of the children, and was instrumental in restoring order and decency in the house. She did not feel quite so lively an interest in this employment as she had formerly done, though her aunt's manner was a complete contrast to what it had formerly been. By her uncle's advice, she put the money she never considered her own into the hands of the much-respected general shopkeeper of the parish, who placed it in the bank, and became a trustee for her. Still she resolved not to touch it, but to keep it, as the property of Laud, until she should be more sure of his death. She had great hopes still that she should one day see him again. She lived with her uncle and aunt, and made herself useful in every possible way; nor did she ever murmur at her condition, though she often sighed over past misfortunes.

In the month of May, 1797, she received a letter from old George Teager, her fellow-servant, which ran thus:—

" MARGARET,

" This comes hoping it may find you well, as it still leaves me, though very deaf. I have got a bit of news for you, which I know you will be glad to hear. I was going down the Wash yesterday, when who should I meet but Will Laud ? He looked uncommon well, and was very civil to me. He asked me many questions about you ; and I set him right about some bad splints and curbs he had got in his head. He told me he should soon manage to see you, so no more from old

" GEORGE TEAGER.

" MARGARET'S GREEN, May 3rd, 1797."

Imagine poor Margaret's anxiety. She waited seven days in such a state of feverish suspense as only those so situated can feel. She rested neither day nor night, but became each morning more anxiously disturbed, until she determined to go herself to Ipswich.

Now Laud had been to Ipswich to purchase some timber, and to dispose of some of his smuggled goods. He had met old Teager, the coachman, and had treated him with a friendly glass, which the old man seldom refused. He had also met an old messmate accidentally ; a good-for-nothing fellow, whom Luff had formerly made use of to deceive Margaret with false reports concerning him. Laud had treated this man to some grog; and in talking over old times, the man disclosed some of Luff's villainy, with which Laud had never before been acquainted; especially his conduct to Margaret on that wretched night in which Laud had sought an interview with her. This fellow, whose name was John Cook, told him that he was one of the sailors bribed to deceive her, and to go backwards and forwards with false reports to the kitchen of St. Margaret's Green.

Laud now saw the reason for poor Margaret's exclamation, " I will have nothing more to do with any sailors ! " The truth broke on him with such conviction, that he resolved to seek out his betrothed the very moment he had fulfilled his engagement at Ipswich. It is a remarkable fact, that, on the very same day on which Laud left the town with the full determination to see and have an explanation with Margaret, she determined to go to Ipswich, to explain (if she could find him) the whole of her conduct. This was on the evening of the 9th of May, 1797. She had frankly explained to her uncle the purpose of her journey; and as to the money in the hands of the trustee, she said, " If a letter comes to you, from me, about it, you can then consult with Mr. Smith about its disposal. I fully expect," she added, " to meet Laud at Ipswich, and whatever his fortunes may be, I am determined to share them with him."

She arrived at Ipswich that afternoon, and took up her abode at her former lodgings at the Widow Syers', a distant relative of her mother's, though by no means a desirable person for Margaret to abide with at such a time. She did not go, as she ought to have done, to her good mistress, who would have instituted every inquiry for her; but she chose to pursue her own course. She saw the old coachman, and learned from him that he had seen Laud at the Salutation, in Carr Street, only the day before. She did not stay to ask any more questions, but off she went towards the public-house in question. On her way, it was her misfortune to meet with that vagabond, John Cook, the very fellow who had so often made a dupe of her before, and who was now the cause of her performing an act that is probably without precedent in female history. Intent but upon one thing, the obtaining an interview with her lover, the mainspring of all her prospects in life, and the centre to which all her hopes, wishes, thoughts, and cares were pointed, she was almost crazy with anxiety to see this worthless object of her idolatry. She had been betrayed into misfortunes by her blindness on this point; and though careful, prudent, and considerate upon almost every other thing, she had been, and was still, the easy victim of any artful machination which had for its bait the sight of her lover. Had she consulted any of her friends, Mr. Stebbing, Mr. Brooks, Mr. Notcutt, or her beloved mistress, she would not have fallen a prey to the artful villainy of a wicked man; but Margaret had forgotten at this time her mistress, and every other consideration, except the all-engrossing subject which filled her heart; and she saw neither danger nor difficulty, right nor wrong, but was ready to go anywhere, or to do anything, provided she could only have an explanation with Laud.

"Why, Margaret, is that you?" said John Cook as he met her, turning the corner of the Chaise and Pair, on the evening of the 9th of May; "why, where have you been all these livelong days? And what are you doing now in Ipswich?"

"I am in search of Laud: have you seen or heard anything of him to-day?"

"Yes, that I have; you are in luck to meet with the only person in the world who could tell you where he is! But this is not the place to be talking secrets. Come with me to the Marquis Cornwallis, where Laud and I have spent a merry time, and I will tell you all about him."

There was no difficulty in persuading her to accompany him, and on arriving at the inn, Margaret found by this fellow's conversation with the landlord, that Laud and he had spent the previous evening at that house. This confirmed her belief in his story, and enabled him to make her the easy dupe of all the vile inventions which were to follow.

They requested that they might have the parlour to themselves; and the ever-liberal Margaret ordered some refreshment, though she could, from her anxiety, partake of nothing herself.

"Well, I promised you I would tell you all about Laud; but first let me tell you that I set him right about your ugly speech that night when you got such a ducking."

"Did you? did you, indeed? What did he say to it? Did he forgive me?"

"Did he? Aye! I'll tell you what, I never saw a fellow so dumb-foundered before. He looked almost like a madman, cursed his stars, and swore they were all confederate against him. He swore you were the best creature in the world, and if he could but see you, he would make you happy."

"Oh, John! how good you were to tell him! But where is he? Is he in Ipswich? Do bring me to him?"

"Hold hard a bit; I must let you into a little bit of a secret. You must know that Laud and I are upon such intimate terms, that we communicate by a kind of expression known only to ourselves. He, as you know, went back to smuggling again after your rap, though that was not intentional on your part. He did not go to sea, but entered upon the timber trade, though he employed about twenty men under him to carry on his traffic. Now I know he would have gone in search of your hiding-place, if he had not been compelled to hide himself. The fact is, he is escaped from an arrest for five hundred pounds which he was bound to pay to the Excise, and but for a very lucky turn he would have been nabbed last night."

"Well, but where is he now?"

" I will tell you where he may be found to-morrow. All I know now is, that he took the mail last night, by the greatest good luck in the world, and went off to London. He is to write to me to-night, and I shall be able to tell you to-morrow."

That this was all a mere invention of this rascal's, to get out of Margaret all he could, the reader will easily believe. Lucky was it for her that she did not tell him what sum of money she had belonging to Laud, or every farthing of it would have gone into this fellow's hands. As it was, he managed to get out of her what little cash she could spare, under the promise of revealing to her the hiding-place of Laud. After chatting with him a long time, and hearing much of herself and her lover, all pure inventions of this fellow's brain, and easily detected by any person with less blindness upon the subject, Margaret took her leave of him, giving him half-a-crown to spend. She returned to the Widow Syers', and, as might be supposed, passed a feverish night, restless with nervous anxiety. Poor girl! she little thought of the mischief then brooding for her ruin.

The morrow came, bringing a letter to John Cook, of a very different description to that which Margaret anticipated. It ran thus:—

" DOG AND BONE, LAMBETH,
" May 8th, 1797.

" JACK,

" I sold the bay mare at Smithfield yesterday. I might ha' got more, but the nabs were about; so I wopt her off for ten. Old Snacks, at the Bone here, got his 'centage. I crabbed the old chap as well as I could; but he's up to snuff. You wouldn't ha' known old Peggy again. We blacked her white legs and popt a white face on to her, gave her a rat's tail, filed her teeth, and burnt her mark, and wop me if I mightent ha' sold her for a six-year old, if I hadn't been in a hurry. But she's off, they tell me, to serve in a foreign country. She's a right good un, though an old'n. All 's honour bright, Jack!

"I say, old boy, we talked o' the brown nag; can ye send him up to Chelmsford? or if to the Dog and Bone, direct to your old chum,

"BOB BUSH,

"Sam Snacks,

"Dog and Bone, Lambeth.

"To JOHN COOK,
　"Marquis Cornwallis,
　　"Ipswich, Suffolk."

This letter, which was found some days later at the inn, and delivered up to the constable of the parish of St. Margaret's, may serve to show the connexion which this fellow had with a gang of horse-stealers, who, at this time, infested the counties of Essex, Norfolk, and Suffolk. The brown nag here mentioned was one which had been turned off in the pastures of St. Margaret's, belonging to John Cobbold, Esq. He was a high-spirited little horse, and aged. The eyes of this rogue had been upon him, and a most diabolical project now entered his brain, of making Margaret Catchpole, whose early feats of riding were not unknown to him, the minister of this theft.

"I shall make something out of her now," said the fellow, "if I can only play upon her feelings. How shall I do it?"

A thought struck him that he would tear off the half of the letter containing the post-mark, and paste one which he would invent, on that half, and sign it for Will Laud. Margaret knew little or nothing of Will's handwriting, so that she could easily be deceived in this respect; and if she knew that it was not his, the fellow was ready enough to swear that he had hurt his hand by the falling of a spar, and so got a friend to write it for him. He put his wits to work, and concocted an epistle as nearly pertinent to what he had made out Laud's case to be, as he could.

He dated it from the same place from whence he received his own, and intended to write to Bob Bush to take the horse off Margaret's hands, if he could get her on to it. He wrote thus :—

"DOG AND BONE, LAMBETH, May 9th, 1797.

"DEAR JACK,

"Hurrah, my boy! Safely anchored, though I had cut my cable, and run; but I have got into a friendly port, and my pursuers shan't easily find me. Precious hard, though, Jack, after just finding out my girl, to have to tack and leave her. You might lend a hand now, just to serve an old friend. Margaret would make my present dull time a little lighter, if you could but find her up, and put her on the right road to find me. I think she would forgive me, if you could explain matters a little to her. Tell her we could get married here, and after a time all would be well. But, Jack, mum must be the order of the day. Don't you fire a volley at me until she's off to London. She must come incog, Jack; aye, in man's clothes, if she can: you know why. A thought strikes me, which if you put it into her head, will just suit her, and me too. Persuade her to borrow the old pony of her master's, from the pasture on the Woodbridge road, or to take it with French leave. It is worth nothing, and will never be inquired after; and if disposed of, will scarcely be missed. And if she was found out, it would only be treated as a good spree! So, Jack, try her; she has a spirit equal to the work, and we shall then be no more parted. Now, do this for

"Your old friend,
"WILL LAUD."

Margaret read this letter with mingled feelings of pain and pleasure, but she implicitly believed every word of it, yet she did not like Laud's plan. "Why not go and borrow the horse of old Teager," said she, "if it must be so? I know he will lend it to me."

"What, and tell him you want his stable-dress to ride to London in? Fine fun he'd make of it, would he not ? No, no, Margaret, that will never do. We must take it with French leave, or let it alone."

"I wish I could see him by some other means. I do not like his plan ; and yet, perhaps, he has none other to offer," said Margaret, as if pondering within herself.

"I can tell you he is not the man to offer it if he has," said Cook. "Once put him off again, and it will be long enough before you ever see or hear of him again."

Margaret felt that such would be the case, and yielded to the artful duplicity of this wicked man, and agreed to meet him the next night to put their wild plan in practice. But as heaven willed that she should have one more chance of escape from the evil which threatened her, the excitement which she suffered brought on an attack of fever that very night, and she was laid up for many days. The warning, however, was in vain ; and so soon as she recovered, she agreed to put their plan in execution.

It was on the 23rd of May that Margaret met John Cook at the place before appointed, having previously bought herself a hat and a pair of boots. But now a new obstacle presented itself, which, like the one just alluded to, might have served as a warning, had any religious feelings found place in Margaret's mind and heart. They went into the meadow, and for more than an hour tried to catch the horse. But it was all in vain ; he would be caught by nobody but old Teager.

What was to be done now ?

"This is a turn I did not bargain for," said John Cook, "and I have written to Laud to say you will be, without fail, at the place I shall tell you of when you are once mounted. A horse we came for, and a horse we will have, for I would not disappoint the captain for a hundred horses ; so follow me, Margaret."

The girl hesitated, and inquired what it was he proposed to do.

"Not many yards off, in yonder stable, there are two noble horses that are worth riding ; you shall take one of them."

"Do you mean the carriage-horses? I dare not ride one of them."

"Nonsense, girl! If you don't come along and just do as I bid you, hang me if I don't write to Laud, and tell him you don't care anything about him. Come along! I must help you over the low wall against the end of the garden. Come along! You have fairly begun the work; don't give it up."

Margaret never wanted courage until that moment, and then she followed, trembling from head to foot.

The fellow got on to the wall and assisted her up and down. He then went across the lawn to the stable-yard with the trembling Margaret at his heels; they found the stable-door locked; but the wicket at the side, by the muck-bin, was unhanked and stood ajar. Margaret got into the stable through this place, and slipped back the bolt of the stable-door; the horses had been accustomed to her coming into the stable for straw for her fire, and she had often spoke to them and patted them, so that her voice now, as she said, "Whoho, Crop!" and "Gently, Rochford!" was familiar to them; and they did not rise up until John Cook entered and began to strike a light.

"Now, Margaret, pull the litter down toward the stable-door, whilst I just look into the harness-house."

Rochford, a fiery grey horse which Mr. Cobbold had lately purchased from Lord Rochford, at Easton, rose up and snorted, and clanked his chains so terribly, that Margaret expected every moment that old George who slept over the stable, would present himself; but the old man was deaf, and heavy in his sleep, and had only returned from Mrs. Proby's, of Stratford, late that evening, and had not been in bed above an hour, so that he was in his first sound sleep.

"Margaret, you must take this lantern, and just move the dark part round, and it will show you where the old boy's stable-dress is; go up the stairs carefully, and bring it down with you."

Margaret did so. She went with breathless step to the bedside of the coachman. His stable dress was upon the floor; she took it up gently, and as cautiously receded with it down to the stable again, closing the door without noise.

"So far so good, Margaret. Now, do you dress yourself there in the empty stall, while I saddle and bridle the further horse."

This, however, was more than John Cook could do, for Rochford was of such a spirit, and sent out at him with such vengeance that he dared not go up to him; nor could he without Margaret's help put the saddle or bridle on to Crop. She dressed herself as quickly as she could in the coachman's stable-dress; he being a little fellow, and Margaret rather tall, they only hung about her a little loosely, but were not too long for her. When she came from the stall, after rolling her own things in a bundle, and putting them into the very bottom of the seed-box, under the manger, and covering them with hay, she looked exactly like a young groom. She went up to the Crop horse and patted him on the neck, whilst her companion saddled and bridled him; she then tied some straw round his feet, so that no noise should be made in the stable-yard, and out the gallant fellow was led, ready for such a journey and for such a rider as never before had mounted his back.

"Now my girl," exclaimed Cook, "screw up your courage to the start! Come into the meadow. I can let you out on to the Woodbridge road, and then off with you."

"But where am I to find him? You have not told me that," exclaimed Margaret.

"Mount! and I will tell you."

Margaret, with his aid, was soon in the saddle, and once there, she felt her own command over her steed.

"Now Margaret," he replied, "mind what I say: you must sell that horse if you can, at Chelmsford market to-morrow morning; if not, you must ride on to the Bull, in Aldgate, London; but if you regard your own and your lover's safety, you will sell the horse first, and then find your way to the Dog and Bone public-house, at Lambeth; there you will find Will Laud expecting you. Sell the horse for all you can get; say he is worth a hundred guineas, and that your master, Squire John Cook, sent you up to sell him."

The horse was a strawberry roan colour, remarkable for his action and the spirit with which he went through a journey. His ears were short enough, for, in accordance with a barbarous practice of that day, they were cropped; few that ever knew the horse could forget him; in harness he carried himself as proudly as if he had been trained to exhibit his beauty, but this was his constant habit; his spirit was such, that he was never touched with a whip, and never exhibited the least disposition to restiveness; free, easy, gentle, noble, swift, untiring, graceful, and grand—he was admired wherever he went; and the short coachman, who occasionally used to ride him, made him, a sixteen-hand horse, look at least a hand higher. What an object was Margaret Catchpole upon him! Her spirit was up as well as Crop's; her resolution to go through all she had undertaken was fixed, and in reply to John Cook's question, when they came to the paddock-gate, "Are you ready, Margaret?" she replied, "Quite ready!"

"And now, off with you," said the fellow, as he opened the gate. "Remember the 'Dog and Bone.' A hundred guineas for the horse, and you will be a happy woman;" and off started poor Margaret at a sweeping pace for the London road.

St. Margaret's clock struck one, just as she passed the front of that house in which she had lived so much respected, and in which, unconscious of her guilt, slept the kindest master and mistress that a servant ever knew.

But Margaret rode on, reckless of all the ills that might await her, and thinking only of the lover that she was to meet at the end of her mad journey.

The guard of the mail-coach observed to the driver of the Ipswich mail, as Margaret met it, about two miles before she reached Colchester, "That's Mr.

Cobbold's Crop horse! There must be something the matter in the family by the pace the groom is going. Did you see the fellow's stable-dress up to his knees? There's something amiss, or the horse is stolen."

When he came to Ipswich, the man mentioned the circumstance at the coach-office, and said he was positive something was wrong.

Mr. Bailey, the postmaster, immediately sent a messenger with a note, to inform Mr. Cobbold that the guard had met some one riding his horse very fast on the London road.

It was five o'clock when the man rang loudly at the porch-bell; the footman came down in a great hurry and carried up the note to his master's room, who quickly ordered him to go to the stable and see if George Teager and the horses were safe. He ran to the stable, and true enough, he found the Crop horse gone. He called out to George, whom, at first, he suspected of having gone off with the horse, "Hullo, George; Crop is gone!"

The old man jumped up. "What's the matter? Who calls?"

"One of the horses is stolen, George; you must come down immediately; it was met two miles this side of Colchester!"

"Come, come, Tom, none o' your tricks! this is only some of your nonsense: can't ye let an old fellow rest in his bed without playing off your boy's tricks? what have you done with my stable dress?"

This made Thomas bolt upstairs.

"I know nothing of your stable-dress; I tell you master will be here in a minute: on with your livery. I'll be whipped if somebody has not stolen the fustians! Come, old boy, this is no fun, it's as true as you are staring there; so up with you."

George found by his companion's earnest manner that he spoke the truth, and putting on his livery he came down; he was, as many a man at his age and in his situation would be, much bewildered. He ascertained, however, that the thief had taken his master's

new saddle and bridle, and a small stick of his own.
He observed that it must have been an old practitioner,
by the straw being littered down to the door, and
pointed out to Thomas that the horse's hoofs had been
covered with straw to prevent them clattering on the
pavement of the yard. His master soon came down
and easily tracked the horse to the paddock gate.
Of course all the family were roused. "Go directly,
George, up to Mr. Spink's, the dealer's, who got this
horse for me, and knows him as well as you do, and order
a post-chaise from the Lion, and bring Mr. Spink here.
You must both of you pursue the thief, even to London.
Be as quick as you can."

In the meantime a handbill was written and sent
to Mr. Jackson's, of the *County Press*, with a request that copies might be struck off immediately, in
time for the nine o'clock coaches to London. It was
to this effect :—

"TWENTY GUINEAS REWARD.

"Whereas, last night, or this morning, May 24th,
a fine strawberry roan grey gelding was stolen out of
the stable of John Cobbold, Esq., of St. Margaret's
Green, Ipswich, together with a new saddle and bridle,
and the coachman's stable-dress. Whoever shall give
information of the robber, so as to lead to the recovery
of the horse, or the conviction of the offender, shall
receive the above reward at the hands of the owner.

"N.B. The horse is sixteen hands high, has cropped
ears, is six years old, has a cut tail, and is very strong
and very fast.

"IPSWICH, May 24th, 1797."

This was struck off as soon as possible, and circulated over the town and through the country, by every
vehicle leaving the town.

It was about seven o'clock when old Teager and
Mr. Spink left Ipswich for Colchester, so that Margaret
had some hours' start of her pursuers. As they went

on they heard at every toll-gate of a young man having gone through on just the description of horse given, so that it was a warm scent before them.

When they arrived at Chelmsford, through a misdirection of some person, they were told that the same horse was seen going on to Maldon, in the hundreds of Essex ; and they had just given the post-boy orders to turn off the London road in pursuit, as Mr. Alston, of Diss, rode into the yard of the Black Boy as the pursuers were in the act of getting into the chaise.

"Pray, sir, may I be so bold as to ask if you came far along the London road ? "

"I left town this morning, and am now on my journey to Manningtree. Why do you ask ? "

"Because I am in pursuit of a thief. You did not chance to meet a man riding a strawberry roan carriage-horse ? "

"Yes, I did ; and remarked at the time that I thought it was the finest shaped horse I had ever seen. He was a crop, with high action and bold crest."

"It is the very horse ! Whereabouts might you meet him, sir ? "

"I met him I should say about five miles on the other side of Romford, near to Ilford. It was about nine o'clock. I remarked to myself, what a fool the lad must be who was riding him, that he did not manage to fasten his overalls down at his ankles, as I could see his stockings up to his knees. Some gentleman I thought was sending him into livery stables."

"We are greatly obliged to you, sir. On, boy, on ! " and the post-chaise dashed out of the yard.

But for the accidental meeting of Mr. Alston it is very probable Margaret would have escaped ; but the information thus given put the pursuers on the right scent, just in the right time.

Meantime let us accompany Margaret on her perilous expedition. She had actually ridden the horse from Ipswich to London in the space of eight hours and a half ; it being seventy miles from that place to the Bull, in Aldgate. She only stopped once on the road, at a small public-house, called the Trowel and Hammer, at Marks Tey, in Essex; here she gave her gallant horse a feed of corn, and had a glass of brandy and water and a biscuit. It was just five o'clock when she baited. She dared not to offer the horse for sale at Chelmsford for fear of detection, at such an early hour. She felt persuaded that a pursuit would be made, and hoped to hide herself in the metropolis before her pursuers could reach her. Accordingly she allowed the horse no more time than was sufficient for him to finish his corn, and off she went again for nearly five hours' further ride. As she approached town many were the eyes directed towards her, both on account of the remarkable character of the horse, and the singular appearance of the rider. Margaret took no notice of any one, but pushed on her willing steed with the same indifference as if she had been sent upon an errand of only a few miles; nor was the horse apparently fatigued in the least when they arrived at the Bull Inn, which they did about half-past nine o'clock.

She rode quietly down the yard, called for the ostler, dismounted, shook her trousers down, and addressed the man in as off-hand a manner as if she were a real groom.

"Rub that horse down well, and get him cool and comfortable; give him a sup of water and a mouthful of hay, and I will come and see him fed."

"Have you rode far, young man?" asked the ostler.

"Not a very great way. I came out of Chelmsford this morning. See and rub his ears dry, ostler. You must make him look as well as you can, for I expect my master up in town to-night; and if I don't meet with a customer for that horse he'll blow me up."

"He's a very fine horse; and if as good as he looks, would be worth any man's money."

"He's better than he looks, ostler: and 'tisn't any man's money that will buy him. He must give a good price for him, whoever buys him. But look well after him. I must go and get a bait myself."

She went into the bar, ordered her breakfast, took

up the newspaper, and with all the airs of a consequen-
tial young jockey sat down to the perusal of it. After
taking some refreshment she got up to see her horse
fed.

The ostler, finding so fine a horse was for sale,
apprised a livery-stable-keeper of his acquaintance,
who on hearing his representation hastened to look at
him. Margaret was called out; the animal exhibited;
under-valued by the dealer in the style so characteristic
of such gentry; and his good qualifications well vouched
for by the young groom.

"Did you ever see a better shape" exclaimed
Margaret. "Look at his fore-end; there's a crest,
there's a shoulder, there's a head! Look at his legs, as
straight and clean as a colt's; and as for quarters,
where will you find such for strength and beauty?
He's six-year old next grass; has never done any hard
work before this day; and you won't find a puff as big
as a pea in any of his sinews. Quiet to ride or drive,
and without a fault. Now, what's the matter with
him?"

This was such a poser to the dealer that he could
only reply by asking, "Can I have a warranty with
him?"

"To be sure you can," said Margaret. "You may
have a written one from me; or, if you like better to
deal with my master, you may wait till he comes up,
and then he'll give you a character, and perhaps you'll
make a better bargain with him than you will with
me."

"Are you authorized to sell the horse?"

"To be sure I am, or else I should not stand here to
talk with you about him."

"Who does he belong to, young man?"

"He belongs to my master, Mr. Cook, of Ipswich,
in Suffolk."

"What do you want for him?"

"One hundred guineas."

"May I take him for a trial?"

"Yes; when you have bought and paid for him.

He is not to go out of my sight until I receive the money for him, or deliver the horse himself into my master's charge."

"I should like to see him down our ride; I could better judge of his paces."

"Clap the saddle on him. I will ride him where you like; or I will let you drive me with him; but I do not trust any one else with him whilst he is in my care."

The saddle and bridle were put on, and Crop came out of the stable free, and ready to trot back again to Ipswich if his rider was so disposed. He was as fresh and joyous as a lark, and sprang up into the air with almost as light a heart. Margaret mounted awkwardly; put her foot into the stirrup the wrong way; and perceiving that this was noticed, she crossed the stirrups over the saddle in front of her, saying,

"My master always makes me ride without stirrups, and I like it best."

In truth she sat the horse better without them; and had she had no saddle, it would have suited her even better still; but this seemed to have the desired effect.

The dealer, however, entertained some suspicions from the awkward manner of the groom, and having already suffered for purchasing a stolen horse, he was more on his guard than he otherwise might have been.

They went out of the stable-yard together, and reached the ride belonging to the dealer, and Margaret turned her horse in as she was directed. The stable lads peeped out to see what kind of nag their master was buying, and were not satisfied with a glance, but looked with much admiration at him.

"Just trot him down the ride, young man."

Margaret dashed down the yard and back again.

"Soho! my fine fellow! Peter," he said to his head man, "just come and look at this nag."

Peter stepped forward, and gave his master a knowing look, as much as to say, "Am I to decry him?"

"Look at his mouth!"

Peter did so.

"How is it, Peter?"

"All right, sir."

"What's his age?"

"Rising six."

"What do you say to him?"

Peter looked at every point, then scratched his head, and again looked at his master; but he received no sign to manœuvre; so he replied, "Why, master, if you ask for truth you shall have it. He's a right good one; that is it."

"Well, young man, now what is the lowest price you will take?"

"I told you his price when you asked me before. You don't expect me to lower the price of my own horse without a bid! What do you say you will give?"

"Why, I don't know! He's not every man's horse! Not easily matched; and not suited for a town horse; but I'll bid you fifty guineas for him."

"Thank you for your bid, sir; but you must come nigh to double that before you'll buy."

"Will you take sixty for him?"

"No; I will not."

"Will you take seventy? Come now, I'll give you seventy. You may go a long way before you'll get such another offer. Say, will you take it?"

"Add another ten to it and it shall be a bargain. I will take eighty."

"Just walk him down again. Peter, what do you think of him?"

"He's worth the money; that's what I say. Buy him, master."

"Well, young man, I'll take the horse; but you must give me a written warranty with him."

"That I'll do; but perhaps you'll not like to conclude the bargain without master's warranty; if so, we had better not exactly conclude the price."

This so took the dealer aback, that it drove away all suspicions, and he said, "No, no; your warranty will do. I'll give you the money." He was in the act of going to the gateway as he saw one of his men come

into the yard, with a paper in his hand, which proved
to be one of the identical hand-bills, offering a reward
of twenty guineas for the very horse he had just bought.
" Peter," he called out, " tell the young man just to walk
that horse once more up the yard, and come you here."

He showed Peter the bill, who said : " It 's the very
horse ! "

" Go you and fetch a constable ; I'll keep him in
play a bit until he comes."

" He 's a charming shaped horse, young man. I'd
just a mind to ask you if you'd throw the saddle and
bridle into the bargain."

" Why, master told me I might sell that if I pleased,
and if I sold well, that should be my perquisite."

" I see 'tis a country-made saddle ; but it looks
pretty good. What will you have for it ? "

" Four guineas for both. Come, I have let you take
the horse at much less than he is worth ; you can
afford to give me a fair price for the saddle and bridle,
which are, you see, quite new."

By this time Peter returned with the constable ; but
Margaret was joking about the saddle and bridle, and
greatly rejoicing at her success, not the least conscious
of the presence of the man of the law, or of the dreadful
fate which awaited her.

" Did you say that horse came from Ipswich, young
man ? " said the dealer.

" I did," said she.

" When did he leave Ipswich ? "

" Yesterday."

" Did you leave with him ? "

" Yes, I did ; I told you so."

" No, you didn't ; you told me you rode him from
Chelmsford."

" So I did ; and from Ipswich too."

" What was your master's name ? "

" Mr. John Cook," said Margaret, who now began
to feel a little uneasy.

" Are you sure it was not Mr. John Cobbold ? Look
at that hand-bill, young man."

Margaret saw only her master's name, and all her fortitude forsook her; she swooned away in a moment, and would have fallen from the horse, had not the constable caught her by her jacket as she was falling; and in endeavouring to support her off the horse the jacket flew open, and to the astonishment of all around, lo, and behold, it was a woman!

Margaret was taken into custody; and such a hubbub was created in the neighbourhood, that the story of a female horse-stealer was soon spread abroad, and people began to crowd into the yard. Among the multitude was a son-in-law of Mr. Cobbold's, who happened to be in town at the time, and identified both the horse and its rider. It was not long before the coachman and Mr. Spink made their appearance, and she was taken before a magistrate, and immediately committed to Newgate, until further evidence could be produced.

CHAPTER XXII

PREPARATION FOR TRIAL

MARGARET CATCHPOLE was taken into custody; and whilst she was spending a dismal night in the dungeon, a letter was on the road to Ipswich, to inform her master of the capture of the thief.

The wretched young woman had now time for rest and reflection. Instead of meeting her lover, for which purpose alone she had undertaken her desperate enterprise, she had now before her eyes the terrors of the law, the certainty of conviction, the probability of a violent and shameful death. Who knew anything of the cause which had induced her to steal the horse, and who would pity her if they did? The secret was known only to herself, and she resolved it should continue so, lest her lover should be involved in the consequences of her guilt.

It will readily be believed that the news of what had happened created no small sensation in the minds of the various members of that family who had so dearly loved the miserable culprit.

It was immediately arranged that both Mr. and Mrs. Cobbold should go to town, and they arrived about nine o'clock in the evening at the Four Swans, Bishopsgate Street.

At the time fixed for the examination of the prisoner before the magistrates, Mr. and Mrs. Cobbold arrived at the Police-office in Whitechapel.

Many gentlemen were present, who having heard the case mentioned, had obtained permission to attend.

The office was crowded, and the street also, for it was understood that Margaret was to be brought up for examination. Hundreds who knew nothing of the parties, but only that a female had stolen a horse, were assembled purely from curiosity to see such a person.

Margaret was brought up in proper custody, and found herself the object of jokes and gibes amidst the thoughtless rabble of the streets. She was conducted into an ante-room adjoining the court, and as a door opened into the passage from the magistrates' private room, she thought she heard her mistress's voice. Another moment convinced her that she saw her. It was to her a moment of great bitterness and agony.

At the request of the prosecutor, she was summoned into the magistrates' private room, before going into the public court. She was terrified beyond measure at the idea of encountering the sight of her mistress. She begged hard not to be taken into her presence, but she was compelled to go in. The moment she saw her she exclaimed: "Oh, my dear mistress!" and fell to the ground. She was lifted up and placed in a chair; and from her dreadful state of agitation, it was agreed among the magistrates that, upon her recovery, her deposition should be taken where she then was. Accordingly, the clerk was summoned from the public office into the private room.

Her mistress as well as herself was greatly affected

at the interview, and deeply touched at her distress.
All the gentlemen present felt more than commonly
interested in the scene.

The girl slowly revived; the gentlemen took their
seats, and the clerk was ordered to take down her
deposition. The magistrate told her that the confession she had made, and might now make, would be
evidence against her on her trial, and that she was at
liberty to speak, or not, as she pleased.

Having implored and obtained forgiveness from her
master and mistress, Margaret became more composed, and made a full confession of her guilt. She
acknowledged that she had been persuaded, and even
compelled, to this act by a man named John Cook,
a sailor at Ipswich, and declared that she stole the horse
by his direction and threats; that she was to have
sold it at Chelmsford, but that she dared not offer it
there. She did not once betray her lover's name, or
mention anything about his hiding-place; but she
described all the particulars of the robbery with which
the reader is acquainted, and stated, as a corrobora-
tive fact, that her own clothes would be found, if not
already removed, under the manger of the empty
stall.

Her deposition having been then read over to her
by the clerk, she signed her name to it. Before they
parted, Mrs. Cobbold spoke to her consolingly, while
she placed before her mind the heinousness of her
offence. Poor Margaret felt better after this, and with
a heart very much humbled, was committed to Newgate by N. Bond, Esq., with an order for her removal
as soon as the forms could be gone through, to the gaol
of the county in which the offence was committed.
Mr. Cobbold was bound over to prosecute, which being
done, that gentleman and his lady returned to their
hotel.

Every effort was made to discover the resort of John
Cook; but that scamp, the moment he heard of the
capture, decamped, nor was he ever after heard of.
He was well known; and the landlord of the Marquis

Cornwallis testified to Margaret's having been at his house with the man, as also his being at the same place with Captain Laud, as he was called, the evening before. But what became of him no one ever knew. The half of a letter from his companion in London was found at the inn, and was adduced to show his connexion with a gang of horse-stealers; but this only served to tell against poor Margaret on her trial.

Margaret was removed to Ipswich by *habeas corpus*, July 6th, 1797, and Mr. Ripshaw, the gaoler, informed her mistress of her arrival.

On the evening of the day Margaret arrived at Ipswich, she wrote the following letter to her mistress. It has been already stated that she had been taught to read and write, and keep accounts, by Mrs. Cobbold, when she superintended the education of her family; and the results of this teaching, as exemplified in the touching epistles which we shall hereafter present to the reader, will doubtless be received with singular interest, copied as they are from the original documents, which are carefully preserved in the family. The following is the first she ever wrote :—

" IPSWICH, Thursday, July 6th, 1797.

" HONOURED MADAM,

" Your wretched servant has this evening arrived at the county gaol. Hope induced me to look forward to an earlier abode near you, that I might have the consolation of your instruction and advice. Oh! my honoured lady, when I look upon that dear spot in which you live, and see those green fields before your house, in which I used to walk and play with your dear children, I think the more deeply of the gloom of my felon's chamber, from which I can even at this moment behold them. They recall to my mind those happy hours in which I enjoyed your approbation and respect. How wretched do I now feel! Oh! what have I not lost!

" I am come to Ipswich to take my trial, and am

already condemned by my own conscience more severely than any judge can condemn me. But yours must be the task to teach me how to escape, not the condemnation of the judge, but of my own heart. Oh, my dear lady! do come and see me! Many people were kind to me at Newgate, and many persons contributed to my necessities; some indeed flattered me, and called me a brave girl for my recent act, which they termed clever and courageous. But if they were so, dear lady, why should I now feel so much fear? I thought them poor consolers, and not half such sincere friends as those who told me, as you did, the greatness of my offence, and the probable extent of ultimate punishment.

"Honoured madam, would you let a messenger go to my dear father and tell him where I am, and how much I desire to see him? I fear you will think me very bold and troublesome, but I know your kind heart will make allowances for my troubled mind. I should like to see my Uncle Leader. But I should, first of all, like to see you, my dear lady. Perhaps it will not be long before I shall see you no more. I wish to make up my mind to the worst, but I am at times dreadfully troubled. I feel it so hard to be suddenly torn away from every earthly bond, and some on earth I do so dearly love; and none more deserves that love than you do. Pray come to me; and ever believe me

"Your grateful, though
"Most wretched servant,
"MARGARET CATCHPOLE.

"P.S.—Mr. Ripshaw has promised to send you this letter this evening. He tells me you have often inquired for me."

The chaplain of the gaol was a friend of Mrs. Cobbold's; she wrote a note to him requesting him to accompany her at any hour most convenient to himself, to see her poor servant. At eleven o'clock the next day, the interview took place between the wretched culprit and this truly Christian lady. She spent some hours with that disconsolate being, whose whole thoughts seemed to be directed with bitter agony to days of past happiness. For though she had endured much mortification in early life, she had experienced the comfort and consolation of a true and disinterested friend and benefactress in the person of that kind mistress, and her naturally intelligent mind had duly appreciated these benefits.

These visits were repeated many times, and with the most beneficial effects on the mind of the culprit. Her present anguish was the keener, because her sensibilities were all so acutely alive to the memory of the past. It was her mistress's endeavour not to suffer her to be deceived with any false hopes. She was well aware that the penalty of her crime was death, and that unless her instigating accomplice could be delivered up to justice, she stood every chance of being made a public example, on account of the great frequency of the crime. To such an extent had horse-stealing been carried on in the counties of Suffolk and Essex, that scarce a week passed without rewards being offered for the apprehension of the thieves.

Margaret's interviews with her father and brother were still more deeply affecting: but to them and to her beloved mistress alone did she make known the real circumstances, attending her stealing the horse. She did not attempt, however, to defend the act, nor would she admit that another's influence was any exculpation of her offence. Mr. Stebbing, the surgeon of the gaol, who had been her first friend in Ipswich, was very kind to her, as was likewise his benevolent daughter, who lent her many useful books. But the being she most wished to see, and from whose memory she had never thought she could have been displaced, came not near her in her adversity. William Laud had been at Nacton, to see her father and brother. The report of her confession had reached him—he had seen it in the newspapers; and it altered all his views and intentions respecting her; so that the very act which she had done in the hope of strengthening his attachment to her, was the direct cause of his deserting her. In fact, he believed that she had committed the act from an attachment to somebody else, and he gave up all idea of her for the future.

But Margaret was still true to *him*. In one of her interviews with Mrs. Cobbold, that kind and good lady, referring to the fact of Laud's not coming near her in her adversity, said earnestly—

"You must endeavour to think less of him, Margaret."

"It is hard, madam," was the reply, "for flesh and blood not to think of one who has been in one's thoughts so many years of one's life. In happy as well as miserable hours, I have thought of him, madam, and have always hoped for the best. He is still in all my prayers!"

"Your hopes of him, Margaret, must now be at an end. It would have been happier for you, if they ended when you lived with me."

"Perhaps so, good lady; perhaps so. Or even earlier. I think now of my poor sister Susan's last words: 'Margaret, you will never marry William Laud.' I had hoped that these words were only the fears of the moment; but, alas! I perceive they will prove too true!"

The only diversion of Margaret's mind at this period, from a fixed and undivided attention to heavenly things, was the one hope of seeing Laud. She clung with tenacity to this, as a sort of last farewell to all things in the world. She said, that had she but one interview with him, she should then have no other wish but to die.

Time flew fast, and the day of her trial approached. She was to depart for Bury, where the assizes were held, early on the morning of the 9th of August; and, on the preceding day, she wrote the following letter to her mistress:—

"IPSWICH GAOL, August 8th, 1797.

"HONOURED MADAM,

"By the time you read this, which I expect will be at your happy breakfast-table to-morrow morning, your poor servant will be at Bury, awaiting the awful moment of her condemnation. I could not leave this place, however, without pouring out my heart to you, my dear and honoured lady; thanking you for your great kindness and Christian charity to my poor soul. I have confessed my guilt to God and man, and I go to my trial with the same determination to plead guilty before both.

"Honoured madam, I am told that the judge will call upon me to know if I have anybody in court to speak to my character. Now, though I cannot hope, and indeed would not urge you to be present in court, considering the state you are now in,[1] yet you have spoken well of me in private, and I know you would never fear to speak publicly that which you have said of me in private. Perhaps a line from you would do that which I want. You well know, my dear madam, that it is not from any hope of its obtaining a pardon for me that I ask it; but it is from the hope that one, whom I shall never see again, may by some means catch a sight of it; and may think better of me than the world at large, who know nothing of me, can do. Pardon this weakness.

"Think not that I have any hope of mercy or pardon here. You have taught me how to hope for both hereafter. You have shown me much mercy and pity here, and the Lord reward you and my dear master for your unmerited compassion to your wretched servant! You have fortified my mind with the riches of consolation in that religion which I hope will be poured with tenfold increase into your own heart, and give you that peace you are so anxious I should possess.

[1] The writer of these pages, one of the sons of that excellent woman, was born on the 9th of September following.

It grieves me to see my fellow-prisoners so unprepared
for the fate which awaits them. Oh, that they had
such friends as I have had! Oh, that they had been
partakers of the same consolation as myself! And
now, dearest lady, I have only to request your mention of me in your prayers. Bless you, my dear madam!
God bless you and your dear children, and may they
live to be a blessing to your old age! Give my kind
thanks to all those friends who may ever inquire about
me. And now, dearest lady, pardon the errors of this
letter, as you have done all the graver faults of your
ever grateful and now happier servant,

" MARGARET CATCHPOLE.

" To MRS. COBBOLD, St. Margaret's Green, Ipswich."

Margaret, with several other prisoners, departed for
Bury assizes in the prisoners' van, which started at
six o'clock on the 9th of August, 1797, under the care
of Mr. Ripshaw, the gaoler, and arrived at that place
about eleven o'clock in the forenoon.

The town was in a bustle, and the prisoners were
received into the borough gaol that day an hour or
so previously to their trial—a day of anxiety to many,
but by too many spent in revelry and folly. The
various witnesses crowded into the town. The inns
were filled on the 8th. Expectation was alive and
active; and the bustle of preparing for business created
a stir throughout that town, which at other times is the
most silent, the coldest, and the dullest place in
England.

CHAPTER XXIII

TRIAL AND CONDEMNATION TO DEATH

THERE are few things that appear in greater and more painful contrast than the general rejoicing which attends the assizes of a country town, and the solemn and awful purposes for which those assizes are held. It may be said, that it is matter of rejoicing when justice is about to be administered ; and that honest people have a right to be glad when the wicked are about to be punished. But there is great difference between a reasonable show of rejoicing, and the overflowings of pomp and parade, levity and folly.

At the assizes at Bury, at the time we speak of, the sheriff's pomp and state was something approaching to regal splendour. His gaudy liveries, his gilded carriage, his courtly dress, and all the expenses attendant upon such a station, made it a heavy burden to the unfortunate country gentleman who should be appointed to such an office. The balls, too, and public entertainments common at such time in the county, formed a striking contrast to the sorrows and despair of the criminals. The judges entered the town, the trumpets sounded, the bells rang, the sheriff's carriage was surrounded with hosts of gapers of all kinds, to see their lordships alight at the Angel steps. The Lord Chief Baron Macdonald and Mr. Justice Heath attended divine service, at St. James's Church, previously to their entering the courts. Who could look down upon that assemblage, and see those grave men, with their white wigs crowned with black patches, their scarlet robes, lined with ermine, preceded by the sheriff's officers, and all the municipal servants of that ancient borough, with their gilt chains, silver maces, and ample robes, and not think of the purpose for which they were assembled !

The best preparation for the scenes met with in

a court of justice, is the house of prayer; though even here there is a strange contrast between the peace and quietness of the church, and the bustle, broil, and turmoil usually attendant on the administration of criminal justice.

At twelve o'clock, on the day of trial, August 9th, 1797, the Lord Chief Baron Macdonald took his seat upon the bench, in the criminal court. Mr. Justice Heath presided in the Nisi Prius. On the right hand of the Lord Chief Baron sat the High Sheriff, Chalonor Archdeckne, Esq., of Glevering Hall, with his chaplain, and a full bench of county and borough magistrates. After the proclamation had been read, the respective lists of the grand jury for the county and the liberty were then called over, as follows :—

FOR THE COUNTY

Lord Viscount Brome.
Sir John Blois, Bart.
Philip Bowes Broke, Esq.
Charles Berners, jun., Esq.
George Golding, Esq.
William Middleton, Esq.
Eleazar Davy, Esq.
John Frere, Esq.
Matthias Kerrison, Esq.
Wolfran Lewis, Esq.
John Sheppard, Esq.

Francis Broke, Esq.
Mileson Edgar, Esq.
Robert Trotman, Esq.
John Bleadon, Esq.
John Cobbold, Esq.
Thomas Green, Esq.
Joseph Burch Smith, Esq.
Thomas Shaw, Esq.
John Vernon, Esq.
James Reeve, Esq.
James Stutter, Esq.

FOR THE LIBERTY

Sir Charles Bunbury, Bart.
Sir Charles Davers, Bart.
Sir Thomas Cullum, Bart.
Sir Harry Parker, Bart.
Sir William Rowley, Bart.
Nathaniel Lee Acton, Esq.
Capel Lofft, Esq.
Samuel Brice, Esq.
William Parker, Esq.
Richard Moore, Esq.

Robert Walpole, Esq.
James Oakes, Esq.
Matthias Wright, Esq.
Abraham Reeve, Esq.
John Oliver, Esq.
John Pytches, Esq.
Thomas Cocksedge, Esq.
John Cooke, Esq.
George Jackson, Esq.
William Kemp Jardine, Esq.

After the names had been respectively answered, the Lord Chief Baron addressed the grand jury, in a most powerful and impressive speech, in which he pointed out to their attention the extraordinary case then about to come on for trial. The grand jury retired. The prisoners were led into the cages, under the body of the court, where the people sat. They could hear all the proceedings, and could see, through an iron grating, all the witnesses in attendance. After the petty jury had been sworn, and had appointed John Bloomfield, auctioneer and farmer, their foreman, they took their seats, and various true bills were handed into court against the prisoners, whose trials then came on. After an hour or two, a paper was handed from the grand jury box, to the clerk of arraigns; it was announced as "a true bill against Margaret Catchpole, for horse-stealing." She presently after heard herself summoned by name; and with trembling hand and foot, ascended the steps of the dock, and stood before the bar. The court was crowded to excess, and upon the bench sat more ladies than gentlemen. The judge cast a severe glance at the prisoner, evidently expecting to find a bold, athletic female, of a coarse and masculine appearance. Margaret was dressed in a plain blue cotton gown, and appeared deeply dejected. She seemed to be inwardly engaged in prayer. Once she looked round the court, to see if she could discover the person of her lover, or the instigator to the crime for which she was arraigned. Her eye rested only upon her aged father and her affectionate brother Edward, who stood beneath her, close to the bar. The workings of nature were too powerful to be resisted, and tears rolled down the old man's cheeks, as he gave his hand to his daughter. She kissed it, and let fall upon it the hot drops of agony.

"Prisoner at the bar, you stand committed upon your own confession, before two of his majesty's justices of the peace for the county of Middlesex, of having, on the night of the 23rd of May last past,

stolen from the stable of your late master, John
Cobbold, Esq., of St. Margaret's Green, Ipswich,
a strawberry roan-grey coach gelding, and of having
rode the same from Ipswich to London that night ;
and being in the act of selling the horse next day following, when you were taken into custody. For this
offence you now stand before the court. How say
you, prisoner at the bar, are you guilty, or not guilty ? "

Margaret looked at her judge, and in a firm though
low voice said, " Guilty, my lord."

" Prisoner at the bar," resumed the judge, " though
you have made this confession, you are at liberty to
retract it, and to plead, ' Not Guilty,' if you please,
and so to take your trial. Your plea of ' Guilty ' will
avail you nothing in the sentence which must follow.
Consider then your answer."

Margaret replied, " I am not able now, my lord, to
plead ' Not Guilty.' "

" Why not ? " said the judge.

" Because I know that I am ' Guilty.' "

This was too sound an argument to be disputed ;
and the judge did not attempt any further explanation.

Margaret's appearance was not remarkable for
beauty, nor was it by any means unpleasing. Her
figure was not masculine. She was tall, and rather
slender. She had a dark eye, dark hair, and a countenance pale from emotion.

The judge then addressed her in the following
words :—" Prisoner at the bar, it is my painful duty
to address one of your sex in such a situation. I cannot
possibly judge of your motives for committing such a
crime. They do not appear in your confession, and
I am at a loss to conceive what can have induced you
to commit it. The sentence to which you have subjected yourself is death. Have you anything to say
why this sentence of the law should not be passed upon
you ? Have you any friends in court to speak to your
character ? "

There was evidently a stir in the body of the court,
and several persons were seen crowding forward to the

witness-box, and all ready to enter it. At this juncture the prisoner expressed a wish to know if she might speak a few words to the judge.

"Prisoner at the bar," said the Chief Baron, "I am quite ready to hear what you have to say."

There was now a hushed and breathless silence in the court, and the prisoner spoke calmly, clearly, and audibly, in the following words :—

"My lord, I am not going to say anything in defence of my conduct, or to make any excuse whatever for my crimes. I told your lordship that I was guilty, and guilty I feel that I am. It is not for my own sake, either, that I am speaking, but that all in this court may take warning from my bad example. A kinder master and mistress no servant ever had, nor had ever master or mistress a more ungrateful servant. I have long since condemned myself, and more severely than your lordship can do it. I know my crime, and I know its punishment. I feel that, even if the law acquitted me, my own conscience would still condemn me. But your lordship may proceed to pass sentence upon my body. I have already felt assurance of some peace and mercy where I alone could look for it, and thanks be to God I have not sought it in vain. It has prepared me for this moment. My master and mistress have forgiven me. Oh! that all against whom I have offended by my bad example could here do the same! I do not ask forgiveness of the law, because I have no right to do so. I have offended, and am subject to the penalty of death. If your lordship should even change my sentence, and send me out of the country for life, I should rather choose death, at this time, than banishment from my father and my friends. Temptation would no longer assail me, and I shall hope to see them, and all whom I now see before me, in a better world. I hope your lordship will forgive my words, though you must condemn me for my actions."

To attempt a description of the effect of these few words upon the court would be impossible. The ladies hoped that mercy would be extended to her. The judge looked at her with mingled astonishment and pity.

"Are there any persons present," said the judge, "who are ready to speak to the previous character of the prisoner?" Whereupon the prosecutor, her master, immediately ascended the witness-box. He stated that the prisoner had, during the time she lived in his service, always discharged her duty faithfully. He had reason to believe that she was neither a hardened nor an abandoned character. He knew from experience that she was most humane and faithful, and ready to risk her own life in the service of another. He here mentioned her presence of mind, and the intrepidity she had so signally displayed in saving the lives of his children. He stated, moreover, that, for his own part, he never should have prosecuted the prisoner but that the magistrates in London had bound him over so to do, and a sense of duty compelled him to adopt this course. He should always entertain, under all circumstances, a grateful recollection of her. He particularly recommended her to mercy, because he did not believe that she had committed the crime in question in conjunction with any gang of horse-stealers, but that she was the dupe of an infamous villain, who had persuaded her to steal the horse for him, and for no pecuniary benefit to herself. He believed her to be a proper object for royal clemency, and hoped that if his lordship could find any mitigating circumstances in her favour, that he would give her the full benefit of them.

George Stebbing, Esq., surgeon, Ipswich, stated that he had known the prisoner from her childhood; that in her earliest years she gave promise of such good character and conduct as would have merited the approbation of all men. He mentioned her riding the pony to Ipswich.

Margaret put her head down upon the bar, and, hiding her face in her hands, sobbed audibly before the whole court.

The doctor stated that, if she was at that moment at liberty, he would take her into his own house. He assured his lordship that it was a romantic hope of seeing her lover, that induced her to listen to the voice of the tempter who induced her to steal the horse. He prayed for mercy for her, and handed a petition to the court, signed by many persons who knew her early history, and bore testimony to her former good character.

Her uncle and aunt Leader next spoke in the highest terms of her general good character. Her first mistress at the Priory Farm gave her also an excellent character for honesty and humanity, and assured his lordship that it was an early but unfortunate attachment which had been the cause of this rash act; adding, that neither she nor her husband would object to take the prisoner again into their service.

Several other persons spoke in her favour, and so cordial and so earnest had been the testimony borne to her character, that in almost every breast a hope began to prevail that mercy would be extended to her.

The judge took an unusually long time for deliberation. He was in conversation with the high sheriff, but what passed between them did not transpire. The longer he delayed his judgement, the stronger grew the hopes of mercy. At last, turning round to the body of the court, he looked for one most awful moment steadfastly at the prisoner; and, when every eye was riveted upon him, he was seen to take the black cap from beneath his desk, and to place it upon his head. That dreadful forerunner of impending condemnation struck forcibly upon the hearts of all the people assembled. Some ladies fainted, and were carried out of court. The most perfect stillness ensued, as the Lord Chief Baron addressed the unhappy creature in the following words:—

"Prisoner at the bar, I have paid attention to your address to me, and to those around you, and am glad to find that you have made a proper use of the time which has intervened between your committal to prison and the present moment. Your words show that you are by no means ignorant of your duty as a member of society, and that you are possessed of strong sense and much good feeling. I earnestly wish that your conduct had not been such as to belie that good sense which you possess. It is, however, the more inexcusable in one who, at the time she was committing an offence, must have known its heinousness. Your sin, prisoner at the bar, has found you out quickly, and judgement as speedily follows. I will not aggravate those feelings of remorse which I am sure you experience, by any longer dwelling upon the painful situation in which your crimes have placed you. I trust your own persuasive words will be long remembered by every one present, and be a warning to all how they suffer themselves to be betrayed into crime. May your early fate warn them in time to keep themselves in the path of rectitude and honesty.

"I must say that, in the whole course of my judicial career, I have never met with a person who so well knew right from wrong, and who so extraordinarily perverted that gift. I must say, likewise, that I have never met with any one who has received so good a former character at such a moment as the present. The representations that have been made of your past conduct shall be forwarded to the king, with whom alone the prerogative of mercy in your case exists.

"It would be cruelty, however, in me did I not candidly tell you, that the crime for which you are now to suffer is one of such frequent, bold, and in this day, daring commission, as to defy the authority of the law; so that persons detected and brought to judgement, as you are, stand but little chance of mercy. It is not in my power to give you any hope of escaping the full punishment of the law, but I will represent your case this very night, before I sleep, to the proper quarter whence any alteration in your behalf can alone be obtained.

"I need scarcely tell you not to rely upon any false hopes which friends may hold out to you, who would grieve the more could they see the danger and distress which they thereby occasion. Let me rather entreat you to continue that attention to the interest of your soul which has already been well instructed and fortified against the present crisis. You have to prepare, prisoner at the bar, for a greater trial, a more awful moment; and I hope you will make good use of the short time which remains in preparation for eternity. You appear to have been well assisted hitherto, and the good instruction seems to have fallen upon productive ground. I hope the increase will continue to the day of your death.

"It only remains for me to fulfil my duty, by passing the sentence of the court upon you, which is—

"That you be taken from the place where you now stand, back to the place whence you came, and thence to the place of execution, and there be hanged by the neck until you be dead; and may God have mercy upon your soul!"

At these last words tears of agony overwhelmed many in the court; but Margaret herself seemed to be less overcome by the sentence than by the kind words of the judge.

She respectfully curtsied to him and the court, and, in the act of retiring, fell into her father's arms. She was conveyed back to the gaol in a swoon.

In the meantime every exertion was made to represent her case favourably to the judge. A petition was signed by many of the grand jury, as well as the petty jury, in her behalf, and strong hopes were entertained of a reprieve.

These things were not mentioned to the prisoner, who returned to the cell of condemned felons, to employ her time in "seeking that peace which the world cannot give."

A keeper constantly attended her, and a female sat up with her all that night. She requested to have a Bible, and pen, ink, and paper: these were granted her. She did not sleep, but read the Sacred Book, sometimes aloud, sometimes to herself. She also seemed to find great relief in writing to her friends. One letter which she wrote to her uncle, and another to her mistress, on that very night, will best evince the state of her mind and feelings.

"MY DEAR UNCLE,

"This will reach you to-morrow before you leave Bury. Give my love and best thanks to my aunt and friends who spoke this day in behalf of your unhappy niece; but, when you arrive at Ipswich, be sure and call and thank that dear old gentleman, Doctor Stebbing. I know he feels very much for me, but tell him not to distress himself, as if I were to be lost for ever. Tell him I hope to see him in a better world. He has been very kind to me in those days when I was most forlorn, and my Saviour, who then guided me to him, will give him his reward. For He says, that a cup of cold water given to one of His most poor and wretched children, shall not be forgotten.

"Dear uncle, show this letter to the gentleman in whose hands you have placed the money which I gave you for such purpose, and tell him that I wish it to be restored to William Laud, its rightful owner, if he can be found, and will receive it again. If he is not found, after my death, within the space of one year, I wish it to be divided into four equal portions: one for my father, one for my brother Edward, one for yourself, and one for my aunt.

"Do not mourn for me, dear uncle, for I sincerely believe in God's forgiveness of my past sins, through the merits of Jesus Christ, my Saviour. My prayer to God is, 'Increase my faith, O Lord! and pardon me, as thou didst the malefactor upon the cross;' for I feel, dear uncle, as if I was justly in that thief's condemnation. I hope soon, very soon, to be in a better state, and in a happier world. I wish you and my aunt to come to Ipswich and see me once more before I suffer. Tell my aunt I wish her to purchase something decent for my funeral. She will find some money in the corner of my box, under the linen. Oh! how little did he, who gave me that money, and who so worthily esteemed me, how little did he think that any portion of it would be devoted to such a purpose! My dear uncle, go and comfort my poor father, and my good young brother: I will write to them before another day is past. I wish my bones to lie beside my mother's and sister's, in Nacton churchyard. I am told that on Saturday week I shall probably suffer death. God grant I may then be prepared!

"We shall all return to Ipswich as soon as the nine prisoners, whom Mr. Ripshaw brought to Bury, shall have been tried. Pray for me, dear uncle! Warn the dear children by my fate. I should like to see them myself. I wish I could impress upon their young minds the dreadful feelings of guilt which I have endured, and so prevent their commission of any crime. I am going to write now to my dear mistress, and, as you return to-morrow, you must take that letter and deliver it. God bless you, dear uncle! God's peace be with you! So no more from your poor affectionate niece,

"MARGARET CATCHPOLE.

"BURY GAOL, August 9th, 1797.
"To MR. LEADER, Six Bells Inn, Bury."

"To MRS. COBBOLD.

"HONOURED MADAM,

"My trial is over, and I dare say my dear master has already told you the fate of your unhappy servant. He cannot, however, tell you what I can, and what will better please your good heart than the account of my trial, namely, that I am not so disconsolate as many persons may think I am. No; God be praised, and thanks to those dear friends who visited me in the Ipswich gaol; and chiefly thanks to you, among them, my dear lady; my heart is consoled with the prospect of soon seeing better things than this wicked world can show me. Oh! my dear lady, I hope to see you among those bright shining spirits who live for ever in harmony and love. Oh! how happy shall we then be, free from fear of pain or grief! I have just been reading that beautiful passage, where it is written, ' God shall wipe all tears from their eyes, and there shall be no more death, neither sorrow nor crying; neither shall there be any more pain.' Oh! what a different world must that be to this; and what should make us grieve to leave this world? It is only the fear of future wrath that can prevent our joyfully looking up to heaven through the valley of death. And, dearest lady, if such a wretched being as I am can hope in that Saviour who died for me and all the world, surely, you, dear lady, must have a bright, a pleasant prospect, before you. Heaven bless you, for all your goodness to me in the days of my prosperity, but more for your Christian charity in the day of my adversity! The judge, who really, I think, reminded me of you, told me I had been well instructed; I wish he knew you, dear madam, and he would then be assured of it. Thank my kind master for his goodness to his unworthy servant. I had no hope of mercy from the first, and the judge told me not to trust in any such idea in this world. He spoke much less severely than I expected; but I was pre-pared for his condemnation, and I am now preparing my mind for the day of execution. I find great com-fort in the Scriptures, because I have no secret pangs of unconfessed guilt, or any wish in my heart to cover or palliate my offences. My trial is over, and the same God who sustained me through it, will, I hope, pre-serve my spirit faithful to the last. Every moment seems valuable to me, dear lady, now that I know them to be so soon numbered; and I scarcely like to lose one even in sleep. Nature, however, is weary with fatigue and anxiety, though my spirit seems so wake-ful. If I go to sleep, it will be in prayer for you and all my friends. That God may bless you and all your dear family, is the heartfelt desire of your unfortunate, though ever grateful servant,

"MARGARET CATCHPOLE.

"BURY GAOL, August 9th, 1797.

"P.S.—My good uncle Leader will bring this, of whom you can ask any particulars, as he was in court during my trial."

On the 11th of August, a letter arrived from the Home Office, in London, giving full powers to the judge to exercise the prerogative of mercy in her case, as he might see fit. The judge was not in court at the time, but in his own rooms. He sent immediately for the sheriff and the prosecutor, Mr. Cobbold, and explained to them the purport of the letter he had received. He thought, however, that some punishment should mark the sense of crime. He therefore commuted the sentence of death for the shortest period of transportation for seven years; and he signed the necessary document for such purpose. He intimated that that period might be shortened by the good conduct of the prisoner in gaol; for as there was great difficulty now in sending prisoners to the new settlement, her portion of confinement would most likely be spent in the Ipswich Gaol. The judge added, that the woman appeared to be a most sensible creature; and he made many most minute inquiries concerning her education and habits. He said that she had conducted herself during her trial in a very becoming manner, and he hoped that her punishment would end with half the term of confinement. This would depend upon the representations of the visiting magistrates.

CHAPTER XXIV

THE REPRIEVE AND REMOVAL

THE feelings of Margaret Catchpole under the new circumstances which now awaited her, will be best explained by a letter written by her to Mrs. Cobbold immediately after the communication of the happy tidings, and her consequent removal to Ipswich Gaol.

"IPSWICH GAOL, Sunday Evening, August 13th, 1797.

"HONOURED MADAM,

"You have heard of your poor servant's reprieve. I had no time to write you word yesterday, because of the bustle of our return, and the general congratulations of the prisoners. Mr. Ripshaw has permitted me to have pen, ink, and paper, this evening, and I hasten to write my heart. Good Mr. Sharp has been warning me against too great exultation in my change, and very kindly says to me in words of truth : 'Sin no more, lest a worse thing come upon thee.' This was his subject in the chapel to-day. I certainly do, even now, feel very different to what I did when I wrote to you last, dear lady, from Bury. I had then made up my mind to die, and hoped to live for ever. I now make up my mind to live ; but I hope not to die for ever. No, dear lady ; if I thought that life being granted to me now was only to make my future dangers greater, I should grieve that I did not rather suffer before this time.

"Life is sweet and to be desired, whilst the hope of becoming good, and doing good in our time, exists. God grant that such hope may be realized in my life ! Oh ! my dear lady, if by living I could only imitate you more nearly, I should then be full of hope. I feel, however, that temptation will assail me, when I leave this place and enter again into the world. Here I am well taught and well guarded against many temptations. I have many dear friends too, who take such an interest in me, that I am afraid of being vain, though God has shown me I have indeed nothing to be vain of, except it be of such as you, dear lady, who take notice of such a creature as myself.

" Oh ! what a happy Sabbath-day has this been to me ! I am so thankful that my heart can sing psalms all the day long. I am very grateful for this paper and pen, that I may be able to speak to you, my dear madam, in this way. You taught me to read and write, and these are my great recreations. Pray lend me some good books to read, and if you would let me see some of your own dear writing, it would be a great blessing to me.

" I have now seven years' confinement to look forward to. Oh ! that I may greatly improve my time ! Beneath your help, what may I not gain in my prison ! It may be some weeks before I see your dear, loved face, as I hear that you are very near increasing your family. I would not have you come into this place at such a time on any account. But, as I am so near you, a word or a message, just to let me know that you, my master, and family are well, would lighten my burden.

" Mr. Ripshaw has promised that I shall have plenty of employment. Work of any sort, you know, dear lady, is always agreeable to me. To be doing nothing is death to me. He tells me, moreover, that if I conduct myself well, he will not fail to represent my case to the magistrates for a shortening of the period of my captivity. I received some hint of this from the chaplains at Bury. You may be sure, dear lady, that I will do all I can to serve Mr. Ripshaw, and to merit the recommendation of the magistrates. I hope your dear children are well. I never was so happy as when nursing Master Roland ; I hope I shall see him soon again.

" Pray, dear madam, give my duty to my master,

and to the young ladies and gentlemen ; and accept the same from your ever grateful servant,

"   MARGARET CATCHPOLE."

Margaret was true to her good intentions.   She became very industrious and trustworthy in the service of Mrs. Ripshaw, the governor's wife ; and made herself useful in every possible way to her new mistress. In fact, she became an invaluable person in the gaol. She exercised a moral influence over those of her own sex who were inmates of the prison, such as no matron could hope to attain.

Her father and brother often came to see her, and occasionally they brought her a luxury which reminded her of the days of liberty—" a harvest cake."

The reader will not be surprised to learn that Margaret still, sometimes, asked after Will Laud.   Her brother could give her but an indifferent account of what he heard of him ; one question, however, of most vital import to the still lingering hopes of poor Margaret, namely—" Is he single still ? "   he could answer in the affirmative.   As a set-off against this, she learned that he was still deeply engaged in smuggling transactions.

In the winter of 1797, Margaret lost her father, who was taken off by a bad fever, which at that time raged fiercely in the neighbourhood.

The following letter to her brother Edward speaks her feelings on this event :—

"   IPSWICH GAOL, December 21st, 1797.

"   DEAR EDWARD,

"   My sins appear to me doubly great, because they have prevented my fulfilling my duties to my dear father in his illness.   They oppress me, because, but for them, I should have found such comfort in being able to wait upon him.   Oh that I had wings to fly from this place to Nacton !   if only for once to be present at the last duties we can any of us pay to those whom we love. But I cannot come, so I send you this letter. My tears fall upon it, whilst I write it. He was such a dear good old man to us all. Can I ever forget him ? Never ! You and he both stood near me upon my trial.

"Ah ! Edward, I do think my ill-conduct has killed him. He was always so fond of me, that I think he has never recovered the shock of that day. Yet he seemed well, and rejoiced to see me, with the hope of happier and brighter times. But he is gone, and all our grief, dear brother, will be useless. If we continue to walk in the right path, we shall meet him hereafter. We shall go to him ; he cannot come to us. Yet, I wish I could join you in the churchyard ; but I may not leave the prison for one moment. It is an indulgence no prisoner is allowed. Mr. Ripshaw has promised me that I shall have the afternoon of to-morrow to myself, which I shall employ in reading, and thinking about the burial service.

"Dear old man ! he promised to spend Christmas-day with me in my cell. He is in a happier place, where joy and peace will make every day his Christmas. I shall think of you to-morrow at two o'clock. Do you remember, Edward, the evening of our mother's funeral ? Do you remember the stranger's visit, and that stranger our brother Charles ? This melancholy time reminds me of him. You will have a dreary home now. Oh that I had power to make it happier !

"I am glad the Cracknells are still near you, and that they are kind to you ; though their misfortunes and mine have kept pace with each other. Never mind, Edward, what cruel people say to you about their prophecies concerning his downfall. They only tell you these things to aggravate you. The time may come when they will impudently say, they prophesied my rise and progress in the world. I hope better days are coming.

"You must come and see me as soon as you can ;

for I feel at this time very low and sorrowful. So my dear brother, do come and see me, when you are able to spare the time. Pray for me, and I will not cease to do so for you. My dear mistress has promised to send this by an especial messenger. How kind of her to think of one so unworthy as your affectionate sister,

"MARGARET CATCHPOLE."

In the spring of 1798, Edward Catchpole, finding the notoriety his sister had obtained occasioned him much annoyance, left the neighbourhood of Ipswich, and went into Cambridgeshire, where he obtained a situation as shepherd, and was always a respectable character. Poor Margaret felt this loss keenly, though a letter from him now and then cheered her spirits.[1]

---

[1] All traces of Edward Catchpole having been lost, the author is obliged to Henry T. Bourne, Esq., of Alford, in Lincolnshire, for making known to him, since the publication of the work, the circumstances which are here briefly narrated.

Edward Catchpole went into Lincolnshire, and resided some time at Sutton-in-the-Marsh. He was always fond of the sea, and for some years became mate of the *Argus* revenue cutter. In this vessel, he was present at the rescue of an English coal brig, from the *Star*, French privateer ; and having put men on board the brig, sufficient to carry her into port, he pursued the privateer, brought her to close quarters, and having only twenty-seven men on board the cutter, he was overpowered, and at ten o'clock at night compelled to surrender, as the privateer had eighty-six men against him.

This was on the 18th September, 1807. He was made prisoner, and having spent seven years in confinement, he made his escape, and reached home in safety.

He was afterwards appointed chief officer of the coast-guard, at Sutton-in-the-Marsh, in the county of Lincoln. Though a very brave man, and a steady officer, he did not appear to have any very serious notions of religion, until he was compelled by a serious wound to keep at home. It was the blessing of God to him, and others, that this

requesting him to come and see her, which he did ; and she then gave him full powers to withdraw the 130 guineas from Mr. Smith, and requested him to pay £100 into the hands of Mr. Ripshaw on a certain day ; namely, the 5th of March, the day previous to Laud's term of imprisonment expiring.

Mr. Leader was well assured that she would never draw the money, except to restore it to Will Laud. He asked her the plain question. She gave him an honest answer. She told him that Will was then in prison, and that his liberty depended upon the punctuality of the payment. Her honesty with her uncle saved her from detection, for, in all probability, had not Mr. Leader had more prudence than she had, it might have been suspected by the gaoler. He at once suggested that Mr. Smith, who was not known to have any connexion with her, should be requested to pay the fine to Mr. Ripshaw, in behalf of the prisoner. It struck Margaret, the moment it was mentioned, and she felt surprised that the hurry and anxiety of her own feelings should have so greatly blinded her as to leave her destitute of common prudence in this matter.

It was on the 3rd of March, in the year 1800, that Margaret was destined to undergo the severest temptation she had ever yet experienced. She had been employed in washing for the prisoners, and was engaged hanging out the linen in the passage on one of the clothes-horses used for that purpose, when she was accosted from the debtors' side in a well-known voice, " Margaret ! what a capital ladder one of those horses would make, if set against the wall ! "

She turned round, and there stood Will Laud. Cautiously she looked along the passage to see if any one was near. She pretended to be busily engaged ; at the same time she said,—

" Ah, William ! I understand you. I wish I could make my escape with you, and I would ; but I fear the thing is too difficult."

" You might manage it, Margaret, when the governor goes to Bury with the prisoners."

" How, William ! How ? "

" You have the horse, and you have the linen line.
Look around the wall, and see if you cannot find a place
of escape. You must be tired of your captivity. I owe
my liberty to you ; and if I can once get you out of
this place, no power on earth shall separate us again."

" But where should I go, William, if I got out ? "

" To my sister's at Sudbourn, Lucy Keeley. I will
tell her to expect you."

" That would do. I will look round and see if it
can be done. On the 19th or 20th of this month, Mr.
Ripshaw goes to Bury with the prisoners. On Monday
the 24th, and Tuesday the 25th, are our two great
washing days. It must be one of those nights. Will
you be waiting for me at the end of the lane, near
St. Helen's Church ? "

" I will be waiting for you, never fear. I will have
a sailor's jacket and hat to disguise you in."

" Well, the trial is worth the risk. I will confide
in you once more, Laud ; but if you deceive me, then,
indeed, I care not what becomes of me. But I will trust
you. Go !—There is some one coming."

Laud departed, and Margaret busied herself with the
linen. That day she had many things given her to
mend. She contrived also to get a candle, under the
pretence of working late. And such was the confidence
which was placed in her, and such the quantity of work
she performed, that she was trusted beyond any other
prisoner in the house.

Margaret knew nothing of the penalty the law would
compel her to pay for breaking out of prison. She
knew nothing of the bond by which the gaoler was
bound, in case of the escape of any of his prisoners.
She saw but her lover and liberty, and did not suppose
it any great offence, even if she should be detected in
the attempt.

Her uncle Leader paid her a visit on the 5th, and
gave her the thirty guineas, telling her that the hundred guineas were lodged in the hands of Mr. Ripshaw
for the discharge of Will Laud.

" I will give William this money myself," thought Margaret; but she breathed not one word of her intended escape to her uncle; and the good man left her with the conscious happiness, that let her term of confinement be what it might, she had been instrumental in procuring the release of her lover.

It was a proud day for Margaret, that 6th of March, 1800. From the felons' side she could see her lover depart out of gaol in company with Mr. Ripshaw. She saw him go to the turnkey's lodge; and with a heart at the same time bounding with the hope of liberty, she walked quietly round the felons' yard, looking anxiously up at those long spikes to see where the widest place could be found for her to get her body through. That very hour she discovered a place where one of the spikes had been broken off. She looked at it and sighed. She was very thoughtful about it. It dwelt upon her mind night and day, till she had fully resolved to make the attempt at that very spot.

At night, and early in the morning, she was at work for herself. Out of one sheet she contrived to make a smock-frock, such as shepherds wear over their clothes. Out of the other she made a pair of sailor's trousers. These she laid upon her bed in such an ingenious manner, that no one going into her cell would discover any difference in the usual make of it.

Anxiously did she watch the hours for the departure of Mr. Ripshaw with the prisoners for trial at Bury. In the very cell next to her own was a felon to be taken away. The anxious time came, and Margaret saw the governor and prisoners take their departure.

Meantime, Laud, directly he left the gaol, went to his sister's house at Sudbourn. He reached that place the same night. He told his sister who it was that had paid the fine for him, and thus completely won her heart for Margaret. His plan was fixed to get off with Margaret in a smuggler's boat, and get a cast to Holland, where he intended to marry and settle. He told

his sister his plan, and she approved it, and promised
to receive Margaret.

He was not long in ascertaining what boats were
expected on the coast. He had an interview with one
David Shaw, the master of a cutter belonging to Captain Merrells, and with him came to an understanding
that, some day after the 25th, when wind and weather
should suit, he should send a boat ashore for him.
A red handkerchief tied round his hat should be the
signal that he was ready. He told him that he should
be accompanied by a friend, whom he wished to go
over the water with him. All these things were arranged, and, as far as they went, were in some sense
honourable. In the meantime he promised to assist
in landing any cargoes along the shore. And this part
of the contract he performed.

On the 19th of March, Mr. Ripshaw, with seven
prisoners, departed for Bury. The business of the
assizes began on Thursday, the 20th, and did not
terminate until that day week, the 27th. On Monday
and Tuesday the wash took place. On these occasions
the female convicts are all locked up in one large
room, from seven o'clock in the morning until seven
in the evening ; their food being brought to them in
the washing-room. At seven in the evening they all
go into the felons' yard for exercise and air. They
usually give their signal that the wash is finished by
rapping the door about seven o'clock. This evening,
Tuesday, the 25th, Margaret contrived by various
means to prolong the wash till nearly eight o'clock,
and as she had some kind of acknowledged authority
and influence among her fellow-convicts, she insisted
upon the signal not being given till the work was
completely finished ; so that at eight o'clock it was
quite dark. They were let out of the room into the
felons' yard at that time for one half hour. Some
were accustomed to saunter about, or to have a
game of romps. Some, when the season admitted,
would weed the flower-beds ; for Mr. Ripshaw was
a great fancy florist, and used to raise the best ranun-

culuses, carnations, and polyanthuses, of any person
in the town. His garden adjoined the felons' walk,
and was only separated from it by a very low paling.
Margaret had continual access to the garden, and used
to take considerable interest in the culture of the
plants.

She was greatly disappointed to find that all the
linen-horses stood on the stone area, between the
debtors' and felons' yards. She had hoped that they
would have been carried by the turnkey to the drying
ground in the garden, as usual, ready for the linen in
the morning. Owing to some cause or other, they
were not there that night.

This was a sad disappointment, for she had made
up her mind to escape that very night. Could she
be suspected ? Had anybody betrayed her ? No, it
was impossible. As the turnkey passed the palings
she cried out to him, " You have not put out the horses
for us to-night ? "

" No, Margaret," he replied, " we have all been
too busy cleaning the cells and yards ; but they shall
be put out the first thing in the morning."

The reply was both satisfactory and unsatisfactory.
It convinced her she was not suspected ; but declared
that she must expect no help from the linen-horses.
She was glad, however, to see that the lines were on
the posts for the coarse linen, and the crotches, or
props, in their proper places.

She looked around for something to help her. The
gaol wall was nearly twenty-two feet high, and the
chevaux de frise three feet from the point of one
revolving spike to its extreme point. What could
she get to assist her ? At one time she thought of
pulling up a portion of the paling for a ladder. She
tried her strength at it, but it was too much for her.
She then turned her eye upon a large frame, which
was used for the flower-beds. It covered a long bed,
and the awning usually placed upon it to keep the
sun off the flowers in the summer was not there. She
tried her strength at this, and lifted the legs upon

which it stood about a foot upwards. This she resolved
to make her ladder. She looked up at the narrow
spot where the iron spike had been broken, and which
was close to the shoulder or prop of the *chevaux de
frise*. Hope beamed brightly upon her as she thought
of her liberty. Margaret resolved to make the attempt
at midnight. At half-past eight the convicts all
went in to supper, and afterwards retired to their cells.
But Margaret, the moment she reached hers, contrived
to slip out of it again, with the things she had made
for her disguise, into the adjoining one, which stood
open ; and she crept under the bed of the felon who
was gone to Bury for trial. She had, as usual, closed
her own door, and lay anxiously waiting in her hiding
place the turnkey's approach. She heard him coming
along, and asking the several prisoners, as he came,
if they were in their cells. They answered his summons, and then she heard them locked up ; and now
came the challenge to her own door.

"Margaret, are you there ? "

She put her lips to the wall of the cell where she was,
and answered, " Yes." It sounded exactly as if she
was in bed in her own cell ; and to her great joy she
heard the key turn in the iron lock, and the bolt shoot
into its place. She breathed for a moment freely,
but the next moment she experienced such a sudden
revulsion as few could have borne without detection.
To her confusion and dismay, the turnkey entered the
very cell where she lay concealed under the bed. He
walked up to the iron-grated window, and, as usual,
the casement stood open for the benefit of air through
the passage, and, in a soliloquizing manner, said,
" Ah ! poor Sarah ! you will never sleep upon this
bed again ! "

In breathless agony did Margaret dread two things
equally fatal to her project. One was, that he should
hear her breath in the stillness of the night, and discover her ; the other, that he should lock the door upon
her. She knew that it was not usual to lock the doors
of those cells which contained no prisoners, but she

dreaded lest the same absence of mind which made him saunter into Sarah Lloyd's cell should make him lock the door. What a state of suspense! How did her blood course through her frame! she could hear her heart beat! She was presently relieved from her suspense, for the turnkey, having completed his duty in locking up all his prisoners, quietly departed out of the cell, and left the door, as usual, standing wide open. Never was relief more opportune or welcome than this to her overcharged heart. The clock struck the hours of nine, ten, and eleven, and Margaret had not stirred. She now rose, took her shoes in her hand, and her bundle under her arm; she then managed to tie it up with an apron-string over her shoulders, and, with the slightest tread, stole along the stone passage. A mouse would scarcely have been disturbed by her as she descended the front of steps that led to the felons' yard.

To her great comfort she found the door unbolted; for the turnkey, having locked every one up, saw no necessity for bolting the yard door. Silently she opened it; it creaked so little, that the wind prevented any sound reaching beyond the precincts of the door. She made her way to the flower-stand in the governor's garden, lifted the frame out of the ground and set it up endways directly under the broken spike. It reached a little more than half way up the wall, being about thirteen feet long. She then went and took the linen line off the posts, and made a running noose at one end of it. She then took the longest clothes-prop she could find, and passed the noose over the horn of it. She mounted the frame by the help of the prop, and standing upon it she lifted the line up and passed the noose over the shoulder of the *chevaux de frise*, then, pulling it tight and close to the wall, it slipped down the iron and became fixed.

Now came the greatest difficulty she had ever overcome in her life. She drew herself up by the line to the top of the wall, and laying her body directly upon the roller where the spike was broken, with the help of one hand grasping the shoulder of iron, she balanced herself until she had pulled up all the line and let it fall down the other side of the wall; then, taking hold of the rope with both hands, she bent her body forward, and the whole body of spikes revolved, turning her literally heels over head on the outer side of the gaol wall. Was there ever such a desperate act performed by any woman before? Had not the fact been proved beyond all doubt, the statement might be deemed incredible. But Margaret Catchpole did exactly as here described; and after the oscillation of her body was over from the jerk, she quietly let herself down in perfect safety on the other side.

Just as she alighted on the earth St. Clement's chimes played for twelve o'clock. It was a gently sloping bank from the wall, and a dry fosse, which she crossed, easily climbed over the low wooden palings against the road, and made her way for the lane against St. Helen's church. There she found Will Laud in readiness to receive her, which he did with an ardour and devotion that told he was sincere.

They fled to an empty cart-shed on the Woodbridge road. Here Laud kept watch at the entrance whilst Margaret put on her sailor's dress. She soon made her appearance on the road with her white trousers, hat, and blue jacket, looking completely like a British tar. They did not wait to be overtaken, but off they started for Woodbridge, and arrived at the ferry just as the dawning streaks of daylight began to tinge the east. Their intention was to cross the Sutton Walks and Hollesley Heath to Sudbourn. Unluckily for them, however, who should they meet at the ferry but old Robinson Crusoe, the fisherman, who, having been driven round the point at Felixstowe, was compelled to come up the Deben to Woodbridge for the sale of his fish. The old man gave them no sign of recognition, but he knew them both, and, with a tact that few possessed, saw how the wind blew. But without speaking to either of them, he proceeded with his basket to the town.

At this they both rejoiced, and as they took their journey across that barren tract of land, it seemed to them like traversing a flowery mead.

CHAPTER XXVI

PURSUIT AND CAPTURE

THE morning after Margaret's escape the turnkey was alarmed by the call of the gardener, who came early to the prison to prune some trees in the governor's garden. He told the turnkey there was a rope hanging down the wall, as if some one had escaped during the night. They soon discovered the frame against the wall; footmarks along the beds, and the linen crotch, all told the same tale. The turnkey then ran to the men's cells, and found them all bolted. He did the same to the women's, and found them likewise fastened just as he left them the night before. He then examined every window. Not a bar was moved. He did this without speaking a word to any one. At the usual hour he called up the prisoners, and marched them out of their cells. Margaret's was the last, at the end of the passage. When he opened it, no one answered his summons. He walked in; no one was there. The bed had not been slept in, and was without sheets. He then made Mrs. Ripshaw acquainted with the facts. Astonishment and alarm were depicted upon her countenance. Her husband's absence made the circumstance the more distressing.

Search was made in every part of the gaol, but no trace of Margaret could be found. The women with whom she washed the day previously all declared that they knew nothing of her escape. They declared that they saw her go before them to the farther end of the passage to her own cell. But how could she escape and lock the door? The turnkey was quite sure he had secured her in her own cell, for that he went into the one adjoining after he had, as he supposed, locked

her up in hers. It came out, however, in the course
of inquiry, that he remembered her asking him about
the horses not being set out for the wash; and the
women declared that Margaret had been very per-
emptory about not giving the signal before eight
o'clock. These things seemed to indicate a design to
escape, and carried some suspicion of the fact.

Mrs. Ripshaw, however, was not satisfied, but sent a
swift messenger on horseback to Bury St. Edmunds,
with a note to acquaint her husband with the circumstances. Mrs. Ripshaw also wrote to Mrs. Cobbold
in the greatest agitation, begging of her, if she knew
where she was, to give information of it, as her husband
and two sureties were bound, under a penalty of five
hundred pounds each, to answer for the escape of any
prisoner from the goal. Such a stir was created in the
town of Ipswich by this event as was scarcely ever
before witnessed. People flocked to the gaol to see
the spot whence Peggy had made her escape, and many
were the reports falsely circulated concerning her.

It is not easy to describe the grief and consternation
which was truly felt by Margaret's dearest and best
friend. She knew the consequences of this rash act;
that, if she was taken, it was death, without any hope
of reprieve.

She ordered her carriage, and went to the gaol, and
was as much, or even more astonished than the inmates
of the prison could be. She soon convinced Mrs.
Ripshaw that she had not the slightest idea of any
such intention on the part of her late servant, neither
could she tell where she was gone. She made inquiries whether she had been seen talking with any of
the male prisoners; but no clue could be gained here.
Mrs. Cobbold was one of those whose decided opinion
was, that she must have had somebody as an accomplice; but every soul denied it. This lady returned
home in the greatest distress and uncertainty. Mes-
sengers were dispatched to Nacton, to Brandiston,
and even into Cambridgeshire, to inquire after her.

When Mr. Ripshaw returned from Bury, he found

some of the magistrates in the gaol. He had formed a very strong opinion in his own mind, and requested the visiting magistrates to examine the turnkey immediately. He was summoned, and examined before Colonel Edgar, Mr. Gibson, and Mr. Neale, and closely questioned. His answers were not deemed satisfactory.

The magistrates remanded him for a time, and conversed together upon the subject. They were of opinion that somebody must have bribed the man, and that he must have let her out, and have put the things as they were found, as a blind to turn suspicion from himself.

He was again summoned, and given in custody, on suspicion of having assisted the prisoner's escape.

In the meantime, every exertion was made to discover the prisoner, but without any success. The following hand-bill was printed and circulated in every direction :—

"FIFTY POUNDS REWARD.

"Whereas, on Tuesday night, the 25th of March, or early on Wednesday morning, Margaret Catchpole, a female convict, confined in the Ipswich gaol, made her escape therefrom, either by scaling the wall, or by the connivance of the turnkey, this is to give notice, that the above reward shall be given to any person or persons who will bring the said Margaret Catchpole to Mr. Ripshaw, the gaoler; and one-half that sum to any person or persons furnishing such information as shall lead to her apprehension. And notice is hereby given, that any person concealing or harbouring the said Margaret Catchpole shall, after this notice, if detected, be, by order of the magistrates, punished as the law directs.

"N.B.—The prisoner is a tall and dark person, with short hair, black eyes, and of intelligent countenance. She had on the gaol dress, and took away with her the two sheets belonging to her bed.

"IPSWICH GAOL, March 28th, 1800."

This notice was circulated far and near, and furnished topics for conversation throughout the county.

It so happened that some of the servants of Mrs. Cobbold mentioned the subject of the reward to the old fisherman, Robinson Crusoe, as he stood at the back-door with his basket of fish.

"Well, Robin, have you heard of the reward? Have you heard of Margaret's escape from the gaol!"

"No; but I think I have seen her, or the foul fiend has played me one of his shabby tricks."

"Seen her, Robin! Where?"

"I saw that fellow Laud, and somebody very like her, go across the Sutton Ferry together. She might deceive anybody else, but the foul fiend showed her to me, though she was in a sailor's dress. I told your mistress, long ago, that no good would come of Margaret."

This news reached the parlour, and was soon communicated to Mr. Ripshaw, who quickly had an interview with Mrs. Cobbold, and from her he learned the intimacy existing between Will Laud, his late prisoner, and Margaret, and could not doubt that he had assisted in her escape. He soon ascertained the probable bearings of Laud's destination, and lost no time in prosecuting the pursuit. He went off for Woodbridge and Sutton Ferry directly. The ferryman corroborated the testimony of old Colson as to two sailors, a slight one and a stout one, passing over the river in his boat, on the morning of the 26th. They went off directly, he said, for Eyke. Thither the gaoler pursued his course, and thence to Sudbourn.

He found out that two sailors had been seen in that neighbourhood such as he described them, and that they lodged at Mrs. Keeley's. He took a constable along with him to the cottage, and at once demanded his prisoner. The woman at first denied all knowledge of the persons he sought, but, after threatening her with taking her off to gaol at once, she confessed that her brother and Margaret were down on the coast, waiting for a boat to carry them off to sea; she even

confessed that Margaret slept with her only the night
before, and that a report having reached them of the
reward offered for her capture, she had put a smock-
frock over her sailor's jacket, and was assisting Keeley,
her husband, in keeping his flock upon the marsh
saltings.

The constable of Sudbourn and Mr. Ripshaw went
off immediately for the saltings. They met Keeley,
the shepherd, returning with his flock, to fold them
upon the fallows; but no one was with him. He was
a shrewd, sharp, surly fellow, and in a moment understood what was in the wind.

Mr. Ripshaw began the attack. "Constable, take
that man into custody."

"Where's your warrant, Mr. Gaoler? 'Old birds
are not to be caught with chaff.' Now, then, your
warrant for my apprehension, and I am the man to go
with you. Come, show me the warrant at once;
or, you no sooner lift your hand against me than I will
show you what resistance is, and you shall take the
consequences of an assault upon my person."

The fellow stood with his brawny limbs displayed
before them, and his two fierce, rough-coated, short,
flap-eared dogs wagging their stumps of tails, and
looking earnestly in their master's face, to see if he
gave the signal for them to attack either, or both the
gaoler and the constable. It was clear that they must
go upon another tack.

The shepherd gave a shrill whistle to his dogs, and on
they dashed, driving the sheep towards the fold.

They proceeded directly along the shingled hardware
to the beach, or rather to the shore of the river-side,
which in those parts much resembles the sea-shore.
The revenue cutter's boat was then going across the
stream of the Alde; they hailed it, and the officer in
command ordered his men to return.

It was young Barry who came on shore from the
boat, and he immediately walked a little way apart
with the gaoler, who explained to him the nature of
his business; and painful as its connexion with Mar-

garet Catchpole made it to Barry, his sense of duty compelled him to render the assistance required. Accordingly, they were soon seated in the stern of the boat, and were rowed by his men towards the spot, where, on the main shore, Laud and Margaret stood, anxiously watching the approach of a boat from a vessel on the sea.

There they stood, not only unconscious of approaching danger, but congratulating themselves upon the prospect of a termination of all their troubles. Joyfully did they watch the boat coming over the billows of the sea, not seeing the other boat approaching them from the river. A few minutes more, and they would have been beyond the reach of gaolers and of prisons.

Neither Laud nor Margaret saw them until they came down upon them, headed by the gaoler, whose voice Margaret instantly recognized. With a wild shriek that made the welkin ring, she rushed into the sea, and would at once have perished, had not Laud caught her, as a wave cast her back upon the beach and suddenly deprived her of sense and speech.

He stood across the seemingly lifeless body of that devoted girl, and with a pistol in each hand cocked, and presented to the foremost men, the officer and the gaoler, he exclaimed, "Let us go—we are not defrauding the revenue—you have no business with us!"

"*You* may go unhurt," replied the gaoler, "if you will deliver up the body of Margaret Catchpole. I must and will have her in my custody."

"If you do, Mr. Ripshaw, it shall be at the peril of your life, or the cost of mine. The first man who approaches to touch her shall be a corpse, or he shall make me one."

There was such determination in his words and attitude, that every one saw he would not flinch. It was a painful moment for young Barry; he wished to save the life of Laud; he did not wish to risk that of any of his men; he stepped forward, and said,—

"Will Laud, let me entreat you to give up the person

of Margaret Catchpole; she has escaped from the custody of the gaoler, and is under sentence of transportation. I promise that you shall depart in safety, and that she shall take no hurt. Do not force me to shed blood—we *must* take her!"

The next instant two pistols flashed, and Laud lay stretched upon the sand. He had first fired at Barry and missed him, and the next moment, in self-defence, Barry was compelled to fire in return. The ball, which was intended only to have disabled his arm, passed through his heart and killed him on the spot. So ended the career of a man who, only in the few latter days of his life, seemed steadily resolved to act fairly by the woman who had devoted her life to him, and to follow some honourable occupation in a foreign land. Poor Susan's words at last proved true: "Margaret you will never marry William Laud."

The bodies of Laud and Margaret were both carried by the sailors to the preventive-service boat, and laid upon the men's cloaks at the bottom of it. After a while, Margaret began to revive, and her awakening dream was, that she was on board the smuggler's boat, which was coming to meet them. But the men in that boat, observing the fearful odds against them, had only rested on their oars to see the fatal result which took place, and then turned back and steered for their own vessel.

Margaret looked wildly round her as the moonlight shone upon the sailors. She whispered, "Laud! Laud!" She saw something lying in a line with herself upon the same cloaks, but could not distinguish anything but a sailor's dress: she heard a voice at the helm which was familiar to her; she recognized it to be Barry's; she lifted her head, and saw the banks of the river on both sides of the water. The truth seemed to flash upon her, for she fell backwards again, fainted away, and became insensible.

She and her lover were conveyed to the Ship Inn at Orford. The sailors who carried her, sensible of the devoted heart of the poor girl, seemed oppressed with heaviness, and could not refrain addressing one another, in their own peculiar style, upon the bad job of that night. Margaret became too soon and too fully acquainted with her situation. She shed tears of the deepest agony; her mind was distracted, and without consolation. She did not speak to any one; but between sobs, and groans, and lamentations upon her loss, she seemed the most melancholy picture of human woe. By what she had heard from some of the pitying sailors around her, she understood that it was young Edward Barry who had shot her lover. When he came into the room where she was seated in an arm-chair, with her head resting in an agony upon her hand, he went up to speak to her. She lifted up her hands, turned her head aside, and exclaimed—

"Begone, wretch! Did you not voluntarily promise you would never hurt him?"

"And so I would, Margaret, if he would have permitted me to do so. But he would not. He first fired at me, and then I returned it; but only with the intention of disarming him."

"You have done a noble deed, and one which will immortalize your name, one which will form a source of happy reflection to you hereafter, most noble man of war! You have killed a harmless man, and have taken captive a poor fugitive female! Happy warrior! you will be nobly rewarded!"

"Do not reproach me, Margaret, but forgive me. I have only done my duty; and, however painful it has been, you would not reproach me, if you did but know how much I really grieved for you."

"Your grief for me will do me about as much good as mine will poor William!" and here Margaret burst into a flood of tears, which words could not in any way repress.

A post-chaise was ordered to the inn-door, and Margaret, apparently more dead than alive, was placed within it, and the gaoler taking his seat beside her, they were conveyed immediately to Ipswich.

She was once more confined within those walls

which she had so recently scaled ; she made no secret of the manner in which she had effected her escape ; she fully confessed her own work, and perfectly exonerated every other person in the gaol.

It was well for the poor turnkey that she was captured. He was immediately released from confinement, and reinstated in his office.

Margaret was now kept in almost solitary confinement, to mourn over her unhappy lot, and to reflect upon the death of one whom she had loved too well.

CHAPTER XXVII

SECOND TRIAL, AND SECOND TIME CONDEMNED TO DEATH

AFTER the arrival of Margaret at the Ipswich gaol, several magistrates attended, at the request of Mr. Ripshaw, to take the deposition of the prisoner. She was summoned into the gaoler's parlour, or, as it was more properly called, the "Magistrates' Room." The depositions of Mr. Ripshaw and of the constable of Sudbourn, were first taken down. The nature of the offence was then for the first time explained to Margaret, and its most dreadful consequences at once exposed. She was taken completely by surprise. She had no idea that, in doing as she had done, she had been guilty of anything worthy of death, and made no hesitation in telling the magistrates so. She told them, moreover, that her conscience did not accuse her of any crime in the attempt, and that she thought it a cruel and bloody law which could condemn her to death for such an act.

" But are you aware," said Mr. Gibson, one of the visiting magistrates, " that you have broken that confidence with Mr. Ripshaw which he placed in you, and that you subjected him and his sureties to the penalty of five hundred pounds each, had he not recovered you, and brought you back to prison ? "

" Had I been aware of such a thing, I should then have thought myself as bad as if I had stolen the money, and should, indeed, have broken the confidence which, with such a knowledge, would have been placed in me, but I knew nothing of such a fact. My master, Mr. Ripshaw, was always kind and indulgent to me, and my mistress the same, but they never hinted such a thing to me. I was not aware that, with regard to my personal liberty, there was any bond of mutual obligation between me and my master. I was always locked up at the usual time, and it never was said to me, ' Margaret, I will rely upon your honour that you will never attempt to escape.' No promise was exacted from me, and I did not think that it was any breach of confidence to do as I have done."

" You do not consider that you might have ruined an innocent man ; that the turnkey was actually committed upon suspicion of having connived at your departure, as nobody would believe that you could have done such an act of your own accord."

" I might not have done it of my own accord, though I certainly did it without the assistance of any human being. He, alas ! is dead who persuaded me to it, though I confess it did not require any very great degree of persuasion ; and I fear that, were he living now, I should almost attempt the same again."

" There you speak contemptuously, and in a very unbecoming manner, young woman."

" I did not mean to be disrespectful to you, gentlemen, especially as you are so kind as to explain to me the nature of the law. I only meant to express my own weakness. But may I ask what law it is that makes the act I have been guilty of so felonious as to deserve death ? "

" You may ask any question you please, but you must not add defiance to your impropriety and guilt. You are sensible enough to be well assured that the magistrates here present are not your judges. They have a duty to perform to their country; and they consider it a privilege and an honour that their sovereign places them in the situation of such an active service as to send prisoners before the judge; that such as transgress the laws, and render themselves unfit to enjoy rational liberty, should be punished, as men not worthy to be members of a well organized and civilized community. By the law of the land you live in, you have once been condemned to death for horse-stealing. By the mercy of your king, you have had a reprieve, and a commutation of that sentence of death for transportation for seven years. The period you have spent in gaol is part of that sentence. Now understand the law :—

"' Any prisoner breaking out of gaol, if he resist his gaoler, may be killed on the spot, in the attempt of the gaoler to restrain him. And any person breaking out after sentence of death, shall be considered liable to that punishment for his original offence, which had been commuted, and shall suffer death accordingly. If he escape through the door of his prison, when left open, it shall not be felony, because it is the negligence of the gaoler; but if he break out, after proper caution exercised for his security, either by force in the day, or by subtlety in the night, then it shall be felony.'

"Such is the law; and though in your case, young woman, you may not consider it just, yet when you reflect upon your example to others, you will see it in a different light. If every prisoner should go unpunished who broke out of prison what continual attempts would be made to escape! I am truly sorry for your case; but the law is made for offenders; and it is our duty to send you to Bury again for trial. In the meantime, the gaoler will be upon the alert, and take good care that you do not commit the same offence again."

Margaret thanked Mr. Gibson for his explanation. She felt very sorry, she said, if she had offended any one, and hoped they would forgive her ignorance and unintentional offence.

She was fully committed to take her trial for the

second offence. Mr. Gibson was much astonished at
her presence of mind and singularly acute understanding, as well as appropriate and becoming form of
speech, which she used as naturally as she felt it. His
words to one deeply interested for Margaret were,
" What a pity that such a woman should not know the
value of her liberty before she lost it ! "

The reader knows the reason why Margaret broke
out of prison, and has seen how she became a second
time amenable to the laws. He will observe, that it
was from her acquaintance with that desperate man,
who had been the cause of misery to her and her family,
from the first days of her acquaintance with him.
But he was now dead. The cause was removed, and
with it died every wish of her heart for life and liberty.

But it was not the place that made Margaret so unhappy. It was the void occasioned by the having no
one now to love, that made her feel as if no one in the
world loved her. In this she was greatly mistaken ;
for though her offence had occasioned much condemnation among those who were interested in her,
yet they were not so lost to pity and compassion as
not to feel for her sufferings. Among the foremost of
those friends was her former mistress, who, in the
true sense of the word, was charitable.

As soon as she heard that Margaret was retaken,
she saw at once all the dreadful consequences which
awaited her, and knew that she would require more
than double attention and care. Her first step was
an application to a magistrate (Mileson Edgar, Esq.,
of the Red House), for an order to visit Margaret in
prison, and the application was immediately granted in
the following letter from that gentleman :—

"RED HOUSE, May 10th, 1800.

" MY DEAR MADAM,

" Any request that you would make would be sure
to meet with prompt attention from me, because I am
well assured that you would not make one which I
could not grant, and which, when granted, would not

give me pleasure to have attended to. Herewith I
send you an order to Mr. Ripshaw to admit you to
visit Margaret Catchpole during her confinement in
the Ipswich gaol. What an extraordinary being she
is! a clever, shrewd, and well-behaved person, yet
strangely perverted in her judgement! She actually
cannot be persuaded that she has offended against the
laws of her country. You will, I trust, my dear
madam, by the exercise of your influence and judgement, convince her of her folly. I am truly glad that
you intend going to see her; for next to the pleasure
derived from granting your request is the comfort I
derive from the prospect of great benefit therein to the
prisoner.

"Believe me, my dear madam,
"Ever yours sincerely,
"MILESON EDGAR.

"To MRS. COBBOLD, St. Margaret's Green, Ipswich."

The visit was soon paid to poor Margaret in her cell,
and it was one of deep interest and importance, inas-
much as it paved the way for a better frame of mind,
and deeper humility, than this wretched young woman
ever before felt. On this account we shall record the
particulars of the interview in detail, as related by
the lady herself.

When Mrs. Cobbold entered the cell, Margaret rose
and curtsied respectfully, and the next moment the
big tears rolled down her cheeks, and her chest heaved
with convulsive emotion, as if her heart would break.
The gaoler placed a chair for the lady, and retired to
the end of the passage. For a long time nothing
could be heard but the occasional sobs of the prisoner.
At length she spoke:—

"Oh! my dear lady, how can you look upon me?
You are good to come and see me; but indeed I feel
as if I was not worthy you should come. I never
dared to ask it of you. I had scarcely any hope of it.
It is only your goodness. I am a poor, ill-fated being,
doomed to sorrow and despair!"

"Margaret, I came to see you from a sense of duty to God, and to you too: I came to try and comfort you; but how can I give consolation to you if you talk of your being ill-fated and *doomed* to despair? Do not say that the doom of fate has anything to do with your present situation. You know as well as I do, that unless you had misconducted yourself, you might have been as happy now as you were when I saw you after your return from Bury. Put your sin upon yourself, and not upon your fate. You know the real cause of this unhappiness."

"Ah! dear lady, what would you have done if you had been me and in my place?"

"I might have done as you did; but I do think, Margaret, knowing what a friend I had always been to you, that you might have placed confidence in me, and have told me Laud was in prison. I observed that you were much disturbed, and not yourself, when I last came to see you, but I could not divine the cause."

"I was afraid to tell you, madam, lest you should persuade me to give up my acquaintance with him, and I had learned much more to his credit than I knew before."

"And so, by following your own inclination, you have brought your lover and yourself to an untimely death. Oh, Margaret! had you confided in me, I should have persuaded you to have tried him until you had obtained your discharge from prison; then, had he been a respectable and altered man, I should have approved of your marriage."

"But think, dear lady, how constant he had been to me for so many years! Surely his patience deserved my confidence."

"And what good did you ever find it do you, Margaret? Look at the consequences."

"I could not foresee them. How could I then look at them?"

"Though you were so blind as not to foresee the consequences, others, with more reflection and forethought, might have done so for you; and, assuredly, had you hinted the matter to me, I should have prevented what has happened."

"I wish indeed, now, that I had done so. I suffer most severely in my mind, not from the fear of punishment, but because I have been the cause of William Laud's death."

"And he will have been the cause of your own, Margaret. Had he not persuaded you to break out of prison, he would not have been killed. He knew the penalty was death to you if you were caught, and he has met that very end to which he has now made you liable. Had he loved you lawfully and honourably, as he ought to have done, he would have waited for your free and happy discharge."

"But it seems to me," said Margaret, "so very strange, something so out of justice, to condemn a person to die for that which does not appear to her to be a crime. I cannot see the blood-guiltiness that I have thus brought upon myself. In God's commandments I find it written, 'Thou shalt not steal.' I stole the horse, and I could see that I deserved to die, because I transgressed that commandment; but I do not find it said, 'Thou shalt not escape from prison.'"

"Now Margaret, your own reasoning will condemn you. You acknowledged that you deserved to die for stealing the horse. Now consider the difference between the sentence you were actually prepared to submit to and the one for which it was in mercy changed. Though justly condemned to death, you are permitted to live and undergo a comparatively mild punishment, yet you cannot see the duty of submitting to it. You should have endured the lesser punishment without a murmur. You appeared to receive the award of it with such thankfulness that it made all your friends rejoice for you. But how deep is their present sorrow! What will the judge say to you now when you are placed before him? Religion teaches you submission to the constituted authorities of your country; and you ought to think with humility, as you once did, that, like the thief on the cross, you suffer justly for your crimes. To my mind, Margaret, you have no excuse whatever. It may be all very well for romantic ideas of fancy to make your lover the excuse; but you were not at liberty to choose to roam over the sea with him until you could do so with a free conscience."

"It is not for me, dear lady, to say a word against your reasoning. I did not look upon my crime in this light."

"You must learn to look upon your crime as one which has done injury to society. Which of your friends, who interceded for you with the judge, and gave you so good a character, can now intercede for you again? I am persuaded, Margaret, that the judge himself will think his former mercy much displaced, and that you will meet with severity and reproach at his hands."

"Dear lady! who can give me comfort? Laud is dead, my father is dead, my brother is at a distance and will probably be so ashamed of me that he will never come to see me again. To whom, then, can I look for help? You, my dear mistress, must be hurt at my conduct, and all my friends likewise. I do not deserve their compassion, and yet I never wanted help so much. Oh! who shall comfort me now?"

"You shall have all the consolation I can give you; I will pray for you continually; I will lend you such books to read as I think may assist you; and were we not now about to remove from St. Margaret's Green to the Cliff again, and in the midst of much bustle, I would come to see you much oftener than I can now do. My family is increasing, and your master says he must return again to the brewery and to business. But I will come and see you many times, and when I cannot come I will write such instructions as, if you pursue them diligently, may, with God's blessing, promote your everlasting benefit. I am glad that you are sensible of your sins. This will go some way towards your deriving consolation from the Word of God. Attend to the precepts of the chaplain, who is a good man, and understands your disposition as well as I do. I shall often communicate with the Rev. Mr. Sharp concerning you. You must indeed be very, very humble, before you can obtain that sweet peace of mind which you once possessed. It will come to you again, if you are sincerely penitent and resigned, but not without."

"You are a dear friend, madam, to the poor destitute, and the only one now left me upon the earth. Oh! how, dear lady, can I be worthy of such kind consideration? Forgive me! oh, pray forgive me!"

"Margaret, I wish the law could as freely forgive you as I do, but you must not expect it. You must fortify your soul with religious consolation alone. Everything else will fail. You must think of far greater love than I can show to you, Margaret; love that has endured inexpressible anguish for you; love that has laid down life for you; and that will teach you how to die. You must think of your Saviour's love—free, unsought, undeserved love. Oh, the depth of His riches! Who can estimate them as he ought? You must look up to Him during every moment of your short existence, and be never weary of praying to Him for forgiveness. But I must now leave you, Margaret. It shall not be long before I see you again. God bless you! Good-bye!"

Margaret could not speak, but she knelt down and prayed inwardly.

For the next three months Mrs. Cobbold became a frequent visitor at the gaol, and found that Margaret made the best use of her time between the period of her committal and her trial. How instructive are the minutes of her progress, which that lady made, during that most engaging period! and how blessedly employed was the enlightened mistress in communicating light to her poor benighted servant! It was now that she made amends, in her own heart, for that too common error among all who exercise power and authority: the neglect of the spiritual welfare of their dependants. She applied her powerful faculties to the strengthening and refreshing of her servant's mind, by humbling herself with her before God. And well was she repaid for this exertion. Abundant was the reward to herself in obtaining that experience in the ways of godliness which strengthened her own faith and increased her charity.

Margaret's mind underwent a complete change. She might be truly said to be a resigned and patient Christian; one who, from that day to her latest moments, never lost the influence of those purest principles and most blessed hopes which were then instilled and rooted in her soul.

On the 1st of August, the day previously to her departure for Bury, Margaret received the following letter from her excellent mistress:—

"CLIFF, IPSWICH, August 1st, 1800

"MARGARET,

"I cannot come and see you, as I had intended this day to have done, having been so unfortunate as to sprain my ankle in getting out of my carriage on to the stone step at the Cliff. But I am so full of thought about you, that my painful foot shall not prevent my willing hand writing to you a few words before you depart. It may be good for you and me that this accident has occurred, however much it may seem our present privation. It may teach us that we never can command events, or tell what a day may bring forth. It may so happen that this letter may do you more good than my visit; if so, I shall not regret the pain I suffer, since I shall have the consolation of its seeming evil being productive of some good. Oh, how I wish that we could look upon all events in the same manner, and be persuaded that all things 'work together for good to them that love God!' Let us (i. e. you and I) be thus persuaded. It will prevent us experiencing any present mortification in the impossibility of our seeing each other at this time.

"I would first speak to you about your conduct at the trial, and my pen does that which my tongue would do. Do not attempt in any way to defend your conduct. Being fully convinced, by God's grace, of the criminality of your act and deed, let no legal sophistry whatever induce you to plead *not guilty*. In a court of justice, you should stand before man in the same way as you would before your Maker, without any covert deceit, any desire to make a bad cause appear a good one.

"Satan is sometimes transformed into an angel of light. He is so eloquent, so engaging, so bold, so devoted, so earnest, so intelligent, so interesting, so persuasive, that a lie comes from him with such apparent grace, that the sons of God are almost deceived by his transformations. But let not any one persuade you to take advantage of his services. Truth, Margaret, needs no fiction to defend it ; for ' whatsoever loveth and maketh a lie shall never enter into the city of truth.' So do not suffer any one who calls himself your friend to persuade you to trust to fallacies. You know yourself guilty. Conduct yourself as a person conscious of your guilt before God and man. I shall not deceive you. The penalty of your crime is death ; and you do not forget the argument that I used upon a former occasion, ' that if a man owns himself justly condemned to suffer death, and has mercy shown to him by giving him a lesser punishment, his duty is to suffer that lesser punishment with the same resignation as he would death. And if he fail in this duty, he justly deserves the former punishment.' So do you justly deserve sentence of death for your present or late sin. And you will be condemned to die !

"Be prepared for much severity at the hands of your offended judge. I say, be prepared ; for unless he should know as much of you as I do, he will think you one of the worst persons alive, and therefore only fit to be made a public example of by a violent death. I know you, however, Margaret ; and though I believe that if you were now restored to liberty you would be a Christian servant, and never more be a guilty slave of sin, yet your judge cannot know this. Indeed, scarcely any of the magistrates know this. It is, therefore, best to be prepared for a severe trial. Do not attempt to call any one to speak to your character. It will be of no use. The representations made by the magistrates at the last assizes will be sufficient testimony up to that time ; and since then, you cannot say that you deserve any defence. You must not expect any mercy, but prepare yourself not only to receive sentence of death, but *prepare yourself to die.*

" If a prisoner who knows himself to be guilty does not prepare himself to die before the sentence of death is passed upon him, his is a very dangerous state, since the period is so short between condemnation and execution that he must be very much distracted.

" You have read through ' The Christian's Consolations against the Fears of Death,' and you tell me that your mind has been greatly strengthened by the piety expressed in this good old book. I agree with you that it touches upon every source of consolation which a Christian man can contemplate. It meets almost every case. But it does not exactly contemplate a female convict, like yourself ; and on this account I would add a very few words of advice to you upon this subject.

" To die a Christian, and as a Christian ought to die, is to have no desire whatever but for the kingdom of God. You suffer justly for your crimes ; and you must not let any one deceive you into any false idea of your own worthiness to live. The penitent malefactor on the tree rebuked the boldness of his brother, who railed upon the Saviour of the world, and used these words of reproof, ' Dost not thou fear God, seeing thou art in the same condemnation ? And we indeed suffer justly ; but this man hath done nothing amiss.' Then he prefers that humble prayer, which should ever be yours, Margaret, up to your latest moment, ' Lord, remember me when thou comest into Thy kingdom !' How infinite in mercy is the

Lord! How loving! How pitiful! How generous to the poor wretch at the moment of his late repentance! We cannot tell, Margaret, how late that repentance was. He might have been convinced of his guilt long before he was lifted up to die. In prison he might have heard, as you have done, of the great, the good, the only Christ. So that men do wrong to take even this example for the success of a death-bed repentance at the last hour. We cannot tell when our last hour may be. Our first should be one of repentance as well as our last. And the whole desire of our lives should be, to be remembered in the kingdom of Christ. The blessed words of our Saviour must have taken away the sting of death from the faithful heart of the penitent: 'This day shalt thou be with Me in Paradise.'

"I conceive that we are justified in taking these words to our own selves in our own contemplation of death, and in considering them as the most blessed words that can be used to destroy the power which the King of Terrors often raises in the minds of weak and sinful mortals. If you are truly penitent, justly sensible of all your sins, and are fully convinced of the meritorious sacrifice which God has once made for your sins and those of the whole world, I see no reason why your faith should not be so fully fixed on these blessed words as to let them be the hope of your heart. It is almost impossible for the true penitent to beg to be remembered in the kingdom of Christ without experiencing comfort from the Saviour's words, 'This day shalt thou be with Me in Paradise.'

"Death frees us from the dominion of sin; that is, if we die in Christ. We are then with Him in Paradise, in that state of innocency in which Adam was before he was driven out of the Garden of Eden. Our spirits know no fear, since we are in love; and 'perfect love casts out fear, because fear hath torment.'

"Your judge, Margaret, will probably tell you to

make good use of the short time you have to live. I
not only tell you this, that you may be fortified against
your sentence of death, but that you may prepare
yourself for entering upon another and a better life.
I am glad to find, by my friend the chaplain, that you
have diligently applied your whole strength to the
Word of God, and have found how weak, how wicked,
how lost you have been all the days of your life. I
hope to be able to come and see you, with him, after
your return from Bury, and to partake with you of
spiritual refreshment. Till then, my poor servant,
I can only pray that you may be rich in grace,
strong in faith, humble in heart, devout in prayer,
lowly and contrite in spirit, watchful against all
temptation, in love, in peace, in charity with all,
praying for all : for your judge, jury, and fellow-
prisoners.

" Oh that your end may be as you wish it, a warning to all your sex, and especially to those in your
situation of life, never to let passion get the upper
hand of virtuous principle ! That God may fortify
you with His spirit, cheer you with His Word, and
comfort you in death, is the earnest prayer of your
former mistress

" And present friend,

" ELIZABETH COBBOLD.

" To Margaret Catchpole."

Margaret fed upon the contents of this letter, and
followed the advice given her ; and with what effect
will be best seen by the account preserved of her
second trial. She went to Bury on the 2nd of August,
and on the 3rd was conducted to the same court, and
appeared before the same judge, as she had done
upon her first trial three years before.

The Lord Chief Baron Sir Archibald Macdonald
was this time accompanied by Sir Beaumont Hotham.
The juries for the county and liberty were the following honourable gentlemen :—

FOR THE COUNTY

Lord Viscount Broome.
Charles Berners, jun., Esq.
B. G. Dillingham, Esq.
P. J. Thelluson, Esq.
George Wilson, Esq.
Matthias Kerrison, Esq.
Wolfran Lewis, Esq.
Mileson Edgar, Esq.
John Cobbold, Esq.

Edward Studd, Esq.
Anthony Collet, Esq.
Joseph Burch Smith, Esq.
John Farr, Esq.
John Dresser, Esq.
William Philpot, Esq.
James Reeve, Esq.
Edmund Barber, Esq.
James Stuttur, Esq.

FOR THE LIBERTY

Sir T. C. Bunbury, Bart.
Sir T. C. Cullum, Bart.
Sir Harry Parker, Bart.
Barnard E. Howard, Esq.
N. Barnadiston, Esq.
Nathaniel Lee Acton, Esq.
Capel Lofft, Esq.
John Mosley, Esq.
Joshua Grigby, Esq.
William Mannock, Esq.

John Wastell, Esq.
Robert Walpole, Esq.
Richard Cartwright, Esq.
Thomas Cocksedge, Esq.
Thomas Mills, Esq.
James Oakes, Esq.
Thomas Gery Cullum, Esq.
Abraham Reeve, Esq.
George Archer, Esq.

William B. Rush, Esq., Sheriff.

The usual forms of the court having been gone through, Margaret Catchpole was again placed at the bar. Margaret was dressed, as formerly, in a plain blue calico dress. She appeared pale and thin, but perfectly free from any of that emotion which she formerly exhibited. There was a calmness of deportment without the least obduracy, and no obtrusive boldness nor recklessness. She did not look round the court with any of that anxiety she formerly exhibited, as if she wished to see any one there who knew her. She knew that Will Laud was gone, and that neither her father nor her brother was there. She was quite indifferent to the public gaze, and with her eyes cast down upon the bar, she saw not that piercing glance which the judge gave her as she took her station before him, though every person in court noticed it, and looked at the prisoner to see if she did not quail before it.

The indictment having been read aloud, once more the clerk of the court addressed her in these terms:

"How say you, prisoner at the bar, are you guilty or not guilty?"

Margaret lifted up her dark eyes once more, and looking her judge calmly in the face, said—

"Guilty, my lord."

There was a perfect stillness in that crowded court, while the judge now addressed her in the following terms:—

"I cannot address you, prisoner at the bar, in the same strain I formerly did, since I am persuaded that you are hardened in your iniquity. I pitied you at that time for your youth; but though young in years, you are old in crime. I considered you then a person who, if you had the chance, would form, for the remainder of your days, an estimable character. In this, however, I have been greatly deceived, and I now look upon you as a person whom I believe to be dangerous to the morals of others, and therefore unfit to live. You have shown your sense of the past mercy extended to you by your bold and daring conduct in breaking out of prison. I had fully intended to have obtained your discharge from the Ipswich gaol at these very assizes, had I heard the good report I received last year confirmed. You may judge, then, of my surprise and indignation when I heard of your escape from the gaol.

"So bold a woman would make a very bad companion for any man. She who, after receiving pardon for her past crimes, in the merciful permission to live when condemned to death, will again be guilty of setting a bad example to all, instead of a good and reformed one: she who will set at defiance the laws of her country, and be so bold as to break out of prison before the period of her confinement had expired, shows such a disregard to all past and present mercies that she is not worthy to live.

"You have, I understand, been the occasion of sudden death to one man, and might have involved others in your guilt. The turnkey of the gaol might have been severely punished for your delinquency. Your gaoler, whose duty it is to attend the prisoners to Bury, and of whose absence you took such a shameful advantage, might have suffered a heavy fine. You had very nearly eluded his activity, and I consider that great credit is due to him for the manner in which he recovered you and has brought you to justice. The magistrates of this county have very properly applauded his zeal; and I consider it a fortunate thing for society, that you are not this moment at large in any part of his Majesty's dominions.

"I will not waste words upon a person so ungrateful as you are. What can you possibly have to say why sentence should not be passed upon you? You may say anything you have to say. It cannot be anything good, or in the least mitigate the severest penalty of the law. Have you anything to say, prisoner at the bar?"

There was such a still silence in the court at this moment that the scratch of a pen might have been heard. The barristers all looked up at the prisoner. Every eye was fixed intently upon her pale face, as she looked up and made such a composed reply to the Lord Chief Baron's speech, that one of the most eminent barristers of that day, afterwards as eminent as a judge, declared it to be the most able and impressive he had ever, under such circumstances, heard. She spoke with perfect ease, and apparently without the slightest tremor, and was heard all over the court.

"My lord, I fully expected that your lordship would condemn me severely for my present offence. I expected severity; but I did not think that I should receive the language of judgement without mercy from one whose former kindness touched my heart. As to my being a hardened offender, I humbly hope that in this respect your lordship is mistaken. I have committed two offences against the laws of my country.

The first I acknowledged, not without a sense of its guilt; the second, when I committed it, I was quite unconscious of the light in which the law viewed it, and I thought it no crime at all. Had not the arguments of one wise as your lordship, and a far dearer friend to the prisoner, convinced me of its enormity, I had this day stood before the court and felt myself condemned as an innocent person. Thank God, such is not the case! and your lordship's accusation of my being a hardened offender is without foundation.

"At this moment of condemnation you refer to your intention of obtaining my discharge at these assizes. At such a time as this, the expression of such an intention might have produced extreme bitterness in my heart, did I not know, that before the last assizes, your lordship received a memorial, signed by all the magistrates who visited the Ipswich gaol, praying for my discharge on account of exemplary conduct up to that time. Had you, then, my lord, attended to that prayer, the offence for which I am now to suffer the severity of the law would never have been committed, the life of the man whom it was my fault to love would have been spared, and I should not have had the anguish of being compelled to speak as I now do, nor this court the pain of hearing me. The bitterness then which your reference to my intended discharge would have given me must remain with your lordship, not with me. You may be well assured, my lord, that I am not hardened, but penitent. In the twinkling of an eye I shall meet your lordship at the tribunal of perfect justice, where we shall both be prisoners at that bar where we shall require, and, I hope, shall find mercy.

"You could not imagine what I should say, and what I do say is not meant as a defence of my improper act, but only in justice to those who may wish me 'God speed' in this court, and who might think from your lordship's language that I was insensible to their or your lordship's past kindness. The day will come, and not long after my departure hence, when your lordship will be convinced that your opinion, now expressed, was not such as the circumstances of my case warranted or called for. Your lordship will then clearly see, that through ignorance, and prompted somewhat beyond the bounds of reason by the force of gratitude to one whom I too dearly loved, I was induced to attempt to gain that liberty which I then felt could only be pleasant in his company.

"Your lordship will, I hope, send me soon to the enjoyment of a liberty with which no laws of man can interfere. I call no persons to speak to my character since the period when your lordship received the testimony of the gaoler, chaplain, and magistrates of the Ipswich division. I humbly beg pardon of you, my lord, and of all this court, if I have said anything which may seem disrespectful to you or any persons present; and I now await your lordship's sentence."

After Margaret had finished speaking, all eyes were turned towards the judge. The barristers who were present whispered together, and his lordship caught the sounds of words like these: "Admirable answer!" "Sensible speech!" "Able reply!" which made the colour come into his face, and it required some degree of judicial self-possession to disperse it. He soon resumed, however, his wonted dignity and calmness, and proceeded to pass sentence upon the prisoner, prefacing the awful terms with these words:—

"Prisoner at the bar, I am glad to say that my opinion may be altered with regard to your hardened state; I may lament, also, that the prayer of that petition made in your behalf was not sooner complied with, as you expected it would have been. This will not, however, excuse your crime. It might be sufficient to establish the propriety of your conduct up to that time, but your subsequent act completely cancelled that character. You have artfully attempted to throw the blame, which rests entirely with yourself, upon me as your judge." Here Margaret looked at him with piercing scrutiny, but uttered not a word. "He will not blame himself again under similar circumstances, having had such occasion to blame himself for too great leniency upon your former trial. You are sufficiently sensible to be aware of the short time you have to live, and of the necessity of making good use of it. I shall add no more than the judgement of this court, which is —— "

Here the judge passed the sentence in the same awful words as he had formerly done.

There were many in that court who felt for the prisoner more than the finest eloquence could express. She received the sentence without any of those deep feelings which she had formerly exhibited ; she looked as mildly and quietly at the judge as if she had only been receiving his advice ; she curtsied respectfully to him and the court ; and then she firmly receded from the dock, and returned to the care of the gaoler.

It was observed by several persons of the court, that the Lord Chief Baron did not rally his wonted cheerfulness during the succeeding business of the day. Whatever may be said of the habit of sternness and indifference to the real promptings of nature, which men who administer the laws of their country usually entertain (and a judge is seldom guilty of any exhibition of human weakness in the act of condemning a fellow-creature to death), yet Chief Baron Macdonald most certainly did feel a strange sensation of nervous sensibility with regard to the unfortunate woman he had that day condemned. He was more abstracted and thoughtful upon her case than upon any other which came before him. He could not dismiss it from his mind with his wonted consciousness of composure. He continually reverted to her extraordinary character whenever a pause in the business of the court afforded him an opportunity to speak to the high sheriff, and he was heard to say—

" I should like to examine the spot whence this wonderful woman effected her escape. The more I think of what I have been told of her, and of what I have heard from her own lips, the more curious I am to inspect the gaol. If I have an opportunity before I return to town, I most assuredly will do so. I wish I could see that woman, and be myself incog. I could then judge of some things which appear to me inexplicable in such a person. Whence does she gain such powers of speech, such simplicity of manners, and yet so truly applicable to her situation? There must be mind and instruction too!"

The high sheriff, who was a man of the most humane disposition, here ventured to tell the judge that many of the magistrates thought that her life would have been spared on account of their former recommendation. This was quite in private conversation, and only came to light after the business of the assizes was over. Let whatever influence may have been exercised with his lordship in behalf of the prisoner, or let it have been simply his own conviction that mercy would not again be unworthily extended, before he left Bury her sentence was once more changed from death to transportation. But this time it was for life, instead of for seven years or for any fixed period.

Margaret received the announcement of this change without any expression of joy for herself or thankfulness to her judge. She regretted that she should have to linger out so many years of her existence in a foreign land, and when told of it as an act of mercy, she replied "that it was no mercy to her."

CHAPTER XXVIII

TRANSPORTATION

MARGARET returned to Ipswich in a very despondent state of mind ; more so, to all appearance, than if her sentence had not been changed from death to transportation. Her feelings on this point are strikingly evinced in the following letter, which she wrote to her mistress soon after her return to gaol :—

"IPSWICH GAOL, August 9th, 1800.

"HONOURED MADAM,

"I am returned from Bury, and I regret to say that I am not to die yet. That day is put off—perhaps that I may be swallowed up by the sea, or be eaten by the savages of Botany Bay. I am to look forward to years of degraded slavery, and to be sent away from my country and my friends. I am so sorrowful, my dear lady, that I require more of your good advice to learn to live than to learn to die. I feel, indeed, as if my judge did it to torment me, and if I had the opportunity, I should certainly tell him so. You told me he would be severe ; he was bitterly so, but it made me feel much less grateful to him than I did the first time. Then I thought him like you, dear lady, but I see no traces of that resemblance now. His words were tormenting, his manners towards me tormenting, and his change of sentence is tormenting. I would really have rather been left to die, though by the hand of the public executioner, than be as I am, soon to be sent out of the country to meet a more miserable death. If I never see you more, I shall never forget you. I told the judge that but for your friendship I should not have been sensible of my sin. He called me a hardened sinner, and said I was not fit to live. I wonder, then, that he did not suffer me to die. Dear lady, I feel so very low, that if you do not come and see me I shall be miserable indeed. Do—oh! pray do, if you can! I hope you are suffering less from the effects of your sprain, and that I shall see you. Forgive your poor servant's boldness and seeming selfishness. I pray earnestly for you and your dear family. Oh that I could see the dear Cliff again! So happy was I when I first lived there, and so should I be now, could I ever hope to see you there again. To be your servant would be something worth living for; but to be a slave in a foreign land! Oh! my dear lady! death would be preferable to

> " Your poor servant,
> " MARGARET CATCHPOLE.

" To MRS. COBBOLD, Cliff, Ipswich."

Her letter was dated on Saturday, the 9th August. It may be seen in the *Ipswich Journal* of the 16th of August, A. D. 1800, that the Lord Chief Baron paid a visit to the Ipswich gaol on Tuesday, 12th of August.

He arrived on the morning of that day in his carriage, and was not personally known to the turnkey. He told the man that he came purposely to inspect the gaol, and wished particularly to see the spot where Margaret Catchpole effected her escape.

" Did you fill the office of turnkey at the time?" inquired the visitor.

" I did, sir," replied the man.

" Then you had a very narrow escape; for, had I been the judge to have tried you, I should have been much inclined to have thought you guilty of connivance in this matter."

" Then I am very glad, sir, that you are not a judge."

The Lord Chief Baron did not tell him at the moment who he was.

The turnkey was quite ready to show him the way in which the escape had been made. He set up the frame exactly as he found it on the day of Margaret's adventure, and showed him the very crotch with which she had fixed the line on the *chevaux de frise.* The broken spike on the roller was pointed out, and he informed the judge of the trousers and smock-frock which the prisoner had manufactured out of the sheets of her bed. After having examined minutely the place and the frame, and having heard the full report of the turnkey, he again said—

" What an artful woman she must be to do this, and to be able to deceive you in the sound of her voice from the adjoining cell ! "

" Aye, sir ; and had she not confessed this, I should have been puzzled, up to this hour, to account for her getting out of her cell, as I swore that I heard her answer from within, before I locked the door."

" She must be a clever person."

" Yes, sir, I believe she is. She owes a very great deal to a lady in this town, who has taken great pains with her."

" So I have heard," said the stranger. " I would give something to see that lady. I understand she is the wife of the gentleman from whom she stole the horse."

" I wish the lady might call while you are here, sir. It is not unlikely that she may. Pray, sir, were you in court at the time of her trial ? "

" Yes, I was."

" Then, perhaps, sir, you could tell us if it be true that she answered the judge who addressed her in such a manner as to confuse him. Our folks say that he was completely set, and felt so much surprised as to be put out by her speech. I do not, of course, know if it be so, but I heard two of our visiting magistrates talking about it the other day, and they seemed to say as much as if it was so."

" It did not strike me to be exactly so. The judge was certainly surprised at what she said, but I do not think he was angry with the prisoner. Is the woman in her cell at this time ? "

" Yes, she is, sir."

" Will you tell Mr. Ripshaw that I should like to examine all the cells of the prison ? "

" Mr. Ripshaw is gone with two prisoners to Portsmouth, sir ; but Mrs. Ripshaw is within, and I can show you the cells."

The Lord Chief Baron followed the turnkey to the door of the governor's house, which was in the centre of the gaol. At this moment the chaplain, the Rev. Mr. Sharp, came to pay his visit to the prisoners. The gentlemen were shown into the parlour, where Mrs. Ripshaw sat, busily engaged at some of the gaol accounts.

The Lord Chief Baron presented his card to the chaplain, who immediately explained to Mrs. Ripshaw who it was.

" I am come purposely to inspect the gaol, Mrs. Ripshaw, and I wish to be quite incog. at present. I have already examined the spot where that extraordinary woman, Margaret Catchpole, effected her escape ; and if you, sir," addressing himself to the chaplain, " are going to visit her, and have no objection to my accompanying you, I should like to be brought in as your friend. You need not address me, but I will join you in your duties. I wish to see this singular woman, if possible, without her recognizing me."

" She is, indeed, my lord," replied the chaplain, " a most extraordinary person. I have found her, up to this second trial, not only tractable, but intelligent and attentive in the highest degree ; but since her return from Bury, she is disappointed and dissatisfied."

" With what ? "

" With her reprieve for transportation."

" With her reprieve ! Does the woman really prefer death to life ? "

" Your lordship will be the best judge of that by the tenor of our conversation, if she should not recognize your lordship. And should she do so, she would not scruple to tell you plainly her opinion."

" I do not think that she can possibly recognize me, if I do not speak to her, and I shall keep strict silence, if I can."

What a strange alteration do robes and wigs make

in the appearance of men of the law! Who could
recognize the Lord Chief Baron of our courts of law
without the robes of his office? Counsel are not
recognized even by their clients when they first see
them in their rooms without their wigs and gowns.
No wonder, then, that Margaret Catchpole should take
her judge for some brother clergyman or friend of the
chaplain's, when he entered the cell, and seated himself upon a chair, which the turnkey placed there for
him.

"Well, Margaret," said the chaplain, "I hope you
are a little more reconciled to your prospects than you
were when I saw you last."

"I wish I could say I am, sir; but my prospects
look very gloomy, and I feel a great deal more anguish
than if I were going to be executed."

"You ought not to do so, Margaret; I consider it
a great mercy that your life is spared."

"Spared! For what, sir? To drag on a wretched
life as a felon, and to live and die, no one knows how
or cares, and then to lie in a felon's grave in a distant
land! Here my body would at least have soon rested
beside my friends and relatives. My sufferings would
have been short, and I think I should have been happy.
Oh, sir! pray forgive my poor broken heart; it will
give utterance to the language of lamentation. Oh!
that cruel judge! He might have let me die, especially
as the bitterness of death had already passed over me.
But he was angry and displeased at me for speaking,
though he asked me if I had anything to say! So he
resolved that I should suffer the most excruciating
torture by killing me by inches in a foreign land! Is
this mercy, Mr. Sharp?"

"You look upon this in an unchristian and too
gloomy a light. You here attribute motives to your
judge of a very improper kind; such as I am fully
persuaded never entered his mind, and never were
inmates of his breast. I am persuaded his thoughts
toward you were those of pity as well as mercy, and
that your change of sentence was meant for your good

and that of others. You have no right to judge of his motives in so unchristian a light."

"My dear sir, again I say, pardon my speech. I speak as I feel. Perhaps, with your help, I may feel differently, but I should then speak differently. Could you, or this gentleman, feel as I do, and were either of you placed in my situation, you would think and argue very differently to what you now do. You sit there, both of you, at liberty to move from this place to the happy associations of kindred, friends, and home. I grant you, a return to their society sweetens life, and teaches you to bear your earthly visitations, whatever they may be, patiently. But let me ask you how you would, either of you, like now to be afflicted with a long, lingering, painful, bodily disease, which permitted you only a few moments' rest, and those troubled and broken, and disturbed by horrid dreams; that, when you awoke each day, it was only to a sense of increased pain? How would you like years of such increased agony? Tell me, would you not prefer a happier, shorter, and speedier termination of your sufferings than that long distant one which must come at last after years of weariness and pain? Yet you find fault with me because I would rather die now than live many years in all the horrors of slavery, and then die without a friend near me!"

"Still I think you wrong, Margaret. You seem to argue as if we had a choice of our own in these matters, and forget that it must be God's will, and not our own, to which we must submit."

"Is it God's will, or is it man's will, that I should lead a life of misery?"

"This question almost makes me think you impious, Margaret. It is God's will that you should live, and I hope for some good: at all events, it is for some wise purpose of His own, either that you may become an instrument of His righteousness or mercy in His hands, or that you may be an example to others. As to the misery you talk of, that will depend much upon your own future individual conduct and character. I have heard that some receive pardon in that country for their good conduct, and they settle in the land ; and instead of being slaves, they become useful members of society."

" That may perhaps be the case with some, sir ; but I am looking at my own present state, and I cannot believe that my judge had any such mercy in his view when he changed my sentence from present momentary suffering to such future wretchedness."

" Of that you can know nothing, neither ought you to take your present state as any other than that of God's decree by His agent, the judge. How can you ascertain the motives of any man's heart ? I do firmly believe that your judge decided most mercifully and righteously in your case. He might really think that if you were removed from this country, you might be instrumental in doing much good. He might hope that, under different circumstances of life, from the very natural force of your character taking another bias, you might become a blessing to yourself and others."

" And so, because I yielded to temptation when I had so many good friends around me, he would throw me into the very midst of temptation, where I have not one friend to help me. Oh ! Mr. Sharp, would it not be far better to choose present release, when such kind friends are near me, than future death, when no comforter or friend can be near ? "

" And is not your God near you, Margaret, in every place, unless you drive Him away by your wickedness ? But how can you tell that He may not raise up some benevolent friend to help you in that country to which you are going ? I hope for the best. At all events, you must cherish better feelings towards your judge than those you now possess, or your state will be dreadful indeed wherever you may be. You seem to have forgotten all the Christian lessons which your dear mistress and I have taken such pains to teach you."

" I would not be ungrateful, sir, though I may now

appear, as I am, so unhappy. I will try by prayer to conquer the prejudice you speak of. I do suffer such extreme horror in my mind from my view of the future, that there is no rest for me by night or day. I see nothing but chains and darkness. I think sometimes of the long, long journey from my native land, of the dangers of the sea, of the companions with whom I may be mixed. I start sometimes in my dreams, and fancy a great shark dashing at me in the waters. Another time I see the native cannibals ready to devour me. Then I think of home, of you, sir, of dear Dr. Stebbing, of my uncle and aunt, and of my dearest mistress, and I find my prison-pillow is wet with my nightly tears."

The tears started in more eyes than her own, as she spoke, in her touching simplicity, of these acute feelings. She suffered intensely; and it took many months of rational and devout conversation, on the part of both her mistress and this worthy man, to eradicate those bitter seeds of despair, and to sow those of cheerfulness and hope. After directing Margaret's mind to Christian duties, the chaplain and the judge left her cell. They conversed some time upon her state of mind and future prospects. The judge declared that he thought her one of the most sensitive persons he had ever seen, with a mind capable of the highest cultivation. He left five guineas with the chaplain to be laid out for her benefit. He stated that she would not, in all probability, leave England till the next summer, and hoped to hear a better account of her some future day. Margaret was not informed of the person who had visited her that day with the chaplain, until she had learned to look upon him and herself in a very different light.

The Lord Chief Baron visited all the cells of the prison, and expressed his approbation of the cleanliness and neatness of the whole place. As he was going away, he told the turnkey that he was the very judge who had tried the female prisoner for breaking out of gaol. The reader may imagine how frightened the poor fellow was at his late boldness of speech. The judge observed his embarrassment, and told him that he had spoken nothing improper; that he had done his duty, and deserved his thanks.

"You may tell your master," he added, "that I am so well satisfied with the appearance of all things under his care, that when I return to town I shall not fail to give a favourable report of the state of the gaol and of his discipline." He made the turnkey a present, and left the gaol.

It was not until May, 1801, that Margaret Catchpole was informed of the day of her departure for Botany Bay. She had been instructed in many things relating to the country to which she was going, and her kind mistress had purchased an assortment of useful articles for her future employment. Her mind had been gradually divested of its miserable horrors, and became fortified for the occasion. It will be seen, however, that as the near approach of the day came, she dreaded and lamented it bitterly. On the 25th of May, 1801, Mrs. Cobbold received the following note from her :—

"Ipswich Gaol, May 25th, 1801.

"Dear and Honoured Madam,

"I am sorry to have to inform you of the bad news. I am going away on Wednesday next, or Thursday at the latest, so I have taken the liberty of troubling you with these few lines. It will be the last time I shall ever trouble you from this place of sorrowful, yet, comparatively with the future, blessed captivity. My grief is very great, now that I am really on the eve of banishment from my own country and from all my dearest friends for ever. It was hard for me ever to think of it. Oh! what must it be to endure it! Honoured madam, it would give me some happiness to see you once more, on the Tuesday previous to my leaving England for ever, if you will not think this request of mine too troublesome. I know your kind heart. I would spare you any anxiety about so unworthy a person as myself, but I must entreat your goodness to consider me in this my severest misery. Have pity upon me! Oh! do come! Only let me see your dear face once more, and it will ever be a comfort and satisfaction to your poor unhappy servant,

"MARGARET CATCHPOLE.

"To MRS. COBBOLD, Cliff, Ipswich."

On Tuesday, the 26th of May, this benevolent lady paid poor Margaret her last visit. She felt that it would be the last time she should ever see her in this world. It was a painful interview, and one that she would have spared herself, had it not been for the hope of comforting the mind of her disconsolate servant. She found her seated upon the chest which she had sent her from the Cliff a few days before. Her eyes were swollen with weeping ; and, as she rose to meet her beloved mistress, she trembled and tottered from the weakness of agitation. Her mistress gently seated her again, and took her seat beside her.

"Oh! my dear lady!" she began, "my time is come, and I feel just as if my heart would burst. Surely this must be worse than death!"

"Do not say so, Margaret. Remember all the advice I have given you, and I have no doubt that you will find yourself rewarded with different treatment to that which you expect."

"But I shall never see you nor any of my dear friends again. This is my sorrow."

"But we shall hear from you often, Margaret."

"And shall I hear from you, dear lady ? Will you remember me ? Will you not forget your poor servant ? Oh! she will never forget you, never cease to bless you!"

"I will write to you, Margaret, as soon as I hear of your arrival."

"Bless you, dear lady! God bless you! But when I look at you, and think of your dear face, it is like the sun for ever hidden from my sight when you leave me."

"The same sun, Margaret, will shine upon us both. He will visit you while I am asleep, and me when you are at rest. The same God who causes him to shine upon us all will be, as he is, alike merciful to us both, though we live in different lands. Let me entreat you, as my last solemn injunction, never to forget your duty to Him. Read your Bible whenever you can. You will have much time and opportunity upon your voyage, and I hope you will employ them to the best purposes. You will find in your chest many good books. They will be a great source of comfort to you."

"Oh! that I will, dear lady! and when I think of you who gave them to me, and of the dear friends who have visited me, and of that good lady you introduced to my cell, Mrs. Sleorgin, who brought me yesterday this packet of books. Oh! how dearly shall I desire to see you and them!"

"Think, too, Margaret, what pleasure it will give us all to hear that you are doing well, that all the instructions of your kind friends have not failed. You will be able to add greatly to my comfort by this. You will also add to my knowledge many things of which I have at present very imperfect information. You will inform me of the state of that new country. Surely this will give you some pleasure, and profit me also."

"Dear lady! you are so good! You make me almost wish to live, if only for the pleasure of serving you. If it were but permitted me to come to England once more, I do think my journey would seem nothing to me. It looks such a dreary prospect to be deprived of all whom we love, that I feel faint at the idea of loneliness in a foreign land."

"Exercise your faith, Margaret, and you will never be alone. All lands will be pleasant to you."

"None so pleasant as my own: but I will try, I do try, I will hope. You are so kind to me, my dear mistress! Give my duty to my good master; my love to all the dear, dear children. Oh! forgive me, my dear lady! I cannot help crying ; tears do me good.''

Those friends (for so, in spite of the difference in their station and their character, we must venture to call them) parted from each other for the last time on earth ; but they lived to correspond, by letter, for many years after, and both felt an increased interest for each other's happiness.

The hour of Margaret's departure arrived. The worthy chaplain was the last person whom Margaret saw in the cell of her prison. Her uncle and aunt Leader saw her the day before. The worthy chaplain presented her with the remainder of the judge's present. She had long learned to look upon his sentence in a different light to that in which she had once viewed it ; and now, with feelings greatly subdued, she knelt with the good chaplain, and prayed earnestly that she might never forget the lessons he had given her. She prayed fervently for pardon for all her sins, and that she might for ever leave them behind her, and thenceforth lead a new and better life. Then, turning to Mr. Sharp, she said—

"One favour more, sir : your blessing."

"May God bless you, Margaret," said the good chaplain, "and make you, for the remainder of your days, an instrument of good, to His own glory and the benefit of your fellow-creatures ! Amen. Farewell.''

On Wednesday, May 27, Mr. Ripshaw left Ipswich with three female prisoners in his charge, Margaret Catchpole, Elizabeth Killet, and Elizabeth Barker. He took them to Portsmouth, and saw them safe on board the convict-ship, bound for Botany Bay.

Margaret had not left the New Gaol, two hours before the turnkey was summoned to the lodge, and opened the door to a tall, thin man, dressed in the poorest garb, who with a voice soft and gentle, meek and melancholy, requested to see Margaret Catchpole.

"She is just departed with the governor for Portsmouth. Who are you ? ''

"I am her brother. My misfortunes are indeed heavy: I am just returned from India. I find my father gone, my brothers gone, and this my only sister, worse than all! Oh, bitter cup! gone in disgrace from the country!"

"Pray walk this way. I will introduce you to our chaplain, and some consolation may be found for you."

The melancholy truth was soon explained. Charles Catchpole, alias Jacob Dedham, alias Collins Jaun, the spy, whom the reader may recognize as mentioned in a former part of this history, returned to his native country literally a beggar. He went out to India, and, upon his arrival in that country, his friend, Lord Cornwallis, had resigned his high office, and returned to England. The account he gave of himself was singularly eventful. He assumed the appearance of a native chief, joined some of the roving tribes of warlike adventurers, and became a conspicuous character. He fell in love with a nabob's daughter, and married her according to the national customs and ceremonies; but 'his ill-assorted match did not long prosper. His origin and connexion with the English were discovered, and the spy had to fly the country for his life. He escaped, gained his passage home, and had spent his last shilling in the very public-house at St. Mary Elms where he received his first as an enlisted recruit. His case was that day mentioned to several individuals, amongst others to Edward Bacon, Esq., who had spent many years in India, who pronounced him no impostor. He employed him many days in taking a view of Ipswich and its environs, which he did with extraordinary accuracy, from Savage's windmill on Stoke Hills. This view was presented by that gentleman to the author of these pages, and it presents all the striking accuracy and patient persevering characteristics of a self-taught artist.

By his own industry, and the generosity of others, he gained a few pounds, with which he determined to settle in one of the colonies. He obtained a passage to the Cape of Good Hope ; but the poor fellow met with a severe accident in falling down the hold of the vessel, broke his back, and died upon the passage.

Thus ended the career of Margaret Catchpole in England, where her virtues will long be remembered, together with her crimes. What remains of her history will serve to show what fruits may be gathered from a faithful spirit, a good heart, a high courage, and a strong understanding, when disciplined in the school of adversity, and under the guidance of good principles, seasonably instilled by kind and judicious monitors. It will be seen that her chief temptation having been mercifully removed, a true repentance, and an entire alteration of life and character, entitled her to the full forgiveness, and even approbation, of her fellow-creatures.

CHAPTER XXIX

BANISHMENT

THE first news which reached England concerning Margaret was contained in a letter written by herself, by which it appears she had obtained a situation at the Orphan Asylum ; and, as it will best explain her feelings and situation at that time, the reader shall be furnished with a copy of it. The sheet upon which it is written contains two letters ; one to her mistress, directed to her master ; the other to Dr. Stebbing.

"SYDNEY, Jan. 21st, 1802.

" HONOURED MADAM,
        "With pleasure I cannot describe, I am permitted to take up my pen and write to you, to acquaint you with my arrival in safety at Port Jackson, Sydney, New South Wales, on December 20, 1801. As I left

the ship, and was about to be landed, the shore, as I approached it, put me very much in mind of the Cliff on the banks of the river Orwell. The houses, backed by the hills, so much resembled that happy spot, that it put me in good spirits; and had I but seen your smile to welcome me, I should have been happy indeed. But I thought of you, of your prayers, your advice, your kindness and consolation; and when I saw land so much like my own dear native home, I really felt as if I was not entirely banished from old England.

"Your advice relative to my conduct on board the convict-ship was strictly followed; and every morning I prayed that I might keep it, and every evening I thanked God for his help. I had much influence with the female convicts who came out with me, and prevented many murmurs and one outbreak among them. So that, you see, dear lady, others reaped the benefit of your instructions as well as myself.

"Captain Sumpter gave me a good character to the governor; so that I was not two days upon the stores, but was taken off them by Mr. John Palmer, a gentleman of the highest respectability in the colony. He came out as purser in the *Sirius*, with Captain Arthur Phillip and Captain John Hunter, in January, 1787. Captain Phillip was the first governor of this place. Mrs. Palmer is very kind to me, and is as benevolent as yourself. She is a niece of a famous physician in London, Sir William Blizzard; and she says, dear lady, that she has heard her uncle speak of you. Only think that I should be so fortunate as to find a good mistress, who had some knowledge of you, even in this distant land! I feel this a great blessing.

"After the loss of the *Sirius*, on a reef off Norfolk Island, Mr. and Mrs. Palmer undertook the management of the Female Orphan Asylum. This institution was established by Governor King, who purchased, for the residence of my master and mistress, the elegant house in which they now live, of Lieutenant Kent, who returned to England two years since in the *Buffalo*.

He had built it entirely at his own expense, but he found that the country did not agree with him.

"You know, my dear lady, how fond I always was of children, and here I have many cheerful young faces around me. We have already sixty female children, who are taken as good care of as if they were all one family belonging to Mrs. Palmer. So you see how happily I am employed. Have I not reason to be thankful to God for His great mercies to so unworthy a creature as myself? I know you will rejoice to hear of my situation. You desired me to write anything I could for your instruction. I wish my opportunities were greater, that my letter might be more entertaining; but Mrs. Palmer has afforded me some facilities, and I hope, when I write again, to give you the benefit of them.

"This country is much more like England than I expected to find it. Garden-stuff of all kinds, except gooseberries, and currants, and apples, are abundant. The gardens, too, are remarkably beautiful; the geraniums run up seven or eight feet in height, and look more magnificent than those which I used to see in your own greenhouse. The country is very woody, so that I cannot go out any distance from Sydney without travelling through woods for miles. They are many of them very picturesque, and quite alive with birds, of such exquisite plumage that the eye is constantly dazzled by them.

"I assure you, my dear lady, that, in taking a ramble through them with my mistress and some of the elder orphans, I felt just as I imagine your own dear children used to feel when they walked with me to the Grove near Hog Island, I was so pleased with the birds, and trees, and flowers. I only wish I could send you one of the beautiful parrots of this country, but I have no means of so doing at present, as my money is all laid out for my future benefit. I have no money given to me for wages. I have board and lodging; and, if I conduct myself well, Mrs. Palmer says she will lay up a little store against the day of my emancipation or my marriage. With God's help, in whom I trust, I am determined to be independent of all men. I have no desire to be married and settled, as some people seem to say I shall be. I have no wish of the kind, neither do I now nor do I hope to desire any better situation than that I now enjoy, unless it were a return to England.

"I grieve to say, my dear lady, that this is one of the wickedest places in the world. I never heard of one, excepting those of Sodom and Gomorrah, which could come up to it in evil practices. People are so bold, so shameless, and so sinful, that even crime is as familiar as fashion in England. Religion is the last thing thought of, even by the government, which sends out criminals that most want it. The Rev. Mr. Johnson, who is almost the only clergyman in the whole country, comes frequently to the Foundling Asylum; but he tells my mistress that the town of Sydney is like a place of demons. Government is at great expense in the police establishment, to keep our poor bodies in subjection; but I am sure, if our souls were but a little more thought of, government would find us ten thousand times better subjects.

"Is it not dreadful, dear lady, that in such a country as this so many souls should utterly perish? Surely it will never be blessed with the blessing from Heaven, until God shall induce our government to send us out some able ministers of the Gospel. I will write more upon this subject at another time. I trust in God, who has brought me over the broad sea, that He will keep me from all evil upon this wide land.

"The wheat harvest was almost over when I landed. Wheat is here eight shillings per bushel at this time. There are two crops, I understand, each summer, one of wheat and another of Indian corn. I am told that the winter is very short; I cannot give you any certain information yet, as I have been only one month in the country. This letter, for the same reason, will be but a poor one; my next will, I hope, be more worthy your perusal. I will make minutes, according to your wishes, of all things which come under my observation. Never, never, my dearest lady, shall I forget your goodness to me, and especially on the last day before I left Ipswich.

"All the things you gave me arrived in safety with me, and are of great service to me. Oh! how I wish that many poor creatures, whom I see around me, had some of the blessings which I have! There are some who have been here for years, who have their poor heads shaved, and are sent up the Coal River. They have to carry coals from daylight until dark. They are badly fed; and though very bad men, who actually sell their rations of bread for three days for a little rum, yet they ought not to be left without instruction, as they totally are, until they perish.

"Norfolk Island is a terrible place to be sent to. Those only who are incorrigible are sent to this place, with a steel collar round their necks, to work in gangs.

"I have no government work to do; nor has the officer of government anything to do with me. When there is a general muster of the convicts, then only I shall have to appear, and give account of myself. Some days I am permitted to go and see a friend at a distance, if I have any, either at Paramatta, twenty miles, Gabley, thirty, or Hawkesbury, forty miles from Sydney; but then I shall have to get a passport, or I should be taken up, and put into prison as a runaway. A very little will get a person into prison here; but it requires a great deal of interest to get him out again.

"I want to say a great deal more, but time will not permit me, for I expect the ship to sail very soon. I have been very ill since I came on shore. At one time I was thought to be dying; but by the blessing of God and the attentions of my mistress, I am now strong again. I was very well during my whole voyage, though we were tossed about tremendously in the Bay of Biscay. I was very glad to see land, after so many months' confinement; yet I should not mind just such another voyage at this moment, if it were but to bring me back again to dear old England. I cannot say yet that I like this country, or that I think I ever shall ; God only knows. The governor has a great many very beautiful cows, and so has Mr. Palmer, who is very partial to agricultural pursuits. There are a great many horses at Sydney, and some very neat whiskeys and little clay-carts. There are a great many passage-boats, but all numbered and registered, and secured, lest the convicts should use them to attempt their escape.

"Pray, my dear madam, let good Doctor Stebbing have the other side of this sheet. I hope this will find you and all your good family well. Pray, my dear lady, do not forget your promise of writing to me by the first transport-ship that comes out ; and direct to me at Mr. Palmer's, Female Orphan Asylum, Sydney ; and with deep love to all my friends, I remain

"Your faithful servant,

"MARGARET CATCHPOLE."

The following is her letter to Dr. Stebbing, written on the same sheet of paper :—

"DEAR SIR,

"This is to acquaint you with our safe landing at Sydney, on the 20th of December, and that we all arrived in good health. Barker bore the voyage the worst of the three, and was so terrified at the sea that she could scarcely bear to look at it ; and whenever it was rough she would never be persuaded to come on deck. She used frequently to cry out that she wished you were near her. She is just the same as ever, now she is on land : I regret to say, no better. Elizabeth Killet lives very near to me, and is very well. She and I were both taken off the stores on the same day. We have not to go to government work, as the horses do ; but we have both obtained respectable places, and I hope we shall continue in them.

"I am sorry to say that Barker has to spin for government, her character not being such as to deserve a good report : she is still upon the stores. But she can get her stint of work done by one o'clock if she chooses to work hard at it, and then her time is her own till six. Pray, sir, give my kind remembrance to all my fellow-prisoners, and tell any of them that may be sentenced to come out to this country not to be dead-hearted, as I was, about Botany Bay; for if they are sent out, and will only conduct themselves well, they will be better off than in prison.

"The greater part of this country is not yet explored; and if inhabited, it is by natives of a very low caste and hideous features. Those that I have already seen are of a very ferocious aspect. They carry along with them spears of great length, made of hard wood, and a sort of hatchet, made of bone, stone, or very hard wood. They look half-starved, and have very long, lank visages, most hideously distorted by various customs; such as knocking out a front tooth to denote their arrival at manhood, painting their brows, and putting quills through the cartilage which separates the nostrils of their wide-distended noses.

"Their females, I am told, are in a very degraded condition, and are generally stolen from other tribes, and brutally treated, being beaten into immediate subjection by their husbands, who steal them. The men seem to me a very subtle race. If they meet an unarmed white man at a distance from home, they will spear and rob him. They behave themselves well enough when they come into the town, and visit, as they do sometimes, the Female Orphan Asylum, where I live. If they did not they would soon be punished; still they are very sly and treacherous, and can take up things with their long toes as easily as we do the same with our hands.

"They often have a grand fight among themselves, either to gratify their leader or to settle some dispute between the tribes. Twenty or thirty join in the fight, whilst all the others look on, as if it was only a game of play; but some of them are sure to be killed. There is nothing said or done to them for killing each other in this manner. What horrible barbarians they must be!

"The crops of wheat are very good in this country. Forty bushels per acre are commonly grown; it is a very fertile place, and fruitful in every respect. I will write more fully of the country another time. Population increases rapidly. Some things, which we cannot obtain, are very dear: tea is 25s. per pound; sugar, 2s.; salt beef, 1s.; and mutton, 2s. per pound. A pair of shoes, 15s.; 10s. a pair of stockings; 5s. for a yard of common print; calico, 3s. per yard; soap, 3s. per pound; onions, 6d. per pound; potatoes, 2d. per pound; a cabbage, 6d.; rum, 5s. per bottle; a quart of porter, 2s. Fish is as cheap as anything we can buy; but we have no money here to trade with.

"Pray, my dear sir, remember me to Mrs. Ripshaw, and tell her that one of Mr. Ripshaw's daughters, who lives up in the country here, paid a visit to the Orphan Asylum last week. She asked me, when she heard my voice, if I was not a Suffolk woman. This led to my knowledge of her being the daughter of Mr. Ripshaw's first wife. Pray, write to me as soon as you can. I shall never forget your goodness to me, from the day I rode the pony to your door till the day I left Ipswich. I shall never forget your dear daughter, so clever, so kind to every one. Remember me to your faithful servant, who was such a friend to me, and give my duty to all inquiring friends. We had not a single death in our ship, though we had near two hundred females on board.

"Just as I am writing this a messenger has come flying into the town to say that the Blacks have killed eight men, women, and children. One man's arms they have cut, and broke his bones, and have done the same by his legs up to his knees. The poor fellow is just now carried past to the hospital, but he looked more dead than alive, and death would be a blessing to him. The governor has sent out troops after them, with orders to shoot all they can find. I hope I may be able to give you a better account of the natives when I write again. Pray send me word if you know where Dinah Parker and her child were sent to. Give my love to my uncle and aunt Leader. My brother Edward should not have deserted me ; I always loved him affectionately. God bless you, dear doctor, and direct your letter to me at Mr. John Palmer's, Female Orphan Asylum, Sydney ; and ever think of me as your faithful and humble servant,

"MARGARET CATCHPOLE.

"To JOHN COBBOLD, ESQ., Cliff, Ipswich.
"Favoured by CAPTAIN SUMPTER."

By her good conduct in her new situation as cook and superintendent over the dairy of Mr. John Palmer, she was found to be a very useful and confidential person, and was soon looked upon as likely to be a very valuable wife for a free settler. Her fondness for children, and her management of them, came under the particular notice of Mrs. Palmer, who, without any family of her own, had from the most humane and benevolent motives undertaken the entire management of the Orphan Asylum. She found Margaret as willing and as well qualified an assistant as she could wish for.

This school was founded in the year 1800, by Governor King. It was for sixty female orphans. A grant of 15,000 acres of land was given to this foundation for the maintenance and support of the children. They were to be educated usefully and respectably, brought up to industrious habits, and to receive the best religious instruction which could be obtained for them. Few things in Sydney gave such general satisfaction as this benevolent institution ; few things at that period more tended to the ameliora- tion of the conduct of those who, from being the offscourings of such a densely-peopled country as England, were of course so deeply depraved as to be very difficult to recover from their evil habits. Desti- tute female children were taken into this establishment. A portion was given to each one brought up in this place of 100 acres of land, on her marriage-day, pro- vided she married a free settler, and was herself a good character. This was a great inducement for the elder ones to set a good example, as well as to induce young free men to be approved of by the governor as worthy to receive so great a boon. Hence, in later days, have arisen many sterling characters in the neighbourhood of Sydney.

In this benevolent arrangement, the governor was mainly prompted and assisted by a free settler, who had been eight years in the colony, and was one of the first who arrived in the *Bellona* transport, in 1793, and settled upon a spot then called Liberty Plains. This was no other than the reader's friend, and we hope his favourite, John Barry, whose steady and upright character was observed by the governor; he was taken into his confidence, and was a most admirable pattern for all settlers. For his strict integrity and early business habits, he was chosen as the great government agent for the distribution of lands; and he it was who suggested to Governor King the plan of forming this Orphan Establishment. In the sale of every 180 acres to free settlers, this gentleman was allowed a certain percentage, which in a short time realized to him a considerable property, in addition to that which he had already acquired.

John Barry was also the first to propose, and to assist with his wealth, the building of the first church, that of St. John's, at Sydney. He often lamented that government would not make a noble grant of land for church purposes, and in that early day he tried hard for a public grant for the Church of England, and mourned over the supineness of colonial legislation upon such a vital subject. Had this good man lived but to see the arrival of a British Bishop of Australia, it would have added one more joy to the many which his good conduct provided for him; indeed, he always said that such would be the case. Mr. Barry had a very handsome house at Windsor, on the green hills of Hawkesbury; also a fine estate, consisting of the most extensive pastures and the finest corn district in the whole region.

John Barry had kept his solemn word with Margaret, and had never entered into any matrimonial alliance, though he was looked upon as the most eligible match in the whole colony.

And this was the person formerly known to the reader as Jack Barry, the young farming lad, the son of the miller at Levington Creek, on the River Orwell. With small means, good introductions, steady conduct, and active habits, this youth rose from the day he purchased his first hundred acres in the colony until the day of his death. Two of his sisters had gone out to him before Margaret's committal to prison for any offence, and all that they could tell him of her was that she was at service at the Cliff at Ipswich, and that Laud was in the British navy. This gave him unfeigned pleasure, though it did not permit him to hope that he should ever see Margaret.

Had he been certified of Laud's death, there is little doubt that he would have returned to England. But his own family, in their correspondence with him, never mentioned either one or the other person.

Indeed, after Margaret became so notorious in the county of Suffolk, they never named her to him, or sent him the papers which mentioned any word concerning her. He very seldom named her to his sisters. He knew nothing of her career, and she had actually been living some years within a short distance of his own residence in Australia, without his either seeing or hearing anything of her. In her most confidential communications with Mrs. Palmer, she had never mentioned his name, or an explanation must have taken place. She had the narrowest chance of meeting him in July, 1803, when Mr. Barry came to inspect the Asylum. A day only before he came, Margaret had been sent to a free settler's, a relation of Mrs. Palmer's, who had the misfortune to lose his wife, and being left with two very small children, he wanted a person like Margaret to take care of them, and to superintend his domestic concerns. Mrs. Palmer consented to let Margaret go, if she would, at least for a time, until her relative could meet with an eligible person. This gentleman's name was Poinder, and his house was at Richmond Hill. Margaret did not raise any objection, though all felt sorry to part with her from the Asylum; she went to oblige her mistress, and received a handsome present from her at parting.

The first money which this faithful creature received was devoted to the purchase of many curious things for her dear mistress in England. These she treasured up, anticipating the pleasure of forwarding them from Sydney, when she had obtained sufficient to fill a chest.

Though many letters and presents had been sent from her friends in England, it would appear by a letter to her uncle Leader, dated December 20, 1804, that she never received any of them. That uncle conveyed her letter to Mrs. Cobbold, who took a copy of it, from which it is here transcribed. Three years had passed away since the date of her first letter, and the poor creature had been vexed greatly at the non-arrival of any tidings from her friends.

"SYDNEY, December 20th, 1804.

"MY DEAR UNCLE AND AUNT,

"With great pleasure I once more take up my pen to write to you, and all your dear children, as well as all inquiring friends, hoping that they may all be in as good health as I am at the time this letter leaves this country. I bless God, dear uncle, for his past and present mercies towards me, which have been and are very great. I am as young as I ever was; indeed I may say that I am in spirit, if not in body, younger, freer, and happier, than I ever was at any former period of my life. I should be almost ready to jump over St. John's Church, which is the first church built in this country, if I could only hear from you, or some of my dear friends in England. You may well suppose how overjoyed I should be to snatch up any tidings of any of you.

"I cannot think why I have not heard from some of

you. England is, I know, in a very disturbed state and engaged in a maritime war. This is the fourth time I have written. I sent a letter by Captain Sumpter, on the return of the vessel I came by; my next I sent by the *Glutton*, and my next by the *Calcutta*. I did hope that I should have received a letter before this time. My anxieties have been so great as almost to make me go out of my mind; for I see so many letters arriving from London, but none for poor me. I should be unhappy indeed if I thought that no friends in England cared for me.

" I am so grieved and disappointed that my dearly loved mistress has not written to me once since we parted ! I cannot bring myself to believe that if she is alive, and is able, she has not already done so. I fear that some accident has occurred to the ship by which she has written to me, and that she is waiting for some reply. Do not neglect me this time, dear uncle, for it makes me very unhappy to think that I cannot hear from you, or any of my friends in England.

" I am in great hopes that, if I continue in the same state that I am now in, and, if it please God, have the same approbation of my employers, who are high in the governor's favour, I shall have the unspeakable joy of seeing you all again. The thought of such a blessing makes my hand tremble, and the tears run down my cheeks so fast, I cannot see the end of my pen. Governor King is a very good man ; he is very merciful to those who deserve it, even to those who are, as I am, transported for life. There are many who have been granted their free pardon with power to settle in the colony. Some who have distinguished themselves by exemplary conduct, and have rendered public service to the settlement, not only receive their free pardon, but are permitted to return, if they wish it, to their native land. The anticipation of such an event would prompt me to any service.

" The young man who brings this letter to England was transported for life. He was in the governor's service, and discovered a robbery of the government stores, for which he has received a full and free pardon. He lived one year at John Palmer's, Esq., where I have been living; his name is William Underwood. He was very much approved while in my master's service, and was taken thence into the governor's establishment. He is a good young man, and was betrayed into a crime by a butler, who employed him to rob his master, in London. He promises to convey this letter to England, and to post it for you, so that I do hope this will certainly come to hand.

"I have left Mrs. Palmer's service for a time, at her own particular request, and am now living as housekeeper to a young friend of hers, who married her niece. He is a free settler. His wife was a very sickly lady, and had, since she resided in this spot, fallen into a rapid decline; indeed she was in a poor state of health during her sea-voyage. She was a good and amiable lady, and her loss is a great misfortune to the young man, and much sorrow to my dear Mrs. Palmer.

"The free settlers are the great farmers of this country; they have one hundred acres of land as a grant, with power to purchase as many more as they can; they have to clear away the woods, and burn up the stumps, before they can grow corn, though the swine thrive well in the thick bush. We begin to set wheat in March or April, and the harvest comes on in November; and as soon as that is cleared off, they set fire to the stubble, and burn it on the land, and then put in fresh corn directly. They do not plough it, but dibble the corn in without cleaning it, as the burning straw destroys the roots of all the weeds.

"In clearing new land, it is broken up by men with very large hoes, and it is the hardest work that is done in the country. A great price is paid for this labour, and men work too hard at it. They frequently destroy their health and their lives, by their over-exertion to get rich enough to buy farms for themselves. This has been done by some robust men, but others fall a prey to the toil.

"This is a very dangerous country at present to settle in. The natives, who are almost black, wear no covering, but go, most of them, in a state of nudity. They paint their bodies with a light-coloured ochre, marking out the ribs and bones so strongly, that at a little distance in the shade they look like so many moving skeletons. They are a most miserable, half-starved race of men, but very active, very treacherous, and very bold. They seem to have no shame. They used to bear a deadly hatred to the white people; and if all I hear be true of some of the dealings of our colonists with these poor wretches, I am not surprised at it.

"They are much more reconciled to us than they were, and actually send some of their young children to be instructed in our schools. I do not think, how-ever, that the race will ever amalgamate with our own, it appears such an inferior and unsettled one. As we advance our settlers towards the Blue Mountains, these people will recede from us, and being divided into many tribes hostile to each other, will never be able to unite their forces against us.

"This country is full of curious animals. I have already collected some skins for my dear mistress at the Cliff. I never get a fresh one without blessing her name, and hoping that, poor as I am, I may yet give her some little pleasure.

"Among the snakes, few are venomous. I have seen but one, which I am told is a very dangerous foe. Him I had a personal conflict with, and thank God I came off victorious. I was walking with two young children of my master's, not very far from the newly-enclosed lands. The children were a few yards in advance of me, gathering flowers for me, when a large black snake flew at me from the foot of a tree, just as if it had been a dog. I had nothing in my hand but a thin stick which I had broken off one of the fresh shoots of a stump of a tree, which had been cut down the last winter; but I was afterwards told that it was the very best weapon of defence that I could have. He rose upon his tail, and darted at my face, as if he aimed at my eyes ; but just as he came within reach, I gave him a cut over a white line at the back of his neck, which attracted my attention ; he made a beautiful curve, like the bending of a fountain, when it has reached its height, and then fell in a straight stiff line, licking the dust.

"It was providential that I hit him where I did, for my master told me it was the only place that I could have killed him on so suddenly. He told me that he was the most venomous snake in the country, and that, had I not broken his neck as I did, either the children or myself would have been killed. His bite is attended with swelling and blackness of the body, and when the sun goes down death ensues. How merciful that the dear children had passed by him without provoking an attack ! The whole of that night I did nothing but lie and think of this event, and thank God for my deliverance.

"Some of the snakes which I have seen are full twelve feet long, and thicker than a stout man's arm. These are not venomous, but they would soon strangle a child. Some of our workmen have had severe encounters with them.

"I have collected a good many curiosities of this country, and have skinned the birds and smaller animals myself, and preserved their skins, as dear Doctor Stebbing directed me ; and if I can once get a letter from England to assure me that I live in the memory of my friends, I will soon pack them off to my good and learned mistress. People laugh at me sometimes for giving the value of a quarter of an acre of land for the skin of a dead animal ; but they know not the pleasure I derive from the joy of pleasing those I love.

"Give my love to my aunt and the dear children, and for their sakes, as well as my own, let them see this long letter. It may teach them to be very thankful to God ; then they will bless poor Margaret, their foster-mother, and feel glad that they are so beloved by one so far away from them.

" This is a very hot country. In the summer, the ground actually scorches the feet whilst we walk upon it, and creates great blisters, especially where shoe-leather, which is very scarce and dear, does not protect the feet. In winter it is very cold. Not that there is any quantity of snow, but there are very white frosts, which penetrate to the inmost recesses of our chambers. It is much colder and hotter than it used to be, since the country is cleared of its shady woods, and is so much more open. It will be a very populous and improving country. Even within a year or two, the people seem to be more moral and domesticated than they were; but it is a terrible place for drunkards.

" We want British clergymen; good men of real steady principles, such as you have in England. The governor orders the Bible to be read at stated times to the different gangs of convicts; but then it is a convict who can read better than the rest, and they make a joke of him! Oh! what a sin it is that so little provision should be made for that which would be the surest way to reform the convicts, and to pre-serve their souls alive! I pray continually for friends to help us.

" The trees grow very fast in this country. A few pear-trees and apple-trees are getting up, and the vine flourishes wherever it is planted. The oak grows luxuriantly; peaches and apricots thrive; but gooseberries and currants do not seem to suit the soil. Money is very scarce. Copper coins are almost the value of silver, and gold is a thing that I seldom see. Those who trade with India or China are the only people in the colony who use it. Tea is dearer here than it is in Old England, though we are so much nearer to the countries where it is grown. It is a matter of luxurious indulgence which convicts and servants do not at present enjoy. The native flax of Norfolk Island is the finest which we can obtain. You must not suppose that we are badly off, though some commodities may be very dear; for this country will be, if the world stand, one of the richest on the

face of the earth : oh that it may be one of the best !
At present it is one of the worst, though improving.

"Sarah, or, as she calls herself, Elizabeth Barker,
and Elizabeth Killet, are both living. One is doing
well ; I regret to state the other does badly.

"If the young man who brings this should write to
you from London, send an answer to him directly.
He intends to return and settle here. He is a good
young man. Singularly enough, he returns to England
to gratify his aged parents with a sight of himself,
and intends to try and persuade one of his female
cousins to come out with him.

"Pray go to my dear Mrs. Cobbold, and tell her
I long to hear of her and her family. The same of
Dr. Stebbing. Be sure and direct your letters for me
at Mrs. Palmer's Orphan Asylum, Port Jackson,
Sydney. Let all your letters be left at Government
House. Mrs. Palmer will take care of any letters for
me. Pray God bless and keep you all, is the constant
prayer of

                    "Your affectionate niece,
                        "MARGARET CATCHPOLE.

"To Mr. WILLIAM LEADER,
        "Brandiston, near Woodbridge. Suffolk,
                                    "England."

By her next letter it appears that Margaret was
housekeeper to a young widower. After living there
about one year, her principles were put to a trial,
under which any less firm and stable than hers would
have succumbed. The young widower, finding what
a valuable person Margaret was, resolved to marry
her. He did not think it at all necessary to pay
court to one who he thought would feel herself honoured
by the proposal ; and as he fully intended to make her
the mistress of his establishment, he at once said to
her—

"Young woman, I am resolved to marry you, and

make you mistress of my house at Richmond Hill. You need not trouble yourself to make any preparations. I will see the Rev. Mr. Johnson, the chaplain, and to-morrow you shall be mistress of my establishment."

Startled as Margaret was by this wholly unexpected offer, and by the terms in which it was couched, she hesitated not a moment in her reply.

"I have no intention, sir, whatever," said she, "to marry any one, but most certainly should not think of marrying you. I was sent here by your relative, Mrs. Palmer, in the capacity of your servant, and I am willing to fulfil the duties of that situation; but I should act with great duplicity towards my mistress, if, without either yourself or me holding any conversation with her upon the subject, I were to marry you. But, to be candid with you at once, sir, I tell you I have no intention to marry, and I will not comply with your demands in this respect."

As may be supposed, the young man was not a little astonished; but all he said was—

"Then, if you do not, you may go back to Mrs. Palmer, and say I sent you."

This was quite enough for Margaret, who immediately packed up her few treasures, and started off for Sydney; and her kind friend, Mrs. Palmer, who was equally astonished and pleased at her conduct, received her again in a more confidential capacity.

One thing poor Margaret had deeply to regret about this time, and it occasioned her many tears of unaffected sorrow. She had, with persevering care, and at serious cost, collected a great many curiosities, seeds of plants, shells, fossils, minerals, skins of birds and lesser animals, all which she had treasured up with the most lively hope that they would one day reach her dear mistress in England. She packed them in a strong box, and paid a man to carry them for her to Mrs. Palmer's, at Sydney; but they never arrived. The man to whom they had been entrusted broke open the box, sold the contents to a settler, and invented a plausible tale of his being robbed by some bushmen.

The name of the gentleman who made Margaret the offer of marriage, above referred to, was Mr. John Poinder. He died about two years afterwards, but left his aunt, Mrs. Palmer, sole executrix of his property, and commended his children to her care. Margaret then returned to Richmond Hill, to superintend the affairs of the house and the management of the children, until they should be sent to school.

It may be here mentioned as one of those singular coincidences to which Margaret Catchpole's life had been subjected, that not only on this occasion of her absence from the Asylum, but on the only other occasion that she had ever been absent from it, Mr. John Barry visited the institution, stayed there some time, and left it, without receiving the smallest intimation that it was, or had been, the residence of the woman on whom his affections had been fixed from the first moment he beheld her, and had never swerved up to the period of which we write ; and the subsequent events which we have to record render this coincidence still more remarkable.

CHAPTER XXX

REPENTANCE AND AMENDMENT

BEFORE Margaret left Sydney the second time for Richmond Hill, she had the inexpressible delight of receiving a ship-chest from England, containing letters and presents from her beloved mistress and friends. The good Mrs. Palmer was requested to be present at the opening of the chest ; and never, never did the eager school-boy unpack his parcel from home with more intense delight than this poor young woman did the box from England.

But her first interest was directed towards the

packet of letters which the box contained ; and, until she had devoured the contents of *them*, all else was a matter of comparative indifference to her. There were letters from her uncle and aunt Leader, from Dr. Stebbing, from several of her fellow-servants at the Cliff ; but above all, in Margaret's estimation, there were letters from her dear mistress—the excellent lady of the Cliff—to whose kindness she owed and felt such lasting gratitude.

The reader need not be troubled with a description of the numerous articles of wearing apparel which the box contained ; nor is it needful to do more than mention that, besides the larger objects, there was an inner case, containing combs, thimbles, needles, netting needles and pins, knitting needles, pins, threads, papers of Dutch tape, of Indian cotton, of coarse threads, pincushions, scissors, knives, and all sorts of those stores which are so precious to a housewife, when at a distance from the ordinary sources where they are to be procured.

Poor Margaret could neither eat nor drink till she had devoured the contents of her letters. She wept so much during their perusal, that she was forced to ask Mrs. Palmer to read them to her. This she did with most sincere pleasure, for they afforded her own good heart instruction as well as gratification. The letters written to Margaret were such as would have gratified any intellectual and benevolent mind. They were much admired by all who read them, but by none more than by the faithful creature to whom they were directed.

The following letter was addressed by Margaret Catchpole to Mrs. Cobbold, shortly after the receipt of the box of treasures just alluded to :—

"October 18th, 1807.

" HONOURED MADAM,

" With the purest pleasure I again seize an opportunity to write to you. I feel it my duty to do so, as you are my dearest friend upon earth. Sincerely do I thank God for your health and happiness, and for that of all your good family. I hope and trust in God that I shall soon hear from you again, for it is my greatest comfort in this distant land. Oh, my dear lady, how grieved I am to tell you that there are so many depraved creatures in this country! I have been robbed of all my collection of curiosities, which I had been saving up, according to your wishes, and which I intended to have sent you by the next ship. I am sure you would have thought them valuable, as they were all so perfect, and the birds in such good order, skinned, and dried, and perfumed. I will endeavour to collect them again; but I am so sorry, when I had collected so many, and had such great pleasure in them, that I should lose them all through the artful conduct of wicked men!

"But I will soon be at work again for you. I have no greater joy than to be waiting upon you; and everything I get, which I think will be valuable to you, gives me increased satisfaction. You can scarcely believe what happiness I experience in devoting any portion of my time to your service. You are never out of my thoughts, and always in my prayers. My ideas turn toward you from every place, and in almost everything I see. When I think of the troubles and trials you must have, with eighteen children around you, I wonder you can at all think of me. But, dear lady, I do feel such an interest about you and your family, that I am thankful whenever you name any of them; and I was so delighted with your description of them all! Always tell me about them. I sincerely desire to know how Miss Anne is, and Miss Harriet, and Miss Sophia.

"Have you any knowledge, my dear lady, of Governor Bligh? Alas! I have lost a good friend in Governor King. I do think that if a petition were presented to him in my behalf, so well known as I am to the late governor, something might be done for me. Every one tells me that he says my conduct has been so uniformly consistent and good that I deserve a reward. But it requires friends near the fountain of mercy to make its stream flow towards such as I. I should be almost ready to die with joy if a pardon were to come to me, with permission to return to England. I would then gladly come, and live and die in your service.

"Since I last wrote to you, I have been living again with Mrs. Palmer. I sent you, by the ship *Buffalo*, a small case, containing the skins of the rarest birds found in this country, together with an opossum, of a dark colour, and very fierce; also a species of rat, which very much resembles a diminutive hyena. You will find two large, magnificent birds, called here the mountain pheasant; they are only like our English bird in size. The plume of feathers in the tail of the cock bird would form the most graceful ornament for a queen's head-dress. Two noble feathers, somewhat like a peacock's, only more brilliant and various in their colours, surrounded by the most glittering silver lines of curving feathers, fine as the prairie grass, and sparkling like the waves of the ocean, ornament the tail of the male bird, whilst the female is only remarkable for the elegance of her shape, and not for the beauty of her plumage.

"In my opinion, this bird is the peafowl of this country, and not a pheasant. Early in the morning, I have seen him spring from the thickest brushwood, and wing his arrow-like flight to the tallest tree, and there he appears to mimic the notes of the various songsters around him. But the most beautiful attitude that I once saw him in beats everything I ever beheld of what men term politeness. I have heard and have read of delicate attentions paid to our sex by men of noble and generous dispositions; but I scarcely ever heard of such devoted attention as I one day witnessed in this noble bird towards his mate. I saw her sitting in the heat of the meridian sun upon her nest, and the cock bird seated near her, with his tail expanded, like a bower overshadowing her; and, as the sun moved, so did he turn his elegant parasol to guard her from his rays. Now and then he turned his bright eye to see if she was comfortable, and she answered his inquiry with a gentle note and rustle of her feathers.

"Was not this a sight calculated to teach us all gentleness ? Dear lady, as I looked upon it, the tears came warmly down my cheeks, as I thought of your good husband and yourself ; and I dreamed of your writing a poem upon this subject, and reading it to the young ladies in the school-room. I had often wondered what use the tail of this bird could be to him. If this be one of its general uses, surely it is truly ornamental and useful. I hope these birds will come safe to hand. Captain Brooks of the *Buffalo*, promised me faithfully that he would himself forward them into Suffolk. The thought that they may reach you and give you pleasure will make me happy for many a long day. Owing to the late floods, every thing is become very dear: pork, 2*s.* ; beef and mutton, 2*s.* 3*d.* ; soft sugar, 6*s.* and 8*s.* ; tea, £1 10*s.* per pound ; a bushel of wheat, £1 5*s.* ; printed cotton, 10*s.* to 12*s.* per yard ; shoes, for females, 13*s.* per pair. Scarcely any linen cloth to be had. Newspapers, of any date, 1*s.* a-piece.

"But your chest, just now arrived, contains so many things of value, that my good Mrs. Palmer has at once proposed that I should at once open a little shop at Richmond Hill. I wrote word, in my uncle's letter, or in my last to you, about my offer of marriage, but the gentleman is since dead, and has left his property to the management of Mrs. Palmer. She says I shall have a cottage of my own, with land attached to it, and begin business for myself. You know not, dear lady, how valuable all those things are which you have sent to me. But your letters, and those of Mrs. Sleorgin—oh, what a comfort they have been to me !

"I had been very ill before their arrival. About eight months ago, I took a long journey, for Mrs. Palmer, to arrange something about Mr. Poinder's children. I walked a distance of thirty miles, and over-exerted and heated myself very much, so that my body threw out large blisters, just as if I had been burnt with small coals, and I was so swelled out that I thought I should have lost my life. I was under the care of a Mr. Mason, a very clever surgeon; and Mrs. Palmer was very kind and attentive to me. Blessing be to God! I recovered; but I am still very subject to cold and inflammation. I am not permitted to go near the fire.

"I am to go to Richmond Hill as soon as I can, which will be very soon. I will write to you again when I am settled there. Only let me thank you, as I ought, for your great goodness to one so unworthy of it. If I should prosper, so as to get enough to keep myself from starving in my old days, how shall I bless God for raising me up such a friend as you have been to me!

"Mrs. Palmer says she is very sorry to part with me, but she wishes to serve me. She is so good to me! She was so pleased to find I was so respected by such friends as the ladies who wrote to me. She said she never read such beautiful letters as yours and good Mrs. Sleorgin's, and asked me to let her take a copy of them. She had a great desire to publish them in the Sydney paper, as she thought they would do so much good to others as well as to myself. She blessed your spirit, and desired me to say, that she considered me worthy of all the favour which your generous hand had bestowed upon me. This was her saying; but it is not my opinion, though I may say I wish I was worthy. She desired me to say, that if you should see Sir William Blizzard, a physician in London, he would tell you all about her. She has promised to do all she can to obtain my restoration to society. If I could once return to my own native land, what a happy woman I should be! You add much to my comfort here; for whenever I have a few moments' spare time, I am sure to be seeking for seeds, shells, insects, or curiosities of any kind; and the thought of whom I am serving makes me feel very happy. Thank God! I keep myself free from all men. I have formed no acquaintance with any man; and I may sincerely confess to you, my dear lady, that my early attachment and deep-felt disappointment have deadened the feelings of my heart to any further matrimonial speculations. I do not think that any man in the colony could persuade me to marry. My dear Mrs. Palmer has often spoken to me on the subject, and I have never concealed the fact, that to my first attachment I owe my present abode in this colony as a convict. I am wise enough now to see my own follies, and I pray to God for His forgiveness. In this colony there are few that remain single from choice, old or young. Girls of fifteen years become mothers before they are able to take care of themselves; and I may state it as a curious fact, that very many whom you would suppose too old to be mothers, have young families increasing around them.

"Vegetation in this clime is very abundant; but there are some fearful drawbacks to our reaping its fruits. We may have a good crop of grain on the ground to-day, and to-morrow it may be all cut down by a hail-storm, or destroyed by a blight, or swept away by a flood. On Monday last, the 16th of this month, a hail-storm passed over this place, and cut down the wheat just as it was in full blossom. The stones which fell from the clouds were as big as pigeons' eggs, and you may imagine the mischief which ensued. Great numbers of fowls and small cattle were killed. The harvest will be about six weeks hence, and will be a lamentably deficient crop. Now begins our hot season. We dread the attacks of ophthalmia, as the surgeons call it; we call it commonly the blight in our eyes. We can find no remedy for it but patience. In one day our eyelids are so swelled that we cannot see. With some it lasts a week, with others a month, according to the state of the constitution of the sufferer. It is a very irritating and painful disease, and none are such dreadful sufferers as those who most deserve it, the habitual drunkards, of which class I regret to state there are too many in this country.

"The natives are much more tractable than they used to be, and not so savage and uncivilized. They will work but little; I can get from them, however, the most rare skins of wild animals, such as the settlers have not patience to pursue. They boast that the white man is made for drudgery, and the black for liberty. He can roam through his native woods and subsist without labour, whilst he supposes that we enjoy no freedom. They have not left off their barbarous habit of fighting and killing each other for a public exhibition. I remember that you used to make the young ladies read of the tournaments in the reign of Elizabeth, and how the knights sometimes killed each other in this way. Surely those ancestors of the English had some such spirit as these free blacks of Australia in this day. These people form a stately circle, and contend most skilfully and magnanimously, by fixed and settled rules of combat; and I assure you, dear lady, that their deportment, at such times, would be no discredit to the most gallant knights of Europe. Gallantry towards their females, however, is at a very low ebb; yet, for the honour of the sex, they take no delight in these pageants of blood and murder. In this respect, degraded as they are in other things, they are not so bad as some were in the ages of chivalry.

"It will not much interest you to know of our farming here, but some of your friends may like to hear a word about it, though from such an ignorant being as myself. The price of farming stock is very high: a sow sells for £10; a ewe for £7; a milch-goat, £3 10s.; a cow from £60 to £70; a good horse from £100 to £150. But things will not continue in this state many years, for this is a most prolific land. You will be more glad to hear of our great variety of botanical plants. My good lady, Mrs. Palmer, has promised that her friend, Mr. Mason, who is a good botanist, shall affix the proper names to each of the specimens which I send.

"Honoured madam, give my duty to Mrs. Sleorgin, and say how happy I am to hear from her, and am glad that she approves of my conduct and pursuits. I love her good advice, and endeavour to keep it. I am so sorry that I was robbed of all my first treasures for you. My tears, however, would not bring them back again. I will try again. Give my duty to dear Doctor Stebbing. Oh that I could see him with his dog and gun, upon some of our plains, or beating in the bush of this country! I would get him to kill me many a beautiful bird to enrich your collection. Give my duty to his daughter. Is poor old Robinson Crusoe alive? and is Jack Whatcheer? Alas! their memory brings back painful recollections. So, my dear lady, hoping to hear from you again, accept the love and duty of your humble and constant servant,

                              "MARGARET CATCHPOLE.

"To J. COBBOLD, Esq., Cliff, Ipswich."

From this letter it appears that Margaret was then upon the eve of leaving Sydney for her cottage at Richmond Hill, some forty or fifty miles up the country. There were a small village and store-rooms on the banks of the river, and Margaret rented a small house and about twenty acres of land of her friend Mrs. Palmer, at a very moderate price. Part of her house was formed into a shop, in which all her little stock in trade was placed and her little capital invested. The goods which were sent her from England formed a valuable assortment; and she began by offering for sale small portions of her general stock, so that her customers might have the same articles upon another application. Her house was situated in a very beautiful spot, commanding an extensive view over a well-watered plain, with the ever-blue mountains in the distance.

Margaret remained at Richmond Hill, as her own independent mistress, for five years. About two years after her residence at this place she wrote again to her mistress, and sent a small drawing of her cottage, which was taken by one of Mrs. Palmer's friends for this very purpose.

The mountain pheasants, which she speaks of in the following letter, duly arrived by the *Buffalo*. They were splendid specimens, and were in a very perfect state. They were preserved in the author's family for many years, and may now be seen at the public museum at Ipswich, in company with many thousands of valuable specimens. The bird itself is now become very scarce. A live specimen has never been brought to England.[1]

"RICHMOND HILL, Oct. 8th, 1809.

"HONOURED MADAM,

"I take up my pen again with new and increased delight, to say that I duly received another box from you, which arrived at Sydney with everything in it, according to the inventory, quite safe. A thousand thanks for it, my dear lady, and all its valuable contents. It was three years last June since I sent you, according to your request, a number of our native productions. I had a cedar case made on purpose,

---

[1] The specimens in question may be seen distinguished by a label attached to them with the following words :—

"MANURA SUPERBA.
"LYRA, OR BOTANY BAY PHEASANT.

"These beautiful birds were sent to the late Mrs. Cobbold, of the Cliff, by Margaret Catchpole, a female servant, who stole a coach-horse from the late John Cobbold, Esq., and rode it up to London in one night. She was in the act of selling the horse when she was taken. She was in man's apparel. She was tried at Bury in 1797, and received sentence of death, which sentence, owing to the entreaties of the prosecutor, was changed to seven years' transportation ; but breaking out of gaol, she was afterwards transported for life.

"Presented to this Museum by R. K. Cobbold, Esq."

strong and stoutly ironed. I was told that it would preserve the goods in a more perfect state than an oaken one; but as you say nothing about its arrival in your letter, I fear that it is lost.

"I sent it on board the *Buffalo*, the ship in which Governor King left the colony. It may, perhaps, yet reach you. I hope it will. There were many of our Sydney newspapers in it, and a host of birds' skins, weapons and knives, and curiosities, which I obtained from the natives near the Blue Mountains. I can see a great part of the chain from my chamber-window. Mrs. Palmer undertook to see the case forwarded to you.

"This is the second great collection I have made for you; and I shall not, dear lady, forward any more until I hear of the safe arrival of the last, it is so very disheartening to find all my labour and love thrown away. Oh! how I wish that I could be permitted to bring a cargo home for you! I would part with everything I have most gladly for such a purpose, but I fear it will never be; and sometimes my poor heart feels broken, as I sit alone, pondering over all my hope and fears.

"My dear landlady, Mrs. Palmer, has given me such a nice drawing of my cottage and the surrounding country for you! I shall send it; and I hope you will not think me presumptuous if I ask for one of the dear, dear Cliff, as I know, my dear lady, that you can so easily do one for me. If one of the young ladies would be so kind as to copy it, then I could give Mrs. Palmer one by way of return. Yours shall hang over my chimney-place; and when I look at it I shall think of those happy days which I spent there with you for my friend and mistress.

"Ah! dear lady, when I was learning so many good lessons under your eye, little did I think that I should reap the profit thereof in a foreign land. Your word of approbation was a sort of foretaste of that which, I hope and trust, we shall both rejoice to hear, 'Well done, good and faithful servant!'"

" Dear lady, I am very contented, and am getting on well, but we have all had severe misfortune in this district : first, by the floods ; secondly, by fire ; and thirdly, by such a hurricane as levelled whole acres of timber-trees of enormous size. We were afraid to remain indoors lest our houses should fall on our heads ; and out of doors we could hardly stand at all. Great trees swept by us as if they had been straws.

" The flood in the month of May distressed us very much ; but that on the 31st of July and the 1st of August, the days after the high wind, was dreadful. It was the greatest ever experienced by any of the settlers, though the natives speak of one which covered all the plain from the mountains, and was deeper than our church is high. The one I have so lately witnessed went over the tops of the houses on the plain ; and many poor creatures were on their chimneys crying out for mercy, and for boats to go to them. It was shocking to hear their cries, and it made me feel so wretched at not being able to relieve them. It was very dangerous to approach them, for sometimes the eddies were so strong round their houses that boats were swept away, or swamped in the attempt. I saw one boat completely sunk by a tree falling upon it, just as it was passing ; and had not another boat been near to take the sufferers off the boughs upon which they had climbed, they must all have perished.

" One man, of the name of Thomas Lacey, and his wife and family, were carried away in a barn. They got upon the mow, and broke a hole through the thatch. I saw them, dear creatures, holding up their hands to heaven as they passed us on the sweeping flood, and imploring our help. It made my spirit rise within me ; and I thought how God had made me instrumental in saving life in former days, and I could not resist the impulse of that which at first the people called my madness. I called to some men who were standing near a boat moored to the bank, and urged them to go with me to the rescue, but they would none of them stir. I took two long linen-lines, and tied them together, and requested the people on the bank to assist me, for I was determined to go alone if they would not go with me.

"I jumped into the boat, and then the men were ashamed, and took their oars, and said they would go without me; but no, that I was determined they should not do; so the man slackened the rope, as we were carried by the stream towards the barn, which had fortunately grounded upon the stump of some large tree which had collected a quantity of earth so as to form a bank near it. We had hard work to get up towards the smooth-water side of the barn; but the men kept the boat close to the side by pushing against the trunk of the tree; and I stood up at the head of the boat, and received the dear children into my arms. They were all taken from the thatch, and we launched again into the eddies.

"Had it not been for the line, we should have been sent down the stream like an arrow from a bow. All our fear was lest the line should break, and if it had we could never have rowed up the stream. Thanks be to the providential mercy of God, we were all hauled safe to land.

"Oh! how the dear children did cling to me! They told me that they saw great alligators come up and look at them; but, poor things! their terrible situation would make them magnify a floating tree into an alligator. Horses, cows, sheep, and all kinds of animals, were hurried along the waters to the sea. I wonder whence all this body of fresh water can come from! We had no previous rains, and yet thousands and thousands of acres were covered ten, fifteen, and twenty feet deep with these floods.

"I brought Mr. Lacey's family to my own house. You know, my dear lady, how fond I am of children. I take care of them, and they assist me, until their father shall have got another habitation to take them to. Some poor creatures expired just as help reached them. They got on to houses, barns, stacks, and trees, and were often swept off all these resting-places.

Many persons were drowned; many lost all their property. We were all fearful at one time that we should be swallowed up. Part of the hill on which my cottage stands began to cave away, and has left a cliff several feet high for a long distance. I was very near losing my own life; for I was standing on the verge of the hill when a part of my own field close by my feet caved in, and was swept away by the flood. It seemed to melt away like sugar in a cup; but, God be praised! I just escaped falling with it. You may believe that it terrified me.

"I have about twenty acres of land from my dear friend, Mrs. Palmer, who sends me one man to help me in the cultivation of it. Some have lost all: my loss is estimated at about fifty pounds. Everything is now so dear in the colony that my little stock in my shop is as much as doubled in its value; so that my loss in one way will be made up in another.

"We are almost afraid of starvation on account of the many thousand bushels of Indian corn carried away by the flood. This corn, mixed with a little wheat, makes most excellent bread. You may imagine, dear lady, how we suffer, when I state that most of the wheat then in the ground was completely rooted up and carried away like sea-weed. All manner of grain has become very dear. Government has issued a certain quantity for each sufferer for seed-corn.

"Clothing of all kinds is very scarce; but whilst I am writing, news has just arrived that a ship has providentially come into port laden with a vast supply, so that it will soon be the cheapest thing we can get. I should have done great things this year but for the flood; but I have every reason to be thankful for that which is left for me.

"My prayers, dear lady, are always for your happiness, and for the good of all your dear family. Pray God that I may have the comfort to hear from you again! It is the comfort of heaven to me to hear that you and yours are well. Give my dutiful thanks to that dear lady, Mrs. Sleorgin, for the handsome present of books which she has sent me, and for the letter of good advice which accompanied it. Assure her, dear madam, that I endeavour to follow her advice every day. How thankful ought I to be to God that I have such dear friends who care for me !

"My health at times is not good, and I am still very thin. Tell Dr. Stebbing that I walk every day farther than the space between his house and Nacton Street. God bless him ! I have got several packages of curiosities for him. The greatest pleasure I have in this country is the hope of hearing from you, dear lady. I shall feed upon this hope for the next twelve months ; and I assure you, when your letters do arrive, I am just as delighted as a child would be to hear from an affectionate parent.

"Give my love and duty to my master, and all the young people who may chance to know my name, and ever believe me to be

"Your affectionate servant,
"MARGARET CATCHPOLE.

"JOHN COBBOLD, ESQ., Cliff, Ipswich."

The last letter received from Margaret *Catchpole* is also dated from Richmond Hill. It breathes the same affectionate attachment and anxiety, and is given here as worthy of the same attention as the former ones :—

"RICHMOND HILL, Sept. 1st, 1811.

"HONOURED MADAM,

"On the 8th of August of this year, 1811, I received my cedar case that Captain Prichard should have brought. It is almost two years ago since he landed the troops at Sydney. Mrs. Palmer, my ever-constant friend, took charge of it for me, until I was enabled to go down myself. When I received tidings of its arrival, I set off from my cottage, and walked the whole way, leaving the eldest child I took from the flood to take care of my house. It is full fifty miles from Richmond Hill to Sydney. Mrs. Palmer could not think where the case could have been all that time.

But your letter, my dear madam, has set all our minds easy upon the subject.

"At first I thought it was the case, and all the things I sent you, come back again. But bless you, dear lady, for thinking of me! I was greatly rejoiced when I found that you had received the birds quite safe, and that they gave you such pleasure. Everything that you have sent me is quite safe, and so delightfully packed, that I could see your own dear handiwork in the whole process. All are, I assure you, very acceptable to me; and many thousand thanks do I give for them. I never can feel sufficiently thankful to heaven and you.

"How deeply do I feel the loss of dear Mrs. Sleorgin! With God's help, I will endeavour to follow her good advice to the day of my own departure, and then I shall meet her again. My loss is, I am persuaded, her own gain. Her blessings have come here, and will be fruitful to her own good soul in a happier world. I am very fond of reading those good books which she has sent me, and I shall always be reminded of the benevolent donor.

"Dear lady, I am grieved to hear of the death of poor Miss Anne that was. She was always the most meek-spirited of all the young ladies. Master Rowland was always my favourite. He was born in those happy days when I lived with you; and he, too, is gone. Your letter conveys very anxious tidings; and though joyful to me to see your dear handwriting, yet I grieve to find that you have been so ill. Oh! if there was anything in this country that would do you good, however difficult it might be to be obtained, I would not cease using all my efforts until I had got it for you. If I can find anything at any time which may be new to you, and please your dear, good mind, anything you have not heard of before, what pleasure it will be to me!

"Oh! never can I be dutiful or grateful enough to you for your goodness to me. God preserve you long to be a blessing to your dear family and friends!

"I am ashamed, my dear madam, to send this hasty scribble into your hands, but the ship is about to sail directly, and I am hard pressed for time. I am pleased to think that you got my long list of dried plants and birds. I am sorry the insects were not better fastened in the case; I will attend particularly to your instructions about them for the future. I am living alone, as I was when I last wrote you, and am getting on well, in a very honest and independent way of life. People wonder why I do not marry. I cannot forget my late trials, troubles, and horrors, and I dread forming any acquaintance with any man. I was happy before such notions entered my mind, and I have been comparatively happy since I have had no more notions of the same sort. So I am single and free.

"The cap you have sent me, which you say is a great favourite of yours, I put on last evening, and drank my tea in it, with some tears of reflection. My heart was so full, to think that the work of your own hands, and that which had graced your own head, should cover such an unworthy one as mine, it made me feel humble and sorrowful, as well as joyful and thankful. I must hastily conclude this letter, as the messenger calls for any ship letters for Sydney. May the blessings and thanks of your grateful servant reach your dear heart, from the soul of

"Your ever devoted servant,
            "MARGARET CATCHPOLE.

"J. COBBOLD, ESQ., Cliff, Ipswich."

It is now time that our attention should be recalled to one whose conduct has, we trust, already gained him a place in the reader's esteem, and who after all must be looked upon as the true hero of our simple story. John Barry (now most worthy to have that old English title of Esquire attached to his name, as being the highest which was acknowledged in the settlement, under the governor) had, as the reader will remember, arrived at New South Wales, and

settled at Liberty Plains. He was among the earliest
free settlers in the land, and was a man of such firmness and steadiness of character, of such integrity and
perseverance, that he succeeded far beyond his own
most sanguine expectations, and established for himself such a character for probity, sagacity, and general
worth, that he was consulted upon all the most interesting concerns of the colony. He it was who
suggested to Governor King the first idea of establish-
ing the "Female Orphan Asylum," and proposed
attaching one hundred acres of land as a marriage
portion for the children. He it was who laid the
second stone of St. John's Church, Paramatta. He
built the first free-trader that was ever launched from
Port Jackson. That he prospered it is needless to
declare, because industry and integrity, with activity
of mind, intelligence, and sincerity, must prosper in
any place. He was a merchant as well as a great corn
grower: he was also, as we have before stated, the
government contractor for land. He never caballed
with any one party against another, for the sake of
increasing the price of land, but honestly, in a straight-
forward way, stated the price per acre, the quantities
that parties might have, and the money expected in
a given time. He had sold for the government many
thousand acres of the finest tract of land, which bor-
dered upon the river Hawkesbury, and retained a
portion for himself at Windsor, by the Green Hills,
for which he strictly paid the highest price that was
then given for land in that district.

His residence, called Windsor Lodge, was situated
on a very commanding spot upon the south bank of
the river. At a short distance from the water he had
built very large granaries, capable of holding an immense quantity of grain, and this spot became the
great corn-mart of the country; the grain was thence
transported to the coast, and supplied every port
connected with the colony. The Hawkesbury is a noble
river, particularly opposite to Windsor Lodge, the
house, or rather mansion, of the owner of the Green

Hills around. If real worth and talent, if public and private benevolence, with the most expansive views of men and things, together with acts of such virtue and dignity as speak the spirit of true nobility, could be found in any one, they existed in the mind and heart of that youth, who left the shores of old England a simple, single-minded Suffolk farmer's son, to become a man of wealth and goodness in a distant land.

It is true that no chivalric deed of arms signalized his career: he was an enterprising, but a peaceful man; he could boast no long line of ancestry higher or more exalted than himself. His parents were good, honest, and virtuous people, and their son bore the same character, but with the possession of superior information; and may we not, in some measure, trace the origin of all this man's virtues and good qualities to that passion which still, as it was in the olden times, is the parent and prompter of all that is great and noble, all that is gentle; all, in short, that distinguishes man from the brutes that perish? Love dwelt, a pure and holy flame, in the breast of this young man; and change of scene, change of condition, increase of knowledge, of wealth, and of circumstances —in short, circumstances which would have changed almost any other being—changed not him.

It may seem strange to many that Mr. Barry should have been so long a leading man in the colony, and in constant communication with England, and never have heard of the fate of Margaret Catchpole. But when they understand that all notice of her career had been studiously excluded from the correspondence of his friends in England; and, moreover, that convicts of all classes, when they came to Botany Bay, were sent to the northward to be employed on the government stores, and that the Hawkesbury was devoted principally to free labourers and settlers, and that the line of demarcation between convict and free settler was extremely strict, their surprise will in a great degree cease.

Beloved and respected by all, as John Barry was,

the wonder with all was that he never married. With every comfort around him, with health and cheerfulness, a goodly person, great repute, and wealth scarcely equalled by any one in the colony, he still remained a lone man ; and but that he evinced a kind, benevolent, and friendly disposition towards all their sex, the females would have set him down as a cold ascetic. He was far from being this kind of person. Love was the ruling principle of his life ; and though he had himself suffered so much from disappointment that he never had the slightest inclination to address his affection to another, yet he encouraged social and domestic virtues in others, and advised many not to follow his bachelor example. His own sisters he had portioned off handsomely ; and one of his greatest relaxations was to visit their abodes and to delight in their happiness and prosperity.

In the year 1811, Mr. John Barry was visited with a deep affliction, in the loss of one of his sisters, who died of fever, leaving a husband and a young family of seven children. But how surely does good spring out of seeming evil ! Fraught as this event was with the most poignant grief to John Barry, it was, nevertheless, the ultimate cause of the consummation of all his hopes, and the completion of that happiness which he had so richly earned. Deeply desiring the welfare of his sister's children, and seeing the forlorn condition to which they were reduced by the death of their excellent mother, he at once acted with an energy and discretion which the afflicted husband could not command. He sought to obtain as speedily as possible some respectable person to take charge of the family, and he remembered that Mrs. Palmer had mentioned to him a valuable person, whom she had sent to Richmond Hill, to take charge of some motherless children related to herself. He therefore went down to Sydney immediately, and obtained an interview with that lady at the Orphan Asylum.

" I think, my dear madam, you mentioned to me, two or three years ago, that you lost a relative who left a young family, and that you sent a confidential female to superintend and take care of the children ?''

"I did, sir, and a most valuable treasure she has always been to me. She lived with the husband of my relative for two years as housekeeper and general superintendent of his establishment. He is, however, since dead."

"And she——"

"Is still living at Richmond Hill, but perfectly independent. It was a curious and unprecedented fact in this country, for a young woman in her situation to refuse the hand of the very man whose family she managed ; but she did so, and to her honour and credit ; for the love she bore me she left his service and returned to live with me. I was, as you may conceive, greatly pleased with her, and took her still more closely into my confidence. Two years after this the husband of my late relative died, leaving his whole property at Richmond Hill to me, for the benefit of his children, and in case of their death, to me and my heirs for ever. The poor children, always sickly, died in this house, and the property is now let to a most respectable tenant. I reserved twenty acres and a cottage for this young woman, who had acted so generously ; and I do not scruple to tell you, that though she pays a nominal rent to me for the cottage and land, yet I have always put that rent into the bank in her name, with the full intention of leaving her the property I mention."

"I am very much obliged to you for the information which you give me. You have heard that I have lost my youngest sister Maria. She leaves a disconsolate husband with seven young children, the eldest only eight years of age. My object in asking about this person was to secure her as guardian of these dear children ; and the manner in which you have spoken of her convinces me that she would be eligible and valuable, if she were but at liberty to come. Do you think you could persuade her to undertake the duty ?

I would send a man to farm her land for her, and devote the whole rent to her remuneration."

"I am afraid she would not leave her present home and occupation. She keeps a small store and lives entirely by herself, except that a little girl, whose life she saved from the great flood, assists her. You would have been very much pleased with her had you witnessed her brave conduct in risking her own life in the attempt to save a Mr. Lacey and his family, who on that day were carried away in their barn. She put to shame the spirits of several men who stood looking on the waters, and refused to go to the assistance of those poor creatures. She would positively have gone alone, and entered the boat with the full determination to do so, if they refused to accompany her. They were at length fairly shamed into going along with her to the spot where the barn had grounded, and thus actually rescued the whole family from their perilous situation. I wonder you did not see the account of it in the *Sydney Gazette*."

"You interest me very much in this person," said Mr. Barry; "she must be a very extraordinary woman."

"She is, indeed. But this is not the most extraordinary feat of her life. She is a convict, and was transported to this country for stealing a horse, and riding it a distance of seventy miles in one night."

"But how came you to know her?"

"She was recommended to me by Captain Sumpter, who conveyed her in his ship to this country, and gave her an excellent character. She was so highly mentioned in his letters, that I took her into the establishment at the Female Orphan Asylum, and found her all that I could desire, and much more than I could have had any reason to expect."

"Do you know what her character was in England?"

"Her whole history has been laid before me. And this I can conscientiously declare, that she was guilty of but one great error, which betrayed her into the commission of an offence for which she was sent to this country. Her besetting sin was misplaced affection, an unaccountable attachment to an unworthy man. She stole a horse from her master to meet this lover in London, and was sentenced to death for so doing. She was reprieved, owing to her previous good character, and would never have been sent to this country, had she not been persuaded by the same man to break out of prison. She effected her escape from gaol, and would have got clear out of the country, but for the activity of a young man (by-the-by, a namesake of yours) in the coastguard, who shot her lover in a skirmish on the sea-shore ; and then she was retaken, tried a second time, and a second time condemned to death ; but her sentence was commuted to transportation for life."

On looking on the countenance of Mr. Barry at this moment, Mrs. Palmer was surprised to see it deadly pale.

"You are ill, sir," she exclaimed ; "pray let me send for assistance."

"No, no, I thank you ; I shall be better presently. A little faintness came over me, doubtless from the interest I feel in the history you have related to me."

With great effort Mr. Barry commanded himself, as he said in a trembling voice, "And the name of this singular person is——"

"Margaret Catchpole," replied Mrs. Palmer, as he seemed to pause.

Overpowered by emotion of the most conflicting kind, Mr. Barry was completely unmanned. Accustomed for so long a time to smother his affections, he now found his heart bursting with the fullness of agony at finding the being so highly recommended to him, and one whom he had never ceased to love—*a convict.*

"Oh, my respected friend ! " he exclaimed, "I loved that woman long before I came to this country. I love her still—I confess I love her now ; I cannot, I do not, from all I know of her, and from all you tell me, believe her to be an abandoned character ;—but she is a convict."

"Alas! she is," replied Mrs. Palmer. "You astonish, you amaze me, Mr. Barry. Does she know your situation in this country?"

"I should think not, for I have had no information of hers up to this time. You must know that I would have brought her out to this country as my wife, but she was then attached to another. That other, I fear, was shot by my brother. He was a smuggler, and my brother was in the preventive service. She may not retain any feeling towards me but respect."

"I have never heard her mention your name, nor had I the slightest hint of these circumstances. I do not think she dreams of your existence. This is a large country, Mr. Barry, and if your name and fame in it have ever reached her ear, depend upon it she does not think that you are the person who once addressed her. But if she should hear it, I can tell you that she is so truly humble a creature, that she would think it presumption even to fancy that you could still love her. She is the meekest and most affectionate creature I ever knew."

"I can believe it, if she is anything like what I remember of her; she is warm-hearted, honest, open, and sincere, but uneducated."

"She is all the first-mentioned, but far, very far from being the last. In some things she is as well informed as ourselves, and in the best of all books she is really well read. She daily reads and understands her Bible. Her mistress, copies of whose letters I can show you, instructed her with her own children; and I can assure you, that in nothing but the want of station is she inferior to the best of her sex."

After the first struggles of his emotion were over, Mr. Barry made a complete confidante of Mrs. Palmer, and at once revealed to her the state of his own feelings respecting Margaret; and she fully explained to him what had been the excellent conduct of the object of his affection since her residence in that country. After hearing her statement, and appearing to consider within himself for a brief space, he said—

" I think I have sufficient interest with the governor to obtain her free pardon. If you can furnish me with the numbers of the *Sydney Gazette* in which she is mentioned, I will urge upon that humane man the policy of rewarding such an example as that which she set in rescuing the lives of Mr. Lacey and his family from the flood. I will take your recommendation, also, to the governor, and see what may be done. In the meantime, I beg you to take the earliest opportunity of mentioning my name to her in any manner you may think best. My mind is made up. If I procure her pardon, and she will listen to me favourably, I will marry her. You may tell her so, if you find her favourably disposed towards me."

That very day the good Mrs. Palmer wrote the following note to Margaret Catchpole :—

" SYDNEY, Sept. 21, 1811.

" MY GOOD MARGARET,

" I desire to see you at Sydney, and have sent a conveyance for you that you may not be oppressed with the journey. I have something particular to communicate, but shall not tell you by letter what it is, that you may not be over-anxious. I shall simply call it a matter of most momentous business, which concerns both you and me, and also a third person. Your attendance here will greatly facilitate the settlement of the affair. And in the meantime, believe me,

" Your sincere friend,
" ELIZA PALMER.

" To MARGARET CATCHPOLE, Richmond Hill."

It was indeed a great piece of news which this kind-hearted woman had to communicate to her husband. Still he was not so surprised as she expected him to have been.

" I have always thought, from his manner, that Mr. Barry had some strong and secret attachment in England. I fancied that he was in love with some damsel of high birth in his native country ; and truly do I think him worthy of any lady's hand. I little dreamed, however, of his real position. He is a good man, and will make a most excellent member of our highest society, and will exalt any woman he may take to be wife. But how do you think Margaret is affected towards him ? "

" It is that very thing I wish to know. I cannot really tell. She has been as great an exclusive in her way as he has been in his ; and I confess that my present opinion is, that she will never marry."

" She would really be to blame if she did not. I think this match would tend to soothe that growing distance and disrespect which exists between the emancipated and the free settlers. At all events, it is highly honourable and noble in our excellent friend."

" I think she would be wrong to refuse such an offer. But she has shown herself so independent, that unless a real affection should exist, I feel persuaded that she will live at Richmond Hill in preference to Windsor Lodge. I expect her here to-morrow, as I have sent the chaise for her."

Mr. Barry repaired to the governor's house and had a long interview with him. He had some general business to speak of and several public matters to arrange ; but he made haste to come to the case of a female convict, Margaret Catchpole, which he laid before the governor with such zeal, that the latter could not help observing the deep interest he took in her behalf.

" Has your honour seen the nature of the offence for which she was transported, or ever heard of the motive which prompted it ? I have brought testimony sufficient to corroborate my account of her. I have the letters of recommendation for good conduct during her voyage to this country. I have the highest character to give of her all the time she has been with Mrs. Palmer, and a particular instance of personal courage and self-devotion, in saving the lives of a whole family in the late dreadful flood. Her present situation is so highly respectable, and exhibits such an instance of moral and religious influence triumphant over the dangers of a degraded position, that, when I heard of it, I could not fail to lay it before your honour."

"And a most admirable advocate would you have made at the bar, Mr. Barry. You have pleaded this young woman's case with such fervour, that positively, but for your well-known character in the colony, I should suspect you had some private interest in obtaining her pardon. I do think, however, that the case is a very proper one for merciful consideration, and highly deserving of the exercise of that prerogative which the government at home has attached to my power; and I shall certainly grant a free pardon. But, without any intention of being too inquisitive, may I candidly tell you, that from the animated manner in which you have spoken of the virtues of this said female, I am induced to ask, why you have taken such a peculiarly personal interest in her favour?"

"I will honestly confess at once that I ask it upon the most self-interested grounds possible: I intend to offer her my hand."

The governor looked all astonishment. "What? Do I really hear it, or is it a dream? You, Mr. Barry, the highest, and wealthiest, and most prudent bachelor in the settlement, one who might return to England and be one of her wealthiest esquires; and here, enjoying more reputation, with less responsibility, than the governor—you about to form a matrimonial alliance with——"

The governor paused; he found his own eloquence carrying him too far; he considered the character of the man before him, knew the excellence of his principles and his heart, and dreaded to wound his generous soul; he changed his tone, but not the earnestness of his appeal.

"Have you well weighed this matter, Mr. Barry? Have you consulted with your friends around you? You are not the man to be caught by outward appearances, nor to be smitten by passing beauty without some qualities of domestic happiness, arising from temper, mind, character, and disposition. How long has this attachment been in existence ? "

" From my youth, your honour : I have not yet seen her since that happy time when she was a free woman in my native land, enjoying that honest liberty which is the pride and glory of England's virtuous daughters of every station in the land. I was then in her own condition of life. We had both to earn our bread by the labour of our hands ; we both respected each other : would I could say that we had both loved each other ! I should not like to see her again until I can look upon her as a free woman, and it is in your power to make her that happy being, upon whom I may look, as I once did, with the warmest affection."

" I ask no more, Mr. Barry, I ask no more. You have been an enigma to many of us ; it is now solved. It gives me real pleasure to oblige you, and in such a case as this the best feelings of my heart are abounding for your happiness. Her freedom is granted. To whom shall I commit the pardon ? "

" Will you permit me to take it ? "

" Most gladly."

The governor's secretary was immediately summoned, and the form of pardon duly signed, sealed, and delivered to the joyful hand of Mr. John Barry.

" And now," said the governor, " permit me to say that we shall at all times be happy to receive you at Sydney ; and in any way in which you can find my countenance and support serviceable, I shall always be ready to give them."

A cordial shake of the hand was mutually exchanged, and Mr. Barry returned that day to Windsor Lodge one of the happiest, as far as hope and good deeds can make a man so, on this changing earth.

He had communicated his success to Mrs. Palmer before he left Sydney. The green hills of Hawkesbury never looked so bright in his eye before, his house never so pleasant.

His servants saw an evident change in his manner, from the anguish of mourning for the loss of a sister, to what they could not quite comprehend; a state of liveliness they had never before witnessed in him. Their master never appeared so interested about the house, the rooms, the garden, and the green lawn. He was most unusually moved; he gave orders for the preparation of his house to receive his brother-in-law's children, to the great amazement of his female domestics, who could not conceive how a bachelor would manage such a family.

He did not breathe a word of his intention to any of his domestics; but every one observed a great change in his behaviour, which all his habitual quietude could not entirely conceal.

He wandered down to his favourite spot upon the river, and indulged in a reverie of imaginary bliss, which, to say the truth, was more real with him than with many thousands who fancy themselves in love.

Margaret arrived at Sydney on the day following the receipt of Mrs. Palmer's letter. She was a little excited at the tone of that epistle, but much surprised at being received in a manner to which she had never been accustomed. Margaret saw in a moment, from Mrs. Palmer's manner, that she had something to communicate of a very different kind to what she had before mentioned, and at once said—

"I perceive, my dear lady, that you have something to say to me which concerns me more than you wish to let me see it does, and yet you cannot conceal it. You need not be afraid to tell me; good or bad, I am prepared for it, but suspense is the most painful."

"The news I have to tell you then is good; to be at once declared—it is your free pardon!"

"This is news indeed, my dearest lady; almost too good news—it comes so unlooked for; forgive my tears." Margaret wept for joy.

"Shall I again see dear old England? shall I again see my dear friends, my mistress, my uncle, aunt, and family? Oh! how shall I ever repay your kindness?

Oh! what can I say to you for your goodness? On my knees, I thank God, my good friend, and say, God be praised for His mercies, and bless you, the instrument thereof!"

"You may thank God; but you must not bless me, Margaret, for I am only the bearer of the news. I have not even got the pardon in my possession; but I have seen it. It is signed by the governor, and I know that you are free."

"Oh! thanks, dear lady, thanks!—but is it not to Mr. Palmer that I am indebted? You must have had something to do with it."

"Nothing farther than the giving you a just character to the governor by the hand of a gentleman, who has interceded with him, and has pleaded your cause successfully."

"Who is the gentleman? Do I know him?"

"Yes, you may know him when you see him. He read the account of your saving the family of the Laceys in the flood; he listened with attention to your former history: he does not live in Sydney, but at Windsor, on the Hawkesbury; yet, from his interest with the governor, he obtained your pardon."

"Bless the dear gentleman! How shall I ever be grateful enough to him? But you say I know him?"

"I say I think you will. I know you did once know him, but you have not seen him for many years."

"Who can it be, dear lady? You do not mean my brother Charles?"

"No."

"Who then can it be? Not my former master, or any of his family?"

"No, Margaret; I must be plainer with you. Do you remember a young man of the name of Barry?"

"John Barry! Yes, I do. What of him? He went to Canada."

"No, he did not. He came to this country, has lived in it many years, and has prospered greatly. He is in the confidence of the governor. He accidentally discovered you were in the country. He it was—yes, he it was—who went that very hour to the governor, and I have no doubt asked it as a personal favour to himself that you should be pardoned. What say you to such a man ? "

" All that I can say is to bless him with a most grateful heart. Oh ! dear lady, he saved my life once, and now he gives me liberty ! He was a good young man ; too good for such as me to think upon, though he once would have had me think more of him. I had forgotten all but his kindness, which I never can forget ; and now it overwhelms me with astonishment. Is he married, and settled in this country ? "

" He is settled, but not married. He has been a prosperous man, and is as benevolent as he is rich ; but he never married, at which we have all wondered."

This declaration made Margaret blush ; a deep crimson flush passed over her cheeks, and was succeeded by extreme paleness. Her heart heaved convulsively, a faintness and dizziness came upon her, and she would really have fallen had she not been supported by the kind attentions of her benefactress.

" He has kept his word ! Oh, Mrs. Palmer ! I never thought to see him again. I mistook the country he left me for. I have often thought of his goodness to me in former days. I am now indebted to him for double life ! "

" Margaret, what if I tell you that for you only has he kept himself single ? "

" There was a time when he might and did think of me ; but that time must be gone by."

" I tell you, he loves you still."

" Impossible ! Oh, if he does !—but it is impossible ! Madam, this is all a dream ! "

" It is a dream, Margaret, from which you will shortly awake, as he is in the house at this moment to present himself with the governor's pardon ! "

" Dear lady, pray be present with me ; I know not how to meet him ! "

The door just then opened, and in came Mr. Barry,

with the governor's pardon in his hand. He approached
Margaret, as she clung to Mrs. Palmer, agitated beyond
measure. She regarded him with more solemn feelings
than she did the judge who condemned her twice to
death. She dropped upon her knees, and hid her face
before her deliverer. He lifted her up and seated her,
and, in the language of gentleness and tenderness,
addressed her thus:—

"Margaret, I have brought you a free pardon from
the governor. Need I remind you that God has mercifully sent me before you in this instance to be your
friend ? To Him I know you will give all the thanks and
praises of a grateful heart."

"To Him I do first, sir ; and to you, as his instrument, in the next place. I am afraid to look upon you,
and I am unworthy to be looked upon by you. I
am a —— "

"You need not tell me, Margaret, what you have
been. I know all. Think not of what you were, but
what you are. You are no longer a convict ; you are
no longer under the ban of disgrace ; you are no
longer under the sentence of the offended laws of man ;
you are now a free subject ; and if your fellow-creatures
do not all forgive you, they cannot themselves hope for
forgiveness. You are at liberty to settle wherever you
please."

"Oh ! dear sir ; and to you I owe all this ! What
will they say to you in England, when I again embrace
my dear friends there, and bless you for the liberty thus
granted me ? "

"Margaret, hear me again. Remember, when I last
saw you, I told you then what I dreaded, if you refused
to come out to this country with me. How true those
fears were, you can now judge. You made a choice
then which gave me anguish to be surpassed only by
the present moment. You speak now of returning to
England. You have got your pardon, and are at
liberty so to do. It may seem ungenerous to me, at
such a moment, to urge your stay ; but hear now my
opinion and advice, and give them the weight only of

your calm judgement. If you return to England, take
my word for it you will not be happy. You will never
be as happy as you may be here. I speak this with
feelings as much alive to your interest now as they
were when I last parted with you. I will suppose you
returned. Your own good heart makes you imagine
that every one would be as glad to see you there as
you would truly be to see them. Your own heart
deceives you. I have known those who so bitterly
lamented their return to England, that they have
come again to settle in this country, and have offended
those friends who would have respected them had they
remained here. When at a distance they felt much
for them ; but when they came near to them, the
pride of society made them ashamed of those who
had been convicts. It may be that some would be
glad to see you ; your good mistress, your uncle and
aunt : but circumstances might prevent their being
able to do you any great service. Your former mistress
has a large family, your uncle the same ; you have no
independence to live upon there. The eye of envy
would be upon you if you had wealth, and detraction
would be busy with your name. People would talk of
your sins, but would never value you for your integrity.
You would probably soon wish yourself in this country
again, where your rising character would be looked
upon with respect, and all the past be forgiven, and in
time forgotten. Here you would have an established
character : there you would always be thought to have
a dubious one. Besides all this, you are here prosper-
ing. You can have the great gratification of relieving
the necessities of your aged relatives, and of obliging
your best friends. You would, believe me, be looked
upon by them with far greater respect and esteem than
if you were nearer to them. Think, Margaret, of what
I now state, and divest yourself of that too great idea
of happiness in England. You are at liberty to go ;
but you will enjoy far greater liberty if you stay in
this country."

   " What you say, sir, may be true in some respects ;

but I think I should die happy if I once more saw my dear friends and relatives."

"God forbid that I should not approve your feeling! I, too, have a father, and mother, and brothers in England, but I hear from them continually, and they rejoice in my welfare. I love them dearly as they do me. Two sisters have come out to me, and both have married and settled in the country. One I have lost, who has left a husband and seven children to lament her loss. I have strong ties, you see, in these young people, to bind me to this country, for they look up to me as they do to their father. But they are without female protection."

"If, my dear sir, I can be of any service to you or them for a term of years, I shall feel it part of the happiness of that freedom you have obtained for me to abide as long in this land. But I own that I still feel that I should like to return one day to England. I am very grateful for all your goodness, and shall ever bless you for the interest you have taken in one so unworthy your favour."

"Margaret, I am deeply interested in these children. They have lost their mother, my sister. Their aunt, now resident in the colony, has ten children of her own, and it would not be fair that she should take seven more into her house. The young man, now left a widower, is in such a delicate state of health, and so disconsolate for the loss of his wife, that I do not think he will be long amongst us. These circumstances made me come to my good friend Mrs. Palmer for assistance and advice. Guess, then, my astonishment to hear you recommended to me: you, above all people in the world, whose presence I could have wished for, whose gentleness I know, and who, if you will, can make both myself and all these children happy."

"My dear sir, I stand in a very different position with regard to yourself to what I formerly did. I do not forget that to your protecting arm I owe the rescue of my life from the violence of one in whom my misplaced confidence became my ruin and his own death.

I never can forget that to you I am a second time indebted for liberty, and that which will sweeten the
remainder of my days: the consciousness of being
restored, a pardoned penitent, to virtuous society.
But I cannot forget that I am still but little better
than a slave: I am scarcely yet free. I am not, as
I was when you first offered me your hand and heart,
upon an equality with yourself. How then can you
ask me to become your wife, when there is such a disparity as must ever make me feel your slave? No,
generous and good man! I told you formerly that if
Laud were dead I might then find it in my heart to
listen to your claims; but I never thought that I
should be in a situation so much beneath you as I am,
so very different to that which I once occupied."

"And do you think, Margaret, that I can ever forget
that I was a fellow-servant with you at the Priory
Farm, upon the banks of the Orwell? It was then
I first made known to you the state of that heart which,
as I told you long ago, would never change towards
you. You say that our conditions are so very dis-
similar: I see no great difference in them; certainly
no greater than when you lived at the cottage on the
heath and I was the miller's son. You are independent
now. Your good friend, Mrs. Palmer, has made you
so, and will permit me to say, that you have already
an independence in this country far greater than ever
you could enjoy in England."

Margaret looked at Mrs. Palmer. That good woman
at once confessed that all the rent that Margaret had
paid for the years she had been in the farm was now
placed in the Sydney bank, to her account, and quite
at her disposal. She added, that she had made over
the estate she occupied at Richmond Hill to her for
ever.

What could Margaret now say? She found herself
on the one hand made free, through the intercession
of a man who loved her, and on the other she was made
independent for life by a lady who had only known
her in her captivity, but who had respected and

esteemed her. That lady now thought it time to speak out.

"Margaret, do not think that I have given you anything more than what you are strictly entitled to. Remember that, from a sense of justice towards me, you refused the hand of a man who probably would have settled all the estate upon you. But you chose to think yourself unworthy of my kindness had you accepted his offer. You acted with great discretion; and in settling this small portion upon you, I was guided by a sense of justice and gratitude, which made me anxious to discharge a just debt, and I do not consider that I have even given you as much as I ought to have done."

"Indeed, you have, dear lady, and you have bound me to you for ever. Have I, indeed, such dear friends in this country? Then do I feel it my duty to remain in it, and I will learn to sigh no longer after that place where I had so long hoped to live and die. You give me, however, more credit for refusing the hand of Mr. Poinder than I deserve: I never could have married a man who, in such an imperious manner, gave me to understand his will. No; I was his servant, but not his slave. And any woman who would obey the nod of a tyrant, to become his wife, could never expect to enjoy any self-estimation afterwards. He told me his intention of making me his wife in such an absolute way that I quite as absolutely rejected him. I deserve no credit for this."

"Margaret," said Mr. Barry, "understand the offer I now make you. If you are not totally indifferent to all mankind, and can accept the offer of one whose earliest affections you commanded, then know that those affections are as honest, and true, and faithful to you this day, as they were when I first addressed you. Think me not so ungenerous as ever to appeal to any sense of gratitude on your part. You cannot conceive what unspeakable pleasure I have always thought it to serve you in any way I might. You cannot tell how dead I have been to every hope but that of being enabled to do good to others. This has been my purest solace under your loss, Margaret; and if in daily remembrance of you I have done thus much, what will not your presence always urge me to perform?

"I sought a servant, a confidential kind of friend, to govern my brother's household: I little thought that I should find the only person I ever could or would make my wife. I offer you, then, myself and all my possessions. I am willing to make over all I have, upon the contract that you become the aunt of those dear children, and I know you too well ever to doubt your kindness to them.

"As to your respectability, I have already declared to the governor my full intention of offering you this hand. He has promised to recognize you as my wife. Your friend here will not like you the less because you are so nearly allied to me; and I will answer for all my relatives and friends. None will ever scorn you, all will respect you, I will love you. Say, then, will you live my respected wife at Windsor Lodge, or will you still live alone at Richmond Hill?"

"It is you must choose," replied Margaret; "I cannot refuse. I never can doubt you. I will endeavour to fulfil the station of a mother in that of an aunt; and if my heart does not deceive me, I shall do my duty as an honest wife."

After this explanation, it is needless, perhaps, to add that Margaret Catchpole changed her name, and became the much-respected and beloved wife of John Barry, Esq., of Windsor, by the Green Hills of Hawkesbury.

CHAPTER XXXI

CONCLUSION

IF true love and constancy are noble qualities in the heart of man, and prompt him to deeds of generous philanthropy, they deserve to be recorded and imitated from the example of John Barry. And if sincerity and repentance be qualities worthy the charitable consideration of good Christians, Margaret Catchpole's career in this life, and especially her latter days, will not afford a bad example of the promise of " the life that now is, and of that which is to come." The remaining history of this singular individual was one of quiet calm, and yet benevolent exertion in all good works of faith and love. She lived highly respected in the situation to which her husband's good qualities and good fortune had raised her. She lived a retired, though not a secluded life, on the banks of the Hawkesbury, fulfilling the duties of her station as a good wife, aunt, sister, and mother, in an exemplary manner. Charitable as she was rich, she never thought she could do enough to relieve the distresses of others.

Not many months after her marriage she received another chest of goods from her benevolent mistress in England, and wrote her last epistle of thanks, dated

" WINDSOR, HAWKESBURY, June 25th, 1812.

" MY DEAR MADAM,

" The contents of this letter will surprise you. I hope that I am not the less grateful for your goodness because God has blessed me with such abundance, that I no longer require that aid from England which has hitherto been such a blessing to me. Indeed, my dearest madam, my good and early friend, I am most grateful for all your past favours, though I do not wish to tax a generosity which I do not now, in the same manner, need. May Heaven bless your warm heart, which will glow with fervent praise to God when you read this letter from your former poor servant!

"Everything that I could wish for, and, oh! how much more than I deserve, have I had granted to me in this place of probation! God grant I may not set my heart too much upon their value! Dearest lady, I have men-servants and maid-servants, horses and cattle, flocks and herds in abundance. I have clothing and furniture above what you can imagine, and a house wide enough to entertain in it all your numerous family. But, more than all this, I have an excellent husband, one whose constancy from his youth has been beyond the praise which I could find language to express.

"You may remember what I once told you of a young man whom I had rejected for a less worthy one. He has proved his love for me in such a manner as I am sure could never have been seen in any but the most noble of his nature. He told me in England that he would never marry any other, and through years of industry and prosperity (and as I have every reason to believe he would have done to the last day of this life) has kept himself single on my account. Did you ever chance to hear of such a case as this? When I reflect upon it, as I often do, I find it more and more wonderful.

"You must remember my telling you of Mr. John Barry's attachment to me. He left me when I lived at Nacton, and came out here among the earliest free settlers in the country, and has prospered beyond his utmost anticipations. He found me out here by accidental inquiries of my dear Mrs. Palmer, and obtained for me my free pardon. My wishes to return again to my native land became absorbed in the sense of duty and obligation to my benefactor, who, when he had obtained that pardon, gave me the option of sharing my life and freedom with him, or of being independent here or elsewhere. Noble generosity! Does it not win your heart? It won mine. I am his faithful wife: happy, happy, as the days are long. He is good, virtuous, amiable, and truly religious; constant in his love to God and man. I could fill many letters in speaking of his virtues; but I forget that you never saw him, though he lived upon the shores of the same river that you do.

"He is very good to me, so that I want nothing more from England. How proud shall I be to send you now anything which this country produces!

"Herewith I send you a sketch of my present beautiful abode, done by Mrs. Palmer. It will give you a slight idea of my situation. I send you also a present of various seeds, skins of animals (one of the ursine opossum), and dried plants, which I think will be valuable to you; and also some curious weapons and instruments of the natives, for my dear friend, Dr. Stebbing.

"What a wonderful life has mine been! You only, my dear lady, know its reality. There may be others equally eventful; but how few are there who find such a place of unmerited repose as I have? My dear sister's words often recur to my mind when she told me whom I should not marry: I wonder if she ever thought of the one I have married. There are many very excellent people in this flourishing country. The governor and his family have received us, and have been very kind to me. My dear friend, Mrs. Palmer, is now staying in my house. She is my benefactress here, as you were in England. Oh! if I could but bring you both together, and could sit quietly listening to your conversation, it would be such an intellectual treat as few could more enjoy! She is, like yourself, very clever. I believe I should die happier if I could see your dear, loved face in this land; but if that never may be, nor I see old England again, then may Heaven bless you; and God bestow His brightest gifts of grace upon you and your children!

"I am this moment engaged, and lay down my pen to give directions concerning the work in that most interesting of all female employments, preparing for the coming of a family of my own. Mrs. Palmer, who sees me writing these words, says, 'How astonished you will be!' You will rejoice in my happiness. I know you will. Forgive, dear lady, all my errors, both of the weakness of my head and heart. Give my love to all my dear friends. Any person coming to this country, with a recommendation from you to me, will find the warmest reception. In justice to my husband, I would forget what I have been, and I speak seldom of my past errors, though, before God, I never cease to lament and repent of them; and did I not know who 'died for the ungodly,' my grief for the past would be without consolation. Blessed faith, that teaches the contrite how to be comforted! Who can value Thee as he ought in this struggling state!

"I can add but a few more words, and I do so with tears and trembling. It is not from pride of heart. Dear lady, you must judge of its propriety. I am likely to increase my family; and I would conceal from them, in future years, their mother's early history, at least those parts which are so unworthy to be mentioned. But I feel that my maiden name cannot be forgotten in your neighbourhood. Hundreds will speak of it when you and I shall be no more. Oh that it could be represented to the world in its proper light, as a warning to that portion of my countrywomen to which I belonged, that they never give way to their headstrong passions, lest they fall as I did! But 'the tender mercies of God are over all His works,' and I can never magnify that mercy too much, as it has been shown to me.

"If, dear lady, as years increase, our correspondence should not be so frequent, because of my altered situation in this country, do not think me proud. Your feelings as a mother will point to the nature of my own. You would not have your children know your faults. Pardon this, perhaps, my greatest weakness.

"Should you ever think fit, as you once hinted in your letter to me, to write my history, or should leave it to others to publish, you have my free permission at my decease, whenever that shall take place, so to do. But let my husband's name be concealed. Change it, change it to any other; not for his sake, for it is worthy to be written in golden characters, but for mine and my children's sake! And now, dear lady, farewell. God's peace be with you! and ever think of me as

"Your grateful and affectionate servant,
"MARGARET BARRY."

So ends the correspondence of Margaret with her mistress. That lady wrote one more letter to her, assuring her of her joy and thankfulness at her providential settlement in the land of her adoption. She told her that she had kept the early facts of her history in such order, that on some future day they might perhaps be published, but that her wishes should be strictly attended to, and her parental anxieties respected. She took an affectionate leave of her in that last letter, promising not to intrude anything of past obligation upon her notice, but leaving it entirely to her own heart to recognize any friends of hers, from the county of Suffolk, who might, either in military, naval, or civil capacity, go out to Sydney. How delicately those wishes were observed, some can well remember.

Margaret Barry lived many years at Windsor, greatly respected and beloved. She had one son and two daughters, who received the best education which England could afford, and returned to settle in their native land. Among the foremost for intelligence, benevolence, activity, and philanthropy, is the distinguished son of Margaret; and in the future history of Australia he will bear no unimportant share in her celebrity and greatness. The daughters are amiable and accomplished, and have married gentlemen of the first respectability in the country.

After fifteen years of the tenderest and most uninterrupted domestic comfort, Margaret had the severe affliction to undergo of losing her devoted and excellent husband, who died September 9th, 1827, leaving the bulk of his property at her disposal. She removed to Sydney in 1828, where she was conspicuous only for the mildness of her manners, and the unostentatious character of her habits of life.

She had a great desire that her son should settle in her native county of Suffolk, and he came over to this country with that view; and when the sale of Kentwell Hall took place, he was nearly the last bidder for it. His resolution, however, seemed to fail him at the last moment, and he did not become the purchaser of the estate. He stayed a year in England, and then returned, with a determination not to settle in any other country than his native one. He returned to close the eyes of his affectionate parent, who died September 10th, 1841, in the sixty-eighth year of her age.

SUPPLEMENT

BY THE AUTHOR

A. D. 1858

SINCE the first publication of the *Life of Margaret Catchpole*, many have been the correspondents who have addressed the author upon the subject of her life and character. Many have been the inquiries made concerning her, and many things, which the author never heard of her, have since come to light. They would fill a volume. The author has no intention of inflicting any further pain upon the sensitive minds of some, who, in writing to him, have quite overlooked the idea that he, the author, had any sensitiveness whatsoever. He has no intention of reviving any feeling of the past, respecting what may or may not be mere local descriptive scenic representation; but there are certain moral representations which the author gave, both of her early respectability and character, which he deems it but a mere act of common justice to her memory to substantiate, and thus furnish the only defence which can ever be in his power to make against those who accused him of wilful misrepresentation. Though all the documents relating to this extraordinary female are duly filed and preserved,—and her own letters in her own handwriting have been transmitted for inspection to several inquirers,—there are some facts which may be interesting as proof positive of the assertions contained in the narrative. To a few of such the author now refers the reader.

The first is a letter from the Reverend William Tilney Spurdens, formerly head-master of the Grammar School at North Walsham, Norfolk; a celebrated scholar, the translator of Longinus, the early and beloved tutor and friend of the author. This gentleman had an uncle at Brandiston in Suffolk, with whom he used to stay, and to that uncle and to Peggy's aunt he refers in this letter.

"NORTH WALSHAM, 30th Oct. 1846.

"MY DEAR FRIEND,

"I cannot delay to put you in possession of my '*love-passages*' with your heroine, albeit, at this present writing, suffering much pain from asthma and chronic bronchitis, which are both aggravated by our foggy air for some days past.

"In my early childhood I had an uncle, an aged widower with no family, who did me the favour of being very fond of me. He had one domestic in his house, and another out of it, the former a female, the latter a male. The former rejoiced in the name of Nanny, I suppose there was another postfixed to it, but of this I am not cognizant: but Nanny had a niece, or cousin, or something of the kind, named *Peggy Catchpole*; and whenever the old uncle's favourite paid him a visit, the maid's paid a visit to her, '*for*,' as Nanny used to say, '*it was so comfortable for the children, like; and the little dears helped to amuse one another;*' and so it was that Peg and I walked together, played together, and slept together.

"I wish I could give you dates, which are the sinews of history, you know. There is one event which my mind connects very exactly with this period, and which will afford you one date. Peggy and her young swain were going on philandering at supper, at the time of the loss of the *Royal George*, at Spithead. The newspaper came in while my good relative was playing a hit at backgammon with his neighbour, the doctor, as was their frequent practice; and by dint of spelling, and a lift or two over hard words, I read to them the mournful narrative. For this I received sixpence, and laid it out in figs, of which Peg and her swain each ate so many as to make themselves ill.

"Now all this would unquestionably have been forgotten, had it not been made fresh in the memory from Peggy's subsequent career. Whilst she was in Ipswich Gaol I made interest with the personage, then usually called '*Old Rip*,' to see her, intending to give her money. I must then have been a young man. She, however, would not know anything of me—in fact, '*cut me*:' and so I kept my money. But I afterwards learned that Ripshaw would not have permitted it to be given! '*And that's all.*'

"I am afraid that, with all the exuberance of your imagination, you would be puzzled to concoct a chapter out of this.

"I am beginning to long for our young friend's visit in order to my introduction to your other heroine.

"Meanwhile I am,
"My dear Sir,
"Yours very truly,
"W. T. SPURDENS."

There is no need to concoct a chapter out of this letter. It is the genuine offering of a kind heart and clear head, and sufficiently explains the purpose in view; viz. that Margaret was regarded in her early career with respect and pure affection, by one who sought to relieve her in her distress, and in a day of degradation and adversity owned her as his early play-mate, and would have ministered to her necessity. Both, I trust, are now awaiting that final day when the cup of cold water, given with a good heart for Christ's sake, shall meet with a blessed reward.

The second letter is from a gentleman in Lincolnshire, a solicitor and banker, and speaks of the career of that brother Edward who is mentioned in the narrative.

" ALFORD, LINCOLNSHIRE, 10th Dec. 1846.

" SIR,

" I have lately read the *Life of Margaret Catchpole*, and was deeply interested in it. Her brother *Edward* was several years in the preventive service in this neighbourhood, at Sutton-in-the-Marsh, about six miles hence, where he died and was buried a few years ago.

" I often saw him in his rounds on the sea-coast, and have had conversations with him. He was rather a tall person, and of stern manners. I could readily obtain a copy of the inscription on his grave-stone, which refers to his former residence at Ipswich, and forward it to you, should you wish it. His widow, who was a Norwich person, still lives in this neighbourhood.

" I remain, Sir,
" Your very obedient servant,
" HENRY T. BOURNE.

" REV. RICH. COBBOLD,
" Wortham Rectory,
" Diss, Norfolk.

" P.S. Since writing the above I have heard that Mr. Edward Catchpole became a decidedly religious character for the last few years of his life, and died a very happy death."

From the same gentleman is the memoir here inserted of Margaret's brother Edward, obtained from an authenticated source, the substance of which is given in a note, page 294.

" Mr. Edward Catchpole was born near Ipswich in Suffolk, in the year 1778. Of his early days we know but little; he was led to choose a sea-faring life in preference to any other line of business; he served an apprenticeship on board a merchant ship. Some time afterwards he became mate on board the *Argus* Revenue Cutter, of Harwich. Whilst in this service, a most interesting circumstance occurred, which deserves to be noticed. Sept. 18th, 1807, the *Argus* succeeded in rescuing an English coal-brig from the *Star*, French privateer. Having put some men on board the brig, elated with success, they go in pursuit of the privateer. They soon fall in with her, and a sharp engagement ensues, and at 10 o'clock at night the captor was captured; they came to close quarters, and, owing to the great disparity in numbers, the privateer having eighty-six men, and the cutter only twenty-seven, they were boarded, overpowered, taken into a French port, and sent to prison. Mr. C. was about seven years in a French prison. Frequently his expectations were raised by hopes of liberation, an exchange of prisoners was often talked of, but still they were kept in bondage and suspense. A favourable opportunity occurring, he made his escape, and came over to England, His arrival at home was so sudden and unexpected to his wife, that he seemed to her almost like one come from the dead. Subsequently he was appointed chief officer in the Coastguards; his last station was at Sutton-in-the-Marsh, in the county of Lincoln; there his health failed, and there he finished his earthly course, and made a good end. His conversion to God was most satisfactory. In his affliction the Lord graciously supported him, he had a hope full of immortality, and his end was peace. He died on the 17th of December, 1836. He changed mortality for life. He was interred in the churchyard at Sutton, and a stone has been placed at the head of his grave, with the following inscription:

IN MEMORY OF
EDWARD CATCHPOLE,
A NATIVE OF IPSWICH,
IN THE COUNTY OF SUFFOLK,
AND LATE CHIEF OFFICER OF THE
COAST GUARD
STATIONED AT THIS PLACE,
WHO DIED DECEMBER THE 17TH, 1836,
AGED 58 YEARS.

As some correspondents have actually accused the author of producing before the public a fictitious character, and in terms of unmeasured reprobation told him plainly that they understood there never was such a person as Margaret Catchpole in existence, the author here gives a copy of the document signed by her judge, the Lord Chief Baron Macdonald. This document was not obtained until after the publication of the work. The original is preserved in the Corporation Chest at Ipswich.

Copy of a Certificate from the Right Honourable Lord Chief Baron Macdonald, to exempt from all parish offices, for having prosecuted Margaret Catchpole at Bury Assizes, Aug. 11th, 1797.

" These are to certify, That at the delivery of the Gaol of our Lord the King, of the County of Suffolk, holden at Bury St. Edmunds, in the County aforesaid, on Wednesday, the ninth day of August instant, before me, whose name is hereunto subscribed, and other his Majesty's Justices, assigned to deliver the aforesaid Gaol of the Prisoners, therein being Margaret Catchpole, late of the Parish of St. Margaret, in the Town of Ipswich, in the County aforesaid, single woman, convicted of feloniously stealing a Gelding, of the price of twenty pounds, of the goods and chattels of John Cobbold, on the twenty-third day of May last, at the Parish aforesaid, in the Town and County aforesaid ; and that the said John Cobbold was the person who did apprehend and take the said Margaret Catchpole, and did prosecute her, so apprehended and taken, until she was convicted of the Felony. Therefore, in pursuance of an Act of Parliament made in the tenth and eleventh years of the reign of his late Majesty king William the Third, *intituled*, An Act for the better apprehending, prosecuting, and punishing of felons that commit burglary, housebreaking, or robbery, in shops, warehouses, coachhouses, or stables, or that steal horses ; I do hereby further certify, that by virtue hereof and of the said Act of Parliament, he, the said John Cobbold, shall and may be, and is hereby, discharged of and from all manner of Parish Offices within the Parish of St. Margaret, in the Town of Ipswich aforesaid, in the County aforesaid.

"In testimony whereof I have hereunto set my hand this eleventh day of August, in the year of our Lord one thousand seven hundred and ninety-seven.

"AR. MACDONALD."

The author now approaches a most painful, and yet he trusts a pleasurable, duty. Painful, because his own mind and that of others have been excessively hurt by a misconception of the identity of that Margaret Catchpole whose life he has written, and pleasurable, because of the opportunity afforded him of contradicting the fact so often asserted, that Mrs. Reibey of New Town, Sydney, was the identical Margaret Catchpole.

The relatives and friends of that highly-esteemed lady, lately deceased, will be glad to read a letter from the late Bishop of Australia, written to one of his clergy, the Rev. H. D. D. Sparling, of Appin, New South Wales, the good Bishop himself, as well as hundreds of others, having been deceived in that identity from a strange but very simple mistake, viz. that of two places bearing the same name in England, though one be in Suffolk, —Bury, and the other in Lancashire—*Bury*.

Hence originated the grand mistake concerning *Mrs. Reibey* who emigrated from *Bury* in Lancashire, and Margaret Catchpole, who was tried at Bury in Suffolk. It appears from original letters in the possession of the author, and from Mrs. Reibey's herself, that Suffolk was totally unknown to her. She was very justly hurt at presents being sent to her, under the idea that she was that poor girl, whose correspondence and gratitude to her benefactress, the late Mrs. Cobbold of Holywells, showed her to be honest and exemplary. She was justly hurt, because therein was the supposition that she had been tried and convicted as a felon, and was transported for horse-stealing.

The friends and relatives of Mrs. Reibey, as well as

all Christians, will be glad to read the amiable Bishops'
letter; and even the author, whom it condemns, gives
it to the public, because his own heart is in full accordance with the charity therein breathed; and he is
even more anxious to turn the hearts of that lady's
relatives in gratitude to that spirit and testimony
which this good man gives of all the branches of their
respectable family.

Notwithstanding the remonstrance conveyed in the
Bishop's letter, concerning the publication of the Life
of the real Margaret Catchpole, over which the author
had *then* no more control than he now has, he cannot
help here expressing his gratitude to all those who,
viewing the narrative in the light of truth, and intention
on the author's part to convey a moral and spiritual
warning and lesson in an easy and instructive style,
have written to him letters of approbation.

The Bishop's letter, whilst it will animate the hearts
of Mrs. Reibey's real relatives, will also speak equally
kindly to the descendants of the real Margaret Catchpole, and will be the author's best proof of his desire
to convey the Bishop's love to them along with his own.
The wildest olive, when grafted into the true stem,
must be productive of good fruit.

Mrs. Reibey, a high-spirited, romantic girl, from the
neighbourhood of Bury in Lancashire, of good family,
with friends and relatives of England's noblest merchants, conceived the idea that she should be happier
in our distant colony than in the Mother Country.
She left England very young, and, like many of her
sex, succeeded in proving that her enterprising spirit
was not unrewarded. She lived respected by her
family and friends in England, and although mistaken
by the good Bishop himself, yet noble testimony is
borne to the excellence of her character. She was a
clever woman of business, and of a noble disposition.
The author can only hope, that all her relatives and
friends who have written to him will thus accept at
his hands the apology for all the mistakes that have
arisen; whilst, at the same time, he rejoices to keep

concealed the name of Margaret's real descendants until they shall themselves divulge it.

"SYDNEY, 18th April, 1845.

"REVEREND SIR,

"I was very much vexed to learn from your letter of the 15th inst. the course which it is intended to be taken with reference to the publication named in the Prospectus which you forwarded, and which is now returned. My opinion entirely coincides with yours and Mr. Hossall's as to the inexpediency of such an undertaking. It would be cruel even to the individual, whoever it may be, to have early offences thus placed permanently on record as a memorial of shame and cause of annoyance to her younger and perfectly innocent connexions. Indeed, if the party meant be the one whom allusions in your letter lead me to conjecture, they who would suffer in their feelings are not only innocent, but praiseworthy in a very high degree for exertions in the cause of religion, and of the Church of England, scarcely to be paralleled by any instance I have ever known. The Bishop of Tasmania would regret equally with myself, perhaps even more, that any pain should be occasioned to parties so worthy of respect. If my conjecture be right, I happened once to be in circumstances which placed other members of the same family (young females just attaining to womanhood) under my close and special attention, and I can truly testify the impression by me was, that they were in character and deportment altogether unexceptionable, and in habits of devotion very exemplary. Others I know, are regarded by the clergyman of their parish as among the best instructed and sober-minded of the communicants in his church.

"My acquaintance with Mr. Cobbold is not such as I think would justify my taking any step which would so carry the air of remonstrance as that of my writing to him would.

"It appears to me that as you have, through various circumstances, been brought into correspondence with him, it would be more proper that you should make a statement of the true facts, and of the view which is taken of his proposal. At the same time, if you think it would strengthen your case if he were acquainted with my sentiments, I can have no objection to your communicating them; as all my statements to you upon the subject have been in accordance with them, and expressive of my satisfaction at witnessing the exemplary conduct of the individuals whom I suppose to be alluded to.

"I remain,

"Reverend Sir,

"Your very faithful servant,

"W. G. Australia.

"Rev. H. D. D. Sparling,

"Parsonage, Appin."

Mrs. Reibey is no more, and the author acknowledges the receipt of very satisfactory letters from her and her relatives, all conveying their free pardon for any unintentional pain, which might have been given to an innocent and praiseworthy individual, but assuredly they did not endure, and never could endure, the pangs which the author himself received at the very thought of giving pain to others.

He ever did admire the conduct of his mother towards her erring servant, believing it to be as magnanimous and Christian-like as that of the Bishop towards her supposed relatives, and though circumstances compelled the prosecution in question, and the very prevalence of the crime at the time made it too notorious to be disregarded,—the years of intercourse, and passing presents to and fro, between the prosecutor and the prisoner, made too deep an impression upon the young heart of the author to be obliterated even in these his old days.

He cannot help thinking that the removal of the *card* which was placed at the foot of the "Manura Superba," the first Lyra Pheasants sent from that country to England, as a present from Margaret

Catchpole to her mistress, and presented by Mrs. Cobbold's eldest son to the Ipswich Museum, simply because it stated the fact of her transportation, was, however kind in intention, a mistake in point of judgement. The object of all records of crime ought to be taken as warnings to others; though the simple fact of such birds being sent as a grateful present from a once poor transport, proves that the heart was not totally devoid of grace, and that we should ourselves be more glad to see such a noble token of love, in the days of poverty, than the most splendid monuments of accumulated wealth.

One duty only remains for the author, and that is the last and very simple one of gratitude to the memory of those who loved his mother, as well as to those living who were subscribers to the monument placed in the Tower Church, Ipswich, to her memory. That duty is simply to record the inscription engraved upon it; and the author does so, because, as years increase, so much the brighter in his mind is the memory of the talents and virtues of the departed.

AS A PUBLIC TESTIMONY OF RESPECT

FOR EXALTED TALENTS AND UNWEARIED EXERTION

IN THE CAUSE OF BENEVOLENCE AND CHARITY

THIS MONUMENT IS ERECTED BY THE GENERAL

CONCURRENCE OF AN EXTENSIVE CIRCLE OF FRIENDS

TO THE MEMORY OF

ELIZABETH COBBOLD

THE BELOVED WIFE OF JOHN COBBOLD, ESQ.

OF HOLYWELLS

SHE DIED OCTOBER XVII, MDCCCXIV

AGED LIX

Rectory, Wortham, Oct. 21st, 1858.

PRINTED IN GREAT BRITAIN AT THE UNIVERSITY PRESS, OXFORD
BY JOHN JOHNSON, PRINTER TO THE UNIVERSITY

A LIST OF THE

WORLD'S
CLASSICS

Oxford University Press

THE WORLD'S CLASSICS

A SERIES in constant progress, containing over four hundred volumes, and offering in a size adapted for the pocket, and at a low price, the most famous works in the English language, with more than a few translations. Many of the volumes contain introductions by the best modern writers.

POCKET SIZE, $6 \times 3\frac{3}{4}$ inches (as this list). Large type, on thin opaque paper, in superfine art cloth.

A NUMBER of the volumes are also obtainable in Pebble grain Moroccoette and in Natural grain Morocco. These are specially recommended for presentation.

THE VOLUMES are obtainable through any bookseller.

IN THE FOLLOWING LIST the books are classified as below:

Anthologies
Autobiography
Biography
Classics—Greek and Roman
Drama
Essays and Belles Lettres
Fiction (Short Stories are grouped separately)
History

Letters
Literary Criticism
Philosophy and Science
Poetry
Politics, Political Theory, and Political Economy
Religion
Short Stories
Travel and Topography

AN INDEX OF AUTHORS is given at the end of the list.

THE
WORLD'S CLASSICS

PRINTED ON OXFORD INDIA PAPER

The following Works are obtainable in superfine
maroon cloth, gilt lettered on back,
gilt top, and marker.

TWO VOLUMES IN ONE

BORROW. Lavengro *and* Romany Rye.

MAUDE (AYLMER). Life of Tolstoy.

TOLSTOY. Anna Karenina. Translated by *Louise*
and *Aylmer Maude.*

TROLLOPE. Last Chronicle of Barset.

„   Orley Farm.

THREE VOLUMES IN ONE

DANTE. The Divine Comedy. Italian text and
translation by *M. B. Anderson.*

ENGLISH SHORT STORIES (Nineteenth and Twentieth
Centuries).

RABELAIS (FRANÇOIS). Gargantua and Pantagruel.

TOLSTOY. War and Peace. Revised translation by
Louise and *Aylmer Maude.*

COMPLETE LIST OF THE SERIES

¶ *Anthologies*

A BOOK OF AMERICAN VERSE. Selected and edited by *A. C. Ward* (428).

A BOOK OF NARRATIVE VERSE. Compiled by *V. H. Collins*. Introduction by *Edmund Blunden* (350).

A BOOK OF SCOTTISH VERSE. Compiled by *R. L. Mackie* (417).

AMERICAN CRITICISM. Representative Literary Essays. Chosen by *Norman Foerster* (354).

ENGLISH ESSAYS, chosen and arranged by *W. Peacock* (32).

ENGLISH ESSAYS, 1600–1900, chosen by *S. V. Makower* and *B. H. Blackwell* (172).

ENGLISH ESSAYS, MODERN. Two Series. Selected by *H. S. Milford* (280, 406).

ENGLISH PROSE from MANDEVILLE to RUSKIN, chosen and arranged by *W. Peacock* (45).

ENGLISH PROSE, chosen and arranged by *W. Peacock* in 5 volumes: I, WYCLIFFE to CLARENDON; II, MILTON to GRAY; III, WALPOLE to LAMB; IV, LANDOR to HOLMES; V, MRS. GASKELL to HENRY JAMES (219–23).

ENGLISH PROSE, Narrative, Descriptive, Dramatic (MALORY to STEVENSON), compiled by *H. A. Treble* (204).

ENGLISH SONGS AND BALLADS, compiled by *T. W. H. Crosland*. New edition, with the text revised, and additional poems (13).

ENGLISH SHORT STORIES (Nineteenth and Twentieth Centuries), selected by *H. S. Milford*. Three Series (193, 228, 315).

ENGLISH VERSE. Edited by *W. Peacock*. I, Early Lyrics to SHAKESPEARE (308); II, CAMPION to the Ballads (309); III, DRYDEN to WORDSWORTH (310); IV, SCOTT to ELIZABETH BROWNING (311); V, LONGFELLOW to RUPERT BROOKE (312).

LETTERS WRITTEN IN WAR-TIME (Fifteenth to Nineteenth Centuries), selected and arranged by *H. Wragg* (202).

A MISCELLANY OF TRACTS AND PAMPHLETS. Sixteenth to Nineteenth Centuries. Edited by *A. C. Ward* (304).

PALGRAVE'S GOLDEN TREASURY, with 188 pages of additional poems from LANDOR to BLUNDEN (133).

READING AT RANDOM. A 'World's Classics' Anthology (410).

¶ *Autobiography*

AKSAKOFF (SERGHEI). Trans. by *J. D. Duff*. A Russian Gentleman (241). Years of Childhood (242). A Russian Schoolboy (261).

CELLINI (BENVENUTO) (300).

DE QUINCEY (THOMAS). Confessions of an Opium-Eater (23).

FRANKLIN (BENJAMIN). The Autobiography, edited from his original manuscript by *John Bigelow* (250).

GIBBON (EDWARD). Autobiography. Introduction by *J. B. Bury* (139).

HAYDON (BENJAMIN ROBERT). The Autobiography. Introduction and Epilogue by *Edmund Blunden* (314).

HUNT (LEIGH). Autobiography. Intro. *Edmund Blunden* (329).

MILL (JOHN STUART). Autobiography. Introduction by *Harold J. Laski* (262).

TOLSTOY. A Confession, and What I believe. Translated by *Aylmer Maude* (229).

TRELAWNY (E. J.). Adventures of a Younger Son. Introduction by *Ethel Colburn Mayne* (289).

TROLLOPE (ANTHONY). Autobiography. Introduction by *Michael Sadleir* (239).

¶ Biography

CARLYLE. The Life of John Sterling. Introduction by *W. Hale White ('Mark Rutherford')* (144).

CRABBE, LIFE OF. By his Son. Introduction by *E. M. Forster* (404).

DOBSON (AUSTIN). Four Frenchwomen: Charlotte Corday, Madame Roland, Princess de Lamballe, Madame de Genlis (248).

EMERSON. Representative Men. (With *English Traits*) (30).

FRANCIS OF ASSISI (ST.). The Little Flowers; and The Life of Brother Giles. Translated into English verse by *James Rhoades* (265).

GASKELL (MRS.). The Life of Charlotte Brontë (214).

HOUGHTON (LORD). Life of Keats (364).

JOHNSON (SAMUEL). Lives of the Poets. 2 vols. (83, 84).

MAUDE (AYLMER). Life of Tolstoy. 2 vols. (383, 384).

SCOTT (SIR WALTER). Lives of the Novelists. Introduction by *Austin Dobson* (94).

TREVELYAN (SIR G. O.). Life of Macaulay. With a new Introduction by *G. M. Trevelyan*. 2 vols. (401, 402).

WALTON (IZAAK). Lives of Donne, Wotton, Hooker, Herbert, Sanderson. Introduction by *George Saintsbury* (303).

¶ The 'Classics', Greek and Roman

AESCHYLUS. The Seven Plays. Translated into English Verse by *Lewis Campbell* (117).

ARISTOPHANES. The Acharnians, Knights, Birds, and Frogs. Translated by *J. Hookham Frere*. Intro. *W. W. Merry* (134).

HOMER. Translated by *Pope*. Iliad (18). Odyssey (36).

SOPHOCLES. The Seven Plays. Translated into English Verse by *Lewis Campbell* (116).

VIRGIL. The Aeneid, Georgics, and Eclogues. Translated by *John Dryden* (37).

—— The Aeneid, Georgics, and Eclogues. Translated by *James Rhoades* (227).

¶ *Drama*

BROWNING (ROBERT). Poems and Plays, 1833–42 (58);
CONGREVE (WILLIAM). Complete Works. Introduction by *Bonamy Dobrée*. I, The Comedies. II, The Mourning Bride, with Letters, Poems, and Miscellanies (276, 277).
EIGHTEENTH CENTURY COMEDY. FARQUHAR'S Beaux' Stratagem, STEELE'S Conscious Lovers, GAY'S Beggar's Opera, FIELDING'S Tom Thumb, GOLDSMITH'S She Stoops to Conquer (292).
EIGHTEENTH CENTURY, LESSER COMEDIES OF THE. Edited by *Allardyce Nicoll*. The five comedies are ARTHUR MURPHY'S The Way to keep him, GEORGE COLMAN'S The Jealous Wife, MRS. INCHBALD'S Everyone has his Fault, THOMAS MORTON'S Speed the Plough, and FREDERICK REYNOLDS'S The Dramatist (321).
FIVE ELIZABETHAN COMEDIES. Edited by *A. K. McIlwraith*. Contains GREENE'S Friar Bacon and Friar Bungay, PEELE'S The Old Wives' Tale, LYLY'S Campaspe, DEKKER'S Shoemaker's Holiday, and the anonymous Merry Devil of Edmonton (422).
FIVE PRE-SHAKESPEAREAN COMEDIES. Edited by *F. S. Boas*. Contains MEDWALL'S Fulgens and Lucrece, HEYWOOD'S The Four PP., UDALL'S Ralph Roister Doister, the anonymous Gammer Gurton's Needle, and GASCOIGNE'S Supposes (418).
GOETHE. Faust, Parts I and II. Translated by *Bayard Taylor*. Intro. by *Marshall Montgomery* and notes by *Douglas Yates* (380).
MARLOWE'S Dr. Faustus (with GOETHE'S Faust, Part I, trans. *J. Anster*). Introduction by *Sir A. W. Ward* (135).
RESTORATION TRAGEDIES. DRYDEN'S All for Love, OTWAY'S Venice Preserved, SOUTHERNE'S Oronooko, ROWE'S Fair Penitent, and ADDISON'S Cato. Introduction by *Bonamy Dobrée* (313).
SHAKESPEARE. Plays and Poems. Preface by *A. C. Swinburne*. Introductions by *Edward Dowden*. 9 vols. Comedies. 3 vols. (100, 101, 102). Histories and Poems. 3 vols. (103, 104, 105). Tragedies. 3 vols. (106, 107, 108).
SHAKESPEARE, Six Plays by Contemporaries of. DEKKER, The Shoemaker's Holiday; WEBSTER, The White Devil; BEAUMONT and FLETCHER, The Knight of the Burning Pestle, and Philaster; WEBSTER, The Duchess of Malfi; MASSINGER, A New Way to pay Old Debts. Edited by *C. B. Wheeler* (199).
SHERIDAN. Plays. Introduction by *Joseph Knight* (79).
TOLSTOY. The Plays. Complete edition, including the posthumous plays. Translated by *Louise* and *Aylmer Maude* (243).

¶ *Essays and Belles Lettres*

BACON. The Essays, Civil and Moral (24).
BROWN (DR. JOHN). Horae Subsecivae (Rab and His Friends, &c.). Introduction by *Austin Dobson* (118).
CARLYLE. On Heroes and Hero-Worship (62). Past and Present. Introduction by *G. K. Chesterton* (153). Sartor Resartus (19).

TRACTS AND PAMPHLETS, from JOHN KNOX to H. G. WELLS (304).
WALTON and COTTON. The Compleat Angler. Introduction by *John Buchan* (430).
WHITE (GILBERT). The Natural History of Selborne (22).
WHITMAN. Specimen Days in America (371).

¶ *Fiction* (For SHORT STORIES see separate heading)

AINSWORTH (W. HARRISON). The Tower of London (162).
AUSTEN (JANE). Emma (129). Pride and Prejudice (335). Mansfield Park (345). Northanger Abbey (355). Persuasion (356). Sense and Sensibility (389).
BLACKMORE (R. D.). Lorna Doone. Introduction by *Sir Herbert Warren* (171).
BORROW (GEORGE). Lavengro (66). The Romany Rye (73).
BRONTË (ANNE). Agnes Grey (141). Tenant of Wildfell Hall (67).
BRONTË (CHARLOTTE). Jane Eyre (1). Shirley (14). Villette (47). The Professor, and the Poems of the Brontës (78).
BRONTË (EMILY). Wuthering Heights (10).
BUNYAN. The Pilgrim's Progress (12). Mr. Badman (338).
BUTLER (SAMUEL). The Way of all Flesh. With an Essay by *Bernard Shaw* (438).
CERVANTES. Don Quixote. 2 volumes (130, 131).
COBBOLD (REV. RICHARD). Margaret Catchpole (119).
COLLINS (WILKIE). The Moonstone. Introduction by *T. S. Eliot* (316). The Woman in White (226).
COOPER (J. FENIMORE). The Last of the Mohicans (163).
DEFOE. Captain Singleton (82). Robinson Crusoe. Part I (17).
DICKENS. Barnaby Rudge (286). Christmas Books (307). Edwin Drood (263) Great Expectations (128). Hard Times (264). Old Curiosity Shop (270). Oliver Twist (8). Pickwick Papers. 2 volumes (120, 121). Tale of Two Cities (38).
DISRAELI (BENJAMIN). Coningsby (381). Sybil (291).
ELIOT (GEORGE). Adam Bede (63). Felix Holt (179). The Mill on the Floss (31). Romola (178). Scenes of Clerical Life (155). Silas Marner, &c. (80).
FIELDING. Jonathan Wild (382). Joseph Andrews (334).
GALT (JOHN). The Entail. Introduction by *John Ayscough* (177).
GASKELL (MRS.). Cousin Phillis, and Other Tales, &c. (168). Cranford, The Cage at Cranford, and The Moorland Cottage (110). Lizzie Leigh, The Grey Woman, and Other Tales, &c. (175). Mary Barton (86). North and South (154). Right at Last, and Other Tales, &c. (203). Round the Sofa (190). Ruth (88). Sylvia's Lovers (156). Wives and Daughters (157).
GOLDSMITH. The Vicar of Wakefield (4).
HARRIS (JOEL CHANDLER). Uncle Remus (361).
HAWTHORNE. House of the Seven Gables (273). The Scarlet Letter (26). Tales (319).

HOLME (CONSTANCE). Beautiful End (431). Crump Folk going Home (419). The Lonely Plough (390). The Old Road from Spain (400). The Splendid Fairing (416). The Things which Belong— (425). The Trumpet in the Dust (409).

KINGSLEY (HENRY). Geoffry Hamlyn (271). Ravenshoe (267). Austin Elliot (407).

LA MOTTE FOUQUÉ. Undine, Sintram, &c. (408).

LE FANU (J. S.). Uncle Silas. Introduction by *Montague R. James* (306).

LESAGE. Gil Blas. Edited *J. Fitzmaurice-Kelly*. 2 volumes (151, 152).

LYTTON. The Coming Race, &c. (327).

MARRYAT. Mr. Midshipman Easy (160). Jacob Faithful (439).

MELVILLE (HERMAN). Moby Dick (225). Typee (274). Omoo (275). White Jacket (253).

MORIER (J. J.). Hajji Baba (238). Hajji Baba in England (285).

PEACOCK (T. L.). Headlong Hall; and Nightmare Abbey (339). Misfortunes of Elphin: and Crotchet Castle (244).

RABELAIS. Gargantua and Pantagruel. Translated by *Urquhart* and *Motteux*, with notes and map. 3 volumes (411-13).

SCOTT. Ivanhoe (29).

SMOLLETT. Roderick Random (353). Humphry Clinker (290).

STERNE. Sentimental Journey (333). Tristram Shandy (40).

STEVENSON (R. L.). Kidnapped; and Catriona (297). The Master of Ballantrae (441). Treasure Island (295).

STURGIS (HOWARD). Belchamber. Introduction by *Gerard Hopkins* (429).

SWIFT. Gulliver's Travels (20).

TAYLOR (MEADOWS). Confessions of a Thug (207).

THACKERAY. Henry Esmond (28).

TOLSTOY. Translated by *Louise* and *Aylmer Maude*. Anna Karenina. 2 volumes (210, 211). Childhood, Boyhood, and Youth (352). The Cossacks, &c. (208). Iván Ilých, and Hadji Murád (432). The Kreutzer Sonata, &c. (266). Resurrection, trans. by *L. Maude* (209). Twenty-three Tales (72). War and Peace. 3 volumes (233-5).

TRELAWNY (E. J.). Adventures of a Younger Son (289).

TROLLOPE. American Senator (391). Ayala's Angel (342). Barchester Towers (268). The Belton Estate (251). The Claverings (252). Cousin Henry (343). Doctor Thorne (298). Dr. Wortle's School (317). The Eustace Diamonds (357). Framley Parsonage (305). The Kellys and the O'Kellys (341). Last Chronicle of Barset. 2 vols. (398, 399). Miss Mackenzie (278). Orley Farm. 2 vols. (423, 424). Rachel Ray (279). Sir Harry Hotspur (336). Tales of all Countries (397). The Three Clerks (140). The Warden (217). The Vicar of Bullhampton (272).

WATTS-DUNTON (THEODORE). Aylwin (52).

WHARTON (EDITH). The House of Mirth. With a new Introduction by the Author (437).

¶ History

BARROW (SIR JOHN). The Mutiny of the *Bounty* (195).

BUCKLE. The History of Civilization. 3 volumes (41, 48, 53).

CARLYLE. The French Revolution. Introduction by *C. R. L. Fletcher*. 2 volumes (125, 126).

FROUDE (J. A.). Short Studies on Great Subjects. Series I (269).

GIBBON. Decline and Fall of the Roman Empire. With Maps. 7 volumes (35, 44, 51, 55, 64, 69, 74).

IRVING (WASHINGTON). Conquest of Granada (150).

MACAULAY. History of England. 5 volumes (366–70).

MOTLEY. Rise of the Dutch Republic. 3 volumes (96, 97, 98).

PRESCOTT (W. H.). The Conquest of Mexico. 2 vols. (197, 198).

¶ Letters

BURKE. Letters. Selected, with Introduction, by *H. J. Laski* (237).

CHESTERFIELD. Letters. Selected, with an Introduction, by *Phyllis M. Jones* (347).

CONGREVE. Letters, in Volume II. See under *Drama* (277).

COWPER. Letters. Selected, with Intro., by *E. V. Lucas* (138).

DUFFERIN (LORD). Letters from High Latitudes. Illustrated (158).

ENGLISH LETTERS. Fifteenth to Nineteenth Centuries (192).

GRAY (THOMAS). Letters. Selected by *John Beresford* (283).

JOHNSON (SAMUEL). Letters. Selected, with Introduction, by *R. W. Chapman* (282).

SOUTHEY. Selected Letters (169).

TOLSTOY. Essays and Letters. Trans. by *L.* and *A. Maude* (46).

WHITE (GILBERT). The Natural History of Selborne (22).

¶ Literary Criticism

AMERICAN CRITICISM. Representative Literary Essays. Chosen by *Norman Foerster* (354).

COLERIDGE (S. T.) Lectures on Shakespeare (363).

ENGLISH CRITICAL ESSAYS. Selected and edited by *Edmund D. Jones*. 2 volumes: I, Sixteenth to Eighteenth Centuries (240); II, Nineteenth Century (206).

HAZLITT (WILLIAM). Characters of Shakespeare's Plays. Introduction by *Sir A. T. Quiller-Couch* (205). Lectures on the English Comic Writers. Introduction by *R. Brimley Johnson* (124). Lectures on the English Poets (255). The Spirit of the Age. (Essays on his contemporaries) (57).

HORNE (R. H.). A New Spirit of the Age (127).

JOHNSON (SAMUEL). Lives of the Poets. 2 volumes (83, 84).

SAINTE-BEUVE. Causeries du Lundi. (In English.) Two Series (372–3).

SHAKESPEARE CRITICISM. (HEMINGE and CONDELL to CARLYLE.) Selected and introduced by *D. Nichol Smith* (212).

SHAKESPEARE CRITICISM. (Twentieth Century.) Selected and introduced by *Anne Bradby* (436).

¶ *Philosophy and Science*

(For POLITICAL THEORY and RELIGION see separate headings)

AURELIUS (MARCUS). Thoughts. Translated by *John Jackson* (60).
BACON. The Advancement of Learning, and the New Atlantis.
    Introduction by *Professor Case* (93). Essays (24).
CARLYLE. Sartor Resartus (19).
DARWIN. The Origin of Species. With a new preface by *Major
    Leonard Darwin* (11). Voyage of a Naturalist (360).
REYNOLDS (SIR JOSHUA). Discourses, &c. Introduction by *A. Dobson* (149).
TOLSTOY. What then must we do? Trans. by *A. Maude* (281).
WHITE (GILBERT). The Natural History of Selborne (22).

¶ *Poetry*

ARNOLD (MATTHEW). Poems, 1849–67 (85).
BARHAM (RICHARD). The Ingoldsby Legends (9).
BLAKE (WILLIAM). Selected Poems (324).
BRONTË SISTERS, THE. The Professor, by CHARLOTTE BRONTË, and
    Poems by CHARLOTTE, EMILY, and ANNE BRONTË (78).
BROWNING (ELIZABETH BARRETT). Poems. A Selection (176).
BROWNING (ROBERT). Poems and Plays, 1833–42 (58). Poems,
    1842–64 (137).
BURNS (ROBERT). Poems (34). Complete and in large type.
BYRON. Poems. A Selection (180).
CHAUCER, The Works of. 3 volumes: I (42); II (56); III, con-
    taining the whole of the Canterbury Tales (76).
COLERIDGE. Poems. Introduction by *Sir A. T. Quiller-Couch* (99).
CONGREVE (WILLIAM). Complete works in 2 volumes. Intro-
    ductions by *Bonamy Dobrée*. I, The Comedies (276); II, The
    Mourning Bride, Poems, Miscellanies and Letters (277).
DANTE. Italian text and English verse-translation by *Melville B.
    Anderson*, on facing pages, with notes. 3 vols. (392–4).
    Translation only, with notes, in one volume (395).
DOBSON (AUSTIN). Selected Poems (249).
ENGLISH SONGS AND BALLADS. Compiled by *T. W. H. Crosland.*
    New edition, with revised text and additional poems, 1927 (13).
ENGLISH VERSE. Vols. I–V: Early Lyrics to SHAKESPEARE; CAM-
    PION to the Ballads; DRYDEN to WORDSWORTH; SCOTT to E. B.
    BROWNING; LONGFELLOW to RUPERT BROOKE. Edited by *William
    Peacock* (308–312).
FRANCIS OF ASSISI (ST.). The Little Flowers of St. Francis.
    Translated into English Verse by *James Rhoades* (265).
GOETHE. Faust, Parts I and II. Translated by *Bayard Taylor.*
    Intro. by *Marshall Montgomery* and notes by *Douglas Yates* (380).
GOLDEN TREASURY, THE. With additional Poems (133).
GOLDSMITH. Poems. Introduction by *Austin Dobson* (123).
HERBERT (GEORGE). Poems. Introduction by *Arthur Waugh* (109).
HERRICK (ROBERT). Poems (16).

HOMER. Translated by *Pope*. Iliad (18). Odyssey (36).

HOOD. Poems. Introduction by *Walter Jerrold* (87).

KEATS. Poems (7).

KEBLE. The Christian Year (181).

LONGFELLOW. Evangeline, The Golden Legend, &c. (39). Hiawatha, Miles Standish, Tales of a Wayside Inn, &c. (174).

MACAULAY. Lays of Ancient Rome ; Ivry ; The Armada (27).

MARLOWE. Dr. Faustus (with GOETHE'S Faust, Part I, trans. *J. Anster*). Introduction by *Sir A. W. Ward* (135).

MILTON. The English Poems (182).

MORRIS (WILLIAM). The Defence of Guenevere, Life and Death of Jason, and other Poems (183).

NARRATIVE VERSE, A BOOK OF. Compiled by *V. H. Collins*. With an Introduction by *Edmund Blunden* (350).

NEKRASSOV. Trans. by *Juliet Soskice*. Who can be happy and free in Russia ? A Poem (213). Poems (340).

PALGRAVE. The Golden Treasury. With additional Poems (133).

ROSSETTI (CHRISTINA). Goblin Market, &c. (184).

SCOTT (SIR WALTER). Selected Poems (186).

SCOTTISH VERSE, A BOOK OF. Compiled by *R. L. Mackie* (417).

SHAKESPEARE. Plays and Poems. Preface by *A. C. Swinburne*. Introductions by *Edward Dowden*. 9 volumes. Comedies. 3 volumes (100, 101, 102). Histories and Poems. 3 volumes (103, 104, 105). Tragedies. 3 volumes (106, 107, 108).

SHELLEY. Poems. A Selection (187).

TENNYSON. Selected Poems. Intro. by *Sir Herbert Warren* (3).

VIRGIL. The Aeneid, Georgics, and Eclogues. Translated by *Dryden* (37). Translated by *James Rhoades* (227).

WELLS (CHARLES). Joseph and his Brethren. A Dramatic Poem. Intro. by *A. C. Swinburne*, and Note by *T. Watts-Dunton* (143).

WHITMAN. A Selection. Introduction by *E. de Sélincourt* (218).

WHITTIER. Poems : A Selection (188).

WORDSWORTH. Poems : A Selection (189).

¶ Politics, Political Economy, Political Theory

BAGEHOT (WALTER). The English Constitution. With an Introduction by the *Earl of Balfour* (330).

BUCKLE. The History of Civilization. 3 volumes (41, 48, 53).

BURKE (EDMUND). Letters. Selected, with an Introduction, by *Harold J. Laski* (237). Works. 6 volumes. I : A Vindication of Natural Society ; The Sublime and Beautiful, &c. (71). II : The Present Discontents ; and Speeches and Letters on America (81). III : Speeches on India, &c. (111). IV : Writings on France, 1790–1 (112). V : Writings on Ireland, &c. (113). VI : A Letter to a Noble Lord ; and Letters on a Regicide Peace (114).

ENGLISH SPEECHES, from BURKE to GLADSTONE. Selected and edited by *E. R. Jones* (191).

MACAULAY. Speeches. Selected, with Introduction and footnotes, by *G. M. Young* (433).

MACHIAVELLI. The Prince (43).

MAINE (SIR HENRY). Ancient Law (362).

MILL (JOHN STUART). On Liberty, Representative Government, and the Subjection of Women (170).

MILTON (JOHN). Selected Prose. Intro. *Malcolm W. Wallace* (293).

RUSKIN. 'A Joy for Ever', and The Two Paths. Illustrated (147). Time and Tide, and The Crown of Wild Olive (146). Unto this Last, and Munera Pulveris (148).

SMITH (ADAM). The Wealth of Nations. 2 volumes (54, 59).

SPEECHES AND DOCUMENTS ON BRITISH COLONIAL POLICY (1763-1917). Ed. *A. B. Keith.* 2 volumes (215, 216).

SPEECHES AND DOCUMENTS ON THE BRITISH DOMINIONS, 1918-31. Selected, with Introduction, by *A. B. Keith* (403).

SPEECHES AND DOCUMENTS ON INDIAN POLICY (1756-1921). Edited, with Introduction, by *A. B. Keith* (231, 232).

SPEECHES ON BRITISH FOREIGN POLICY (1738-1914). Edited by *Edgar R. Jones, M.P.* (201).

TRACTS AND PAMPHLETS, A Miscellany of. Sixteenth to Nineteenth Centuries. Edited by *A. C. Ward* (304).

TOLSTOY. What then must we do ? Translated, with an Introduction, by *Aylmer Maude* (281).

¶ *Religion*

THE OLD TESTAMENT. Revised Version. 4 vols. (385-8).

APOCRYPHA, THE, in the Revised Version (294).

THE FOUR GOSPELS, AND THE ACTS OF THE APOSTLES. Authorized Version (344).

THE NEW TESTAMENT. Revised Version (346).

À KEMPIS (THOMAS). Of the Imitation of Christ (49).

AURELIUS (MARCUS). Translated by *John Jackson* (60).

BUNYAN. The Pilgrim's Progress (12). Mr. Badman (338).

KORAN, THE. Translated by *E. H. Palmer.* Introduction by *Reynold A. Nicholson* (328).

TOLSTOY. Translated by *Aylmer Maude.* A Confession, and What I believe (229). On Life, and Essays on Religion (426).

¶ *Short Stories*

AFRICA, STORIES OF. Chosen by *E. C. Parnwell* (359).

AUSTRIAN SHORT STORIES. Selected and translated by *Marie Busch* (337).

CRIME AND DETECTION Two Series (301, 351). Stories by H. C. BAILEY, ERNEST BRAMAH, G. K. CHESTERTON SIR A. CONAN DOYLE, R. AUSTIN FREEMAN, W. W. JACOBS, EDEN PHILPOTTS, 'SAPPER', DOROTHY SAYERS, and others.

CZECH TALES, SELECTED. Translated by *Marie Busch* and *Otto Pick* (288). Nine stories, including two by the BROTHERS CAPEK.

DICKENS. Christmas Books (307).

ENGLISH SHORT STORIES. Three Series. Selected by *H. S. Milford*. Introduction by *Prof. Hugh Walker* in Vol. I (193, 228, 315).

FRENCH SHORT STORIES. Eighteenth to Twentieth Centuries. Selected and translated by *K. Rebillon Lambley* (396).

GASKELL (MRS.). Introductions by *Clement Shorter*. Cousin Phillis, and Other Tales (168). Lizzie Leigh, The Grey Woman, and Other Tales, &c. (175). Right at Last, and Other Tales, &c. (203). Round the Sofa (190).

GERMAN SHORT STORIES. Translated by *E. N. Bennett*, with an Introduction by *E. K. Bennett* (415).

GHOSTS AND MARVELS and MORE GHOSTS AND MARVELS. Two Selections of Uncanny Tales made by *V. H. Collins*. Introduction by *Montague R. James* in Series I. (284, 323.)

HARTE (BRET). Short Stories (318).

HAWTHORNE (NATHANIEL). Tales (319).

IRVING (WASHINGTON). Tales (320).

PERSIAN (FROM THE). The Three Dervishes, and Other Stories. Translated from MSS. in the Bodleian by *Reuben Levy* (254).

POE (EDGAR ALLAN). Tales of Mystery and Imagination (21).

POLISH TALES BY MODERN AUTHORS. Translated by *Else C. M. Benecke* and *Marie Busch* (230).

RUSSIAN SHORT STORIES. Chosen and translated by *A. E. Chamot* (287).

SCOTT. Short Stories. With an Introduction by *Lord David Cecil* (414).

SHORT STORIES OF THE SOUTH SEAS. Selected by *E. C. Parnwell* (332).

SPANISH SHORT STORIES. Sixteenth Century. In contemporary translations, revised, with an Introduction, by *J. B. Trend* (326).

TOLSTOY. Nine Stories (1855–63) (420). Twenty-three Tales. Translated by *Louise* and *Aylmer Maude* (72).

TROLLOPE. Tales of all Countries (397).

¶ Travel and Topography

BORROW (GEORGE). The Bible in Spain (75). Wild Wales (224). Lavengro (66). Romany Rye (73).

DARWIN. Voyage of a Naturalist (360).

DUFFERIN (LORD). Letters from High Latitudes (158).

MELVILLE (HERMAN). Typee (294). Omoo (275).

MORIER (J. J.). Hajji Baba of Ispahan. Introduction by *C. W. Stewart*, and a Map (238).

SMOLLETT (TOBIAS). Travels through France and Italy in 1765. Introduction (lxii pages) by *Thomas Seccombe* (90).

STERNE (LAURENCE). A Sentimental Journey. With Introduction by *Virginia Woolf* (333).

INDEX OF AUTHORS, ETC.

Further Volumes are in preparation.

January 1936